PENGUIN BOOKS

THE PENGUIN BOOK OF
AUSTRALIAN SHORT STORIES

The Penguin Book
of Australian Short Stories

EDITED AND INTRODUCED BY
HARRY HESELTINE

PENGUIN BOOKS

Penguin Books Australia Ltd,
487 Maroondah Highway, P.O. Box 257
Ringwood, Victoria, 3134, Australia
Penguin Books Ltd,
Harmondsworth, Middlesex, England
Penguin Books,
40 West 23rd Street, New York, N.Y. 10010, U.S.A.
Penguin Books Canada Ltd,
2801 John Street, Markham, Ontario, Canada
Penguin Books (N.Z.) Ltd,
182-190 Wairau Road, Auckland 10, New Zealand

First published by Penguin Books Australia, 1976
Reprinted 1978, 1980, 1981, 1983
This collection copyright © Harry Heseltine, 1976

Typeset in Monotype Times by Dudley E. King, Melbourne

Made and printed in Australia by
Dominion Press Hedges & Bell

CIP

The Penguin book of Australian short stories
ISBN 0 14 004303 9

1. Short stories, Australian. I. Heseltine,
Harry P., ed.

A823.01

CONTENTS

Acknowledgements   7

Introduction   9

'Price Warung' (William Astley) (1855–1911)
HOW MUSTER-MASTER STONEMAN EARNED
HIS BREAKFAST   32

'Steele Rudd' (Arthur Hoey Davis) (1868–1935)
WHEN THE WOLF WAS AT THE DOOR   41

Henry Lawson (1867–1922)
SEND ROUND THE HAT   45

Barbara Baynton (1862–1929)
SQUEAKER'S MATE   63

Edward Dyson (1865–1931)
THE HAUNTED CORNER   78

Katharine Susannah Prichard (1883–1969)
HAPPINESS   87

Les Robinson (1886–1968)
THE GIRAFFE'S UNCLE   101

Vance Palmer (1885–1959)
THE RAINBOW-BIRD   105

Frank Dalby Davison (1893–1969)
RETURN OF THE HUNTER   112

Marjorie Barnard (b. 1897)
THE PERSIMMON TREE   126

Gavin Casey (1907–1964)
TALKING GROUND   130

Peter Cowan (b. 1914)
NIGHT   136

Alan Marshall (b. 1902)
TELL US ABOUT THE TURKEY, JO   143

'Brian James' (John Tierney) (1892-1972)
SHOTS IN THE ORCHARD   147

E. O. Schlunke (1906–1960)
THE COWBOY FROM TOWN   154

John Morrison (b. 1904)
A MAN'S WORLD   168

Hal Porter (b. 1911)
FIEND AND FRIEND   178

Patrick White (b. 1912)
DOWN AT THE DUMP   190

Elizabeth Harrower (b. 1928)
ENGLISH LESSON   220

Desmond O'Grady (b. 1929)
BARBECUE   227

Thelma Forshaw (b. 1923)
THE DEMO   236

Dal Stivens (b. 1911)
WARRIGAL   235

Frank Moorhouse (b. 1938)
FIVE INCIDENTS CONCERNING THE
FLESH AND THE BLOOD   255

Michael Wilding (b. 1942)
AS BOYS TO WANTON FLIES   274

Peter Carey (b. 1943)
REPORT ON THE SHADOW INDUSTRY   282

Notes on the Authors   287

ACKNOWLEDGEMENTS

FOR permission to reprint the stories specified we are indebted to:

E. D. Davis for Steele Rudd's 'When the Wolf Was at the Door'

Angus & Robertson Publishers for Barbara Baynton's 'Squeaker's Mate', from *Bush Studies*

Angus & Robertson Publishers for Edward Dyson's 'The Haunted Corner', from *The Golden Shanty*

R. Throssell for Katharine Susannah Prichard's 'Happiness'

Macquarie Head Press for Les Robinson's 'The Giraffe's Uncle', from *The Giraffe's Uncle*

Aileen and Helen Palmer for Vance Palmer's 'The Rainbow Bird'

Angus & Robertson Publishers for Frank Dalby Davison's 'Return of the Hunter', from *The Road to Yesterday*

Curtis Brown (Aust.) Pty Ltd, Sydney, for Marjorie Barnard's 'The Persimmon Tree'

Angus & Robertson Publishers for Gavin Casey's 'Talking Ground', from *Short Shift Saturday*

Peter Cowan for his story 'Night'

Thomas Nelson (Australia) Ltd for Alan Marshall's 'Tell Us About the Turkey, Jo', from *Short Stories*

Angus & Robertson Publishers for Brian James' 'Shots in the Orchard', from *The Big Burn*

Angus & Robertson Publishers for E. O. Schlunke's 'The Cowboy from Town', from *The Village Hampden*

John Morrison for his 'A Man's World'

Angus & Robertson Publishers for Hal Porter's 'Fiend and Friend', from *Selected Stories*

Curtis Brown (Aust.) Pty Ltd for Patrick White's 'Down at the Dump'

Elizabeth Harrower for her story 'English Lesson'

Desmond O'Grady for his story 'Barbecue'

Angus & Robertson Publishers for Thelma Forshaw's 'The Demo', from *An Affair of Clowns*

Dal Stivens and Curtis Brown (Aust.) Pty Ltd for Dal Stivens' 'Warrigal'

Angus & Robertson Publishers for Frank Moorhouse's 'Five Incidents concerning the Flesh and the Blood', from *The Americans, Baby*

Michael Wilding for his 'As Boys to Wanton Flies'

University of Queensland Press for Peter Carey's 'Report on the Shadow Industry', from *The Fat Man in History*

INTRODUCTION

SOME of the writers who appear in this anthology virtually selected themselves. A collection of Australian short stories without, for instance, Henry Lawson or Vance Palmer, Hal Porter or Patrick White, would be as unthinkable as a comparable American volume without Melville or Hawthorne, Hemingway or Faulkner. A nucleus of indispensable authors, however, creates almost as many problems as it solves. In a book of strictly limited dimensions, in particular, it immediately reduces the space available to all the other first-class writers jostling for inclusion. Within the necessary limits, I have nevertheless endeavoured to bring together a set of stories as rich and various as possible in both themes and techniques. I have, too, arranged these twenty-five tales chronologically, in accordance with their dates of first publication in book form, with the aim of presenting a practical, exemplary history of short prose fiction in this country.

To claim for a set of twenty-five stories chronologically arranged the force of an exemplary history is clearly to assume that there is a history to be exemplified. Most students of our literature would agree that the Australian short story has indeed a discernible development beginning in the 1890s and enjoying a second major flowering during the 1940s. They would probably also accept that Henry Lawson is the first of our short story writers with anything like a real claim to greatness, and that since the period of his most intense creativity – the 1890s – the form in general has been the vehicle of much that is quintessentially Australian in our literature.

The argument for the special significance of the short story in Australian literary history may be in part a quantitative one. Denton Prout in his biography, *Henry Lawson: The Grey Dreamer*, records that during the 1890s there were some 300 successful prose writers at work in Australia: for many of them, the short narrative was a principal mode of expression. *The Bulletin Story Book*, edited in 1901 by A. G. Stephens and the first important anthology of its kind, drew upon sixty contributors, only a small proportion of the writers who had appeared in the famous weekly during the previous decade. Similar numerical evidence might be adduced to support the idea of something like a renaissance in the 1940s. Beatrice Davis, thus, editor of the 1942 *Coast to Coast*, noted in her Foreword that in order to arrive at the 21 pieces she finally selected, she had been required to sift through some 300 submissions. In the following year, Frank Dalby Davison reduced some 550 stories to the 24 he finally printed. The sheer weight of such numbers is, to be sure, remarkably impressive. Yet it is necessary, as always, to treat statistical evidence with some reservations. Were comparable statistics sought from England and America in the 1890s, for instance, they might make Prout's figures seem rather less remarkable than, at face value, they appear to be. Even some gross sampling of evidence within Australia can place a different complexion on the importance of the short story to our total literary effort in either the 1890s or the 1940s. Grahame Johnston's *Annals of Australian Literature*, thus, lists some twenty-one books of short stories in the years 1890–1901, constituting roughly 16 per cent of the total literary output of the period; in the decade 1940–49, the figure was approximately 8 per cent, in the previous ten years some 8·6 per cent, and for 1950–59, 6 per cent.

Neither the patterns of literary history, however, nor particular aesthetic excellence can ever be determined by statistics. Even the very rough quantitative analysis offered here must be subject to some kind of qualitative adjustment. For the 1890s such an adjustment would involve at least some study of the range of alternative entertainments available to Australians apart from the short story, some appreciation of the complex sociology of literary production and consumption, and, at a quite basic level, a grasp of the economics of book production, sales, and distribution. With all such allowances made, however, historians of Australian literature have almost certainly been right in their assigning of a place of particular pre-eminence to the short story, and in the special importance they have ascribed to the 1890s and 1940s.

Where there is more room for debate – and where debate has sometimes raged – is in the interpretation of the finer details of the status and value of the Australian short story. The form, it is agreed, has a history; about the details of its historiography, there is a good deal less than agreement. One view of its development, for instance, might stress its radical tradition, its endorsement of working-class attitudes and experience and corollary condemnation of middle- and upper-class wealth and culture snobbery. Another view might see the democratic-nationalist theme at the heart of the tradition. Yet another thematic account of the form might locate its central concern in an engagement with the opposed lifestyles of the city and the outback – Sydney or the bush. A formal critic of the same set of stories might produce a history which derived its coherence from a continuing adherence to the conventions of social realism. Another might place the techniques of the yarn-spinner, the laconic raconteur, at the centre of the tradition; another might insist on the basic importance of certain kinds of comedy.

If the chief versions of the historical development of the Australian short story have any one point in common it is probably an acceptance that Henry Lawson was not only the chronological founder of the tradition but that he is the *source* of most that is imaginatively important in it. If there is any shared failure, it is probably an inability to account for the rise to prominence in the 1960s of two of our most distinguished practitioners of the form, Hal Porter and Patrick White. The whole corpus of White's fiction has indeed demanded not only the best efforts of our evaluative criticism but also some large scale re-adjustments of our literary historiography. White himself plainly sensed his opposition to the canonical tradition in his famous pronouncement about his intentions in writing *The Tree of Man:* 'Above all I was determined to prove that the Australian novel is not the dreary, dun-coloured off-spring of journalistic realism.' By now there can be no doubt that criticism has gone a considerable distance towards accommodating White's novels to a distinctively Australian tradition, and it to them. The relation of his short stories to any possible tradition has been less satisfactorily investigated. Such an investigation, it seems to me, is of crucial importance not only as part of the effort to do the highest kind of critical justice to our only Nobel Prize winning author but also in reaching the fullest possible understanding of a major aspect of our literary culture.

The situation of Hal Porter, at least in respect of the short story, is hardly more satisfactory. In his own way, he is arguably as good a short story writer as Patrick White; he remains even more seemingly alien to any of the commonly accepted versions of the traditions of short narrative prose in this country. Indeed, perhaps the greatest challenge to historical criticism of the Australian short story is to generate a reading of its development which will accommodate Henry Lawson at one end of the continuum and Hal Porter and Patrick White at the other without misrepresenting any one of the three or any of the scores of first class writers who fall between them. Either such a reading is possible, or it must be accepted that two completely idiosyncratic figures arose in the 1960s who are quite inaccessible to culturally genetic explanation. To the literary historian, the latter alternative is always the more desperate; in the present instance, I believe, more desperate than need be. Perspectives are available on the Australian short story which will afford its major representatives some kind of cultural coherence without either imposing on them new and perverse interpretations or absolutely disintegrating the old patterns of understanding. Such perspectives are, it seems to me, discernible in the twenty-five stories brought together in this anthology; it will be useful to describe them with some explicitness, and for two good reasons. In the first place, I wish to make it absolutely clear that any interpretation I offer of the rise of the Australian short story grew out of, did not dictate, the lengthy process of selection. In the second place, all twenty-five stories are, I am persuaded, of high literary merit in their own right; that merit can more fairly and openly proclaim itself if any burden of historical interpretation is unequivocally borne by the Introduction. The responsibility for such interpretation clearly belongs then to the editor; the literary merit, equally clearly, to the authors alone.

I take, then, Hal Porter as my basic reference point in the

perspective on the Australian short story I can no more than outline in the remainder of this Introduction: Porter, because even more flamboyantly than Patrick White he seems to flaunt his idiosyncrasies in the face of the settled traditions of the form. His dandyism, his sometimes *recherché* diction, his emotional sophistication arrange themselves into an art which is, on the face of it, as far removed as possible from Henry Lawson's. Yet the two writers do share, I believe, one common and important attitude in their approach to the short story, an attitude which forcefully identifies itself in Porter's autobiography, *The Watcher on the Cast-Iron Balcony**. In *The Watcher* Porter repeatedly asserts – and in this he appears to be at his most quixotic, most paradoxical – his lack of imagination. 'I am fundamentally more realistic than imaginative,' he writes on p. 118; 'I am an unimaginative boy,' on p. 150; 'having no imagination, I do not understand people,' on p. 93. The personal tone and temper of Porter's fiction seem to make such a claim utterly preposterous. In the long run, however, one comes to accept the shrewdness of Porter's self-analysis, and to see in it a crucial, if unexpected, clue to the right interpretation of his fictional prose. The boy Hal Porter was more realistic than imaginative in the sense that he found in language the greatest reality, was 'inclined . . . to find words more convincing than anything else'. Denied, as he believed, an entrée into the world of imagination, he developed 'a greed for abundance and information' (p. 205). Language, the most vivid reality he could conceive, became the nexus between himself and the external world, a world immeasurably more compelling than any of the images of his own mind. In discovering the experienced quality of his total environment as the great subject of his writing, making the authentication of that experience (to himself and to others) the prime responsibility of his language, Hal Porter placed himself at one with the major creative impulses which have brought the Australian short story into being since its inception.

The one absolutely sure foundation that even the forerunners of the major tradition laid down, indeed, was the necessity of a factual fidelity to the experience offered them by their Australian world. What I have called the pre-history of the Australian

* Faber & Faber edition, London, 1963.

13

short story begins with John George Lang's *Botany Bay*, of which the symptomatic sub-title is *True Stories of the Early Days of Australia*. In a work of largely undistinguished writing, some of the few pages to exhibit the force of compulsion and the shock of truth are to be found in the Introduction. 'It behoves me to inform the English reader', Lang wrote, 'that ... the entire contents of this volume are founded upon truth.' He went on to admit, to be sure, that names, dates and localities had been altered, and that his 'object in making such alterations was to spare the feelings of the surviving relatives of the various persons alluded to' in his narratives. No such tender scruples guided Marcus Clarke in writing *Old Tales of a Young Country* (1871). Yet the Preface he appended to his collection of stories announces a motive for their composition basically akin to that of Lang:

[The stories] were dug out by me at odd times during a period of three years, from the store of pamphlets, books, and records of old times, which is in the [Melbourne] Public Library; and in their narration I lay claim but to such originality as belongs to a compiler ...

The short story writer as compiler of a social record – the formulation is more sophisticated than Lang's, but the idea is in essence the same. Where Clarke went beyond the author of *Botany Bay* was in his determination to tell the whole truth about the horror which had been the early reality of life in colonial Australia:

I have done my best to secure accuracy in names, dates, and minute particulars; but the meagreness of the early colonial newspapers, the wanton destruction or mutilation of many of the early colonial official documents, the jealousy with which the colonial families guard the secret histories bequeathed to them by their ancestors, and the fact that the rude, adventurous life of those early colonial days prevented the registration of the very romances which it induced, render it difficult to obtain correlative evidence of many statements quoted, and have compelled me to accept the narrative as correct on the sole authority of the first and only narrator.

Clarke's researches were, as he admits, sporadic and of comparatively brief duration – fitted into the manifold busyness of a journalist's life. There was soon to appear in Sydney, however, a near contemporary so greedy for information about the earliest social actualities of white Australian society that acquiring it became an all consuming preoccupation. Writing in 1892, in the Introduction to *Tales of the Convict System*, 'Price Warung' had this to say:

There is not one [of these stories] in which the motive has not been suggested by, or based upon, fact. They have been submitted to Australian readers as the first fruits, in literary form, of nearly twenty years' study of the sources of Australian history, and however far his works fall short of the standard of graphic story-telling, the writer feels that he can honestly claim that he has sought to communicate to it the quality of historic truth ... To this end he has directed analytic research and systematic industry.

From Lang to Clarke to 'Warung' the line of continuity is clear: so overweening a sense of the importance of experienced actuality as to make the truthful registration of its structure the fundamental responsibility of the narrator's craft. What makes 'Warung' so much more interesting than either Lang or Clarke is the personal pressure which prompted him and the imaginative skill which enabled him to transform his craft into an art. The society he so diligently researched was, he was convinced, central to the experience of the Australian people: 'The Transport System has knotted itself into the fibres of our national being ... The convict past of Australia cannot be shut out of sight.' At the same time, however, his artist's instinct told him that the reality of the System had been so special that some deliberate manoeuvre of language and the imagination would be needed to transform it into literature.

His chosen tactic was ironic melodrama: melodrama in action and event, irony in heightened moral judgement and appalled emotional response. The application of the tactic to the material produced tales of which the literary merit depends above all on the transmitted sense of an appalling social actuality. It might incidentally be argued that they suggest the superiority of the short story over the novel for repeated traffic with that actuality. In *For the Term of His Natural Life*, Marcus Clarke produced an unrepeatable success (even then threatened by the palpable melodrama of its full-length plot). 'Warung', on the other hand, could go on repeating his horrendous glimpses of the System month after month, year after year, with unabated flair. By combining the tactic of ironic melodrama with deliberately abbreviated selections from the truth with which he was obsessed, he contrived to do more than produce a number of notably successful collections of short stories; he invented a major method for giving profound national experience the power and permanency of art.

'Warung' published nearly all his convict tales (including 'How Muster-Master Stoneman Earned His Breakfast') in the Sydney *Bulletin*, and of course no other periodical publication is more intimately connected with the rise of the Australian short story in the 1890s. 'Warung', however, was not in every respect typical of the kind of storyteller it encouraged and fostered. It has been often enough pointed out that the paper's editorial policy had a good deal to do with the characteristic brevity of the stories of the period. But 'Warung's' subject matter was more a matter of personal discovery than *Bulletin* urging. If anything, the *Bulletin* was more likely to look favourably on stories derived from experience of the continent's unique physical reality – the bush. The natural world, however, no less than the System, afforded so special an experience that for those who wished to write seriously of it the exercise of the imagination remained a superfluous activity.

Many of the *Bulletin's* bush writers, it must be admitted, were neither serious nor even especially gifted. They filled the necessary (and honourable) role of entertainers, making of the outback a locale for adventure. Of these middle level writers, Ernest Favenc might be thought of as a fair representative; his *The Last of the Six* appeared in 1893, the same year as John Arthur Barry produced *Steve Brown's Bunyip*, another example of short story-telling as a popular entertainment. Of all the writers who used the natural world as a trigger to excitement and adventure none was more competent than Louis Becke. His stories, collected in 1894 under the title of *By Reef and Palm*, continue the tradition established by Lang of seeking their sanction in an appeal to truth, but have the great advantage of the allure of a South Pacific setting. Probably no volume illustrates better a tendency inherent in the *Bulletin* formula of the 1890s to satisfy the escapist tendencies in that wanderlust which forms so important a part of the national character.

It would be obviously unfair to leave the impression that the best (or even the majority) of the *Bulletin* stories were merely escapist fictions. There was at least one important class of them which, sharing with the adventure stories the desire to ameliorate the experience of the physical world, rose to a distinctive and important kind of artistic achievement. I refer, of course, to the comic stories. Comic writing in the 1890s did not seek its reality in the deliberate research of a Clarke or a 'Warung' but in the abundance of an accumulating folklore. If the System had instilled into the national mythology a profound concern with human cruelty and sadistic harshness, the natural world offered enough of wonder and the extraordinary to allow the growth of an exaggerated appetite for experience which expressed itself in the tall story. This mode of comic narrative, indeed, appears to touch so enduring a quality in Australian culture that, by no means limited to the nineteenth century, it has received some of its classic expressions in the twentieth: Lance Skuthorpe's 'The Champion Bullock Driver', for instance, or Alan Marshall's 'They Were Big Men on the Speewah', or Gavin Casey's 'The Hairy Men from Hannigan's Halt'.

The comic tale involved many other elements besides a sense of wonder at a startlingly unique natural environment; among the most important was the sense of heroic endeavour that folklore often discovers in the battles of puny men against the forces of Nature. In nineteenth-century Australia, however, such battles must have been lost as often as they were won. Hence the development of another characteristic mode of the humorous short story: the tale in which comedy is used as a defence against despair. The supreme examples of such an attitude are the stories of 'Steele Rudd' (Arthur Hoey Davis), the earliest (and probably best) of which are collected in *On Our Selection* (1899). 'Rudd' had no need to research the materials of his writing; he had lived them out in the Queensland bush where he spent his youth. Nevertheless, *On Our Selection* owes its classic status to neither the accuracy of its reporting nor the authenticity of its characterization but to the toughly defensive tone of its comedy. The circumstances he depicted were so uniformly calculated to defeat his protagonists that 'Rudd', no less than Porter, must have deemed the imagination superfluous. All that was needed to translate this hard-earned information into art was a language which would make the quality of the reported life at once accurate and bearable. To have found such a language is the comic triumph of *On Our Selection*. It rebuffs the worst that man or nature can bring against it with a fortitude that turns endurance into a kind of conquest.

Not all the realities of bush life could be controlled by a comic art. The despairs, the joys, the crises, even the *longueurs* of outback existence demanded their serious laureate, and found him in Henry Lawson. Lawson's immense contribution to and influence on the Australian short story are scarcely to be gainsaid; their exact substance and shape remain a matter for lively discussion. To many he is the representative, *par excellence*, of the code of mateship, that loosely coherent male ethos which, having more than survival value, gave to the life of the out-back worker both dignity and worth. Others especially associate his achievement with the attitudes summed up in Furphy's famous slogan, 'Temper democratic – bias offensively Austral-ian'. Others hear most clearly in his work the voice of radical protest, while yet others (and more recently) have developed powerful arguments in favour of the high aesthetic achievement of his tales, pointing to a tactful but unobtrusive control of style, perspective, point of view, and so on.

Plainly all these matters are elements in Lawson's total achievement. Yet, it seems to me that any useful judgement of his success as a serious short story writer must start out from two quite simple and demonstrable facts: (i) the complete canon of his prose fiction is very large indeed, and (ii) it contains only a handful of pieces more than four to five pages in length. In spite of certain statements of intention, Lawson never attempted let alone completed a full length novel – the nearest he came to one is probably the sequence of Joe Wilson stories. In effect, it is impossible to ascribe Lawson's lack of staying power in the art of prose narrative simply to some external cause like the *Bulletin's* editorial policy; it was a basic condition of his creativity.

This quality in Lawson has sometimes been held to constitute a limitation to his powers; and by the sternest critical tests, it probably is. In practical terms, however, and in relation to the

matters which most vitally engaged him, it was an advantage.
Like Porter, Lawson was not an imaginative man; one can almost
see him, especially in his later years, gathering 'copy' for his
stories (like Porter, that is to say, he needed to collect information). Unlike Porter, his talent was not for abundance but for
austerity – the spareness of his writing is a major factor in
creating its aura of more than reality, of truth. Unlike Porter,
finally, his major career was accomplished in a period of poverty
rather than plenty, a quality of life often so grindingly hard that
sustained inspection, front-on, would blind the gaze to its
actualities rather than illuminate. Given this quality of known
life, given the definition of his personal talent, Lawson was
forced back on the same fundamental device as that used by
'Warung' and 'Rudd' – irony. Where with the two other writers
it was merely a tactic, for Lawson it became a whole strategy.
Where 'Warung's' irony was farouche and hyperbolic, 'Rudd's'
savage and deadpan, Lawson's was at its best subtle, tactful,
and oblique. Being subtle, it could achieve a much greater range
of emotional effects; being tactful, it could apply itself to a much
wider range of materials; being oblique, it operated best in the
swift impression, the sidelong glance which registers a whole
scene but reveals little of the beholder. The strength of Lawson's
stories, it seems to me, resides no more in their yarn spinner's
conventions than in a tone so minimally emotional as to state
almost nothing while implying everything. The last sentence of
'That Pretty Girl in the Army', a piece notably charged with
feeling and moral valuation, simply runs, 'I looked at Mitchell
hard, but for all his face expressed he might only have said,
"I think it's going to rain" .' The statement might serve as a
paradigm for an Australian realism which forgoes the effects of
the imagination because language adequately applied to the
quality of experience is already more than enough.

It is in brief the modality of Lawson's stories as much as any
of the ethical attitudes which gives them their high place of
honour in the artistic history of the genre. If there is any sub-
stantive element in his writing of equal importance, it is less the
outback mateship, the urban protest, the radical politics than a
quality which might be described as his distinctly Australian
humanism. It is a quality which again, I should like to argue, he

shares with so apparently distant a writer as Hal Porter. On the very first page of *The Watcher on the Cast-Iron Balcony* Porter sets down this comment: 'I am born a good boy, good but not innocent.' For all its superficial idiosyncrasy, the assertion is no more eccentric or paradoxical in the context of the Australian short story than his denial of the imagination.

It is, thus, both true and pertinent to claim of many of Lawson's tales that they are good but not innocent. Many of his comic pieces, for example, depend on the infliction of pain or the practice of a thoughtless irresponsibility. At the same time Lawson's stories are, it might be argued, profoundly Australian in their thoroughly secular temper, their lack of concern with man as a metaphysical being. He clearly wished his prose works to endorse a certain range of ethical attitudes, yet the resources which he could tap to carry out that task were limited indeed. With little or no formal instruction in politics, philosophy, or ethics, he had, as it were, no intellectual bank account on which to draw for his ideas. Wholly reliant on a highly vulnerable sensibility, his personal capital was exhausted well before he had concluded his business with literature; hence the slow, sad decline of his later years.

If Lawson had the humanistic need to be good without the metaphysical capacity to be innocent, Barbara Baynton in *Bush Studies* (1902) was interested in neither goodness nor innocence. No writer has written more intensely of the experienced despairs of pioneer life on the small selection. The actualities of her tales not only did not require the application of the imagination; they could not tolerate it. Even as matters stand, one of the most sophisticated literary techniques of her period can barely confine the material of *Bush Studies* within the boundaries of what can be borne. In page after page, the ordinary opens out into nightmare, the familiar is transformed into the bizarre. The horrors of 'Warung's' System may have been different in kind, but they were scarcely more unendurable than those visited on the protagonists of these half dozen extraordinary stories. The particular horror of 'Squeaker's Mate', printed here, is the unremitting zeal with which Baynton presses home the necessities of the situation to the very last point of extremity. After *Bush Studies* nothing more need be said about life in the old bark hut; nothing more, indeed, could be said.

Bush Studies appeared in 1902, *The Bulletin Story Book* in 1901. In the years after the turn of the century, however, the short story, like so much of Australian literature, lost much of the impetus which had carried it through the previous decade. Such advances as were made were limited, and on a narrow front. Edward Dyson's *Fact'ry 'ands* (1906) for instance, made some small contribution to the possibilities of the form. In 'The Golden Shanty', set on a worked-out goldfield, Dyson had already produced one of the classic comic stories of the 1890s. In *Fact'ry 'ands* he turned his attertion to the urban proletariat. He was probably right to claim (as he did in his Introduction) that the mere fact of his treatment of this segment of the Australian population was in itself an innovation. In retrospect, however, it was his treatment of urban speech which was his most important contribution to the imaginative history of the short story. In his dialogue he achieved a combination of comic panache and accurate recording which is fairly mirrored in 'The Haunted Corner'. The other important feature of the piece is the transference of the tall story conventions to an industrial environment, and a fusion of those conventions with considerable narrative energy to produce a singular effect of comic fantasy.

It was the energy as much as anything else which moved Norman Lindsay to praise Dyson when he edited a selection of his stories in 1963. The elements of fantasy and humour are, however, more regularly repeated by some of the storytellers who succeeded Dyson in the first two decades of the twentieth century. There was, for example, another of Lindsay's protégés, Hugh McCrae, or 'Kodak' (E. F. O'Ferrall), remembered today largely for the single story, 'The Lobster and the Lioness'. In journalism, there was Lennie Lower. The possibilities of fantasy, however, were cultivated most notably not in any comic writing but in Christina Stead's sophisticated and manysided *The Salzburg Tales* (1934), a work I particularly regret having been unable to represent in this anthology.

Stead's achievement in *The Salzburg Tales* was a reminder in the middle 1930s of the significant contribution being made by women to the Australian short story. As early as 1890 'Tasma' (Mrs A. Couvreur) had produced the not very distinguished *A Sydney Sovereign*. From a later generation Henry Handel Richardson wrote a number of sensitive and enduring pieces.

After Christina Stead would come a long roll call of first class writers – Margaret Trist, E. A. Gollschewsky, Thelma Forshaw, Judith Wright, to name only a few. Only two years before *The Salzburg Tales*, however, there had appeared a collection of short stories by a woman who was, in many respects, a dominant figure in Australian letters during the first half of the twentieth century – Katharine Susannah Prichard's *Kiss on the Lips*, (1932). That work included 'Happiness', the story printed in this anthology. In 'Happiness' what I have suggested as a relationship between the imagination and reality special to the Australian short story notably re-asserts itself. There is, for instance, the same greed for information which had characterized the tradition from its inception. In 1967, in the Foreword to a collection of her stories, Prichard wrote of 'The Cooboo' (another of her Aboriginal tales) that 'An incident released casually so inflamed my imagination that I travelled to an isolated cattle station, four hundred miles beyond the railway, to be sure of authentic details.' A like motive informs the story 'Happiness'. In the same 1967 Foreword, Prichard identified as one of her central aims the effort 'to use the living speech of our people, guarding against a dialogue effect, and making the context of a sentence give the meaning of an unusual word or phrase'. In the interlocking of those two impulses – her greed for authenticating information and her trust in language to turn that information into art – Katharine Susannah Prichard defined her central place in the Australian tradition of short prose narrative.

One of Prichard's great contemporaries once defined his attitude towards language in a manner almost identical to her own. 'My purpose in writing', said Vance Palmer as bluntly as possible, 'is to set down Australian rhythms.' Palmer and Prichard were, of course, not only contemporaries but also close friends and literary colleagues. Prichard was more doctrinally committed to left-wing, radical politics than Palmer ever was – Vance's attitudes were more of a piece with (perhaps in part derived from) Lawson's humanist ethics, though with a considerable leavening of intellectual sophistication. Between them Palmer and Prichard set the tone of a good deal of Australian writing – not only in the short story – in the years between the wars.

Palmer in particular established himself as one of the masters of sensitive, subdued storytelling in the 1920s and 1930s. The political and social complexion of the 1930s, however, might have been expected to produce writers more immediately attracted to the radical posture of Prichard than to Palmer. Nobody can doubt the scale and intensity of the misery that the Depression years brought to Australians; oddly enough, however, they produced very little left-wing writing of real aesthetic merit or lasting interest. If there was a vintage year for the short story during the 1930s Johnston's *Annals* suggests that it was 1934, which saw the publication of Henry Lamond's *Tooth and Claw*, Palmer's *Sea and Spinifex*, Henry Handel Richardson's *The End of a Childhood* and Christina Stead's *The Salzburg Tales*. None of these, however, is significantly radical in either substance or sentiment. A case, indeed, might fairly be made out that the left-wing tradition in Australian culture generally has never fully realized itself in literature. Why this should be so I do not feel able to explain, but at least it can be said of the 1930s that if the decade failed immediately to produce many good stories of social protest it seems to have served as a matrix out of which such stories might come when memory and a long creative stir had done their work. In this connection some of the works of John Morrison or Frank Hardy or Judah Waten come readily to mind.

Of all the new voices of the 1930s which spoke with the accents of protest and social conscience, probably the most important was that of Gavin Casey. Many of his early stories – collected in *It's Harder for Girls* (1942) and *Birds of Feather* (1943) – are founded on his knowledge of deep level mining on Kalgoorlie's Golden Mile. Of his generation, no writer more successfully wedded what might be called the Lawson-populist tradition to a deeply felt critique of capitalist democracy. A few years younger than Casey was Dal Stivens, who also started to establish himself as one of the recognized short story men during the 1930s. Less closely attached to social actuality than Casey's, his work from the outset was marked by a unique combination of personal panache and an ironic play of wit. Another of the new men of the Depression years whose career continued well beyond that time was Frank Dalby Davison. His first book of stories, *The Woman at the Mill*, published in 1940, evinced an intelligence at once tough in its social judgements and capable of some subtlety in its rendering of personal relationships. His most individual variation on the Lawson tradition lay in his clinically unsentimental awareness of animal behaviour, given its most famous expression in the full length works *Man-Shy* (1931) and *Dusty* (1946) but also clearly displayed in 'Return of the Hunter', the piece selected for this anthology.

Appearing in 1940, *The Woman at the Mill* stands on the threshold of what is widely regarded as the second major period in the history of the short story in this country. That the period is rich in achievement is undeniable, so rich indeed that it is virtually impossible to single out any one year as undeniably more significant than the rest. Nineteen forty-four, however, might be thought of as summing up the wealth of the decade, less a vintage year than a representative one. In 1944 there appeared volumes by Peter Cowan, Don Edwards, 'Brian James', Ronald McCuaig, Douglas Stewart, Katharine Susannah Prichard. To assemble some of the other notable names of the period will further reinforce the sense of its variety and accomplishment: Margaret Trist, Ken Levis, James Hackston, Cecil Mann, R. S. Porteous, Alan Marshall, John Morrison, Ethel Anderson, John Ewers, Xavier Herbert. To tabulate the achievement is easy enough; to account for it, a much more difficult matter. It may be that sufficient time had elapsed after the traumas of the 1930s to permit their metamorphosis into art; it is certain that the short story was caught up in the dynamic urgency which swept over nearly all the literary activity of an Australia in imminent peril of invasion and military defeat. The accent on the short story, too, may have been a practical consequence of a shortage of paper and the conditions of publishing in a wartime economy; the temper of the writing was patently influenced by the increasing sophistication of Australian writers about literary and intellectual movements overseas, their increasingly assured capacity to absorb and benefit from acquaintance with foreign masters. Peter Cowan, for instance, (one of the men of the 1940s who has continued to write with unabated vigour and an assured maturity in all the decades since), early demonstrated his ability to profit from an acquaintance with such American writers as Hemingway and Dos Passos.

Whatever circumstances combined to produce the efflorescence of the 1940s, the period was, like the 1890s, fortunate in having a focal point for its short story writers. The *Bulletin* had continued as both influence and arena throughout the twentieth century; in 1941 it was joined by *Coast to Coast*, an annual anthology published by Angus and Robertson. The later history of *Coast to Coast* evinces some faltering and uncertainty, but between 1940 and 1950 it provided both a splendid record of and a major encouragement to the best of the short story writing that was being practised throughout the continent. During those ten years the anthology had some distinguished editors, none more than Vance Palmer, who edited the volume for 1944. In his Foreword Palmer described the prevailing sense of the short story in these terms:

We no longer demand that it shall have a formal beginning, a middle and an end; that it shall contain a plot as easily extracted as the backbone of a fish; one able to be served (to juggle a little with the image) as an anecdote at the dinner-table. Nowadays a short story may be a dream, a dialogue, a study of character, a poetic reverie; anything that has a certain unity and the movement of life.

In sum, the idea of the story as an epiphany had taken root in Australia; and to judge from some of the best known *Coast to Coast* stories of the 1940s, with a vengeance. One thinks of Peter Cowan's 'Living' and Margaret Trist's 'What Else Is There?', both in Palmer's 1944 *Coast to Coast*; or Marjorie Barnard's 'The Persimmon Tree', from 1942; or Palmer's own pieces, like 'Josie' (1941) or 'Mathieson's Wife' (1949–50).

If the subtle revelation of a tender sensibility is one of the nodes around which the stories of the 1940s characteristically cluster, the initiation theme, it might be suggested, is another. In many instances, as in some of the stories of Palmer or Trist, the two themes overlap; if the initiation motif, however, took on any distinct national coloration it was probably in a tendency to make the acquisition of new levels of knowledge coincide with or depend upon a transition from the bush to the city. The depth to which the theme penetrated the national mythology is attested by its continuance well beyond the 1940s; indeed, one of its classic statements, Ray Mathews' *A Bohemian Affair*, appeared as late as 1961.

By simple number count, the 1950s might seem to have made a contribution to the Australian short story scarcely less valuable than that of the previous decade. That there was some weakening in the thrust of the genre is indicated by the fact that most of the new titles were by writers who had already built their reputations: Judah Waten's *Alien Son* (1951), Dal Stivens' *The Gambling Ghost* (1951) and *Ironbark Bill* (1955), Vance Palmer's *Let the Birds Fly* (1955), Alan Marshall's *How's Andy Going?* (1956), Peter Cowan's *The Unploughed Land* (1957). There were, nevertheless, at least two writers closely associated with the 1950s who brought to their work qualities not elsewhere exploited with the same enthusiasm or skill: 'Brian James' (John Tierney) and E. O. Schlunke. Neither was a young man when he published his first book ('James' was 52, Schlunke, 49), and in a sense the virtues of their writing were slightly old fashioned. Both dealt with rural communities, both knew how to make comic capital out of upsetting conventional attitudes towards city and country and the relationships bteween them. Most particularly, however, both delighted in the fact that a short story is not only short but can also tell a story; in other words, they consistently developed the narrative possibilities inherent in their material through finely constructed plots. A master's manipulation of an ingeniously invented tale is a merit easily overlooked in an age of creative experiment and sophisticated criticism; it is not easily set aside in the work of either 'Brian James' or E. O. Schlunke.

While 'James' and Schlunke demonstrated the vitality that still resided in some of the long established conventions of the Australian short story, some of the younger writers were discovering the rewards of examining Australian attitudes in collision with those of other cultures. Peter Shrubb, for example, wrote with some élan of the impact of overseas travel on a sharply observant young Australian. Desmond O'Grady, who lived for some years in Rome, responded vitally to the impact of European experience. The title of his collection, *A Long Way from Home* (1966) suggests the emphasis of a good deal of his work, notably the long, ironic study of the Australian writer abroad, 'A Dedicated Young Man'. Similar interests, viewed from the perspective of a lifetime's humane learning, are displayed in the volume,

Disquiet (1969), by Manning Clark, one of Australia's great historians.

In 1964 Donald Horne published an account of contemporary Australian society which was soon to provide a portmanteau tag for cultural commentators – *The Lucky Country*. In the decade or so before the appearance of Horne's book, Australia had been indeed a lucky country, simply in its settled and expansive material prosperity. The literary record bespeaks a commensurate growth in variety and self-confidence. Of the short story in particular it might be said that, where it had begun in poverty and known the virtues of austerity, it had now come to enjoy the pleasures of abundance. The diverse talents which, in the 1950s, had consolidated the gains of the 1940s would soon be joined by other names of widely differing concerns and attitudes. Frank Hardy, for instance, published *Legends from Benson's Valley* in 1963, Judith Wright *The Nature of Love* in 1967. In 1961 Charles Osborne celebrated the opening of the new decade with his anthology, *Australian Stories of Today*. If ever circumstances conspired to bring Hal Porter's highly individual talent into harmonious relation with the public prestige system of Australian literature it was surely in the early 1960s. No more propitious moment could have been chosen for the publication of his first major volume of stories, *A Bachelor's Children*, than 1962.

In an obvious sense Porter had had to wait something like thirty years for his countrymen to catch up with, accept him. Even then the intricate elegance of his manner could, to many, still make him appear an exotic. Yet it has been the burden of this essay that since 1962 Porter has defined himself closer and closer to the centre of our culture rather than at its periphery. In the years since the appearance of *A Bachelor's Children* we have known conditions more favourable than ever before for making us see in the contours of his work a deep image of ourselves. A writer who subordinates his imagination to his own reality (of words), who is greedy for abundance and information, who reveals himself as good without ever having been innocent, such a writer we can now see as peculiarly representative of our whole national experience.

We have learned, too, to recognize in Porter other particulars which make of this seemingly idiosyncratic artist a deeply representative figure: his understanding of Australian family life, for instance. Nothing is better done in *The Watcher on the Cast-Iron Balcony* than the gathering of the Porter clan at Sale, in Victoria – 'the hubbub and braggadocio and seeming confidence of the family', composed of 'the most complex, double-sided and deceiving, and maybe even deceitful elements' (pp. 107–110). (Just how representative is his understanding of the Australian family is succinctly confirmed by story after story in Thelma Forshaw's *An Affair of Clowns*, published in 1967.) It may be, further, that Porter's recognition of sex as 'not a game but something more dangerously exhilarating, more deadly, more victimizing, a disease of the feelings, an itch, a rage, a mania' (p. 156) is the reverse side of that coin in our literary currency which, for most of our history, has been a massive silence or incompetence upon the subject. It needed a greed for information operating in a period of creative abundance to explicate an insight which had hitherto been too dangerous or dimly apprehended properly to express. But perhaps Porter is no more firmly bound to the indigenous culture than in that temper of mind which, in the immediate sense, makes his stories so uniquely his own. He recalls in *The Watcher* one of the first occasions on which he wept: 'they are the first tears I shed for the world and its people, for shapes and their shadows, for sounds and their shadows, for life and its shadows, running and pouring away like water from a tap not to be turned off' (p. 47). They are pre-eminently the tears of a sensitive humanist whose goodness is of a secular world unsanctioned by any deep-seated tradition of religious understanding.

Porter, then, is a writer whose relationship to his society ceased, as I would argue, in the 1960s to be oblique and became instead piercingly direct. In a way, Patrick White's relation to Australia is just as direct, but his writing throws back markedly different images from its complex planes and surfaces. The relationship of *The Burnt Ones* (1964) to Australian society is not only direct but adversary. The stories that it brings together help us to interpret ourselves by virtue of their unsparing critique of some of our least admirable traits. They tell us less how we are ethically right or wrong than how we are aesthetically or

28

spiritually inadequate, crass in the conduct of our everyday lives. Concerned intermittently for our social goodness or our innocence, they reveal to us the metaphysic of our corruption. The bourgeois, city-dwelling Australian has never been closer to the centre of major art than in White's stories, and has never had better reason for feeling discomfort at being so located.

Yet *The Burnt Ones* consists of more than sardonic satire. Appearing, like *A Bachelor's Children*, in an age of plenty, it has, like Porter's book, a plenitude of its own. The theme of cultures in collision, for instance, is pervasively present, especially in White's fascination with Greek experience; the complex rewards of suffering are centrally portrayed; and, in such a story as 'Down at the Dump', there is a celebration of life, even in defeat, even at Sarsaparilla, which has few peers in our prose fiction. Adversary, then, the relation most certainly is, but it is much more than that. It encompasses every ambiguity of the love-hate attraction that brought White home from England after the Second World War. 'There is the possibility', as he wrote in 'The Prodigal Son', 'that one may be helping to people a barely inhabited country with a race possessed of understanding.' And arguably White's simple presence in the polity of our literature must have encouraged, made possible even, an extension of the creative vitality of Australian writing through the 1960s into the present decade. In particular, it has probably strengthened the resolve of some of our younger writers to maintain their adversary stance in the face of contemporary mores. Events in the late 1960s and early 1970s, to be sure, provided rich materials for artists critical of accepted values and lifestyles: Vietnam, for instance, the whole thrust to a more permissive social morality. The challenges of these new subjects and circumstances have already been convincingly met, in the short story as in the other literary forms. Frank Moorhouse, for example, has already proved himself a sharply observant chronicler of the latest generation of Australian adults. There is a good deal more, however, to books like *The Americans, Baby* (1972) and *The Electrical Experience* (1974) than sharp-eyed observation. The best of his stories realize in the texture of their incident and dialogue a sophisticated and exact appreciation of the experienced quality of his environment. His treatment of the lives at the leading edge of our social culture has a concern for sexuality oddly akin to Hal Porter's: 'a disease of the feelings, an itch, a rage, a mania'. The story selected for this anthology, furthermore, 'Five Incidents of the Flesh and the Blood' provokes tears for the impermanence of life and things quite as poignant as Porter's and with as individual a manner. Moorhouse, like the best short story writers anywhere, subsumes his tradition almost invisibly into his personal registration of the pitch and beat of his own generation's sensibility.

The same point might be advanced with respect to Michael Wilding. In some of his tales he ventures into much the same social territory as Moorhouse, but the true élan of his writing is, in my view, to be felt in the gothic narratives of which 'As Boys to Wanton Flies' is so ripe an example. The title, with its wittily perverse allusion to *King Lear*, hints at a sardonic, unruffled intelligence behind the narrative invention; but the invention itself vibrates to a *frisson* of the genuinely macabre, imposes a vision of horror which has nothing to do with hollow melo-dramatics. Even more fantastically disturbing are some of the stories that Peter Carey has collected in *The Fat Man in History* (1974), and represented here by 'Report on the Shadow Industry'. A piece like 'Withdrawal' (regrettably too long for inclusion) provides horror of almost every kind except the cheap thrill. There is at large in Carey's writing a spirit wholeheartedly subversive of the humanist pieties in which the Australian short story has most regularly found its values, both ethical and aesthetic.

To say as much is to admit that in a contemporary voice like Carey's (and arguably in Wilding's and Moorhouse's as well) can be heard a quite fundamental challenge to the whole tradition I have been outlining. He would, plainly enough, be a stupidly doctrinaire historian, or merely a stupid one, who would not admit the possibility of such a challenge. Of Carey and Wilding, however, it can be suggested that their tales constitute a kind of latter-day tribute to the grotesque and arabesque. And Edgar Allan Poe was a pervasively important influence on nineteenth-century Australian poetry, if not its fiction. It may be that after a history of close on a hundred years the Australian short story is now firmly enough based to venture towards insights and concerns that have hitherto been the exclusive province of our poetry. It may be, too, that the ambiance of Carey's and Wilding's prose suggests not only a specific analogy with Poe but a continuity with the Romantic tradition of prestige assigned to the imagination.

I began these remarks by drawing attention to Hal Porter's seemingly quixotic claim that he subordinates the imagination to the pressure of the actual, and have suggested that such a subordination, far from being unique to Porter, has been endemic in our shorter fiction from its first stirrings; that the experienced quality of reality has, in effect, rendered the imagination superfluous. Perhaps, however, the outlines of the historical development of the Australian short story might come into clearer focus in postulating not an abandonment of the imagination but an active re-definition of the term and of its uses. If the imagination is to be subordinated to one's own reality (whatever that may be), it can no longer be conceived of as a special compartment of the mind, an achieved quality of a successful work of art. It must be seen as the process of understanding and creation, the integrated engagement of all the powers of the artist with a world no solipsistic impulse can negate. That, I take it, is the real burden of Porter's claim; that is the principle by which the best of our shorter fiction has been, and continues to be, written. Australian literature has never been much at ease with theoretical speculation, but in their practice our storytellers have proven against the pulse of a unique national experience the force of Wallace Stevens's dictum: 'the best definition of true imagination is that it is the sum of our faculties.'

'Price Warung'

HOW MUSTER-MASTER STONEMAN
EARNED HIS BREAKFAST

I

AN unpretentious building of rough-hewn stone standing in the middle of a small, stockaded enclosure. A doorway in the wall of the building facing the entrance-gate to the yard. To the left of the doorway, a glazed window of the ordinary size. To its right a pane-less aperture, so low and narrow that were the four upright and two transverse bars which grate it doubled in thickness no interstice would be left for the admission of light or air to the interior. Behind the bars – a face.

Sixteen hours hence that face will look its last upon the world which has stricken it countless cruel blows. In a corner of the enclosure the executioner's hand is even now busy stitching into a shapeless cap, a square of grey serge. Tomorrow the same hand will use the cap to hood the face, as one of the few simple preliminaries to swinging the carcass to which the face is attached from the rude platform now in course of erection against the stockade fence and barely twenty yards in front of the stone building.

The building is the gaol – locally known as the 'cage' – of Oatlands, a small township in the midlands of Van Diemen's Land, which has gradually grown up round a convict 'muster-station', established by Governor Davey. The time is five o'clock on a September evening, fifty-five years ago. At nine o'clock on the following morning, Convict Glancy, No. 17,927, transportee ex ship *Pestonjee Bomanjee* (second trip), originally under sentence for seven years for the theft of a silk handkerchief from a London 'swell', will suffer the extreme penalty of the law for having, in an intemperate moment, objected to the mild discipline with which a genial and loving motherland had sought to correct his criminal tendencies. In other words, Convict Glancy, metaphorically goaded by the wordy insults and literally

32

by the bayonet-tip of one of his motherland's reformatory agents – to wit, Road-gang Overseer James Jones – had scattered J.J.'s brains over a good six square yards of metalled roadway. The deed had been rapturously applauded by Glancy's fellow-gangers, all of whom had the inclination, but lacked the courage, to wield the crowbar that has been the means of erasing this particular tyrant's name from the paysheets of His Britannic Majesty's Colonial Penal Establishment. Nevertheless and notwithstanding such tribute of appreciation, H.B.M.'s Colonial representatives, police, judicial and gubernatorial, have thought it rather one to be censured and have, accordingly, left Convict Glancy for execution.

This decision of the duly constituted authorities Convict Glancy has somewhat irrelevantly (as it will seem to us at this enlightened day) acknowledged by a fervent 'Thank God!' – an ejaculation rendered the more remarkable by the fact that never before in his convict history had he linked the name of the Deity with any expression of gratitude for the many blessings enjoyed by him in that state of penal servitude to which it had pleased the same Deity to call him. On the contrary, he had constantly indulged in maledictions on his fate and on his Maker. He had resolutely cursed the benignant forces with which the System and the King's Regulations had surrounded him, and he had failed to reverence as he ought the triangles, the gang-chains, the hominy, the prodding bayonet, and the other things which would have conduced to his reformation had he but manifested a more humble and obedient spirit. No wonder, therefore, as Chaplain Ford said, that it has come about that he has qualified for the capital doom.

Upon this doom, in so far as it could be represented by the gallows, Convict Glancy was now gazing with an unflinching eye. On this September evening he stands at his cell-window looking on half-a-dozen brown-clothed figures handling saw, and square, and hammer, as they fix in the earth two sturdy uprights, and to those a projecting cross-beam; as they bind the two with a solid tie-piece of knotless hardwood; as they build a narrow platform of planks around the gallows-tree; as they fasten a rope to the notched end of the cross-beam; and as they slope to the edge of the planks, ten feet from the ground, a rude ladder. All the drowsy afternoon he had watched the working party, though Chaplain Ford had stood by his side droning of the grace which had been withheld from him in life, but might still be his in death. He had felt interested, had Convict Glancy, in these preparations for the event in which he was to act such a prominent part on the morrow. He had even laughed at the grim humour of one of the brown-garbed workers who, when the warder's eye was off him, had gone through the pantomime of noosing the rope end round his own neck – a little joke which contributed much to the (necessarily noiseless) delight of the rest of the gang.

Altogether, Convict Glancy reflected as dusk fell, and the working party gathered up their tools, and the setting sun tipped the bayonets of the guard with a diamond iridescence, that he had spent many a duller afternoon. If the Chaplain had only held his tongue, the time would have passed with real pleasantness. He said as much to the good man as the latter remarked to the warder on duty in the cell that he would look in again after supper.

'You may save yourself the trouble, sir,' quoth, respectfully enough, Convict Glancy. 'You have spoilt my last afternoon. Don't spoil my last night!'

Chaplain Ford winced at the words. He was still comparatively new to the work of spiritually superintending a hundred or so monsters who looked upon the orthodox hell as a place where residence would be pleasantly recreative after Port Arthur Settlement and Norfolk Island; and the time lay still in the future when, being completely embruted, he would come to regard it as a very curious circumstance indeed that Christ had omitted eulogistic reference to the System from the Sermon on the Mount. Consequently, he winced and sighed, not so much – to do him justice – at the utter depravity of Convict Glancy as at his own inability to reach the reprobate's heart. But he took the hint; he mournfully said he would not return that evening, but would be with the prisoner by half-past five o'clock in the morning.

II

When Chaplain Ford entered the enclosure immediately before the hour he had named, he at once understood, from the

excitement manifested by a group assembled in front of the
'cage', that something was amiss. Voices were uttering fearful
words, impetuously, almost shriekingly, and hands swung
lanterns – the grey dawn had not yet driven the darkness from
the stockade – and brandished muskets furiously. A very brief
space of time served to inform the reverend functionary what
had gone wrong.

Convict Glancy had made his escape, having previously
murdered, with the victim's own bayonet, the warder who had
been told-off to watch him during the night. This latter circumstance was, of course, unfortunate, but alone it would not have
created the excitement, for the murder of prison-officials was a
common enough occurrence. It was the other thing that galled
the gesticulating and blaspheming group. That a prisoner,
fettered with ten-pound irons, should have broken out of gaol
on the very eve of his execution – why, it was calculated to shake
the confidence of the Comptroller-General himself in the
infallibility and perfect righteousness of the System. And,
popular and authoritative belief in the System once shattered,
where would they be?

The murdered man had gone on duty at ten o'clock, and very
shortly afterwards he must have met with his fate. How Glancy
had obtained possession of the bayonet could only be con-
jectured. As was the custom during the day or two preceding a
convict's execution, he had been left unmanacled, and ironed
with double leg-chains only. Thus his hands were free to per-
petrate the deed once he grasped the weapon. Glancy, on his
escape, had taken the instrument with him, but there was no
doubt that he had inflicted death with it, the wound in the dead
man's breast being obviously caused by the regulation bayonet.
Possibly the sentinel had nodded, and then a violent wrench of
the prisoner's wrist and a sudden stab had extended his momen-
tary slumber into an eternal sleep. The bayonet had also been
used by Glancy to prise up a flooring-flag, and to scoop out an
aperture under the wall, the base-stones of which, following the
slipshod architecture of the time, rested on the surface and were
not sunk into the ground.

The work of excavation must have taken the convict several
hours, and must have been conducted as noiselessly as the

manner of committing the crime itself. A solitary warder occupied the outer guard-room, but he asserted that he had heard no sound except the exchange of whistle-signals between the dormitory guard at the convict-barracks (a quarter of a mile away at the rear of the gaol stockade) and the military patrol. The night routine of the 'cage' did not insist upon the whistle-signal between the men on duty, but they passed a simple 'All's well' every hour. And this the guardroom-warder maintained he had done with the officer inside the condemned cell, the response being given in a low tone, from consideration, so the former thought, for the sleeping convict so soon to die. Of course, if this man was to be believed, Glancy must have uttered the words. It was not the first time the signal which should have been given by a prison officer had been made by his convict murderer.

The murder was discovered on the arrival of the relief watch at five o'clock. The last 'All's well' was exchanged at four. Consequently the escapee had less than an hour's start. The scaling of the stockade would not be difficult even for a man in irons, and once in the bush an experienced hand would soon find a method of fracturing the links.

It must be admitted that this contumacious proceeding of Convict Glancy was most vexatious. Under-Sheriff Ropewell, now soundly reposing at the township inn, would be forthcoming at nine o'clock with his Excellency's warrant in his hands to demand from Muster-Master Stoneman the body of one James Glancy, and Muster-Master Stoneman would have to apologize for his inability to produce the said body. The difficulty was quite unprecedented, and Stoneman, as he stood in the midst of his minions, groaned audibly at the prospect of having to do the thing most abhorrent to the official mind – establish a precedent.

'Such a thing was never heard of!' he cried. 'A man to bolt just when he was to be turned off! And the d—d hypocrite tried to make his Honour and all of us think that he was only to happy to be scragged. It's too d—d bad!'

It certainly did seem peculiar that Glancy, who had apparently much rejoiced at the contemplation of his early decease, should give leg-bail just when he was to realize his wishes. He had told the judge that 'he was – glad they were going to kill him right off instead of by inches', and yet he had voluntarily thrown off the noose when it was virtually round his neck. Was it the mere contrariness of the convict nature that prompted the escape? Or, was it the innate love of life that becomes stronger as the benefits of living become fewer and fewer? Had the craving for existence and for freedom surged over his despair and recklessness at the eleventh hour?

Such were the inquiries which Chaplain Ford put to himself as, horrified, he took in the particulars of No. 17,927's crowning enormities from the hubbub of the group.

'Damn it!' said the Muster-Master at last, 'we are losing time. The devil can't have gone far with those ten-pounders on him. We'll have to put the regulars on the track as well as our own men. Warder Briggs, report to Captain White at the barracks, and –'

Muster-Master Stoneman stopped short. Through the foggy air there came the familiar sound as of a convict dragging his irons. What could it be? No prisoners had been as yet loosed from the dormitory. Whence could the noise proceed?

Clink – clank – s-sh – dr-g-g – clink – clank – dr-g-g. The sound drew nearer, and Convict Glancy turned in at the enclosure gateway – unescorted. He had severed the leg-chain at the link which connected with the basil of the left anklet, but had not taken the trouble to remove the other part of the chain. Thus, while he could take his natural pace with his left foot, he dragged the fetters behind his right leg.

A moment of hushed surprise, and then three or four men rushed towards him. The first who touched him he felled with a blow.

'Not yet,' said he, grimly. 'I give myself up, Mr. Stoneman – you don't take me! I give myself up – you ain't going to get ten quid[1] for taking me.' And then Convict Glancy laughed, and held out his hands for the handcuffs. He laughed more heartily as the subordinate hirelings of the System threw themselves upon him like hounds on their prey.

'No need to turn out the sodgers now, Muster-Master – not

1. 'Ten quid': the reward of ten pounds paid by Government on the recapture of an escaped prisoner.

till nine o'clock.' Once more his hideous laugh rang through the yards. 'You had an easier job than you expected, hadn't you, Stoneman, old cove?'

Muster-Master Stoneman had been surprised into silence and into an unusual abstinence from blasphemy by the reappearance – quite unprecedented under the circumstances! – of the doomed wretch. But the desperado's jeering tones whipped him into speech.

'Curse you!' he yelled, 'I'll teach you to laugh on the other side of your mouth presently. You'd better have kept away.' He literally foamed in his mad anger.

'Do you think I couldn't have stopped away if I'd wanted to, having got clear?' A lofty scorn rang out in the words. 'But do you think I was going to run away when I was so near Freedom as that?' And the wretch jerked his manacled hands in the direction of the gallows. 'You d—d fool!'

No one spoke for a full half-minute. Then: 'Why did you break gaol then?' asked the Muster-Master.

'*Because I wanted to spit on Jones' grave!*' was the reply.

III

Muster-Master Stoneman was as good as his word. Death couldn't drive the smile from Glancy's face. That could only be done by one thing – the lash.

When next the Muster-Master spoke it was to order the prisoner a double ration of cocoa and bread. And, 'Briggs,' he continued, 'while he is getting it, see that the triangles are rigged.'

'The triangles, sir!' exclaimed Officer Briggs and Convict Glancy together.

'I said the triangles, and I mean the triangles. No. 17,927 has broken gaol, and as Muster-Master of this station, and governor of this gaol, and as a magistrate of the territory, I can give him 750 lashes for escaping. But as he has to go through another little ceremony this morning I'll let him off with a "canary" – (a hundred lashes).'[2]

2. Muster-Master Stoneman had doubtless in his mind's eye when he made this remark the decision of a Sydney Court which had legalized the infliction, by an official holding a plurality of offices, of a sentence passed by him in each capacity, but for the one offence.

'You surely cannot mean it, sir!' exclaimed Parson Ford.

'Mean it, sir! By G—, I'll show you I mean it,' replied the M.M., whose blaspheming no presence restrained save that of his official superiors. 'Give him the cocoa, Warder Tuff, give the doctor my compliments, and tell him his attendance is required here. Tell him he'd better bring his smelling salts – they may be wanted,' he sneered in conclusion.

'You devil!' cried Glancy. The reckless grin passed away, and his face faded to the pallor of the death he was so soon to die.

As Muster-Master Stoneman turned on his heel to prepare the warrant for the flogging, he looked at his watch. It was half-past six.

At seven o'clock the first lash from the cat-o'-nine-tails fell upon Convict Glancy's back.

At 7.30 his groaning and bleeding body, which had received the full hundred of flaying stripes, lay on the pallet of the cell where he had murdered the night-guard but a few hours before.

At eight o'clock Executioner Johnson entered the cell. 'I've brought yer sumthink to 'arden yer, Glancy, ol' man. I'll rub it in, an' it'll help yer to keep up.' So tender a sympathy inspired Mr Johnson's words that anyone not knowing him would have thought he was the bearer of some priceless balsam. But Convict Glancy knew him and, maddened by pain though he was, had still sensibility enough left to make a shuddering resistance to the hangman as he proceeded to rub into the gashed flesh a handful of coarse salt. 'By the Muster-Master's orders, sonny,' soothingly remarked Johnson. 'To 'arden yer.'

At 8.15 Under-Sheriff Ropewell, who had been apprised while at breakfast of the murder and escape, appeared on the scene escorted by his javelin-men. This gentleman, too, had been greatly perplexed by Convict Glancy's proceedings. 'Really it was most inconsiderate of the man,' he said to the Muster-Master. 'I do not know whether I ought to proceed to execution, pending his trial for this second murder.'

'Oh,' said the latter functionary – flicking with his hand-kerchief from his coat-sleeve as he spoke a drop of Convict Glancy's blood that had fallen there from a reflex swirl of the lash, 'I think your duty is clear. You must hang him at nine o'clock, and try him afterwards for the last crime.'

And as Convict Glancy, per *Pestonjee Bomanjee* (second), No. 17,927, was punctually hanged at 9.5, it is to be presumed that the Under-Sheriff had accepted this solution of the difficulty.

At 10.15 a mass of carrion having been huddled into a shell, and certain formalities, which in the estimation of the System served as efficiently as a coroner's inquest, having been duly attended to, Muster-Master Stoneman bethought himself that he had not breakfasted.

'I'll see you later, Mr. Ropewell,' he said, as the latter was endorsing the Governor's warrant with the sham verdict; 'I'm going to breakfast. I think I've earned it this morning.'

'Steele Rudd'

WHEN THE WOLF WAS AT THE DOOR

THERE had been a long stretch of dry weather, and we were cleaning out the waterhole. Dad was down the hole shovelling up the dirt; Joe squatted on the brink catching flies and letting them go again without their wings, a favourite amusement of his; while Dan and Dave cut a drain to turn the water that ran off the ridge into the hole – when it rained. Dad was feeling dry, and told Joe to fetch him a drink.

Joe said, 'See first if this cove can fly with only one wing.' Then he went, but returned and said, 'There's no water in the bucket – Mother used the last drop to boil the punkins,' and renewed the flycatching. Dad tried to spit, and was going to say something when Mother, half-way between the house and the waterhole, cried out that the grass-paddock was all on fire. 'So it is, Dad,' said Joe, slowly but surely dragging the head off a fly with finger and thumb.

Dad scrambled out of the hole and looked. 'Good God!' was all he said. How he ran! All of us rushed after him except Joe – he couldn't run very well, because the day before he had ridden fifteen miles on a poor horse, bare-back. When near the fire Dad stopped running to break a green bush. He hit upon a tough one. Dad was in a hurry. The bush wasn't. Dad swore and tugged with all his might. Then the bush broke and Dad fell heavily upon his back and swore again.

To save the cockatoo-fence that was round the cultivation is what was troubling Dad. Right and left we fought the fire with boughs. Hot! It was hellish hot! Whenever there was a lull in the wind we worked. Like a windmill Dad's bough moved – and how he rushed for another when that was used up! Once we had the fire almost under control, but the wind rose again, and away went the flames higher and faster than ever.

'It's no use', said Dad at last, placing his hand on his head and throwing down his bough. We did the same, then stood and watched the fence go. After supper we went out again and saw it still burning. Joe asked Dad if he didn't think it was a splendid sight. Dad didn't answer him; he didn't seem conversational that night.

We decided to put the fence up again. Dan had sharpened the axe with a broken file, and he and Dad were about to start when Mother asked them what was to be done about flour. She said she had shaken the bag to get enough to make scones for that morning's breakfast, and unless some was got somewhere there would be no bread for dinner.

Dad reflected, while Dan felt the edge on the axe with his thumb.

Dad said, 'Won't Mrs Dwyer let you have a dishful until we get some?'

'No,' Mother answered, 'I can't ask her until we send back what we owe them.'

Dad reflected again. 'The Andersons, then?' he said.

Mother shook her head and asked what good there was in sending to them when they, only that morning, had sent to her for some.

'Well, we must do the best we can at present,' Dad answered, 'and I'll go to the store this evening and see what is to be done.'

Putting the fence up again, in the hurry that Dad was in, was the very devil! He felled the saplings – and such saplings – *trees* many of them were – while we, all of a muck of sweat, dragged them into line. Dad worked like a horse himself and expected us to do the same. 'Never mind staring about you,' he'd say, if he caught us looking at the sun to see if it were coming dinner-time. 'There's no time to lose if we want to get the fence up and crop in.'

Dan worked nearly as hard as Dad until he dropped the butt-end of a heavy sapling on his foot, which made him hop about on one leg and say that he was sick and tired of the dashed fence. Then he argued with Dad, and declared that it would be far better to put a wire fence up at once, and be done with it, instead of wasting time over a thing that would only be burnt down again. 'How long,' he said, 'will it take to get the posts?

Not a week,' and he hit the ground disgustedly with a piece of stick he had in his hand.

'Confound it!' Dad said. 'Haven't you got any sense, boy? What earthly use would a wire fence be without any wire in it?'

Then we knocked off and went to dinner.

No one appeared in any humour to talk at the table. Mother sat silently at the end and poured out the tea while Dad, at the head, served the pumpkin and divided what cold meat there was. Mother wouldn't have any meat – one of us would have to go without if she had taken any.

I don't know if it was on account of Dan's arguing with him, or if it was because there was no bread for dinner, that Dad was in a bad temper. Anyway, he swore at Joe for coming to the table with dirty hands. Joe cried and said that he couldn't wash them when Dave, as soon as he had washed his, had thrown the water out. Then Dad scowled at Dave, and Joe passed his plate along for more pumpkin.

Dinner was almost over when Dan, still looking hungry, grinned and asked Dave if he wasn't going to have some *bread*. Whereupon Dad jumped up in a tearing passion. 'Damn your insolence!' he said to Dan. 'Make a jest of it, would you?'

'Who's jestin'?' Dan answered and grinned again.

'Go!' said Dad furiously, pointing to the door. 'Leave my roof, you thankless dog!'

Dan went that night.

It was only when Dad promised faithfully to reduce his account within two months that the storekeeper let us have another bag of flour on credit. And what a change that bag of flour wrought! How cheerful the place became all at once! And how enthusiastically Dad spoke of the farm and the prospects of the coming season!

Four months had gone by. The fence had been up some time and ten acres of wheat had been put in; but there had been no rain, and not a grain had come up, or was likely to.

Nothing had been heard of Dan since his departure. Dad spoke about him to Mother. 'The scamp,' he said, 'to leave me just when I wanted help. After all the years I've slaved to feed him and clothe him, see what thanks I get! But, mark my word, he'll be glad to come back yet.' But Mother would never say anything against Dan.

The weather continued dry. The wheat didn't come up, and Dad became despondent again.

The storekeeper called every week and reminded Dad of his promise. 'I would give it to you willingly,' Dad would say, 'if I had it, Mr Rice, but what can I do? You *can't* knock blood out of a stone.'

We ran short of tea, and Dad thought to buy more with the money Anderson owed him for some fencing he had done. But when he asked for it, Anderson was very sorry he hadn't got it just then, but promised to let him have it as soon as he could sell his chaff. When Mother heard Anderson couldn't pay, she *did* cry, and said there wasn't a bit of sugar in the house, or enough cotton to mend the children's bits of clothes.

We couldn't very well go without tea, so Dad showed Mother how to make a new kind. He roasted a slice of bread on the fire till it was like a black coal, then poured the boiling water over it and let it draw well. Dad said it had a capital flavour – *he* liked it.

Dave's only pair of pants were pretty well worn off him; Joe hadn't a decent coat for Sunday; Dad himself wore a pair of boots with soles tied on with wire; and Mother fell sick. Dad did all he could – waited on her, and talked hopefully of the fortune which would come to us some day – but once, when talking to Dave, he broke down, and said he didn't, in the name of Almighty God, know what he would do. Dave couldn't say anything – he moped about, too, and home somehow didn't seem like home at all.

When Mother was sick and Dad's time was mostly taken up nursing her, when there was hardly anything in the house, when, in fact, the wolf was at the very door, Dan came home with a pocket full of money and swag full of greasy clothes. How Dad shook him by the hand and welcomed him back! And how Dan talked of tallies, belly-wool, and ringers, and implored Dad, over and over again, to go shearing, or rolling up, or branding – *anything* rather than work and starve on the selection.

But Dad stayed on the farm.

Henry Lawson

SEND ROUND THE HAT

> *Now this is the creed from the Book of the Bush –*
> *Should be simple and plain to a dunce:*
> *'If a man's in a hole you must pass round the hat –*
> *Were he jail-bird or gentleman once.'*

'Is it any harm to wake yer?'

It was about nine o'clock in the morning, and, though it was Sunday morning, it was no harm to wake me; but the shearer had mistaken me for a deaf jackeroo, who was staying at the shanty and was something like me, and had good-naturedly shouted almost at the top of his voice, and he woke the whole shanty. Anyway he woke three or four others who were sleeping on beds and stretchers, and one on a shake-down on the floor, in the same room. It had been a wet night, and the shanty was full of shearers from Big Billabong Shed which had cut out the day before. My room mates had been drinking and gambling overnight, and they swore luridly at the intruder for disturbing them.

He was six-foot-three or thereabout. He was loosely built, bony, sandy-complexioned and grey-eyed. He wore a good-humoured grin at most times, as I noticed later on; he was of a type of bushman that I always liked – the sort that seem to get more good-natured the longer they grow, yet are hard-knuckled and would accommodate a man who wanted to fight, or thrash a bully in a good-natured way. The sort that like to carry some-body's baby round, and cut wood, carry water and do little things for overworked married bushwomen. He wore a saddle-tweed sac suit two sizes too small for him, and his face, neck, great hands and bony wrists were covered with sunblotches and freckles.

'I hope I ain't disturbin' yer,' he shouted, as he bent over my bunk, 'but there's a cove –'

'You needn't shout!' I interrupted, 'I'm not deaf.'

'Oh – I beg your pardon!' he shouted. 'I didn't know I was yellin.' I thought you was the deaf feller.'

'Oh, that's all right,' I said. 'What's the trouble?'

'Wait till them other chaps is done swearin' and I'll tell yer,' he said. He spoke with a quiet, good-natured drawl, with something of the nasal twang, but tone and drawl distinctly Australian – altogether apart from that of the Americans.

'Oh, spit it out for Christ's sake, Long-'un!' yelled One-eyed Bogan, who had been the worst swearer in a rough shed, and he fell back on his bunk as if his previous remarks had exhausted him.

'It's that there sick jackeroo that was pickin'-up at Big Billa-bong,' said the Giraffe. 'He had to knock off the first week, an' he's been here ever since. They're sendin' him away to the hospital in Sydney by the speeshall train. They're just goin' to take him up in the wagonette to the railway-station, an' I thought I might as well go round with the hat an' get him a few bob. He's got a missus and kids in Sydney.'

'Yer always goin' round with yer gory hat!' growled Bogan. 'Yer'd blanky well take it round in hell!'

'That's what he's doing, Bogan,' muttered Gentleman Once, on the shake-down, with his face to the wall.

The hat was a genuine cabbage-tree, one of the sort that 'last a lifetime'. It was well coloured, almost black in fact with weather and age, and it had a new strap round the base of the crown. I looked into it and saw a dirty pound note and some silver. I dropped in half a crown, which was more than I could spare, for I had only been a green-hand at Big Billabong.

'Thank yer!' he said. 'Now then, you fellers!'

'I wish you'd keep your hat on your head, and your money in your pockets and your sympathy somewhere else,' growled Jack Moonlight as he raised himself painfully on his elbow and felt under his pillow for two half-crowns. 'Here,' he said, 'here's two half-casers. Chuck 'em in and let me sleep for God's sake!'

Gentleman Once, the gambler, rolled round on his shake-down, bringing his good-looking dissipated face from the wall.

He had turned in in his clothes and, with considerable exertion he shoved his hand down into the pocket of his trousers, which were a tight fit. He brought up a roll of pound notes and could find no silver.

'Here,' he said to the Giraffe, 'I might as well lay a quid. I'll chance it anyhow. Chuck it in.'

'You've got rats this mornin', Gentleman Once,' growled the Bogan. 'It ain't a blanky horse-race.'

'P'r'aps I have,' said Gentleman Once, and he turned to the wall again with his head on his arm.

'Now, Bogan, yer might as well chuck in somethin',' said the Giraffe.

'What's the matter with the — jackeroo?' asked the Bogan, tugging his trousers from under the mattress.

Moonlight said something in a low tone.

'The — hehas!' said Bogan. 'Well, I pity the —! Here, I'll chuck in half a — quid!' and he dropped half a sovereign into the hat.

The fourth man, who was known to his face as 'Barcoo-Rot', and behind his back as 'The Mean Man', had been drinking all night, and not even Bogan's stump-splitting adjectives could rouse him. So Bogan got out of bed, and calling on us (as blanky female cattle) to witness what he was about to do, he rolled the drunkard over, prospected his pockets till he made up five shillings (or a 'caser' in bush language), and 'chucked' them into the hat.

And Barcoo-Rot is probably unconscious to this day that he was ever connected with an act of charity.

The Giraffe struck the deaf jackeroo in the next room. I heard the chaps cursing Long-'un for waking them, and Deaf-'un for being, as they thought at first, the indirect cause of the disturbance. I heard the Giraffe and his hat being condemned in other rooms and cursed along the veranda where more shearers were sleeping; and after a while I turned out.

The Giraffe was carefully fixing a mattress and pillows on the floor of a wagonette, and presently a man, who looked like a corpse, was carried out and lifted into the trap.

As the wagonette started, the shanty-keeper – a fat, soulless-looking man – put his hand in his pocket and dropped a quid into the hat which was still going round, in the hands of the

47

Giraffe's mate, little Teddy Thompson, who was as far below medium height as the Giraffe was above it.

The Giraffe took the horse's head and led him along on the most level parts of the road towards the railway-station, and two or three chaps went along to help get the sick man into the train.

The shearing season was over in that district, but I got a job of house-painting, which was my trade, at the Great Western Hotel (a two-storey brick place), and I stayed in Bourke for a couple of months.

The Giraffe was a Victorian native from Bendigo. He was well known in Bourke and to many shearers who came through the great dry scrubs from hundreds of miles round. He was stakeholder, drunkard's banker, peace-maker where possible, referee or second to oblige the chaps when a fight was on, big brother or uncle to most of the children in town, final court of appeal when the youngsters had a dispute over a foot-race at the school picnic, referee at their fights, and he was the stranger's friend.

'The feller as knows can battle around for himself,' he'd say. 'But I always like to do what I can for a hard-up stranger cove. I was a green-hand jackeroo once meself, and I know what it is.'

'You're always bothering about other people, Giraffe,' said Tom Hall, the Shearers' Union secretary, who was only a couple of inches shorter than the Giraffe. 'There's nothing in it, you can take it from me – I ought to know.'

'Well, what's a feller to do?' said the Giraffe. 'I'm only hangin' round here till shearin' starts agen, an' a cove might as well be doin' something. Besides, it ain't as if I was like a cove that had old people or a wife an' kids to look after. I ain't got no responsibilities. A feller can't be doin' nothin'. Besides, I like to lend a helpin' hand when I can.'

'Well, all I've got to say,' said Tom, most of whose screw went in borrowed quids, etc.; 'all I've got to say is that you'll get no thanks, and you might blanky well starve in the end.'

'There ain't no fear of me starvin' so long as I've got me hands about me; an' I ain't a cove as wants thanks,' said the Giraffe.

He was always helping someone or something. Now it was a bit of a 'darnce' that we was gettin' up for the girls; again it was Mrs Smith, the woman whose husban' was drowned in the flood in the Bogan River lars' Crismas, or that there poor woman down by the Billabong – her husband cleared out and left her with a lot o' kids. Or Bill Something, the bullocky, who was run over by his own wagon, while he was drunk, and got his leg broke.

Towards the end of his spree One-eyed Bogán broke loose and smashed nearly all the windows of the Carriers' Arms, and next morning he was fined heavily at the police court. About dinner-time I encountered the Giraffe and his hat, with two half-crowns in it for a start.

'I'm sorry to trouble yer,' he said, 'but One-eyed Bogan carn't pay his fine, an' I thought we might fix it up for him. He ain't half a bad sort of feller when he ain't drinkin'. It's only when he gets too much booze in him.'

After shearing, the hat usually started round with the Giraffe's own dirty crumpled pound note in the bottom of it as a send-off, later on it was half a sovereign; till in the end he would borrow a 'few bob' – which he always repaid after next shearing – 'just to start the thing goin' goin'.'

There were several yarns about him and his hat. 'Twas said that the hat had belonged to his father, whom he resembled in every respect, and it had been going round for so many years that the crown was worn as thin as paper by the quids, half-quids, casers, half-casers, bobs and tanners or sprats – to say nothing of the scrums – that had been chucked into it in its time and shaken up.

They say that when a new Governor visited Bourke the Giraffe happened to be standing on the platform close to the exit, grinning good-humouredly, and the local toady nudged him urgently and said in an awful whisper, 'Take off your hat! Why don't you take off your hat?'

'Why?' drawled the Giraffe, 'he ain't hard up, is he?'

And they fondly cherish an anecdote to the effect that, when the One-Man-One-Vote Bill was passed (or Payment of Members, or when the first Labour Party went in – I forget on which occasion they said it was) the Giraffe was carried away by the general enthusiasm, got a few beers in him, 'chucked' a quid into his hat, and sent it round. The boys contributed by force of habit, and contributed largely, because of the victory and the beer. And when the hat came back to the Giraffe, he stood holding it in front of him with both hands and stared blankly into it for a while. Then it dawned on him.

'Blowed if I haven't bin an' gone an' took up a bloomin' collection for meself!' he said.

He was almost a teetotaller, but he stood his shout in reason. He mostly drank ginger-beer.

'I ain't a feller that boozes, but I ain't got nothin' agen chaps enjoyin' themselves, so long as they don't go too far.'

It was common for a man on the spree to say to him:

'Here! here's five quid. Look after it for me, Giraffe, will yer, till I get off the booze.'

His real name was Bob Brothers, and his bush names, Long-'un, The Giraffe, Send-round-the-hat, Chuck-in-a-bob, and Ginger-ale.

Some years before, camels and Afghan drivers had been imported to the Bourke district; the camels did very well in the dry country, they went right across the country and carried everything from sardines to flooring-boards. And the teamsters loved the Afghans nearly as much as Sydney furniture makers love the cheap Chinese in the same line. They loved 'em even as union shearers on strike love blacklegs brought up-country to take their places.

Now the Giraffe was a good, straight unionist, but in cases of sickness or trouble he was as apt to forget his unionism, as all bushmen are, at all times (and for all time), to forget their creed. So, one evening, the Giraffe blundered into the Carriers' Arms – of all places in the world – when it was full of teamsters; he had his hat in his hand and some small silver and coppers in it.

'I say, you fellers, there's a poor, sick Afghan in the camp down there along the –'

A big, brawny bullock-driver took him firmly by the shoulders, or rather by the elbows, and ran him out before any damage was done. The Giraffe took it as he took most things, good humouredly; but, about dusk, he was seen slipping down towards the Afghan camp with a billy of soup.

'I believe,' remarked Tom Hall, 'that when the Giraffe goes to heaven – and he's the only one of us, as far as I can see, that has a ghost of a show – I believe that when he goes to heaven, the first thing he'll do will be to take his infernal hat round amongst the angels – getting up a collection for this damned world that he left behind.'

'Well, I don't think there's so much to his credit, after all,' said Jack Mitchell, shearer. 'You see, the Giraffe is ambitious; he likes public life, and that accounts for him shoving himself forward with his collections. As for bothering about people in trouble, that's only common curiosity; he's one of those chaps that are always shoving their noses into other people's troubles. And as for looking after sick men – why! there's nothing the Giraffe likes better than pottering round a sick man, and watching him and studying him. He's awfully interested in sick men, and they're pretty scarce out here. I tell you there's nothing he likes better – except, maybe, it's pottering round a corpse. I believe he'd ride forty miles to help and sympathize and potter round a funeral. The fact of the matter is that the Giraffe is only enjoying himself with other people's troubles – that's all it is. It's only vulgar curiosity and selfishness. I set it down to his ignorance; the way he was brought up.'

A few days after the Afghan incident the Giraffe and his hat had a run of luck. A German, one of a party who were building a new wooden bridge over the Big Billabong, was helping unload some girders from a truck at the railway-station when a big log slipped on the skids and his leg was smashed badly. They carried him to the Carriers' Arms, which was the nearest hotel, and into a bedroom behind the bar, and sent for the doctor. The Giraffe was in evidence as usual.

'It vas not that at all,' said German Charlie, when they asked him if he was in much pain. 'It vas not that at all. I don't cares a damn for der bain; but dis is der tird year – und I vas going home dis year – after der gontract – und der gontract yoost commence!'

That was the burden of his song all through, between his groans.

There were a good few chaps sitting quietly about the bar and veranda when the doctor arrived. The Giraffe was sitting at the end of the counter, on which he had laid his hat while he wiped his face, neck, and forehead with a big speckled sweat-rag. It was a very hot day.

The doctor, a good-hearted young Australian, was heard saying something. Then German Charlie, in a voice that rung with pain:

'Make that leg right, doctor – quick! Dis is der tird pluddy year – und I must go home!'

The doctor asked him if he was in great pain.

'Neffer mind der pluddy bain, doctor! Neffer mind der pluddy bain! Dot vas nossing. Make dat leg vell quick, doctor. Dis vas der last contract, and I vas going home dis year.' Then the words jerked out of him by physical agony: 'Der girl vas vaiting dree year, and – by Got! I must go home.'

The publican – Watty Braithwaite, known as Watty Broadweight, or, more familiarly, Watty Bothways – turned over the Giraffe's hat in a tired, bored sort of way, dropped a quid into it, and nodded resignedly at the Giraffe.

The Giraffe caught up the hint and the hat with alacrity. The hat went all round town, so to speak; and as soon as his leg was firm enough not to come loose on the road German Charlie went home.

It was well known that I contributed to the Sydney *Bulletin* and several other papers. The Giraffe's bump of reverence was very large, and swelled especially for sick men and poets. He treated me with much more respect than is due from a bushman to a man, and with an odd sort of extra gentleness I sometimes fancied. But one day he rather surprised me.

'I'm sorry to trouble yer,' he said in a shamefaced way. 'I don't know as you go in for sportin', but One-eyed Bogan an' Barcoo-Rot is goin' to have a bit of a scrap down the Billybong this evenin', an' –'

'A bit of a what?' I asked.

'A bit of a fight to a finish,' he said apologetically. 'An' the chaps is tryin' to fix up a fiver to put some life into the thing. There's bad blood between One-eyed Bogan and Barcoo-Rot, an' it won't do them any harm to have it out.'

It was a great fight, I remember. There must have been a couple of score blood-soaked handkerchiefs (or sweat-rags) buried in a hole on the field of battle, and the Giraffe was busy the rest of the evening helping to patch up the principals. Later on he took up a small collection for the loser, who happened to be Barcoo-Rot in spite of the advantage of an eye.

The Salvation Army lassie, who went round with the *War Cry*, nearly always sold the Giraffe three copies.

A newchum parson, who wanted a subscription to build or enlarge a chapel, or something, sought the assistance of the Giraffe's influence with his mates.

'Well,' said the Giraffe, 'I ain't a churchgoer meself. I ain't what you might call a religious cove, but I'll be glad to do what I can to help yer. I don't suppose I can do much. I ain't been to church since I was a kiddy.'

The parson was shocked, but later on he learned to appreciate the Giraffe and his mates, and to love Australia for the bushman's sake, and it was he who told me the above anecdote.

The Giraffe helped fix some stalls for a Catholic Church bazaar, and some of the chaps chaffed him about it in the union office.

'You'll be taking up a collection for a joss-house down in the Chinamen's camp next,' said Tom Hall in conclusion.

'Well, I ain't got nothin' agen the Roming Carflicks,' said the Giraffe. 'An' Father O'Donovan's a very decent sort of cove. He stuck up for the unions all right in the strike anyway.' ('He wouldn't be Irish if he wasn't,' someone commented.) 'I carried swags once for six months with a feller that was a Carflick, an' he was a very straight feller. And a girl I knowed turned Carflick to marry a chap that had got her into trouble, an' she was always jes' the same to me after as she was before. Besides, I like to help everything that's goin' on.'

Tom Hall and one or two others went out hurriedly to have a drink. But we all loved the Giraffe.

He was very innocent and very humorous, especially when he meant to be most serious and philosophical.

'Some of them bush girls is regular tomboys,' he said to me solemnly one day. 'Some of them is too cheeky altogether. I remember once I was stoppin' at a place – they was sort of relations o' mine – an' they put me to sleep in a room off the verander, where there was a glass door an' no blinds. An' the first mornin' the girls – they was sort o' cousins o' mine – they come gigglin' and foolin' round outside the door on the verander, an' kep' me in bed till nearly ten o'clock. I had to put me trowsis on under the bed-clothes in the end. But I got back on 'em the next night,' he reflected.

'How did you do that, Bob?' I asked.

'Why, I went to bed in me trowsis!'

One day I was on a plank, painting the ceiling of the bar of the Great Western Hotel. I was anxious to get the job finished. The work had been kept back most of the day by chaps handing up long beers to me, and drawing my attention to the alleged fact that I was putting on the paint wrong side out. I was slapping it on over the last few boards when:

'I'm very sorry to trouble yer; I always seem to be troublin' yer; but there's that there woman and them girls —'

I looked down – about the first time I had looked down on him – and there was the Giraffe, with his hat brim up on the plank and two half-crowns in it.

'Oh, that's all right, Bob,' I said, and I dropped in half a crown.

There were shearers in the bar, and presently there was some barracking. It appeared that that there woman and them girls were strange women, in the local as well as the Biblical sense of the word, who had come from Sydney at the end of the shearing-season, and had taken a cottage on the edge of the scrub on the outskirts of the town. There had been trouble this week in connection with a row at their establishment, and they had been fined, warned off by the police, and turned out by their landlord.

'This is a bit too red-hot, Giraffe,' said one of the shearers. 'Them — s has made enough out of us coves. They've got plenty of stuff, don't you fret. Let 'em go to —! I'm blanked if I give a sprat.'

'They ain't got their fares to Sydney,' said the Giraffe. 'An', what's more, the little 'un is sick, an' two of them has kids in Sydney.'

'How the — do you know?'

'Why, one of 'em come to me an' told me all about it.'

There was an involuntary guffaw.

'Look here, Bob,' said Billy Woods, the rouseabouts' secretary, kindly. 'Don't you make a fool of yourself. You'll have all the chaps laughing at you. Those girls are only working you for all you're worth. I suppose one of 'em came crying and whining to you. Don't you bother about 'em. *You* don't know 'em; they can pump water at a moment's notice. You haven't had any experi-ence with women yet, Bob.'

'She didn't come whinin' and cryin' to me,' said the Giraffe, dropping his twanging drawl a little. 'She looked me straight in the face an' told me all about it.'

'I say, Giraffe,' said Box-o'-Tricks, 'what have you been doin'? You've bin down there on the nod. I'm surprised at yer, Giraffe.'

'An' he pretends to be so gory soft an' innocent, too,' growled the Bogan. 'We know all about you, Giraffe.'

'Look here, Giraffe,' said Mitchell the shearer. 'I'd never have thought it of you. We all thought you were the only virgin youth west the river; I always thought you were a moral young man. You mustn't think that because your conscience is pricking you everyone else's is.'

'I ain't had anythin' to do with them,' said the Giraffe, drawling again. 'I ain't a cove that goes in for that sort of thing. But other chaps has, and I think they might as well help 'em out of their fix.'

'They're a rotten crowd,' said Billy Woods. 'You don't know them, Bob. Don't bother about them – they're not worth it. Put your money in your pocket. You'll find a better use for it before next shearing.'

'Better shout, Giraffe,' said Box-o'-Tricks.

Now in spite of the Giraffe's softness he was the hardest man in Bourke to move when he'd decided on what he thought was 'the fair thing to do'. Another peculiarity of his was that on occasion, such for instance as 'sayin' a few words' at a strike meeting, he would straighten himself, drop the twang, and rope in his drawl, so to speak.

'Well, look here, you chaps,' he said now. 'I don't know anything about them women. I s'pose they're bad, but I don't suppose they're worse than men has made them. All I know is that there's four women turned out, without any stuff, and every woman in Bourke, an' the police, an' the law agen 'em. An' the fact that they is women is agenst 'em most of all. You don't expect 'em to hump their swags to Sydney! Why, only I ain't got the stuff I wouldn't trouble yer. I'd pay their fares meself. Look,' he said, lowering his voice, 'there they are now, an' one of the girls is cryin'. Don't let 'em see yer lookin'.'

I dropped softly from the plank and peeped out with the rest.

They stood by the fence on the opposite side of the street, a bit up towards the railway-station, with their portmanteaux and bundles at their feet. One girl leant with her arms on the fence rail and her face buried in them, another was trying to comfort her. The third girl and the woman stood facing our way. The woman was good-looking: she had a hard face, but it might have been made hard. The third girl seemed half defiant, half inclined to cry. Presently she went to the other side of the girl who was crying on the fence and put her arm round her shoulder. The woman suddenly turned her back on us and stood looking away over the paddocks.

The hat went round. Billy Woods was first, then Box-o'-Tricks, and then Mitchell.

Billy contributed with eloquent silence. 'I was only jokin', Giraffe,' said Box-o'-Tricks, dredging his pockets for a couple of shillings. It was some time after the shearing, and most of the chaps were hard up.

'Ah, well,' sighed Mitchell. 'There's no help for it. If the Giraffe would take up a collection to import some decent girls to this God-forgotten hole there might be some sense in it . . . It's bad enough for the Giraffe to undermine our religious prejudices, and tempt us to take a morbid interest in sick Chows and Afghans, and blacklegs and widows; but when he starts mixing us up with strange women it's time to buck.' And he prospected his pockets and contributed two shillings, some odd pennies, and a pinch of tobacco dust.

'I don't mind helping the girls, but I'm damned if I'll give a penny to help the old —,' said Tom Hall.

'Well, she was a girl once herself,' drawled the Giraffe.

The Giraffe went round to the other pubs and to the union offices, and when he returned he seemed satisfied with the plate, but troubled about something else.

'I don't know what to do for them for tonight,' he said. 'None of the pubs or boardin'-houses will hear of them, an' there ain't no empty houses, an' the women is all agen 'em.'

'Not all,' said Alice, the big, handsome barmaid from Sydney. 'Come here, Bob.' She gave the Giraffe half a sovereign and a look for which some of us would have paid him ten pounds – had we had the money, and had the look been transferable.

'Wait a minute, Bob,' she said, and she went in to speak to the landlord.

'There's an empty bedroom at the end of the store in the yard,' she said when she came back. 'They can camp there for tonight if they behave themselves. You'd better tell 'em, Bob.'

'Thank yer, Alice,' said the Giraffe.

Next day, after work, the Giraffe and I drifted together and down by the river in the cool of the evening, and sat on the edge of the steep, drought-parched bank.

'I heard you saw your lady friends off this morning, Bob,' I said, and was sorry I said it, even before he answered.

'Oh, they ain't no friends of mine,' he said. 'Only four poor devils of women. I thought they mightn't like to stand waitin' with the crowd on the platform, so I jest offered to get their tickets an' told 'em to wait round at the back of the station till the bell rung. An' what do yer think they did, Harry?' he went on, with an exasperatingly unintelligent grin. 'Why, they wanted to kiss me.'

'Did they?'

'Yes. An' they would have done it, too, if I hadn't been so long. Why, I'm blessed if they didn't kiss me hands.'

'You don't say so.'

'God's truth. Somehow I didn't like to go on the platform with them after that; besides, they was cryin', and I can't stand women cryin'. But some of the chaps put them into an empty carriage.' He thought a moment. Then:

'There's some terrible good-hearted fellers in the world,' he reflected.

I thought so too.

'Bob,' I said, 'you're a single man. Why don't you get married and settle down?'

'Well,' he said, 'I ain't got no wife an' kids, that's a fact. But it ain't my fault.'

He may have been right about the wife. But I thought of the look that Alice had given him, and –

'Girls seem to like me right enough,' he said, 'but it don't go no further than that. The trouble is that I'm so long, and I always seem to get shook after little girls. At least there was one little girl in Bendigo that I was properly gone on.'

'And wouldn't she have you?'

'Well, it seems not.'

'Did you ask her?'

'Oh, yes, I asked her right enough.'

'Well, and what did she say?'

'She said it would be rediculus for her to be seen trottin' alongside of a chimbly like me.'

'Perhaps she didn't mean that. There are any amount of little women who like tall men.'

'I thought of that too – afterwards. P'r'aps she didn't mean it that way. I s'pose the fact of the matter was that she didn't cotton on to me, and wanted to let me down easy. She didn't want to hurt me feelin's, if yer understand – she was a very good-hearted little girl. There's some terrible tall fellers where I come from, and I know two as married little girls.'

He seemed a hopeless case.

'Sometimes,' he said, 'sometimes I wish that I wasn't so blessed long.'

'There's that there deaf jackeroo,' he reflected presently. 'He's something in the same fix about girls as I am. He's too deaf and I'm too long.'

'How do you make that out?' I asked. 'He's got three girls, to my knowledge, and as for being deaf, why, he gasses more than any man in the town, and knows more of what's going on than old Mother Brindle the washer-woman.'

'Well, look at that now!' said the Giraffe, slowly. 'Who'd have thought it? He never told me he had three girls, an' as for hearin' news, I always tell him anything that's goin' on that I think he doesn't catch. He told me his trouble was that whenever he went out with a girl people could hear what they was sayin' – at least they could hear what she was sayin' to him, an' draw their own conclusions, he said. He said he went out one night with a girl, and some of the chaps foxed 'em an' heard her sayin' "don't" to him, an' put it all round town.'

'What did she say "don't" for?' I asked.

'He didn't tell me that, but I s'pose he was kissin' her or huggin' her or something.'

'Bob,' I said presently, 'didn't you try the little girl in Bendigo a second time?'

'No,' he said. 'What was the use. She was a good little girl, and I wasn't goin' to go botherin' her. I ain't the sort of cove that goes hangin' round where he isn't wanted. But somehow I couldn't stay about Bendigo after she gave me the hint, so I thought I'd come over an' have a knock round on this side for a year or two.'

'And you never wrote to her?'

'No. What was the use of goin' pesterin' her with letters? I know what trouble letters give me when I have to answer one. She'd have only had to tell me the straight truth in a letter an' it wouldn't have done me any good. But I've pretty well got over it by this time.'

A few days later I went to Sydney. The Giraffe was the last I shook hands with from the carriage window, and he slipped something in a piece of newspaper into my hand.

'I hope yer won't be offended,' he drawled, 'but some of the chaps thought you mightn't be too flush of stuff – you've been shoutin' a good deal; so they put a quid or two together. They thought it might help yer to have a bit of a fly round in Sydney.'

I was back in Bourke before next shearing. On the evening of my arrival I ran against the Giraffe; he seemed strangely shaken over something, but he kept his hat on his head.

'Would yer mind takin' a stroll as fur as the Billerbong?' he said. 'I got something I'd like to tell yer.'

His big, brown, sunburnt hands trembled and shook as he took a letter from his pocket and opened it.

'I've just got a letter,' he said. 'A letter from that little girl at Bendigo. It seems it was all a mistake. I'd like yer to read it. Somehow I feel as if I want to talk to a feller, and I'd rather talk to you than any of them other chaps.'

It was a good letter, from a big-hearted little girl. She had been breaking her heart for the great ass all these months. It seemed that he had left Bendigo without saying good-bye to her. 'Somehow I couldn't bring meself to it,' he said, when I taxed him with it. She had never been able to get his address until last week; then she got it from a Bourke man who had gone south. She called him 'an awful long fool', which he was, without the slightest doubt, and she implored him to write, and come back to her.

'And will you go back, Bob?' I asked.

'My oath! I'd take the train tomorrow only I ain't got the stuff. But I've got a stand in Big Billerbong Shed an' I'll soon knock a few quid together. I'll go back as soon as ever shearin's over. I'm goin' to write away to her tonight.'

The Giraffe was the ringer of Big Billabong Shed that season. His tallies averaged a hundred and twenty a day. He only sent his hat round once during shearing, and it was noticed that he hesitated at first and only contributed half a crown. But then it was a case of a man being taken from the shed by the police for wife desertion.

'It's always that way,' commented Mitchell. 'Those soft, good-hearted fellows always end by getting hard and selfish. The world makes 'em so. It's the thought of the soft fools they've been that finds out sooner or later and makes 'em repent. Like as not the Giraffe will be the meanest man outback before he's done.'

When Big Billabong cut out, and we got back to Bourke with our dusty swags and dirty cheques, I spoke to Tom Hall:

'Look here, Tom,' I said. 'That long fool, the Giraffe, has been breaking his heart for a little girl in Bendigo ever since he's been outback, and she's been breaking her heart for him, and the ass didn't know it till he got a letter from her just before Big Billabong started. He's going tomorrow morning.'

That evening Tom stole the Giraffe's hat. 'I s'pose it'll turn up in the mornin',' said the Giraffe. 'I don't mind a lark,' he added, 'but it does seem a bit red-hot for the chaps to collar a cove's hat and a feller goin' away for good, p'r'aps, in the mornin'.'

Mitchell started the thing going with a quid.

'It's worth it,' he said, 'to get rid of him. We'll have some peace now. There won't be so many accidents or women in trouble when the Giraffe and his blessed hat are gone. Anyway, he's an eyesore in the town, and he's getting on my nerves for one . . . Come on, you sinners! Chuck 'em in; we're only taking quids and half-quids.'

About daylight next morning Tom Hall slipped into the Giraffe's room at the Carriers' Arms. The Giraffe was sleeping peacefully. Tom put the hat on a chair by his side. The collection had been a record one, and besides the packet of money in the crown of the hat there was a silver-mounted pipe with case – the best that could be bought in Bourke – a gold brooch, and several trifles, besides an ugly valentine of a long man in his shirt walking the room with a twin on each arm.

Tom was about to shake the Giraffe by the shoulder when he noticed a great foot, with about half a yard of big-boned ankle and shank, sticking out at the bottom of the bed. The temptation was too great. Tom took up the hair-brush, and, with the back of it, he gave a smart rap on the point of an ingrowing toe-nail, and slithered.

We heard the Giraffe swearing good-naturedly for a while, and then there was a pregnant silence. He was staring at the hat we supposed.

We were all up at the station to see him off. It was rather a long wait. The Giraffe edged me up to the other end of the platform.

He seemed overcome.

'There's – there's some terrible good-hearted fellers in this world,' he said. 'You mustn't forgit 'em, Harry, when you makes a big name writin'. I'm – well, I'm blessed if I don't feel as if I was just goin' to blubber!'

I was glad he didn't. The Giraffe blubberin' would have been a spectacle. I steered him back to his friends.

'Ain't you going to kiss me, Bob?' said the Great Western's big, handsome barmaid, as the bell rang.

'Well, I don't mind kissin' you, Alice,' he said, wiping his mouth. 'But I'm goin' to be married, yer know.' And he kissed her fair on the mouth.

'There's nothin' like gettin' into practice,' he said, grinning round.

We thought he was improving wonderfully; but at the last moment something troubled him.

'Look here, you chaps,' he said, hesitatingly, with his hand in his pocket, 'I don't know what I'm going to do with all this stuff. There's that poor washer-woman that scalded her legs liftin' the boiler of clothes off the fire –'

We shoved him into the carriage. He hung – about half of him – out the window, wildly waving his hat, till the train disappeared in the scrub.

And, as I sit here writing by lamplight at midday, in the midst of a great city of shallow social sham, of hopeless, squalid poverty, of ignorant selfishness, cultured or brutish, and of noble and heroic endeavour frowned down or callously neglected, I am almost aware of a burst of sunshine in the room, and a long form leaning over my chair, and:

'Excuse me for troublin' yer; I'm always troublin' yer; but there's that there poor woman . . .'

And I wish I could immortalize him!

Barbara Baynton

SQUEAKER'S MATE

THE woman carried the bag with the axe and maul and wedges; the man had the billy and clean tucker-bags; the cross-cut saw linked them. She was taller than the man, and the equability of her body, contrasting with his indolent slouch, accentuated the difference. 'Squeaker's mate', the men called her, and these agreed that she was the best long-haired mate that ever stepped in petticoats. The selectors' wives pretended to challenge her right to womanly garments, but if she knew what they said, it neither turned nor troubled Squeaker's mate.

Nine prospective posts and maybe sixteen rails – she calculated this yellow gum would yield. 'Come on,' she encouraged the man; 'let's tackle it.'

From the bag she took the axe, and ring-barked a preparatory circle, while he looked for a shady spot for the billy and tucker-bags.

'Come on.' She was waiting with the greased saw. He came. The saw rasped through a few inches, then he stopped and looked at the sun.

'It's nigh tucker-time,' he said, and when she dissented, he exclaimed, with sudden energy, 'There's another bee! Wait, you go on with the axe, an' I'll track 'im.'

As they came, they had already followed one and located the nest. She could not see the bee he spoke of, though her grey eyes were as keen as a black's. However, she knew the man, and her tolerance was of the mysteries.

She drew out the saw, spat on her hands, and with the axe began weakening the inclining side of the tree.

Long and steadily and in secret the worm had been busy in the heart. Suddenly the axe blade sank softly, the tree's wounded edges closed on it like a vice. There was a 'settling' quiver on its

63

top branches, which the woman heard and understood. The man, encouraged by the sounds of the axe, had returned with an armful of sticks for the billy. He shouted gleefully, 'It's fallin', look out.'

But she waited to free the axe.

With a shivering groan the tree fell, and as she sprang aside, a thick worm-eaten branch snapped at a joint and silently she went down under it.

'I tole yer t' look out,' he reminded her, as with a crowbar, and grunting earnestly, he forced it up. 'Now get out quick.'

She tried moving her arms and the upper part of her body. Do this, do that, he directed, but she made no movement after the first.

He was impatient, because for once he had actually to use his strength. His share of a heavy lift usually consisted of a make-believe grunt, delivered at a critical moment. Yet he hardly cared to let it again fall on her, though he told her he would, if she 'didn't shift'.

Near him lay a piece broken short; with his foot he drew it nearer, then gradually worked it into a position, till it acted as a stay to the lever.

He laid her on her back when he drew her out, and waited expecting some acknowledgement of his exertions, but she was silent, and as she did not notice that the axe she had tried to save, lay with the fallen trunk across it, he told her. She cared almost tenderly for all their possessions and treated them as friends. But the half-buried broken axe did not affect her. He wondered a little, for only last week she had patiently chipped out the old broken head, and put in a new handle.

'Feel bad?' he inquired at length.

'Pipe,' she replied with slack lips.

Both pipes lay in the fork of a near tree. He took his, shook out the ashes, filled it, picked up a coal and puffed till it was alight – then he filled hers. Taking a small firestick he handed her the pipe. The hand she raised shook and closed in an uncertain hold, but she managed by a great effort to get it to her mouth. He lost patience with the swaying hand that tried to take the light.

'Quick,' he said, 'quick, that damn dog's at the tucker.'

He thrust it into her hand that dropped helplessly across her chest. The lighted stick, falling between her bare arm and the dress, slowly roasted the flesh and smouldered the clothes.

He rescued their dinner, pelted his dog out of sight – hers was lying near her head – put on the billy, then came back to her.

The pipe had fallen from her lips; there was blood on the stem.

'Did yer jam yer tongue?' he asked.

She always ignored trifles, he knew, therefore he passed her silence.

He told her that her dress was on fire. She took no heed. He put it out, and looked at the burnt arm, then with intentness at her.

Her eyes were turned unblinkingly to the heavens, her lips were grimly apart, and a strange greyness was upon her face, and the sweat-beads were mixing.

'Like a drink er tea? Asleep?'

He broke a green branch from the fallen tree and swished from his face the multitudes of flies that had descended with it.

In a heavy way he wondered why did she sweat, when she was not working? Why did she not keep the flies out of her mouth and eyes? She'd have bungy eyes, if she didn't. If she was asleep, why did she not close them?

But asleep or awake, as the billy began to boil, he left her, made the tea, and ate his dinner. His dog had disappeared, and as it did not come to his whistle, he threw the pieces to hers, that would not leave her head to reach them.

He whistled tunelessly his one air, beating his own time with a stick on the toe of his blucher, then looked overhead at the sun and calculated that she must have been lying like that for 'close up an hour'. He noticed that the axe handle was broken in two places, and speculated a little as to whether she would again pick out the back-broken handle or burn it out in his method, which was less trouble, if it did spoil the temper of the blade. He examined the wormdust in the stump and limbs of the newly-fallen tree, mounted it and looked round the plain. The sheep were straggling in a manner that meant walking work to round them, and he supposed he would have to yard them tonight, if she didn't liven up. He looked down at unenlivened her. This changed his 'chune' to a call for his hiding dog.

'Come on, ole feller,' he commanded her dog. 'Fetch 'em back.'

He whistled further instructions, slapping his thigh and pointing to the sheep.

But a brace of wrinkles either side the brute's closed mouth demonstrated determined disobedience. The dog would go if she told him, and by and by she would.

He lighted his pipe and killed half an hour smoking. With the frugality that hard graft begets, his mate limited both his and her own tobacco, so he must not smoke all afternoon. There was no work to shirk, so time began to drag. Then a 'goanner' crawling up a tree attracted him. He gathered various missiles and tried vainly to hit the seemingly grinning reptile. He came back and sneaked a fill of her tobacco, and while he was smoking, the white tilt of a cart caught his eye. He jumped up. 'There's Red Bob goin' t' our place fur th' 'oney,' he said. 'I'll go an' weigh it an' get the gonz' (money).

He ran for the cart, and kept looking back as if fearing she would follow and thwart him.

Red Bob the dealer was, in a business way, greatly concerned, when he found that Squeaker's mate was "avin' a sleep out there 'cos a tree fell on her'. She was the best honey-strainer and boiler that he dealt with. She was straight and square too. There was no water in her honey whether boiled or merely strained, and in every kerosene-tin the weight of honey was to an ounce as she said. Besides he was suspicious and diffident of paying the indecently eager Squeaker before he saw the woman. So reluctantly Squeaker led to where she lay. With many fierce oaths Red Bob sent her lawful protector for help, and compassionately poured a little from his flask down her throat, then swished away the flies from her till help came.

Together these men stripped a sheet of bark, and laying her with pathetic tenderness upon it, carried her to her hut. Squeaker followed in the rear with the billy and tucker.

Red Bob took his horse from the cart, and went to town for the doctor. Late that night at the back of the old hut (there were two) he and others who had heard that she was hurt, squatted with unlighted pipes in their mouths, waiting to hear the doctor's verdict. After he had given it and gone, they discussed in whispers, and with a look seen only on bush faces, the hard luck of that woman who alone had hard-grafted with the best of them for every acre and hoof on that selection. Squeaker would go through it in no time. Why she had allowed it to be taken up in his name, when the money had been her own, was also for them among the mysteries.

Him they called 'a nole woman', not because he was hanging round the honey-tins, but after man's fashion to eliminate all virtue. They beckoned him, and explaining his mate's injury, cautioned him to keep from her the knowledge that she would be for ever a cripple.

'Jus' th' same, now, then fur 'im,' pointing to Red Bob, 't' pay me, I'll 'ev t' go t' town.'

They told him in whispers what they thought of him, and with a cowardly look towards where she lay, but without a word of parting, like shadows these men made for their homes.

Next day the women came. Squeaker's mate was not a favourite with them – a woman with no leisure for yarning was not likely to be. After the first day they left her severely alone, their plea to their husbands, her uncompromising independence. It is in the ordering of things that by degrees most husbands accept their wives' views of other women.

The flour bespattering Squeaker's now neglected clothes spoke eloquently of his clumsy efforts at damper making. The women gave him many a feed, agreeing that it must be miserable for him.

If it were miserable and lonely for his mate, she did not complain; for her the long, long days would give place to longer nights – those nights with the pregnant bush silence suddenly cleft by a bush voice. However, she was not fanciful, and being a bush scholar knew 'twas a dingo, when a long whine came from the scrub on the skirts of which lay the axe under the worm-eaten tree. That quivering wail from the billabong lying murkily mystic towards the East was only the cry of the fearing curlew.

Always her dog – wakeful and watchful as she – patiently waiting for her to be up and about again. That would be soon, she told her complaining mate.

'Yer won't. Yer back's broke,' said Squeaker laconically. 'That's wot's wrong er yer; injoory t' th' spine. Doctor says that means back's broke, and yer won't never walk no more. No good not t' tell yer, cos I can't be doin' everythin'.'

A wild look grew on her face, and she tried to sit up.

'Erh,' said he, 'see! yer carnt, yer jes' ther same as a snake w'en ees back's broke, on'y yer don't bite yerself like a snake does w'en 'e carnt crawl. Yer did bite yer tongue w'en yer fell.'

She gasped, and he could hear her heart beating when she let her head fall back a few moments; though she wiped her wet forehead with the back of her hand, and still said that was the doctor's mistake. But day after day she tested her strength, and whatever the result, was silent, though white witnesses, halo-wise, gradually circled her brow and temples.

' 'Tisn't as if yer was agoin' t' get better t'morrer, the doctor says yer won't never work no more, an' I can't be cookin' an' workin' an' doin' everythin'!'

He muttered something about 'sellin' out', but she firmly refused to think of such a monstrous proposal.

He went into town one Saturday afternoon soon after, and did not return till Monday.

Her supplies, a billy of tea and scraps of salt beef and damper (her dog got the beef), gave out the first day, though that was as nothing to her compared with the bleat of the penned sheep, for it was summer and droughty, and her dog could not unpen them.

Of them and her dog only she spoke when he returned. He d—d him, and d—d her, and told her to 'double up yer ole broke back an' bite yerself.' He threw things about, made a long-range feint of kicking her threatening dog, then sat outside in the shade of the old hut, nursing his head till he slept.

She, for many reasons, had when necessary made these trips into town, walking both ways, leading a pack-horse for supplies. She never failed to indulge him in a half pint – a pipe was her luxury.

The sheep waited till next day, so did she.

For a few days he worked a little in her sight; not much – he never did. It was she who always lifted the heavy end of the log, and carried the tools; he – the billy and tucker.

She wearily watched him idling his time; reminded him that the wire lying near the fence would rust, one could run the wire through easily, and when she got up in a day or so, she would help strain and fasten it. At first he pretended he had done it, later said he wasn't goin' t' go wirin' or nothin' else by 'imself if every other man on the place did.

She spoke of many other things that could be done by one, reserving the great till she was well. Sometimes he whistled while she spoke, often swore, generally went out, and when this was inconvenient, dull as he was, he found the 'Go and bite yerself like a snake,' would instantly silence her.

At last the work worry ceased to exercise her, and for night to bring him home was a rare thing.

Her dog rounded and yarded the sheep when the sun went down and there was no sign of him, and together they kept watch on their movements till dawn. She was mindful not to speak of this care to him, knowing he would have left it for them to do constantly, and she noticed that what little interest he seemed to share went to the sheep. Why, was soon demonstrated.

Through the cracks her ever watchful eyes one day saw the dust rise out of the plain. Nearer it came till she saw him and a man on horseback rounding and driving the sheep into the yard, and later both left in charge of a little mob. Their 'Baa-baas' to her were cries for help; many had been pets. So he was selling her sheep to the town butchers.

In the middle of the next week he came from town with a fresh horse, new saddle and bridle. He wore a flash red shirt, and round his neck a silk handkerchief. On the next occasion she smelt scent, and though he did not try to display the dandy meerschaum, she saw it, and heard the squeak of the new boots, not bluchers. However he was kinder to her this time, offering a fill of his cut tobacco; he had long ceased to keep her supplied. Several of the men who sometimes in passing took a look in, would have made up her loss had they known, but no word of complaint passed her lips.

She looked at Squeaker as he filled his pipe from his pouch, but he would not meet her eyes, and, seemingly dreading something, slipped out.

She heard him hammering in the old hut at the back, which served for tools and other things which sunlight and rain did not hurt. Quite briskly he went in and out. She could see him through the cracks carrying a narrow strip of bark, and understood, he was making a bunk. When it was finished he had a smoke, then came to her and fidgeted about; he said this hut was too cold, and that she would never get well in it. She did not feel cold, but, submitting to his mood, allowed him to make a fire that would roast a sheep. He took off his hat, and, fanning himself, said he was roastin', wasn't she? She was.

He offered to carry her into the other; he would put a new roof on it in a day or two, and it would be better than this one, and she would be up in no time. He stood to say this where she could not see him.

His eagerness had tripped him.

There were months to run before all the Government conditions of residence, etc., in connection with the selection, would be fulfilled, still she thought perhaps he was trying to sell out, and she would not go.

He was away four days that time, and when he returned slept in the new bunk.

She compromised. Would he put a bunk there for himself, keep out of town, and not sell the place? He promised instantly with additions.

'Try could yer crawl yerself?' he coaxed, looking at her bulk.

Her nostrils quivered with her suppressed breathing, and her lips tightened, but she did not attempt to move.

It was evident some great purpose actuated him. After attempts to carry and drag her, he rolled her on the sheet of bark that had brought her home, and laboriously drew her round.

She asked for a drink, he placed her billy and tin pint besides the bunk, and left her, gasping and dazed, to her sympathetic dog.

She saw him run up and yard his horse, and though she called him, he would not answer nor come.

When he rode swiftly towards the town, her dog leaped on the bunk, and joined a refrain to her lamentation, but the cat took to the bush.

He came back at dusk next day in a spring cart – not alone – he had another mate. She saw her though he came a roundabout way, trying to keep in front of the new hut.

There were noises of moving many things from the cart to the hut. Finally he came to a crack near where she lay, and whispered the promise of many good things to her if she kept quiet, and that he would set her hut afire if she didn't. She was quiet, he need not have feared, for that time she was past it, she was stunned.

70

The released horse came stumbling round to the old hut, and thrust its head in the door in a domesticated fashion. Her dog promptly resented this straggler mistaking their hut for a stable. And the dog's angry dissent, together with the shod clatter of the rapidly disappearing intruder, seemed to have a disturbing effect on the pair in the new hut. The settling sounds suddenly ceased, and the cripple heard the stranger close the door, despite Squeaker's assurances that the woman in the old hut could not move from her bunk to save her life, and that her dog would not leave her.

Food, more and better, was placed near her – but, dumb and motionless, she lay with her face turned to the wall, and her dog growled menacingly at the stranger. The new woman was uneasy, and told Squeaker what people might say and do if she died.

He scared at the 'do', went into the bush and waited.

She went to the door, not the crack, the face was turned that way, and said she had come to cook and take care of her.

The disabled woman, turning her head slowly, looked steadily at her. She was not much to look at. Her red hair hung in an uncurled bang over her forehead, the lower part of her face had robbed the upper, and her figure evinced imminent motherhood, though it is doubtful if the barren woman, noting this, knew by calculation the paternity was not Squeaker's. She was not learned in these matters, though she understood all about an ewe and lamb.

One circumstance was apparent – ah! bitterest of all bitterness to women – she was younger.

The thick hair that fell from the brow of the woman on the bunk was white now.

Bread and butter the woman brought. The cripple looked at it, at her dog, at the woman. Bread and butter for a dog! but the stranger did not understand till she saw it offered to the dog. The bread and butter was not for the dog. She brought meat.

All next day the man kept hidden. The cripple saw his dog, and knew he was about.

But there was an end of this pretence when at dusk he came back with a show of haste, and a finger of his right hand bound and ostentatiously prominent. His entrance caused great excitement to his new mate. The old mate, who knew this snake-

71

bite trick from its inception, maybe, realized how useless were the terrified stranger's efforts to rouse the snoring man after an empty pint bottle had been flung on the outside heap.

However, what the sick woman thought was not definite, for she kept silent always. Neither was it clear how much she ate, and how much she gave to her dog, though the new mate said to Squeaker one day that she believed that the dog would not take a bite more than its share.

The cripple's silence told on the stranger, especially when alone. She would rather have abuse. Eagerly she counted the days past and to pass. Then back to the town. She told no word of that hope to Squeaker, he had no place in her plans for the future. So if he spoke of what they would do by and by when his time would be up, and he able to sell out, she listened in uninterested silence.

She did tell him she was afraid of 'her', and after the first day would not go within reach, but every morning made a billy of tea, which with bread and beef Squeaker carried to her.

The rubbish heap was adorned, for the first time, with jam and fish tins from the table in the new hut. It seemed to be understood that neither woman nor dog in the old hut required them.

Squeaker's dog sniffed and barked joyfully around them till his licking efforts to bottom a salmon tin sent him careering in a muzzled frenzy, that caused the younger woman's thick lips to part grinningly till he came too close.

The remaining sheep were regularly yarded. His old mate heard him whistle as he did it. Squeaker began to work about a little burning-off. So that now, added to the other bush voices, was the call from some untimely falling giant. There is no sound so human as that from the riven souls of these tree people, or the trembling sighs of their upright neighbours whose hands in time will meet over the victim's fallen body.

There was no bunk on the side of the hut to which her eyes turned, but her dog filled that space, and the flash that passed between this back-broken woman and her dog might have been the spirit of these slain tree folk, it was so wondrous ghostly. Still, at times, the practical in her would be dominant, for in a mind so free of fancies, backed by bodily strength, hope died slowly, and forgetful of self she would almost call to Squeaker her fears that certain bees' nests were in danger.

He went into town one day and returned, as he had promised, long before sundown, and next day a clothes-line bridged the space between two trees near the back of the old hut; and – an equally rare occurrence – Squeaker placed across his shoulders the yoke that his old mate had fashioned for herself, with two kerosene-tins attached, and brought them filled with water from the distant creek; but both only partly filled the tub, a new purchase. With utter disregard of the heat and Squeaker's sweating brow, his new mate said, even after another trip, two more now for the blue water. Under her commands he brought them, though sullenly, perhaps contrasting the old mate's methods with the new.

His old mate had periodically carried their washing to the creek, and his mole-skins had been as white as snow without aid of blue.

Towards noon, on the clothes-line many strange garments fluttered, suggestive of a taunt to the barren woman. When the sun went down she could have seen the assiduous Squeaker lower the new prop-sticks and considerably stoop to gather the pegs his inconsiderate new mate had dropped. However, after one load of water next morning, on hearing her estimate that three more would put her own things through, Squeaker struck. Nothing he could urge would induce the stranger to trudge to the creek, where thirst–slaked snakes lay waiting for someone to bite. She sulked and pretended to pack up, till a bright idea struck Squeaker. He fastened a cask on a sledge and, harnessing the new horse, hitched him to it, and, under the approving eyes of his new mate, led off to the creek, though, when she went inside, he bestrode the spiritless brute.

He had various mishaps, any one of which would have served as an excuse to his old mate, but even babes soon know on whom to impose. With an energy new to him he persevered and filled the cask, but the old horse repudiated such a burden even under Squeaker's unmerciful welts. Almost half was sorrowfully baled out, and under a rain of whacks the horse shifted it a few paces, but the cask tilted and the thirsty earth got its contents. All Squeaker's adjectives over his wasted labour were as unavailing as the cure for spilt milk.

It took skill and patience to rig the cask again. He partly filed it, and, just as success seemed probable, the rusty wire fastening the cask to the sledge snapped with the strain, and, springing free, coiled affectionately round the terrified horse's hocks. Despite the sledge (the cask had been soon disposed of) that old town horse's pace then was his record. Hours after, on the plain that met the horizon, loomed two specks: the distance between them might be gauged, for the larger was Squeaker.

Anticipating a plentiful supply and lacking in bush caution, the new mate used the half-bucket of water to boil the salt mutton. Towards noon she laid this joint and bread on the rough table, then watched anxiously in the wrong direction for Squeaker.

She had drained the new tea-pot earlier, but she placed the spout to her thirsty mouth again.

She continued looking for him for hours.

Had he sneaked off to town, thinking she had not used that water, or not caring whether or no? She did not trust him; another had left her. Besides she judged Squeaker by his treatment of the woman who was lying in there with wide-open eyes. Anyhow no use to cry with only that silent woman to hear her.

Had she drunk all hers?

She tried to see at long range through the cracks, but the hanging bed-clothes hid the billy. She went to the door, and, avoiding the bunk looked at the billy.

It was half full.

Instinctively she knew that the eyes of the woman were upon her. She turned away, and hoped and waited for thirsty minutes that seemed hours.

Desperation drove her back to the door. Dared she? No, she couldn't.

Getting a long forked propstick, she tried to reach it from the door, but the dog sprang at the stick. She dropped it and ran.

A scraggy growth fringed the edge of the plain. There was the creek. How far? she wondered. Oh, very far, she knew, and besides there were only a few holes where water was, and the snakes; for Squeaker, with a desire to shine in her eyes, was continually telling her of snakes – vicious and many – that daily he did battle with.

She recalled the evening he came from hiding in the scrub with a string round one finger, and said a snake had bitten him. He had drunk the pint of brandy she had brought for her sickness, and then slept till morning. True, although next day he had to dig for the string round the blue swollen finger, he was not worse than the many she had seen at the Shearer's Rest suffering a recovery. There was no brandy to cure her if she were bitten.

She cried a little in self-pity, then withdrew her eyes, that were getting red, from the outlying creek, and went again to the door. She of the bunk lay with closed eyes.

Was she asleep? The stranger's heart leapt, yet she was hardly in earnest as she tip-toed billy-wards. The dog, crouching with head between two paws, eyed her steadily, but showed no opposition. She made dumb show. 'I want to be friends with you, and won't hurt her.' Abruptly she looked at her, then at the dog. He was motionless and emotionless. Besides if that dog – certainly watching her – wanted to bite her (her dry mouth opened) it could get her any time.

She rated this dog's intelligence almost human, from many of its actions in omission and commission in connexion with this woman.

She regretted the pole, no dog would stand that.

Two more steps.

Now just one more; then, by bending and stretching her arm, she would reach it. Could she now? She tried to encourage herself by remembering how close on the first day she had been to the woman, and how delicious a few mouthfuls would be – swallowing dry mouthfuls.

She measured the space between where she had first stood and the billy. Could she get anything to draw it to her? No, the dog would not stand that, and besides the handle would rattle, and she might hear and open her eyes.

The thought of those sunken eyes suddenly opening made her heart bound. Oh! she must breathe – deep, loud breaths. Her throat clicked noisily. Looking back fearfully, she went swiftly out.

She did not look for Squeaker this time, she had given him up.

While she waited for her breath to steady, to her relief and surprise the dog came out. She made a rush to the new hut, but he passed seemingly oblivious of her, and, bounding across the plain, began rounding the sheep. Then he must know Squeaker had gone to town.

Stay! Her heart beat violently; was it because she on the bunk slept and did not want him?

She waited till her heart quieted, and again crept to the door.

The head of the woman on the bunk had fallen towards the wall as in deep sleep; it was turned from the billy, to which she must creep so softly.

Slower, from caution and deadly earnestness, she entered.

She was not so advanced as before, and felt fairly secure, for the woman's eyes were still turned to the wall, and so tightly closed she could not possibly see where she was.

She would bend right down, and try and reach it from where she was.

She bent.

It was so swift and sudden, that she had not time to scream when those bony fingers had gripped the hand that she prematurely reached for the billy. She was frozen with horror for a moment, then her screams were piercing. Panting with victory, the prostrate one held her with a hold that the other did not attempt to free herself from.

Down, down she drew her.

Her lips had drawn back from her teeth, and her breath almost scorched the face that she held so close for the staring eyes to gloat over. Her exultation was so great that she could only gloat and gasp, and hold with a tension that had stopped the victim's circulation.

As a wounded, robbed tigress might hold and look, she held and looked.

Neither heard the swift steps of the man, and if the tigress saw him enter, she was not daunted. 'Take me from her,' shrieked the terrified one. 'Quick, take me from her,' she repeated it again, nothing else. 'Take me from her.'

He hastily fastened the door and said something that the shrieks drowned, then picked up the pole. It fell with a thud across the arms which the tightening sinews had turned into steel. Once, twice, thrice. Then the one that got the fullest force bent; that side of the victim was free.

The pole had snapped. Another blow with a broken end freed the other side.

Still shrieking 'Take me from her, take me from her,' she beat on the closed door till Squeaker opened it.

Then he had to face and reckon with his old mate's maddened dog, that the closed door had baffled.

The dog suffered the shrieking woman to pass, but though Squeaker, in bitten agony, broke the stick across the dog, he was forced to give the savage brute best.

'Call 'im orf, Mary, 'e's eatin' me,' he implored. 'Oh corl 'im orf.'

But with stony face the woman lay motionless.

'Sool 'im on t' 'er.' He indicated his new mate who, as though all the plain led to the desired town, still ran in unreasoning terror.

'It's orl er doin',' he pleaded, springing on the bunk beside his old mate. But when, to rouse her sympathy, he would have laid his hand on her, the dog's teeth fastened in it and pulled him back.

Edward Dyson

THE HAUNTED CORNER

THE packer was entertaining Pepper Ned, from Whimble's pickle mill, in the Wharf-side bar. There were threepenny beers and spring-onions lunch, and the talk had taken a scientific turn, it bore upon molecular disturbances of the atmosphere, set up by the popular esculent, and the carrying power of certain breeds of onions, on all of which matters Pepper discoursed oracularly as an expert. The young man from the pickle mill was reminded of the pathetic case of one Artie Coutts, a sensitive soul who had been driven by stress of circumstances and the unfortunate remissness of his people at Home in the matter of remittances, to take service at Whimbles and who had become obsessed by onions in the course of a few weeks. It seemed that Artie was a man whose natural refinement had survived a demoralizing weakness that sacrificed everything else for whisky of Scotch extraction, and fate threw him into that department of the factory where the onions were flayed.

' 'N' me lord juke fair stooed in atter iv onyins,' said Ned. 'Ev'ry one else got 'ardened t' ther hum iv onyins, but Artie he never cud. It fair turned him up, 'n' he'd go er pale pea-green when er bunch iv busy girls got er rush on er ton iv young uns', 'n' th' ink-pink began t' rattle ther windows, 'n' push ther slates off ther roof. Youse don't know what ther little pickle onyin's capable of till yev met er ton of 'em stripped fer bizness in a 'ot room. Artie began t' look like er man with er settled sorrer after er week of it. "My Gord! my Gord!" he used t' say, slappin' his bald 'ead with his two 'ands, "what's t' become iv me?" 'N' then he'd sneak er gulp of whisky, 'n' face it agin like a 'ero. I 'eard afterwards that he got a sort iv idea how he was 'aunted by ther concentrated hodor iv Whimble's onyin branch. He took it 'ome with him. It follered him everywhere. He couldn't shake

it. He took t' sprintin' in ther streets, thinkin' t' outrun it 'n' ide'
where it couldn't find him, 'n' twice he was run in fer gallopin'
wild through ther city without his 'at, 'n' with ther light iv
madness in his eye, thinkin' in his addled 'ead how he was makin'
er break from ther orful smell iv Whimble's. Then he took t'
shriekin' out iv nights when he woke 'n' found th' 'orrid hodor
in his room, 'n' ther people 'ud find him crouched down in one
corner in his nightie, tremblin' all over, 'n' moanin' erbout ther
purple 'n' green smells what was comin' at him down ther
chimbley.

'He said they was some nine foot high,' continued Ned, ' 'n'
they was breathin' pestilent fumes on him, 'n' he couldn't get
no sleep fer ther noise they made trampin' erbout in ther 'obnailed
boots. Then came a Sunday when he went out on ther roof in
his shirt, explodin' the lan'lord's gun, 'n' when ther p'lice pulled
'im down, he said he was shootin' ther big, red onions with ther
livid eyes, what was comin' down in millyins 'n' millyins t' stifle
ther town. They put poor Artie in er padded cell, but ther smell
gave him no peace, 'n' he died of it eventual, sayin' he was goin'
t' 'ell, 'n' 'ell was er pickle fact'ry, jist like Whimble's, where ther
scent iv onions without end rolled over ther souls iv ther damned
fer ever 'n' ever, amen!'

Feathers was deeply impressed by the story of Artie. He
sipped his beer with a thoughtful air. 'Yes,' he said, 'I kin under-
stan' that lad bein' 'aunted by a nodor. I've known ther time
when I've thort there was somethin' spooky 'n' soopernatural
erbout er pertickler weird 'n' unaccountable erfluvium, 'n' I
wasn't ther on'y one, ther whole bloomin' fact'ry got er bit ratty
erbout it, 'n' was thinkin' iv givin' ther grip brusher, 'n' goin'
inter Co. with ther unemployed.'

The wharf-labourers, and the sailor-men, and the hands from
Egg Lane drew their beer about the packer. Feathers had some
reputation as a yarn spinner. His low-comedy style was popular,
and it was admitted that with education and opportunity he
might have become eminent – he might even have aspired to be
an auctioneer.

'Spats' fact'ry's got er bend in it, yeh know, 'n' 'twas round
in ther west corner be ther lift well we first got up agin that
"whoof",' continued the packer. ' 'Twas er mos' curious ink-

pink, sorter unearthly – ther kinder thing yeh might expect t'
biff yeh in ther feelin's when ther trap lid iv ther bottomless is
lifted t' hadmit one more dead 'ead t' ther pit. For er few days it
loitered round there, gatherin' force, 'n' preparin' fer ther attack,
'n' that part iv ther buildin' became very unpop'lar. Fuzzy, ther
foreman, went down with reports ev'ry arf hour 'r so, 'n' ther
new smell created er good deal iv talk. His gills would come
battlin' down ther flat, full iv bisness 'n' good intentions, ez he
always is, 'n' butt up agin ther new flavour, what was takin' on
fresh developments each day, 'n' he'd fetch up, 'n' sniff round
'n' round, like er startled terrier, with er new idear erbout rats.
Then he'd claw up his bunch iv cobwebs, 'n' sample her agin.
Then he'd say: 'Seems t' me they's somethin' a bit queer, George
'Enery;" 'n' he'd paw erbout, 'n' scratch 'n' dig ermong ther
stacks iv bags 'n' ther cuttin's 'n' stuff, more like er terrier 'n' ever.
Lummie! I used t' wonder ther beggar didn't bark.'

Feathers moistened his lips with two-thirds of a long-sleever,
and Pepper Ned leaned on his pint, and sighed heavily. The
interval between drinks promised to be protracted.

'Well, them hatmospheric 'ints grew more pointed, 'n' presently
they began t' clamour. They crep' down on ther pasters, 'n'
eventual they raided Fuzzy's end, 'n' drifted out into ther street
t' disturb ther traffic. It was midsummer, 'n' she raised her voice
to er yell, 'n' ther whole fam'ly iv hodors jined in ther chorus.
By'n bye she was screamin' perlice 'n' blue murder, 'n' you
couldn't hear a bloomin' iron tank drop above ther general din
'n' hodoref'rousness. Down comes Fuzzy, 'n' whacks into it
agin, 'n' he gives er sad cry, 'n' drops his bundle, 'n' goes pluckin'
et his 'air, 'n' bedevillin' his whisks, 'n' barkin' his bleedin' shins
over things, 'n' comin' up out iv ther tangle presently, wet 'n'
dusty, 'n' pale ez death, with one 'and pressed on his "Darby
Kell", 'n' the other holdin' himself down, 'n', "George 'Enery,"
he sez, petulant like, "they must be a leak," sez he. Er leak!
Mother iv Moses! 'twas more like er Niagarer or er barrel iv
litherfracture bustin' in er condemned graveyard.

' "Er leak!" I sez, "I think 'er whale's gone bad on ther firm's
'ands."

' "Can't yeh do somethin'?" wails he, more in sorrow than in
anger.

'I asked t' be excused fer me old mother's sake, me not havin' a sound 'eart. "Send fer ther Board iv Health 'n' ther corporation shifters iv detestable objects," I sez; "I ain't no dealer in remains."

' "Somethin' must be done," whimpers Fuzzy, very pitiful. "Somethin' mus' be done;" 'n' he makes ernother break, 'n' spills over er tub iv paste, 'n' nex' minit he's giggin round ermong ther Beauts, tryin' t' bustle 'em inter takin' on ther job iv searchin' fer ther disturbin' element, 'n' removin' it beyond ther city limits. Ther toms bucked like mules. Kitty Coudray said she was wanted 'ome, th' 'ouse being afire, 'n' Rickards 'n' nine others guv him er week's notice with their compliments, but some iv ther wages 'ands took it on; 'n' presently there was er procession iv pale, sick girls on ther stairs goin' 'ome t' bed.

'Meanwhile, that strange, houtlandish smell was reachin' out 'n' developin', same ez Goatie's candle mill with ther lid off, 'n' our foreman was gettin' so worked up he couldn't sleep iv nights. Ther toadstools 'n' things was growin' on that pale blue hodour in ther 'aunted corner like mussels on er mudbarge, 'n' et this point up comes his gills, ther junior partner, Duff, come on er voyage iv discovery 'n' in er spirit iv scientific inquiry. 'Twas his juty t' hinvestergate 'n' draw up er report. He tried samples from nine points iv view, 'n' then he looked tired, 'n' withdrew frim ther commission, holdin' affectionately to his wishbone, 'n' mutterin' like er man in er dream.

'Ther respected proprietor. His Whiskers, was disgusted with what he called this hefferminate weakness on ther part iv Suety, 'n' he 'eaded fer ther shockin' outbreak on his own. Bizness was suspended on ther spot, every eye was on Odgson. He passed me with his 'ead up, 'n' his nose high, 'n' his cady balanced on ther bridge iv it. He came into collision with ther thick end iv ther distressin' event unexpected, 'n' it took his breath erway. He sorter bounced off it. But ther boss is Scotch and stubborn. He put his 'ead down, 'n' ducked in, 'n' fer arf er minit there was er catch-ez-cats-can contest 'tween him 'n' ther reek iv after judgement, 'n' His Whiskers was beat. He come up out iv it, lookin' white 'n' weak, leavin' his bell-topper in ther possession iv th' enemy, 'n' he leaned 'eavily on my board 'n' breathed hard. Presently he called t' Ellis in er weak voice, 'n' Fuzzy come stumpin down ther aisle, cryin' "Yessir! Yessir!" every stride.

' "Huh, dammit all, man, what's yonder?" sez Odgson, speakin' like er man who's jist done his 'undred yards in ten secs.

' "I'm erfraid it's er leak, sir," stammers Fuzzy.

' "Er leak, yeh idjit!" yells Spats. "Are none iv ther girls missin'?" Then he turns t' me. "Come back t'night, Mills," sez he, "you 'n' Don, ther carter, 'n' shift those bales. 'Unt it out! 'Unt it out!" I had t' do it 'r resign me grip on ther spot, 'n' blime if he didn't send me in fer his 'at.

'Wot er night we 'ad – Jimmy Jee, wot er night! Fuzzy pegged out after ther first hour, 'n' ther Don 'n' me shifted bales 'n' stacks, 'n' ate dust, 'n tainted our himmortal bloomin' souls with the hum of old Tophet, 'n' nothin' come iv it 'septin' ther discovery iv er mysterfyin' noise wot cud be 'eard when you leaned up agin ther wall in ther 'aunted corner. Er creepy, unaccountable kinder noise, like ther faint, far off tickin' iv er clock shop. We tried t' track it down, but couldn't. It seemed t' come outer ther bricks. That was more ghostly than ther smell, 'n' it started my thatch walkin' tiptoe all over me napper, though I ain't ther man t' take long odds erbout ghosts happenin' up anywheres 'r anyhow.

'When ther Beauts got onter that mystery tickin' erway in the wall then ther plot thickened. You couldn't get one iv 'em back fer night work fer gold 'n' di'monds, 'n' they shied from ther 'aunted corner in ther shades iv evenin', 'n' still ther odour grew, so et life wasn't worth livin' up on ther top flat. There was talks iv er general strike, 'n er bunch iv ther pasters interviewed Odgson, 'n' pointed out how they'd wanter be paid time 'n' er half t' carry on ther firm's bizness in ther supernatural hatmosphere what was prevailin' upstairs. Neighbourin' firms was complainin' bitterly, 'n' people was cryin' out in ther street, sayin' Spats' biz orter come under ther head iv noxious trades, 'n' be shifted out inter ther tannery 'n' glue mill district. This stirred the boss up, 'n' he got in workmen t' punch er hole in ther wall, 'n' locate that spook odour, imaginin' ther queer tickin' might be ther furious smell gnawin' its way inter ther buildin'.

'Er gang was on ther job for four days, goin' inter ther hinfected arear in shifts iv short dooration, one man down th' other come on, but, blime, they discovered nothink. They broke 'oles in ther wall, but ther mystery never shifted, ther tickin' went on just ther same, 'n' ther erfluvium become more 'n' more denser. The Board iv 'Ealth was warned be this, 'n' it come down, 'n' stood round, wearin' little patent respirators, 'n' lookin' wise, but it couldn't do nothin' towards solvin' ther problem, so after measurin' ther density iv ther smell with scientific hinstruments, 'n' takin' its longertude 'n' lattertude, 'n' selectin' some samples fer analysis, it went down, 'n' gave Spats legal notice t' have ther tincture iv fiends removed frim his premises within three days, 'r suffer ther hextreme penalty iv ther law.

'Well, that smell got inter ther papers. Ther evenin' organ was quite excited erbout it, 'n' spoke iv it ez er marvellous ferno-menon, goin' on t' say how Spats was evidently ther centre iv some new manifestation iv natural forces, 'n' callin' on ther Govment t' pass er Act iv Parliament without delay. Er perfessor writ er wonderful letter, sayin' proberly the eruption was due t' er earth fissure under ther buildin', what was lettin' ther fumes iv er suppressed volcaner leak out. He said it was er most curious, 'n' interestin' subject, but gor blime, he didn't 'ave t' live in it!

'Erbout here 'n' now, Apps 'n' Winterbee, ther plumbers, had their perfeshional curiosity excited, 'n' they come erlong with er offer iv ther loan iv their boy Sniff et er quid er time. It seems this 'ere boy Sniff 'ad er gift. He was a hexpert smeller out iv things, 'n' was ther firm's greatest treasure. Spats was asked t' take pertickler care iv him. When Apps 'n' Winterbee was called in ter ferrit out er gas leak what 'ad defied all ther other firms in town, it put Sniff on ther job, 'n' Sniff was never known t' fail. He was sent inter all sorts iv dark 'n' dusty places, over ceilin's, 'tween walls, under floors, up channels, anywheres, 'n' he went gaily enough, like er bally foxie after er rat, 'cause it was his speciality, 'n' he was proud iv his great erbility. Sniff was what yeh'd call er hinfant progidy, sniffin' out mysteries was his big hit. 'E was er genius at it, but he didn't look it.

'T' see Sniff, you wouldn' think he was er champion in his class. He was erbout fourteen, 'n' very small fer his age. They kep' him small with gin 'n' 'ard trainin', I think, so's he could creep inter any kind iv er rat 'ole in pursuit iv his callin'. He had er dull eye, 'n' er vacant face, 'n' no chin, his face jist slippin' off where his chin should iv come in, but 'e had er bonzer nose. He'd fair run t' nose. You never see such er nose on er 'uman face. 'Twas habnormally over-developed, so t' speak. Lookin' et that nose, you was sure Sniff wouldn't live long. 'Twasn't in ther nature iv things he could go on sustainin' sich a snich.

'Sniff was turned loose on ther fact'ry flat, 'n' 'e went over it like er tradesman. Other folks was turned end on be one gust iv it, but I think Sniff was 'appy. He was in his helement. He sorter prowled erbout all ther mornin', gettin' ther lay 'n' drift iv ther varyis currents 'n' odours, 'n' makin' his plans; but after lunch he got goin', 'n' how did he 'unt! Nothin' could 'old 'im. He was full iv er sort iv artistic frenzy, 'n' 'e chased trails with his long nose feelin' ther way before him fer all ther world like er 'ound after er 'erring. In two hours he'd run down four gas leaks, three old rats, 'n' two escapes frim ther pickle mill nex' door. Then 'e got out after ther King odour, but that puzzled him. He'd come up agin ther brick wall with er bunt every time, then he'd listen t' ther tick-tackin' fer er bit, 'n' get back on his tracks, 'n' chase her agin. No use, she alwiz brought him up short agin ther bricks in ther 'aunted corner.

'After ther fifth run he stayed there, studyin'. He went down ther wall, 'n' up ther wall, 'n' then er glad light broke over him.'

' "Bring er ladder!" he sez.

'Ther ladder was brought, 'n' Sniff went up it, hot on ther trail. Ther top iv that wall was jist er wide, flat shelf iv brick, on which ther big tye-beams rested. Ther roof over-shot it. On this shelf, back agin one iv ther rafters, was er parcel what couldn't be seen frim below. 'Twas erbout ther size iv er candle box, 'n' ther wrapper was ther tin lining out iv er case, 'n' this tin was polished like silver with ther paws iv ther ten thousan' famished rats what had been spendin' ther brightest years iv their lives, tryin' t' get in. Would yeh believe it, that tin was tickin' like forty watches, 'n' when Sniff stirred it, you'd think it was full iv live dried peas, 'n' was rattlin' on its ace.

'Sniff pulled ther tin parcel out, 'n' he let her drop, 'n' she bust open on ther floor. Boys, I'm done! Here's where I fail. Mother iv Murphy! how did that parcel fogue! Ther volume iv smell smashed ther winders, it rattled ther town, clocks stopped, 'n' trams bolted, fire brigades was called out, 'n' perlice were

sent fer in all directions. Ther hinstruments up et ther hob-
servatory recorded er earthquake iv great vi'lence, ther Lord
Mare resigned his office, 'n' all ther cats left town. Shrieks 'n'
cries was heard in ther streets 'n' people ran 'n' hid in ther cellars,
thinkin' ther end iv ther world was come. Benno fell down in er
fit, 'n' I had ter drag him frim under be ther legs. I was a bit
ratty meself fer seven days, 'n' beer ain't never tasted ther same
ter me since.

' 'N' after all 'twas on'y er cheese, er good-sized, fat, New
Zealan' cream cheese, what some one 'ad pinched frim ther
produce stores in Egg Lane, 'n' wrapped up in tin ter keep ther
rats off, 'n' hid on ther top iv ther wall, till er good charnce
come t' mooch with it. I suspect er lad name iv Creegan – Nipper
Creegan – what got ther sudden jerk fer punchin' ther boss er
clinker in ther whiskers. He got fired so prompt he 'adn't time
t' shift his cheese, 'n' it was lef' there t' ripen 'n' rot, 'n' set up
er storm centre iv cyclonic odorif'rousness what knocked ther
street out iv plumb, 'n' redooced unimproved land values t' nex'
t' nixie.

'Oh, ther tickin'? That was ther cheese mites what bred 'n'
mustered in that cheese, on'y these wasn't mites, they was
monsters, 'n' it was ther tin wrapper what we'd bin hearin' fer
weeks. When ther package broke loose on ther floor, ther ball iv
mites bust, 'n' went skippin' erbout ther flat like er flight iv ole
man kangeroos. They was fearsome things t' meet in ther dark,
I'm tellin' yeh, pale, dreadful grubs ez big ez concertinas, with
long grey hair, 'n' no features exceptin' two dead black eyes.
They could jump five yards, 'n' had er 'ide on 'em like er blonde
pig. They was turnin' up, fright'nin' ther paint off ther girls fer
weeks after, 'n' we 'ad t' set rabbit traps 'n' lay poisoned bate for
'em all over ther place.

'Ther remains iv ther cheese was removed be divers in full
dress, 'n' Sniff got ther Ryle Humane Society's medal fer 'erosim,
'n' was rewarded with er public subscription. There's still er flavor
iv that cheese lingerin' in ther fact'ry t' prove what I've bin tellin'
yeh's gorspel.'

Feathers lifted up his empty pewter, looked into it, knocked
it on the counter in an inverted position, as if to shake out the
dust of dry days, and then said reproachfully to the Aberdeen

engineer off the donkey engine on the wharf, whose turn it was to 'spring': 'Blime, cobber, er yer givin' ther barmaid er perpetual 'oliday 'r what?'

Katharine Susannah Prichard

HAPPINESS

NARDADU, grandmother of Munga, was singing as she gazed before her over the red plains under blue sky. Singing, in a low wandering undertone, like wind coming from far over the plains at night:

> *'Be-be coon-doo-loo*
> *Multha-lala coorin-coorin . . .'**

She was sitting beside the stockyard fence in the offal of a dead beast. There had been a kill the night before. A stench of blood and filth flowed through the air about her. On an old hide rotting in the sun, a little lizard lay quite still. Nardadu plucked over a length of entrail and set it aside. She reached for another, grey-green, and dark with blood.

A small squat woman, with broad square features, wide jawbone, short hair in greasy strands packed with mud and bound by a dirty white rag, she sat there singing, and picking over all that was left of the dead bullock. A gina-gina, blue for a length, almost black with dust and grease, showed her bony legs and feet. Her face all placid satisfaction, the black sticks of her arms and fingers swung backwards and forwards, disturbing flies. Flies clung at the sunken wells of her eyes; but she plucked on over the mess of blood and dung, singing:

> *'Be-be coon-doo-loo, coon-doo-loo,*
> *Be-be, be-be coon-doo-loo,*
> *Multhalala, la-la, lala, lala,*
> *`Coorin-coorin, coorin-coorin.'*

* 'Cuddle your nose into my breast
And know happiness.'

Across a stretch of ironstone pebbles the buildings of Nyedee homestead were clear in the high light of early morning. There were trees round the long white house with verandas where John Gray slept and ate with his women and children. Megga had planted the trees long ago, the tall dark ones, those bushes with curds of blossom, and the kurrajongs whose leaves were light green and fluttering just now.

Megga had ridden and worked with John when he first camped by Nyedee well. Tall and gaunt and hard, she had cooked in the mustering and droving camps, driven men and beasts through long dry seasons. Eh-erm, she drove John. He was still her little brother.

Half a mile away, Nardadu could see every plank and post of the veranda; white hens stalking across it; harsh green of cabbages, onions, turnips surging beside the big windmill; the mill, its wheel and long fine lines ruled against the sky; and the little mill on mulga posts with gauge stuck out like the tail of a bird. Kinerra and Minyi came out from the house for water. Slight, straight figures in dungaree gina-ginas, they moved slowly to the little mill. But it was out of order: would not give water except in a high wind.

White hens scattered and flew before Megga as she came along the veranda, Meetchie behind her, John after them both. A shrill screaming and flow of women's voices reached Nardadu; the throb and deeper reverberation of John's voice, as he came between the women, throwing a word or two before him. Small and stiff as chalk drawings her people had made on rocks in the hills, John and the two women rocked and moved with sharp little gestures before the house.

Nardadu knew what it was all about. She had heard that screaming and quarrelling of women and the anger of John's voice so often before. She smiled to herself and went on with her singing. Winding and rumbling through her, on and on it went, the eerie, remote melody. Nardadu remembered her mother singing that song. It did not belong to Nyedee people. Nardadu had brought it with her to Nyedee from beyond those wild tumbling hills which stood on the edge of the plain, north-east. Her mother had sung the little song to Nardadu when she was a cooboo. Nardadu had sung it to Beilba and Munga. Always it came fluttering out of her when she was pleased or afraid.

She was pleased this morning to have found something she could cook in the ashes of her fire to satisfy the hunger of Munga when he came in from the dogging. All the men of the uloo had been out trapping dingoes while John was away. But John was home again, and the men would be in soon. The old, high, four-wheeled, single-seated buggy in which John had come from Karara station, with Chitali and old Tommy, still stood red with dust, out before the shed. Horses which had drawn the buggy, rough hair streaked and matted with dust and sweat, were feeding beneath the acacias and mulga, beyond the stockyards.

The little windmill would be mended. There would be the good smell of meat roasted on ashes, in the evening air, down by the uloo. When the men had eaten, talk would be made of dingoes: of wild dogs caught, or too cunning for any trap. Wongana would make a song about a dingo, clicking kylies beside his camp-fire. There would be singing: singing and sleeping in the warm, starlit darkness.

On other stations Nardadu knew, men of the camp would not have gone dogging and left their women at the uloo. Wiah! A curse threaded the words of her song. But Nyedee was not like other places. John Gray left the uloo to the ways of the uloo. Megga? Eh-erm – Nardadu guessed Megga was responsible for that. By her will it was, John did not drink whisky until his legs would not carry him; or take a gin even when old men of the camp sent her to him.

Nardadu did not understand how a woman came to have such power with a man that her will should be stronger than his. But Megga – Nardadu understood something of her and her will, having lived so long with her. Had she not made men of the uloo even wear wandy-warra, and the women grass and leaves from a string round their waists, before there were gina-ginas or trousers and boots on Nyedee? But that John should come under her will so, John who was a man of men! Nardadu clucked and threw out her hands in the native gesture of surprise.

Master he might be of all the country which lay before her

old brown eyes, from the wedge of red and yellow purple-riven hills along the west, to those wild and tumbled timbered ridges north and east, beyond which stretched the country of her people and the buck spinifex flats, away and away inland. Yet John he was to her: John the all-powerful to be sure, giver of food and clothing, whose anger and boot you avoided; but who laughed and made fun with you, good-humouredly, when all went well with him.

She had come through the gorge of Nyedee hills with him, how long ago? Nardadu could not count beyond three. 'Plenty years,' she would say it was since John Gray had first brought cattle through the gorge of Nyedee hills, over there where the great koodgeeda's eyes made a pool of fresh drinking-water. Trembling, she remembered the great silver lidless eye in the shadow of dark rocks. How it had flashed at her, glimmered from beneath the water when she went down with her jindie! They had camped quite near, and Wagola, her man, had sent her down to the pool for water because he said the koodgeeda would not hurt a gin. He had made her sleep on the side nearest the pool, too. How terrified she had been, plenty years ago, when she first came to Nyedee with John Gray!

Wagola, her man, had been speared over there on the range by one of her own people. Wagola's brother claimed her. She had grown Beilba then; and Munga was Beilba's son. Her eyes wavered to the creek gums and burying-ground of the uloo, railed places and mounds covered with bark and branches. Her voice had the shrill anguish of wailing for her daughter.

Now she was an old woman, had bulyas on her hands, and led the women's singing in the corroborees. She had no husband to concern herself about, only Munga, her grandson, who put up her low humpy of boughs and hide. And the cows. Nardadu was cow-woman on Nyedee, drove the milkers from their night wandering on wide plains where the windgrass was yellow, and acacias, in their young green, stood against hills blue as the dungaree of a new gina-gina.

While a coolwenda was putting his slow melodious notes across the vast spaces of hill and plain, and stars were still in the sky, she went scurrying after the cows, and brought them through the Two-mile gate to the yards, red heifers and calves, a huge white cow who charged whenever she got a chance, and the old red bull, lumbering and sulky. Nardadu ruled the cows. A drab gnomish figure in dirty gina-gina and the old felt hat which had been Wagola's, she shambled swiftly over the stones, banging two tins to make the cows hurry: proud of herself, of being on the strength of the station, old woman though she was, cow-tailer.

She had not been away since first she came to Nyedee. She had never been pink-eye; but then none of the Nyedee people went pink-eye. Other tribes came to pink-eye on Nyedee every year. There were corroborees, and youths for hundreds of miles about were made men in the widespreading scrub of mulga and minnerichi which stretched to the foot of the dog-toothed range.

The hut of mud-bricks, baked in the sun, on the place where Nyedee homestead now stood – Nardadu had helped to build that. After its walls were up Megga had not ridden out with the men. She had stayed at the hut to watch the sinking of wells, raising of windmills and stockyards. Every plank was set under her eyes: the windmills, with their great wheels and wedge tails of blue-grey iron, stretched taut against the sky.

Then camels bringing stores and sheets of ribbed iron had come over the creek! Again and again they had come, the great beasts, so savage and evil-smelling, yet led by a little stick through the nose and rope reins, bringing more and more sheets of iron and painted wood, flour, sugar, tea, gina-ginas; trousers, boots and hats for the men who went riding with John, pipes, tobacco and boiled lollies. Such days they were, great days of bustle and excitement, from the first fluting of the butcher-bird before stars paled in the eastern sky, until the sun went away behind the back of the hills.

The first room of mud-bricks was kept for a kitchen and the new house grew out from it, with verandas, doors, wire cages for rooms. Megga had sent old men, women and children from the uloo to gather white clay in a creek bed, miles away, and had showed them how to paint the house. But to Nardadu, it still seemed, that the long white house among trees had reared itself by magic on the floor of the dead sea. Far out across the plains she had seen a mirage lying across it, reflections of a house in the sky, and had sung her song as a movin against evil, any evil magic could do an old woman by stealing her wits, when she was minding cows by herself, far away from her kin and the uloo of her people.

Megga herself had worn white clothes when the house was finished. The gins washed them, hung them out to dry and pressed them smooth with irons made hot in the fire. She had gathered about herself, too, china dishes and pots which broke when you dropped them, bringing down Megga's wrath as nothing had ever done.

Then the chickens came. Small fluffy creatures Megga had loved and tended until they were neat white hens, which if a dog killed – eh-erm, there was hell to pay.

Nardadu remembered the killing of one of those hens by Midgelerrie, her own dog, a brindle kangaroo hound, as dear to her almost as Munga. There was no better hunter on Nyedee; but he had pounced on and devoured one of those hens. Lowering, Megga, she remembered, had sent John out with his gun and he had shot the dog. John had told everybody in the uloo he would shoot any dog if it ate Megga's hens; but Nardadu had never forgiven Megga for the shooting. She did not blame John. He did as he was told.

Nothing had been the same on Nyedee since the chickens came. Nardadu believed that Megga's hens were the cause of all that went awry on Nyedee afterwards. Nardadu's was not the only dog John shot because he had eaten one of Megga's hens. The uloo bore Megga a grudge because of her hens, and the dogs John had shot for eating them.

It was beyond anything natural to men and women, Nardadu had decided, the way John and Megga lived in their new house among the trees, with an abundance of food and clothing, shade from the sun and shelter from the rain. They looked about them with pride and contentment. John strutted out from the house to the stockyards and blacksmith's shop, and stretched reading on the veranda when he was not away mustering, or on the road with bullocks for market. Megga cooked, sewed, watched over her china and sat on her chairs, teaching girls from the uloo to scrub, polish, make gina-ginas for themselves. Only two of the youngest gins were allowed into the house, after they had scrubbed their heads and bodies all over with soap and water, every morning, and put on fresh dresses. Other women from the uloo were permitted to sweep round the veranda, in turn, or to help with the washing; but that was all. And always there were new sheds going up, sheds for harness and tools, a butcher miah, shade miah for the hens even.

The station was growing and prospering. John and Megga were growing old with the station; but still, there were no children on Nyedee except children from the uloo who played about the stockyard and woodheap sometimes. Down at the uloo they were concerned about it. The old women suggested that both John and Megga should be advised to take a mate. But Megga, it was agreed, was beyond the age of childbearing.

The men asked John why he did not get a woman. They did not understand his not having a woman except his sister, who was not a wife, to live with him. John laughed and said he had been too busy making the station to think about a wife and family. Men of the uloo believed what he said. They had seen him so often, after a day's hard riding, eat, and sleep as soon as he rolled in a rug beside his campfire. They understood he had thought of nothing but his station and cattle for years.

But the seasons were good. It rained – how it· rained that year! It had not rained since on Nyedee as it had rained then. Nardadu herself, and all the other old women in the camp, had gone down to the creek and beaten it back with green branches when the muddy water swirled over its banks towards the uloo. They had been busy patching their huts to keep the rain out. Grass was green on the plains in a day or so; thick and deep in no time. The cows grew fat. Nardadu clucked with pleasure over their milk and calves, thick-set and sturdy. Megga, busy and masterful, directed everybody and everything, looking stouter, more good-humoured, every day. Since the hens and chickens had come, she seemed to have nothing left to wish for.

John went off mustering after the rain, taking all the boys, two or three gins and most of the horses with him. The grass and herbage everywhere made him gay and light-hearted. He talked now and then in easy familiar fashion with Chitali and the boys as he rode along; or when they camped for the night, he by his fire, they by theirs, at a little distance.

They were chasing breakaways in the back hills when the boys came on tracks of wild blacks from the other side of the range.

Nyedee boys said these were cousins of theirs. John Gray visited the camp, talked to the old men, and in the evening when Nyedee boys were sitting singing round the camp-fire of the strangers, a young gin was sent to John Gray's camp by way of courtesy to an honoured guest.

Nyedee boys marvelled when she did not return, immediately, as others had always done from John Gray's fireside.

And in the morning, John had presented the old men of the camp with pipes, tobacco, and a couple of blankets.

Somehow Megga heard of it. The boys talked when they got back to the uloo. They told their women and the old men, who chuckled, laughing, and smelling what was to follow.

Megga had been angry with Minyi for breaking a cup. Minyi, to make her angrier and to take her mind off the cup, had told Megga of the gin John kept by his camp-fire that night in the Nyedee hills. Megga was furious. The girls heard her talking to John about it. John had been angry, too, angry and sulky. He walked up and down the fence for hours afterwards. For many nights, he walked the fences, morose and restless. Out on the run it was just the same, the boys said, John did not sleep as he used to: threw wood on the fire half the night, and walked about.

The blacks watched him fight out his trouble. They knew well enough what was the matter with him. His mouth took a hard line. Nardadu had seen John striding backwards and forwards at night, sombre and angry as her old bull when he went moaning and bellowing along the fences, separated from the herd. John scowled at everybody who spoke to him during the day. He could not break the habits Megga had imposed on him; would not drink more whisky than he did usually, or have gins about him. But after he had been south with cattle that year he brought back the kurrie.

She was with him in the old high buggy he had driven over from Karara in; and John looked as pleased with himself as Megga had looked when the new house sat, all built-up and whitewashed, on the plains. He had got what he wanted.

And Megga! Nardadu saw Megga's face, as though by lightning, so bleached and stiff it was. Megga had not known John would bring this other woman with him to Nyedee. He kissed Megga and said.

'I've got a surprise for you, Meg. This is my wife.'

Megga did not speak, while the other laughed, saying in a high, singy voice:

'My name's Margie!'

John went on, as if he had done something as much for Megga's sake as his own:

'It was getting a bit lonely for you, Meg, with no white woman to talk to. You and Margie'll be company for each other.'

Nardadu could see and hear them still as if they were corroboreeing before her. Megga, fat and dumb, in front of the girl on slight, bare-looking legs; Meetchie – which was the uloo's way of saying 'Mrs Margie' – in her light frock and hat, holding a red sunshade: John between them, proud and pleased with himself.

They were delighted with the kurrie at the uloo; delighted and excited by her light, brightly coloured dresses, patterned with flowers; her necklaces, high-heeled shoes, the songs she sang, and the tookerdoo she gave them, sweet stuff covered in brown, sticky loam. John himself stepped with a jaunty kick and swing as he walked; his eyes laughed out at you. Nardadu gurgled and chuckled after him, and men of the uloo were very satisfied. Nobody worked very much in those days; and John was easy to get on with. He went about whistling in a queer, tuneless way. Nardadu had even heard him trying to whistle her own little song:

'*Be-be coon-doo-loo, coon-doo-loo . . .*'

How the gins laughed, and he with them, though Nardadu blackguarded him furiously when he took her calves off their milk too soon, so that the kurrie should have plenty of cream and milk in her tea! Black tea was all the gins ever tasted. But the chatter and giggling round the woodheap where they drank their tea and ate their hunks of bread and meat and jam when it was suspected why John was concerned about milk for the kurrie!

He was angry if Nardadu did not drive the cows through the Two-mile gate. Useless to explain she was afraid of the narlu who haunted the mulga thickets beyond the gate: the narlu who had led Wagola from the tracks and hunting-grounds of his people, along the dog-toothed range. John laughed and joked with her good-naturedly enough; but he would have the cows taken where the grass was good. To be sure, he had sent Munga to mind the cows with her, and such days they had been for Nardadu and her grandson, out there on the wide plains, yellow with wind-grass, or in the dove-grey mulga thickets, under blue skies, she teaching Munga how to pick up tracks, and the movins against evil spirits and bullets; to find water, snare bungarra and dig for coolyahs.

Good days! Only in Megga's face the satisfaction faded; and the kurrie became wan and sickly in the hot weather. Nobody saw her during the day; but in the evening, when the sun had gone down behind the hills, she wandered about the veranda and garden. Wandered, wailing and complaining about the heat, the dust-storms, flies and mosquitoes. Up and down she walked: wept and lamented.

John was very tender with the kurrie in her weakness and sickness; as kind as he knew how to be, trying to soothe her when she cried: 'Take me away from this dreadful place, John. I loathe it. Life here, it's so bare, and hard and ugly!' although it hurt him to hear her talk like that about Nyedee. Nyedee, with its wells and windmills, comfortable homestead, garden and bathrooms! What more did a woman want?

Against Megga, though, he would hear no word of complaint. She was mistress of her brother's house: had always been: would always be, he said. She cooked, was storekeeper, accountant, provisioned the parties of well-sinkers, fencers, musterers, rationed the blacks, and saw the gins kept the house clean and in order. There was nobody like her. Two men could not do what she did. She knew every well and windmill and what stock they carried. Megga must go on as she had always done. Meetchie could never do what she did, but she was his boogeriga, his little green parrot, his love-bird.

When Meetchie went away to have her baby the days flowed on at Nyedee as they had always done. Long, quiet days, filled by the riding out, or riding in, of John and the boys with cattle or horses: the arrival and departure of gangs to repair windmills, sink new wells, make fences, while Megga baked bread, prepared the meals, salted meat after the first day of a kill, figured in her account-books, sewed, worked in the garden, read and slept.

Meetchie came back with her baby, bringing cretonne dresses and sweets for the gins. There was a new, older more obstinate look on her face. She did not wail so much or sing so often; but soon the end of the house was regarded as hers and the baby's.

Within a few years there were three children in those rooms at Meetchie's end of the house: one a girl with hair the colour of the tasselled mulga blossom, a little, fleet, wild creature who watched the plains for dust of John's horse when he had been away and ran to meet him when the gins cried: 'John comin'!' No horse on Nyedee would have let John take the child on his saddle, or have stood while she flew up by his stirrup; but always John dismounted to meet his daughter, gave his reins to one of the boys, and, catching her up in his arms, carried her home on the back of his neck, his face as childishly joyous as hers.

But Megga and Meetchie barely spoke to each other. Years only deepened the animosity between them, although Megga loved the children as though they were her own; and Meetchie knew she loved them.

As Nardadu looked at it, the house seemed to be cramped down over one of those dark, slimy, fungus growths which poison the air about them. At the uloo, when the women quarrelled and fought together, their shrieks drifted away; bad feeling was lost in a day and forgotten. But there, in the house, misery and bitterness crouched and clung. You knew they were about when you went near the place and saw the women: Megga's face set to her contempt and repressed indignation: the young wife's face moody and resentful.

For ten day's tramping there was no other building like this John had made in the bed of a dead sea: no other house under those wide, blue skies: no other white women to talk to each other but those two.

John left the house to the women as much as possible. He was out on the plains and in the hills for weeks at a time. The shadow lifted from his face as soon as he was out of sight of the homestead, although he cried out in pain and anger sometimes as he slept under the stars.

The conflict which had been going on for years took a step forward when the kurrie seized Megga by the throat with her fierce white hands and would have crushed life out of her had not John come between them. Then Megga had gone to live in the old store-room near the creek.

Meetchie said she could do all Megga had done. She would cook, manage the housekeeping, order stores, provision the camps, feed the blacks. For months she worked to convince John she could do as well as Megga; but she could not. She had neither strength nor liking for what she had undertaken: she struggled on, overburdened, distraught, screaming at the hens and the gins, losing her soft young beauty, becoming almost insane in her weariness and discontent. John took as much as possible out of her hands. But bread would not rise, store-orders were forgotten, tucker-bags lost. He was cross and impatient. Why couldn't Meetchie have left Megga to run the place as she had always done? The station could not afford to have its work messed up in this way.

And Megga, living alone in her hut by the creek, sat gazing over the plain, day after day, strong, capable hands idle before her; the light gone out of her eyes. Deprived of her work, what had she to live for? She had given everything she had to the station, helping it to grow. She had reared and trained it, as she had John. And the seasons were going from bad to worse. Would it ever rain again? She could see, and John knew only too well, how he would need her to relieve him of all the little odd jobs he did now round the homestead, in the dry season ahead. He would have to be out on the run, moving cattle from well to well, wherever there was a picking, all through the blazing heat and dust storms.

Nardadu could hear them talking over at the house, Megga, Meetchie and John. Their voices came to her, clashing and clanging against each other.

'Your sister means more to you than I do!'

'What is it you want?' John's voice was surly and menacing. 'Meg has left you the house. You want her to clear off of Nyedee, is that it?'

Meetchie made a long wail of grievances. Megga was always interfering, setting the children against their mother, and the gins would only do as she said. Meetchie had told Kinerra to catch and kill a hen for the children's dinner, and Megga had said no more hens were to be killed. It was always the same. If Meetchie told the gins to do one thing and Megga told them to do another, they obeyed Megga. 'Either she goes or I go!'

'Turn my sister out for you?' John shouted. 'Not on your life! She went to the hut of her own accord. But further she shan't go.'

John had left the house and was striding across the red earth and ironstone pebbles towards Nardadu.

Beside the little windmill Kinerra and Minyi, who had been listening to and watching the quarrel, turned to get water. There was no wind; the mill-fans hung motionless; Kinerra, climbing wooden stays of the mill, swung the wheel; Minyi pumped, and filled the fire-blackened kerosene buckets. Two slight, straight figures, buckets on their heads, the girls moved slowly back to the house.

John walked to the shed before which the buggy was still standing. Nardadu had her affections, superstitions. They stirred as she watched John coming from the house towards her. His back was straight: he swung along with as steady, direct steps as when she had first known him, although his body had thickened and swelled in the white moleskin pants and faded blue shirt beneath. But the face under his wide hat-brim, fatter, redder, was sullen and heavy now: the blue of his eyes, burned deeper for the years out there on the plains working cattle under bare skies, held only passion and defeat.

The beat of his heels and spurs, as they clicked on the pebbles with a little silver tinkling, made Nardadu shiver. She remembered she should have been away beyond the gates with her cows: that John would shake his fist and yell angrily, if he saw her. Her song quavered into a queer, gurgling laughter.

But John did not see her. He was calling Chitali and old Tommy, who had driven over from Karara with him.

Nardadu listened. John told the boys to put horses in the buggy again.

When the buggy drew up before the house Meetchie hurried forward and climbed into it. John lifted the children in beside her. He took the reins and they drove away, Megga, standing on the veranda, watched them go. Nobody called to her. The buggy whirled off in dust.

'Wiah!' Nardadu muttered, getting to her feet. Her instinct, sure and sensitive, told her Megga had won, and lost, in the fight which had been going on so long in John's house. Megga had got back the place and work which were hers and driven the kurrie off.

But John had brought the kurrie to Nyedee because he wanted a kurrie. And there were the children. Had he not loved and played with his children as men of the uloo loved and played with their children?

More than ever now, he would wander along the fences at night, like that sulky old bull from the herd: his face turn to Megga as it did this morning: misery and bitterness crouch under the long, white house, with its back to the blue, wild hills.

Against the sky-film, thin, clear blue, soft as the ashes of mulga and minnerichi, dust moved.

A cry rose in Nardadu's throat. She watched that dust grow against the sky and the edge of mulga scratching the sky. The tagged tail of horsemen swept out from it. Men of the uloo were returning from the dogging.

They swerved in a wide curve towards the stockyards, young horses before them. Nardadu could see Munga in charge of the packhorses: Munga on his white horse, ginger with dust, packhorses before him. The bay mare, a bucket lashed to her back, made for the troughs, and Munga, after her. The swing-in of dark, slender legs and flying tails through red mist of dust; bodies of men and horses joined, free-flying, galloping; all wildness and grace! Nardadu exulted. The horseman her Munga would be! And how pleased with the meat she had to feed him from her fire that night, as though he were a man!

The song of her gladness trembled, ranged its high minor notes and went wandering out to Munga:

> *'Be-be coon-doo-loo, coon-doo-loo,*
> *Multha-lala coorin-coorin.'*

100

Les Robinson

THE GIRAFFE'S UNCLE

AMONG other new arrivals at a certain zoo was a remarkably thin giraffe. It appeared to be suffering from granulation of the eyelids, a perpetual inclination to giggle, and a desire to be thought clever. It was a present to the zoo from Fiddleup & Fanticides' Disinfected and Inextricably Mingled Circus and Menagerie, permanent address Soudan Avenue, off Little Sahara Street, Mbomozambombo.

In this particular locality, wild animals are sometimes to be won in lotteries, but may also be obtained in exchange for cigarette cards and the tin tags off plug tobacco. Ground-rents in Mbomozambombo do not amount to more than fourteen king-beetle skulls a year, payable in monthly instalments. It will thus be seen that everything possible is done to foster circuses and encourage the spread of menageries, it being recognized that these industries, more especially when inextricably combined, provide intellectual recreation and a wealth of harmless exercise for animals which would otherwise spend their time in chasing, outwitting if possible, and in murdering their kind friend man, as well as each other.

The price of admission to Fiddleup & Fanticides' Disinfected and Inextricably Mingled Circus and Menagerie was one bird's foot (unsoiled), and in proof of the popularity of this form of entertainment and its unprecedented run in Mbomozambombo and adjacent townships, not a bird could be found with more than one foot, while others were obliged to keep on flying because they had no feet at all. The number of king-beetles, engaged in a fruitless search for their skulls, inclined one also to the belief that closer settlement was extremely popular.

All this information, and a great deal more besides, the newly arrived giraffe imparted to his fellow zoo-mates, in the misguided

101

belief that it helped to beguile the tedium inseparable from life in captivity. As a matter of fact, nothing bored and annoyed the other animals quite so much as the incessant chatter and giggle of the giraffe. They were not interested in forests, deserts, veldts, or any other manifestations, by description, of wild, untrammelled nature. Considering that, with the exception of the giraffe, all had been captive-bred, we should not let this circumstance surprise us.

The giraffe, however, being self-centred, did not notice the lack of esteem in which he was held, nor the open dislike which greeted his loquacity from the very first day of his arrival at the zoo. Not that it would have made any difference even if he had noticed anything. He would still have continued to talk, and his habit of giggling was an heirloom.

'Forest-life, as you describe it,' remarked a toothless, tired, and aged lion, 'is exceptionally unattractive, my friend. There would be the fatigue, for example, of searching every afternoon, possibly in vain, for one's meat, for it is evident to me, that, in these forests and vast plains of which you speak, there are no attendants to wait upon one and to ring a bell whenever it is four o'clock. Pray save yourself the trouble, therefore, of enlightening us further with regard to such places.'

If it had been possible to murder the giraffe, not a stone in the zoo would have been left unturned. But stones, although on view from the cages, were only to be seen through iron bars, and, although iron bars, as a poet has contended, do not make a cage, they are noticeably efficient in preventing anything from getting out of one.

The giraffe, oblivious to the contumely with which he was unanimously regarded, continued to converse aloud, at great length, and with more frequency than ever, concerning the vast, sandy regions, where, prior to extracture, his life had been one incessant gallop in pursuit of happiness.

One evening, having supplemented his bran-mash with the addition of a trimmed straw hat, grabbed that afternoon from a visitor who had strayed too near the enclosure, the giraffe, feeling particularly happy, gave unasked an exhibition of the true, unexpurgated desert-tango and giraffe-trot. For it was another of his delusions that onlookers might spend much money and endure considerable fatigue without witnessing such an excellent all-star entertainment as this one provided by him. What he overlooked, however, was that there were no onlookers. The specimens contained in the other cages and enclosures, in order to forget the giraffe and to miss the true unexpurgated desert-tango and giraffe-trot, had either gone to sleep, or were plunged in gloomy introspection.

Although, at last, he did notice it, this, however, did not depress the performer. He attributed the inattention and absence of applause to ignorance, which is not always voluntary and may sometimes be traced to parental neglect. Any animosity that, under other circumstances, he might have shown, would, he felt, therefore, have been not only out of place, but unjust.

Unfettered by thoughts of his own pusillanimity, and without further preamble (unless a fit of giggling may be regarded in that light), the giraffe reverted once more to his favourite topic – the pleasures of life amid the wide, unfilmed expanses of unsoiled sand and impenetrable banana-forest, belonging to his uncle, the rich giraffe of Mpwampwampwapwapwopwa.

'Yes' he remarked, in continuation of a previous narrative, 'My uncle, though insane, was clever and extremely fleet of hoof. He would gallop interminable distances, for instance, without provocation of any kind at all, and was one of the few giraffes able to distinguish between a pool of water and a piece of some explorer's looking-glass left lying on the sand. It was not long, therefore, before, by a most ingenious subterfuge, he succeeded in making his escape from Fiddleup & Fanticides' Menagerie, swearing at the same time never to be captured again, nor to allow himself to be treated with disrespect.'

'In spite of which,' remarked an elderly gorilla who occupied a cage adjoining the giraffe's pen, 'your rich uncle found himself back at Fiddleup & Fanticides' the very next day. You said so yourself yesterday, and I trust that you will not now attempt to deny it.'

'I am unable to,' answered the giraffe. 'But,' he added, with a far-away look in his eye, 'if uncle had not sprained his foot, the lassoers would never have caught up to him.'

It was at this point that the gorilla managed to unfasten the bolt
on the door of his cage, and leaping into the giraffe's pen, tied
that tedious animal's tail into a knot that could never afterwards
be undone. Having satisfied himself of this, the gorilla then
administered to the possessor of the tail a vigorous kick in the
hindquarters.

'It seems to me,' he said, 'that in a community already overburdened with persons of inferior intellect who do little except
talk, drastic measures of discouragement should always be
resorted to when dealing with the imported article.'

By way of illustrating this theory, and as an antidote to the
giggles, the elderly gorilla then gave the giraffe another vigorous
kick in the hindquarters.

Vance Palmer

THE RAINBOW-BIRD

ALL afternoon as she bent over her slate, Maggie's mind had
been filled with a vision of the bird. Blue-green shot with gold,
its tail an arrow. Her hair fell over her intense, grape-dark eyes;
she hardly knew what she was writing. It was the same every
day now. The hands crawled down the cracked face of the clock
with aggravating slowness; the teacher's voice droned on and on
like a blowfly against the windowpane; the other children
squirmed in their seats and folded paper darts to throw across
the room. But all she lived for was the moment when she would
again see the coloured shape skim from its cavern in the earth,
making her catch her breath as if its wings had brushed across
her heart.

As soon as school was out she flashed a look at Don, racing
down to the bottom fence and along through the bushes that
covered the side of the hill. Don was a little behind, limping
because of his sore toe; flushed and breathless Maggie had
reached the bottom of the gully before he emerged from the
undergrowth. One stocking had fallen over her ankle and her
hat was at the back of her neck, held by the elastic around her
throat, but she cared for nothing but getting away.

From the bottom of the playground she could hear the other
girls calling her.

'Wait on, Maggie! We're coming, too.'

She tried to shut their voices from her ears. None of them
must find out her secret. She hated their empty faces, their coldly-
mocking eyes; they made fun of her because she carried beetles'
wings and cowries about in her matchbox to stare at under the
desk.

'Come on, Don,' she called back impatiently, 'they'll all be
on us soon.'

He growled as he caught up with her.

'It's all right for you – you got boots on. This prickly grass hurts like blazes. Why didn't you go down the road?'

'This is nearly half-a-mile shorter . . . Come on.'

They panted up the other hill and across a cleared paddock that lay between them and the beach. Before the eyes of both of them was the deep cleft left by the store-truck when it was bogged months before, and the little round hole with a heap of sand in front of it. Such a tiny tunnel in the side of the rut that no one would notice unless he saw the bird fly out. They had come on it together when they were looking for mushrooms; there had been a sudden burr of wings almost beneath their feet, a shimmer of opal in the sunbright air, and then a stillness as the bird settled on the she-oak thirty yards away, making their hearts turn over with the sheer beauty of its bronze and luminous green.

A rainbow-bird! And it had come from that rounded tunnel in the sandy earth where the couch-grass was growing over the old rut. Don had wanted to put his hand in and feel if there were any young ones, but Maggie had caught his arm, her eyes desperate.

'No, don't! She's watching. She'll go away and never come back – never.'

She wanted just to stand and let her eyes have their fill. That stretch of cropped turf, with the she-oak on a sandy rise above the beach and the miraculous bird shining out of the greeny-grey branches! It was only rarely they surprised her in the nest, for she usually seemed to feel the pattering vibration of their feet along the ground and slip out unobserved. But they never had to look far for her. There in the she-oak she shone, flame-bright and radiant, as if she had just dropped from the blue sky. And sometimes they saw her mate skimming through the air after flies, taking long, sweeping curves and pausing at the top of the curve, a skater on wings, a maker of jewelled patterns, body light as thistledown, every feather blazing with fire and colour. The vision came back to Maggie each night before she closed her eyes in sleep. It belonged to a different world from the school, the dusty road, the yard behind the store that was filled with rusty tins and broken cases.

'That girl!' her mother said, hearing her mutter on the pillow. 'It's a bird now.'

They hurried across the road, past the spindle-legged house with no fence around it, past the red-roofed cottage where there were bathing-suits hung out to dry. Surely this afternoon the little birds would be out in front of the nest! The day before when they had lain with their ears close to the ground they had heard something thin but distinct, a cheeping and twittering. It had come to them through the warm earth, thrilling them with intense life. Those bits of living colour down there in the dark – how wonderful it would be when they came out into the light!

Maggie pulled up suddenly in the final run, clutching at Don's arm.

'Wait!... Someone's there... Don't go on yet.'

Breathing hard, Don stood staring at the big, dark figure on the slope overlooking the sea.

'It's Peter Riley watching if the mullet are coming in.'

'No, it isn't. It's Cafferty. I know his hat.'

'Cafferty?'

'Yes, Cafferty the Honey Man.'

The man was standing almost on the nest, looking down into the she-oak by the beach, his body still as a wooden stump, his eyes intent as their own. He moved slightly to the right; they saw he had a gun at his side. Horror laid an icy hand on the girl's heart. What was he doing with a gun there?

Suddenly she started to run.

'Come on! I believe he's found the nest. I believe ...'

Her slim legs twinkled like beams of light over the turf, her print frock blew up over her heated face, and Don found it hard to keep up with her. She was out of breath when she reached Cafferty and her eyes were points of fire. He was too occupied to notice her; he was shifting the gun in his hands and watching the she-oak tree. She saw a lump in the pocket of his shirt, a stain of blood.

Words came thickly from her throat.

'What're you doing with that gun?'

'Eh?' he said, hardly looking round.

'You – you've been shooting something... What's that in your pocket?'

Cafferty let his eyes rest on her stolidly, a slow grin parting his lips.

'Guess.'

'It's not . . . It's a bird.'

'Right. Right, first shot. Most people'd have thought it was a rabbit . . . Ever see one of those coloured bee-eaters, little girl? Her mate's somewhere about. I'll get him, too, before long.'

He took the crumpled bird from his pocket and dangled it before her proudly. Through a blur she saw the ruffled bronze and emerald of its plumage, the film over its eyes, the drop of blood oozing from its beak. Then she threw herself on the turf.

'Beast! That's what you are . . . A b-beast.'

Cafferty looked from her small, sobbing figure to that of the boy, a sheepish bewilderment in his eyes. He was a hulking, slow-witted fellow, who lived in a humpy on the other side of the creek, surrounded by his hives and a thick growth of tea-tree.

'What's the trouble?' he asked. 'That bird is it?'

Don had no reply. He was confused, half-ashamed of his sister.

'Lord, you don't want to worry about vermin like that,' said Cafferty. 'Death on bees, them things are – hanging round the hives and licking 'em up as they come out. And they're not satisfied with robbing you like that, the little devils; they'll go through a flying swarm and take out the queen. It's a fact. Dinkum . . . I'd like to wipe the lot of 'em off the face of the earth.'

He went over to the tiny opening of the tunnel and bruised the soft earth down over the face of it with his heavy boot. There was a dull passion in his absorbed eyes, a sense of warring against evil.

'No, you don't want to trouble about the likes of them. Unless it's to go after them with a shanghai. There's sixpence a head waiting for any you fetch me. Tell the other youngsters that – a tanner a head. I'm going to clear the lot of 'em out this winter.'

Shouldering his gun he moved off down the beach, a lumbering heaviness in his gait. Maggie was still stretched prone on the turf, her face in her arms, and Don watched her awhile, awkward and ill-at-ease. But the superiority of one who has not given himself away was slowly asserting itself. Picking up the dead bird that Cafferty had thrown on the grass he fingered it clumsily, wondering if there were any bees in its crop. It was still warm, but its plumage was ruffled and streaky, and it didn't look nearly so wonderful as when it had shot into the air, the light on its wings. Death on bees, the Honey Man had said. He began to feel a contempt for it.

'Come on, Mag! He's gone now. And the other kids'll be coming along soon.'

She rose from the grass, tossing back her hair and looking at the bird with reddened eyes.

'Chuck it away.'

'Why? I'm going to take it home and skin it.'

'Chuck it away!' she stormed.

He hesitated a moment, and then obeyed her. They trailed over the grass toward the store, Don swinging his bag and whistling to show he didn't care. There must be a lot of rainbow-birds about, and if the Honey Man kept his promise ... Sixpence a head! He could go out with the other boys on Saturday mornings, looking all along the sandy banks. But he wouldn't use a shanghai – no fear! His new Bayard was three times as good.

Maggie took no more notice of him than if he were merely a shadow behind her. Their father was standing waiting for them at the bowser outside the store, and Don had to go for orders on his pony. Maggie trudged upstairs to the room over the shop and flung herself down on the bed. Darkness had fallen over her life. Whenever she closed her eyes she could see the Honey Man's evil face, the broken, tobacco-stained teeth revealed in a grin through the ragged growth of beard. Hatred welled up in her as she thought of him squatting among the tea-tree on the other side of the creek, his gun between his knees, his eyes watching the leaves above. Devil! Grinning devil! If only forked lightning would leap out of the sky and char him to ashes.

When the evening meal was over she went upstairs again without waiting to do her homework. Her mother's voice followed at a distance, dying behind the closed door:

'What's the matter with Maggie now? ... The way that girl lets herself get worked up.'

Lying awake, Maggie tried to imagine herself running down the slope and stopping suddenly to see the rainbow-bird whirling round over three spots of colour on the grass. But no! She could only see the soft earth around the nest, squashed by the Honey Man's boot, and the dead bird lying on the grass with a drop of blood on its beak. Wonder and magic – they had gone out of everything! And Don was swaggering round, pretending he didn't care.

A light rain had begun to fall, making hardly any sound upon the roof, dropping with a faint insistent tinkle into the tanks. There were people coming and going in the store below. Between broken drifts of sleep she heard voices running on and on, the telephone's muffled burring, the occasional hoot of a car. But all noises were muted, coming through a pad of distance, of woolly darkness. A funeral, she thought vaguely. They were burying the rainbow-bird.

Near morning, or so it seemed, she heard someone come upstairs, and there was a blare of light in her eyes. Her mother was bending over her with a candle.

'Not asleep yet, dear? Have those people kept you awake?'

The drowsy aftermath of feeling made Maggie's voice thick.

'N-no; it wasn't that. It was because . . . Why do they all come here now?'

Her mother tucked an end of the quilt in.

'They brought Mr Cafferty to the shop to wait for the ambulance. He had a little accident and had to be taken in to the hospital . . . Go to sleep now.'

Maggie's eyes were wide open.

'He's dead?'

'Good gracious, no! Nothing to worry about. He must have been dragging the gun after him as he climbed through the wire-fence across the creek, but they found him soon after it happened. Only in the thigh the wound was.'

Through Maggie's mind flashed a sudden conviction.

'He will die. I know he will . . . Serve him right, too.'

'You don't understand what you're talking about, child,' said her mother in a formal, shocked voice. 'Everyone's fond of the Honey Man and hopes he'll be all right soon . . . You've been lying awake too long. Go to sleep now.'

She faded away, leaving Maggie to stare up at the ceiling in the dark. But the vision of a world oppressed by a heavy, brutal heel had vanished. Her mind was lit up again; everything had come right. She could see the cropped slope by the sea, the overgrown wheel-rut, the small, round tunnel with the heap of sand in front of it. And it was the man with the gun who was lying crumpled on the grass. Above him sailed the rainbow-bird, lustrous, triumphant, her opal body poised at the top of a curve, shimmering in the sunbright air.

Frank Dalby Davison

RETURN OF THE HUNTER

TUG Treloar was skinning the big half-breed dingo he had just shot. His sharp little knife glinted brightly in the moonlight as he lifted it after the first opening slit along the belly and turned the limp warm carcass to get at the inside slit up the hind-leg. He screwed round on his heel once to pat Topsy, the little black kelpie bitch, straining at the end of the length of greenhide by which she was tethered to the butt of a scrubby sandalwood. She had been tied there alone for three hours, an innocent lure, while Tug lay about forty paces off in the deep shadow of a solitary brigalow, waiting for a shot at the wild dog. Now she was straining toward him, whining her delight at his return, almost squealing her ecstasy. She could just manage to push him in the small of his back with her muzzle.

A brief grin cracked Tug's features as he leant back to pat her, then, with lips closed, he turned again to getting the pelt off the dog. He pulled the first hind-leg free, taking care to retain the paw, for beside the bounty-money the skin would make a trophy worth having. He slewed the body round to get at the other hind-leg. He was deeply and subtly excited, triumphant, and was breathing through his nose with a faint whistling sound.

A lot of Tug's life centred around this moment. He didn't realize this detachedly, for he was not very aware of his mental processes, but as he worked his mind was busy with images, retrospective and anticipatory; Tug Treloar, sniper, lying in a forward position, waiting to pick off a man; Tug Treloar's name attached to the pelt, on view at Linklater's store; Tug using the bounty money to buy his wife the pony and sulky she had been wanting; and nearer and more immediately poignant than any of these, Tug arriving back at the camp in a very short while to exhibit the scalp to Bonny, in triumph.

There was an image of Tug that was temporarily forgotten in the excitement of the moment. This was the Tug who sometimes regretted having married, who was irked by the plodding sameness of a settler's life, who would have liked to be away buffalo shooting in the Northern Territory or better still, gold-seeking in the mountains of New Guinea. This image of Tug had faded from mind when the dog hunt began. Tug craftily studying the habits of a wild dog that half a dozen men were after, Tug setting a lure, Tug lying in wait, his trusty rifle pushed forward and ready, all linked up to Tug, the man of daring, worming his way out alone into no-man's-land to establish a sniping post. This Tug was a compensation for Tug grubbing trees and digging post holes on the selection. In speculative enterprise Tug had found temporary forgetfulness of the might-have-been.

Lying in the shade of the brigalow, his eyes on Topsy, he had been aware, of course, that the wild dog mightn't answer the lure, even that his reading of tracks might have been faulty, and that he might be waiting for the wrong dog. The first doubt was set at rest when he saw Topsy prick her ears and, looking where she was looking, saw a shadow stir among the shadows in the scrub beyond the moonlit stretch of open ground. Both doubts were set at rest when the dog, evidently suspicious, came slowly into the open and stood looking at Topsy where she was crouched, whining softly. With curbed excitement Tug tasted again the climax of craft and patience, the planned kill. His forefinger closed slowly and steadily on the trigger, and when the report of his rifle shattered the quiet of the night, echoing and re-echoing, he had no doubt that his aim had been true. The wild dog raised his head as if he didn't know what had happened, didn't know he had been mortally hit. He walked a pace or two towards Topsy, then his legs crumbled under him and he lay quite still.

Tug hurried forward rifle in hand, oblivious at first to Topsy's joyful barking at his return, and stooped to examine the body, while feeling for his scalping knife. It was the black dingo, all right, and by gosh, he was a size! He was a beauty! Tug dropped on one knee, put down his rifle, and was soon busy with the bright little blade. His haste to get the hide off was conditioned only by the need of making a clean and careful job. He even forgot the pipe which had been waiting in his pocket, ready filled with tobacco, this last two hours.

In mind he was doing half a dozen other things besides skinning the dingo; he was being nonchalantly in evidence near Linklater's store the day the skin was put on exhibition; he was modestly receiving the bounty money from the hands of the secretary of the Farmers and Settlers' Association; he was handing the money over to Charlie Munro in return for that pony and sulky Charlie had for sale; he was presenting the pony and sulky to Bonny, who was appropriately melting with gratitude; but most of all, because it was nearest in point of time, a first instalment of the rewards of success, he was stumping back to the camp to cast the pelt at Bonny's feet with a triumphant flourish.

That fifteen pounds should be offered for the pelt of the half-breed dingo who had been making a nuisance of himself in the neighbourhood fitted in with the details of Tug Treloar's life as no other happening within the bounds of likelihood could have. In the first place it gave him fair cause to abandon temporarily the humdrum of selection life for the thrill of the hunt; not that Tug was averse to exertion; on the contrary, he was capable of great and sustained effort, but he liked it with a sporting content. Then again, because of his reputation as a sharpshooter, the reward offered was something of a personal challenge. A number of men would be after the dog. Tug valued his reputation, the legend that had gathered about his name since his return from the war. This was a time to take practical thought of it.

As well, there was the matter of the pony and sulky that Bonny wanted. When once Bonny got an idea into her head an act of parliament couldn't get it out again. She had taken a notion that she wanted a sulky to drive about in and visit her friends. She had made up her mind that the Treloars weren't well enough regarded by the right sort of people, and she felt that this could be remedied if she could drive into the township in an appropriate vehicle, if she could take the baby of an afternoon and drive off to pay calls.

There was only the buckboard on the selection and Tug had pretty well brought that to ruin in the early months of the settlement, hauling heavy loads of fence-posts, fence wire, timber, and galvanized iron. Even if she wanted to use it, it would happen as often as not that the two horses-of-all-work would either be busy on the selection or having a much needed rest. She wanted a pony and sulky. Tug had no money to get her what she wanted. All the money he had had left after the rather extravagant wedding Bonny had insisted on, all he could borrow, and all the tick he could raise with the big store in Wilgatown, was laid out in the selection.

Bonny had a way of harping about things she wanted, as if, like the woman in Scripture, she would be heard for her much speaking. She didn't directly complain to Tug, but if she decided that there was an unreasonable lack in her life she let her needs be known frequently. Bonny had her funny ways. She had a trick of dramatizing ideas, with herself in the leading role. Sometimes she would make a flying attack on the perpetual household disorder in which the Treloars lived. She would make beds and wash up directly after breakfast, and have a vigorous sweep-out, pushing rubbish out of sight as she went, scrub the baby's face red with a damp cloth and then establish herself on the veranda with a woman's journal. She was Good Housekeeping. At another time, on the inspiration picked up from some other woman, she would subject the child to a daily dose of some blood purifying beverage – for three of four days. That was Maternal Solicitude. In the matter of driving about in a sulky she wanted to dramatize herself as Gentility.

Tug was in a difficult position because of Bonny's passion for a vehicle of her own. As he said himself, he'd give her his hide for a bedside mat if she wanted it, but he couldn't raise the price of a pony and sulky. It was only their second year on the selection; the season was winter – dry. They had only eight cows milking and being milked only once a day at that. The bill at Wilgatown store was creeping up; they were still living partly on tick. Bonny ought to understand that.

Bonny had applied for help to her widowed mother, who ran a hand laundry in Wilgatown; but Mrs Meadows, who had three younger children coming along, and who, in any case, had been generous to the young settlers, had replied that the matter troubling Bonny was one for Tug to contend with. Temporarily Bonny was quietened, and for a while drew consolation from an image of herself as the Heroic Wife of the Struggling Pioneer – the Woman of the West. That concept had entertained and sustained her during the first year or so on the selection, but it was now rather worn with use. It was time to be making progress; so presently she resumed talk of the pony and sulky.

She affirmed that the Treloars were regarded as riff-raff, and that something must be done to correct the impression. Her statement didn't quite accord with the truth. The Treloars were respectfully and even affectionately regarded by their neighbours. It was just that they had a gift for unconscious humour. Sometimes something Bonny herself said would raise a smile. She would join in the smile at the moment, and brood over it afterwards.

Experience had taught Tug that patience paid in dealing with Bonny, and he generally kept the fact in mind; but occasionally the natural man took control of his behaviour and he would begin a protest in pleading vein, 'Now look, Bonny. For gawd's sake can't you see. . .?' This invariably worked up to a scene in which Tug would be swearing at the top of his voice, while Bonny threw things at him and the baby yowled with fright at the noise.

Cessation of hostilities would be marked by Bonny addressing him as 'Tug, darling', in a voice like cream and with a smile like a dewy morning; but this would be only after an interval of three or four days, during which he was completely cut off from domestic communion. It is possible that the root of the trouble on these occasions was deeper than either of the participants suspected; that it had less to do with the ostensible cause of dispute than with the inherent capacity of the sexes for disappointing each other. But at all events these times were very trying for Tug, especially with his ears ringing with the recollection of the dreadful language he had used. During the currency of the trouble Bonny would give an effective dramatization of Offended Delicacy, Protective Motherhood, and Love Withdrawn!

On all counts the fifteen pounds' bounty looked like a way out for Tug, so after a word with Bonny he arranged with a neighbour to take over his milking cows for a week or so while he went after the warrigal. In broaching the matter to Bonny, in calculating the prospects of success, he had been as careful of his words as in the days when he had discussed with his superiors the prospects

of a proposed sniping-post. He was eager for the attempt, but
the result of unpropitious circumstances was not going to be laid
at his door in case of failure. 'A man might fluke it, you know.'
He was thinking of the range of country the wild dog had to hide
and hunt in, as well as of the other men who would be on his track.

Bonny seized on the idea and thought of the dingo as already
dead. Her Tug was going to get him! Bonny loved a little
notoriety. Not least of Tug's charms for her at the time of their
courtship had been that he was a local hero, with something
about him in almost every issue of the Wilgatown papers. It was
going to be that way again. The depredations – as the *Bugle* and
the *Argus* called them – of the black dingo had become something
of a local sensation. When Tug shot him there would be a piece
about it in the paper. The name Treloar would once again be
in men's mouths, for there is something in most men that
applauds the prowess of the hunter. Bonny was all for that.

Tug told her that if he was successful he would buy her the
pony and sulky Charlie Munro had for sale. Bonny was so sure
of his success that she would have liked to send word at once to
Charlie that they would take his sulky, but she didn't quite dare
to suggest that course to Tug.

Tug had intended to go hunting the black dingo by himself;
a single man, unhampered, getting meals on the strength of the
sporting sympathy of the settlers, would have a much better
chance than a man encumbered with a full camp; but Bonny
assumed that she would be going with him. She had seized on
the enterprise with such eagerness, and was so confident of his
success, that he hadn't the heart to mention that his idea had
been for her to wait at home. So the buckboard, loaded with
camp gear, left the Treloar selection with Tug, Bonny, the baby
and Topsy on the driving seat.

The half-breed, possibly the result of someone's misguided
experiment in dog-breeding, had appeared on the new settlement
a few months previously. He caused a public stir. It began when
Bert Gifford came across a mangled calf in his paddock with
outsize dog tracks near by. For a dingo to tackle a stray calf was
nothing strange; it happened fairly often in time of drought
when the wild dogs were driven in from the back country, but
this had happened in a good season. No one noticed that until

another settler, and then another, reported similar loss. It was evident then that the newcomer was something out of the ordinary. He was daring, too; he killed a calf on Paddy O'Shaughnessy's place within a hundred yards of the house, and when the two homestead dogs went for him he fought them off, sending one howling back to the house with a piece torn out of his shoulder.

Then people began to report having seen the dog by daylight, sneaking across the paddocks, lurking on the edge of the scrubs, a dark dog – from which he got his name, the black dingo – and as big as a mastiff, some of them said. It is doubtful if so many really saw him – imagination can do a lot with charred tree-stumps in a half-light; but when old Dan Crewe, who was snaring on Back Creek, reported seeing him, it was taken as authentic. 'Dark brown, with yellowy underparts,' said Dan, 'and a fair bit bigger than an ordinary dingo.'

It took Tug five days to get onto the tracks of the black dingo. He studied the record of his kills, the conditions of the waterholes and dams in the district, and the distribution of cover, the lay of the big scrubs. When he heard that a kill had been made the night before on Christmas Creek, he drove immediately to the adjoining watershed, Tommy's Creek, and made camp there. He picked up the tracks of a large dog in the belah scrub on the ridge dividing the two creeks, found identical tracks in the mud of the waterhole on Tommy's Creek, and reckoned he was getting close to success.

That the moon was close to full had entered into Tug's calculations from the start. It had also entered into his calculations that Topsy could be trusted to draw attention to herself. He had kept her tied up during most of the time since they had left home, so that she was beside herself with delight when he – carrying his rifle – took her for a walk one evening after tea; and she was beside herself with disappointment when he left her tied to a little dead tree at a lonely spot, and walked on without her. She was shrilly vocal about her disappointment, yapping, whining and straining after his retreating back, at the end of her tether; making a disturbance that would undoubtedly be audible to canine ears for a mile around, and would as undoubtedly be recognized as feminine.

Topsy was so incredulous at Tug's treachery that when her first excitement died down she didn't know what had become of him. Creeping back to lie at full length in the shadow of the brigalow, Tug realized this. Topsy was looking in all directions. She couldn't see him, even at the short distance that separated them, because of the hummocky ground behind him. Gradually she settled down, crouched in uneasy, watchful quiet, emitting just a whine or two at intervals. That was good. If she became too quiet it would be easy to start her off again by snapping a twig, or by tossing a stick out into the moonlight, some distance behind her.

Tug raised his rifle to his shoulder and sighted on a stump about forty yards away. He had taken the precaution of whitening the tip of his foresight. He wriggled forward until the muzzle of his rifle, when raised for firing, protruded a few inches into the moonlight. That was better.

He lowered the rifle and looked about him. He had a fine clear range of vision between where he was lying and the edge of the scrub from which the black dingo would appear.

Lying in wait, asprawl, his weight on his elbows, his hands loosely supporting his rifle, his eyes on the gleam of Topsy's coat, his ears pricked, Tug was content. He thought of the lead he had on other men who were after the quarry, of the fresh signs he had seen near by on the side of the hill. The prospects for success were fairly good. He took out his pipe, then remembered himself, and put it away again. He did so without regret, rather with pleasure. Lying like this, with a wild craving for a smoke gnawing at him, brought back old times.

Watchful waiting reminded him of the Tug he had been happiest with, sniper Tug, the Tug he liked most to recall. For a few seconds his thoughts dwelt on his life as a selector, then flitted to the mountains of New Guinea, where Mick Brannigan and Tom Hollis, old war-time mates, were gold seeking, then came back to himself. In his present enterprise he felt temporarily compensated for not being with Mick and Tom.

Aboard ship, returning to Australia, he had fixed up with Mick and Tom to go buffalo shooting in the Northern Territory. The price of hides was high. Tug knew nothing about the game, but from Mick's description it sounded fine; excitement, a gambling chance, some notoriety, a season of work and daring, and then a bit of a spree. It looked like retaining in peace the better part of war; an orange without the bitter rind of curtailed liberty, or the pips of monotony.

Tug had had a fairly spectacular career in the army, and in some ways demobilization had loomed rather cheerlessly, a descent from glory. Before the war he had swung a pick in the ranks of municipal employees, and he had no desire to return to that unexciting and undistinguished pursuit. Buffalo shooting looked like a way out, but in the interval of a visit to his native Wilgatown, before rejoining his mates for further adventures, he met Bonny Meadows, and the first thing he knew he was a simple, hardworking selector, with a wife and baby.

Bonny in place of a buffalo hunter's life had seemed far more than a fair exchange until, one day, after about a year of married life, he happened to see in the papers a short news item to the effect that Messrs Brannigan and Hollis had struck it rich on a new field they had discovered in the interior of New Guinea. So that was what they were up to! They hadn't gone just buffalo hunting but farther afield. Tug felt chagrined. He didn't care about their striking it rich, it was the life he was thinking about. He couldn't quite imagine it, but he reckoned that tropic forests, savages, and strange rivers stood for something that would have suited him fine.

He brooded over it while at work on his selection and at length evolved a plan. He decided to broach it first to Mrs Meadows. If he could win her over he might manage Bonny with her help. He put it to Mrs Meadows one week-end when, on his especial urging, she came up from Wilgatown to visit the settlers. The plan was simple. It was that Mrs Meadows should give up the laundry – of which she must be very weary! – and come and live on the selection. She and Bonny could run the selection between them while Tug went off to seek for gold in New Guinea. 'There's money in it, mother,' urged Tug. 'I might make a fortune for all of us!' They were sitting together on the edge of the veranda.

Mrs Meadows, an intelligent woman who had accumulated much wisdom in the course of a hard life, considered the matter for a moment. When she spoke there was a look of affection as well as an ironic gleam in her eye. 'Something sure and steady is best, I think, Tug,' she said. 'You know, there's the baby to think of now, as well as Bonny.'

Yes, there was the baby to think of. Tug had to admit it. As a matter of fact there was another baby on its way. Tug had decided not to mention that. It was one of the things he had counted on Bonny and Mrs Meadows managing between them when the time came. He saw, now that Mrs Meadows had refused help, that he would have to think of some other plan.

He hadn't much time to do so, for as soon as Mrs Meadows had gone Bonny challenged him.

'What was that you and mother were talking about on the veranda?' she asked.

In the face of frontal attack Tug had to explain.

'The idea!' exclaimed Bonny, after he had finished.

She thought for a moment, and then, as if suddenly struck by another aspect of the matter, looked at him more sharply than she had ever looked before. 'Do you think I'd be waiting for you when you came back?' she demanded.

Tug thought these words over as he went about his work. He had known Bonny to abuse him roundly, he had seen her eyes ablaze with wrath and venom, but never had she spoken as directly as then, never had her eyes been so cold and deadly. Her utterance, he realized, was from the bedrock of her nature.

He brooded. He knew Bonny had him there. For some reason he couldn't determine the knowledge put him in a secret rage. He was puzzled. He had never doubted that he was the captain of his soul, and yet somehow life had run a fence round him. He felt angry and baffled. He couldn't get it all straightened out in his thoughts. He felt like two men instead of the one and indivisible man he had naturally assumed himself to be. In his distress he turned for consolation and relief to dwell upon the comforting image of the man he liked most to recall, the man his pride affirmed as himself; not Tug Treloar sweeping out the cow bails, nor Tug Treloar carrying buckets of pig swill, but Tug Treloar the lone-hand sniper.

In imagination he saw himself going over the top, just before dawn, to his day of secret deadly work between the lines. He heard again the muttered 'So-long' and 'Good luck, Tug' of less enterprising men. He tasted again the little drama of his return after nightfall. His night of undisturbed rest was sacrosanct. No irritating, trifling night watches in his life. He recalled with satisfaction the way other men looked at his rifle and at the two decorations on his breast, the way his superiors treated him practically as an equal when questioning him and discussing his plans with him, the way he was pointed out by his officers to visiting officers from brigade and divisional headquarters.

Lying out in front, it had been his habit to go over these things ruminatively, chewing a quiet cud of satisfaction. He had never been able quite to make out how the obscure Tug he remembered in civil life had come to be a famous chap, didn't know that in large measure it was due to his lack of imagination. There was a war on, and when Tug had reason to suppose that a man had dropped after the crack of his rifle he was scarcely more impressed than if it had been a kangaroo, just a little more elated. Neither did anything serious happen to his imagination when he thought of being hit himself. He hadn't the nervous mechanism to be moved by anything he hadn't actually experienced, and not even the sight of other men laid out could make good the lack. Some fellows got wounded or killed. Tough luck! Getting knocked was something you avoided if you could, but otherwise it was just being knocked! His imagination couldn't effectively distinguish between being struck by a flying lump of shell or a muddy football. His thoughts couldn't encompass the idea of his own non-existence. At twenty-eight, powerfully and actively built, with a flawless nervous system and a body as hard as the trunk of a gum-tree, Tug was well fitted for his trade.

His rewards for skill and daring were garnered not only in the firing line. Back in billets he was granted small indulgences, such as being excused fatigue duties, a freedom he valued highly. Then he had the fun of showing himself at the different *estaminets*, where he was treated by other men with a touch of deference, like a successful boxer or a prominent roughrider. He liked the mademoiselles, too, especially the kind that didn't expect a lot of beating around the bush. *Très bon!* Tug had a lot of good things to chew over while lying in watch for the enemy to betray himself.

It happened that Tug was the first returned soldier to reach his native Wilgatown. He immediately received an official call from the mayor, at his home, accompanied by compositor-reporters from rival papers, the *Bugle* and the *Argus*, and by an amateur but very zealous photographer. For a couple of weeks he was feted and feasted, made free of the pubs, stared at in the street, engaged in conversation by people who wouldn't ordinarily have noticed his existence, and written up in the press.

It was the first time Tug had seen himself referred to in print, and it surprised him to discover what an interesting life he had lived. What a different light fell on his schooldays when an old teacher at whom he had once thrown his slate recalled him as a 'high-spirited lad'. Even the job his father had forced him into in his indolent teens, driving a cart for old Pentwhistle the butcher, looked different when the *Bugle* put it that he 'had accepted a position with Pentwhistle and Sons'. Best of all Tug liked the way the press ended up by reporting his intention to 'engage in buffalo hunting in the Northern Territory, a hazardous but lucrative career for which his prowess with a rifle and taste for daring exploits mark him out as eminently fitted'. This was evidence for all men to see that Tug, who was now a conspicuous figure in the streets of the town, who had found himself in war, was not going to lose himself in dullness and drab anonymity.

While yet awaiting word from Mick, appointing a rendezvous from which the three mates would set forth, while yet he supped on fame, Tug suddenly became aware of a vision of surpassing feminine loveliness beaming at him invitingly from among the encircling throng of admirers – Bonny Meadows!

Bonny was eighteen, in full bloom, and more than ordinarily buxom. Though many turned their noses up at her, she was the belle of the town. She was also a problem. From one or two things that had come to her notice – happily before any harm was done – Mrs Meadows had decided that it would be best to marry Bonny off at the first reasonable chance. In the meantime it was necessary to see that she was kept properly busy by day, and that she came straight home from the pictures, and that she didn't go to picnics unless Mrs Meadows went too. After studying Tug briefly but shrewdly, Mrs Meadows welcomed him as a man of serious intentions.

Tug had seen Bonny once on the street and once at the house of a friend before becoming a caller at her home. From the beginning he was unable to take his eyes off her. Always an admirer of a full figure, Tug was goggle-eyed before the exclamatory nature of Bonny's feminine characteristics. She had such a lot of everything. They were married just as soon as Tug had made the necessary arrangements to become a selector instead of a buffalo hunter. The baby's arrival dated from the engagement rather than the wedding, but this was something that nice people were expected not to notice.

Tug, despite his yearning for adventures in New Guinea, was still enamoured of his bride. 'Do you think I'd be waiting for you when you came back?' These words, uttered with such deadly calm and certitude, echoed and re-echoed in his ears as he went about his selection. He thought of himself as gone, already in New Guinea, or rather, affectionately in New Guinea and watchfully at home, at one and the same time. It wouldn't work. Bonny wouldn't wait. He knew that. He almost wished that Bonny's charms weren't quite so sumptuous. He would feel safer about leaving her. He didn't feel safe about that, so his spirit warred with itself. Altogether, the appearance of the black dingo on the settlement was cause for thankfulness.

The skinning of the black dingo was finished, and Tug, his pipe alight, was well on the way to the camp. He was stumping along in high spirits, living over again the moment when his finger had closed on the trigger. Neither then, nor during the long wait in the shadow of the brigalow, had any sense of fellowship with the warrigal stirred in his mind. It was hunter and hunted, and when his shot rang out the hunter had triumphed.

He stopped and stooped to pat Topsy, frisking round and round him in her delight at his return, her release and their homeward progress. He resumed his way, his face beaming with self-approval. It had been a great wheeze, tying Topsy out like that as a lure. Trust Tug! He knew a thing or two!

He stopped and held up the hide of the dingo, examining it by the light of the moon, dangling limply from the scruff. It was not unimpressive. Paws, tail and head – the latter retained for more careful skinning by light of day – gave it something the appearance of life. The ears were pricked, the eyes still scarcely glazed, the lips drawn back a little as if, in a dim way, following the impact of the bullet, the outlaw had recognized death and would have turned at bay. Perhaps more thoughtfully than he had ever looked upon anything, Tug studied the scalp dangling limply at the end of his up-thrust arm; the coat, the bloom of life still in it, gleaming dimly in the moonlight. A skin without a dog in it. Rather funny! Just for a moment a vague sense of kinship with his trophy troubled him; but the connection eluded him. His brow cleared.

He turned on his way, his thoughts leaping forward to the moment of his arrival at the camp. He would be in sight of it from the top of the next ridge. When they got within fifty yards or so, Topsy, as she always did, would rush on ahead, and into the tent, to announce her return with joyful whining, pawing and tail-wagging. Bonny would most likely be in bed, dozing, with the hurricane lamp still burning. Topsy's tempestuous entry would rouse her. Then would follow Tug. He would hold the black dingo's scalp up at arm's length, as he had done just then, and exclaim, 'There you are!' Bonny would raise bare white arms to him. Her pleasure and approval would be unbounded.

Marjorie Barnard

THE PERSIMMON TREE

I saw the spring come once and I won't forget it. Only once. I had been ill all the winter and I was recovering. There was no more pain, no more treatments or visits to the doctor. The face that looked back at me from my old silver mirror was the face of a woman who had escaped. I had only to build up my strength. For that I wanted to be alone, an old and natural impulse. I had been out of things for quite a long time and the effort of returning was still too great. My mind was transparent and as tender as new skin. Everything that happened, even the commonest things, seemed to be happening for the first time, and had a delicate hollow ring like music played in an empty auditorium.

I took a flat in a quiet, blind street, lined with English trees. It was one large room, high ceilinged with pale walls, chaste as a cell in a honey comb, and furnished with the passionless, standardized grace of a fashionable interior decorator. It had the afternoon sun which I prefer because I like my mornings shadowy and cool, the relaxed end of the night prolonged as far as possible. When I arrived the trees were bare and still against the lilac dusk. There was a block of flats opposite, discreet, well tended, with a wide entrance. At night it lifted its oblongs of rose and golden light far up into the sky. One of its windows was immediately opposite mine. I noticed that it was always shut against the air. The street was wide but because it was so quiet the window seemed near. I was glad to see it always shut because I spend a good deal of time at my window and it was the only one that might have overlooked me and flawed my privacy.

I liked the room from the first. It was a shell that fitted without touching me. The afternoon sun threw the shadow of a tree on my light wall and it was in the shadow that I first noticed that the bare twigs were beginning to swell with buds. A water colour, pretty and innocuous, hung on that wall. One day I asked the silent woman who serviced me to take it down. After that the shadow of the tree had the wall to itself and I felt cleared and tranquil as if I had expelled the last fragment of grit from my mind.

I grew familiar with all the people in the street. They came and went with a surprising regularity and they all, somehow, seemed to be cut to a very correct pattern. They were part of the mise en scene, hardly real at all and I never felt the faintest desire to become acquainted with any of them. There was one woman I noticed, about my own age. She lived over the way. She had been beautiful I thought, and was still handsome with a fine tall figure. She always wore dark clothes, tailor made, and there was reserve in her every movement. Coming and going she was always alone, but you felt that that was by her own choice, that everything she did was by her own steady choice. She walked up the steps so firmly, and vanished so resolutely into the discreet muteness of the building opposite, that I felt a faint, a very faint, envy of anyone who appeared to have her life so perfectly under control.

There was a day much warmer than anything we had had, a still, warm, milky day. I saw as soon as I got up that the window opposite was open a few inches, 'Spring comes even to the careful heart,' I thought. And the next morning not only was the window open but there was a row of persimmons set out carefully and precisely on the sill, to ripen in the sun. Shaped like a young woman's breasts their deep, rich, golden-orange colour, seemed just the highlight that the morning's spring tranquillity needed. It was almost a shock to me to see them there. I remembered at home when I was a child there was a grove of persimmon trees down one side of the house. In the autumn they had blazed deep red, taking your breath away. They cast a rosy light into rooms on that side of the house as if a fire were burning outside. Then the leaves fell and left the pointed dark gold fruit clinging to the bare branches. They never lost their strangeness – magical, Hesperidean trees. When I saw the Fire Bird danced my heart moved painfully because I remembered the persimmon trees in the early morning against the dark windbreak of the loquats. Why did I always think of autumn in springtime?

Persimmons belong to autumn and this was spring. I went to the window to look again. Yes, they were there, they were real. I had not imagined them, autumn fruit warming to a ripe transparency in the spring sunshine. They must have come, expensively packed in sawdust, from California or have lain all winter in storage. Fruit out of season.

It was later in the day when the sun had left the sill that I saw the window opened and a hand come out to gather the persimmons. I saw a woman's figure against the curtains. *She* lived there. It was her window opposite mine.

Often now the window was open. That in itself was like the breaking of a bud. A bowl of thick cream pottery, shaped like a boat, appeared on the sill. It was planted, I think, with bulbs. She used to water it with one of those tiny, long-spouted, hand-painted cans that you use for refilling vases, and I saw her gingerly loosening the earth with a silver table fork. She didn't look up or across the street. Not once.

Sometimes on my leisurely walks I passed her in the street. I knew her quite well now, the texture of her skin, her hands, the set of her clothes, her movements. The way you know people when you are sure you will never be put to the test of speaking to them. I could have found out her name quite easily. I had only to walk into the vestibule of her block and read it in the list of tenants, or consult the visiting card on her door. I never did.

She was a lonely woman and so was I. That was a barrier, not a link. Lonely women have something to guard. I was not exactly lonely. I had stood my life on a shelf, that was all. I could have had a dozen friends round me all day long. But there wasn't a friend that I loved and trusted above all the others, no lover, secret or declared. She had, I suppose, some nutrient hinterland on which she drew.

The bulbs in her bowl were shooting. I could see the pale new-green spears standing out of the dark loam. I was quite interested in them, wondered what they would be. I expected tulips, I don't know why. Her window was open all day long now, very fine thin curtains hung in front of it and these were never parted. Sometimes they moved but it was only in the breeze.

The trees in the street showed green now, thick with budded leaves. The shadow pattern on my wall was intricate and rich. It was no longer an austere winter pattern as it had been at first. Even the movement of the branches in the wind seemed different. I used to lie looking at the shadow when I rested in the afternoon. I was always tired then and so more permeable to impressions. I'd think about the buds, how pale and tender they were, but how implacable. The way an unborn child is implacable. If man's world were in ashes the spring would still come. I watched the moving pattern and my heart stirred with it in frail, half-sweet melancholy.

One afternoon I looked out instead of in. It was growing late and the sun would soon be gone, but it was warm. There was gold dust in the air, the sunlight had thickened. The shadows of trees and buildings fell, as they sometimes do on a fortunate day, with dramatic grace. *She* was standing there just behind the curtains, in a long dark wrap, as if she had come from her bath and was going to dress, early, for the evening. She stood so long and so still, staring out – at the budding trees, I thought – that tension began to accumulate in my mind. My blood ticked like a clock. Very slowly she raised her arms and the gown fell from her. She stood there naked, behind the veil of the curtains, the scarcely distinguishable but unmistakeable form of a woman whose face was in shadow.

I turned away. The shadow of the burgeoning bough was on the white wall. I thought my heart would break.

Gavin Casey

TALKING GROUND

THE trouble between Bill Lawton and Jim Sparrow was that the former knew the weakness of his mate. They had worked together for a year and been cobbers off the lease before Bill made the discovery that was to change the character of their relationship. But it had to come, and it came on the evening when the shift-boss took them from the face on the seven hundred level, and set them to work in the big stope at the twelve.

Bill knew the mine. He had worked in the stope before, and it was all the same to him. He led the way, because he knew every foot of the level and could make progress without peering ahead into the beam of his lamp. He voiced a warning of the locality of the chute as they left the plat, and when they were a quarter of a mile from the shaft, and the faint mutterings that had always distinguished the rickety old twelve hundred became audible, he thought nothing of it. He emerged from the tunnel into the great shadowy cavity, talking over his shoulder.

'It's a good level, Jim. There's plenty of air, and I like a place where there's plenty of air,' he said, and then looked back. Jim was not there.

For a moment Bill was startled, but the sound of moving stones and a glow in the distance reassured him. Jim came out of the darkness, and stood his lamp on a rock behind him so that it shone on his back and his face was still in the gloom.

'What happened to you?' asked Bill. 'You gave me a fright.'

'Nothing,' said his mate. 'Just strange to the place.'

Bill, who had moved off without waiting for an answer, was halted by something shaky in his tone. He swung his light so that the beam shone bright on Jim's face. Jim did not blink. His eyes remained wide and fixed, tense and alert as his white, drawn features.

' 'Strewth!' said Bill. 'You look like someone's ghost. What the hell's the matter?'

'Nothing,' said Jim again. 'She – she talks a lot down here, don't she?'

Bill's laugh of relief rumbled among the crevices and mingled with stifled, faraway grunts that indicate the minute movements of hundreds of tons of earth. The chuckle cut its way into Jim's paralysed mind like an echo of the menace that he felt around him; but it could not have been suppressed. The man was frozen with frig: ., and Bill was amused. The very idea of a miner, one who had toiled in the depths for years, even noticing what he himself had long ago dismissed from his mind as the baffled bluff of ground held in check by its masters was funny. For the first time he had a warming, elating sensation of superiority over the mate who had never before shown a weakness, except of the kind that is admired among men.

'Snap out of it!' he said. 'It's talked a lot for twenty years, and it'll talk a lot for another twenty. That's what it is – all talk, and the safest place on the Mile. You ought to know better, feller.'

Jim knew it, but it was a flush of resentment that brought the colour back to his cheeks. He said nothing, but picked up his lamp, and soon they were making their insignificant contributions to the toil of the underground together.

But from out of the great black void of the stope the voice of the earth continued to protest. Whispers grew into muffled groans, and occasionally the hollow rattle of a little falling stone, diving down a rock wall, hitting the broken rock, and spinning and leaping to the bottom of a rill, made an exaggerated clatter in its higher key. Whenever this happened Jim's already taut muscles would stretch till they hurt, startled sweat would bead his forehead, and he would take a new grip of tattered nerves before he could go on.

But for Bill, Jim would have quit before the first week was out. He had walked off his last job – a good one, on profitable contract rates – before any one had discovered the reason. There, too, the ground had 'talked', threatening and shifting about behind its deceptive face, day and night. It had creaked and groaned and grated above and around him, until it was no longer an interesting phenomenon, but a promise of doom. It had developed voices, suggestions of impending catastrophe that were almost articulate. The rock had pressed around him, stifling and startling, before he had decided not to go down into it again. He had got into a habit of staring, hypnotized, at a wall of solid stone until it first melted into vague, swirling, dark masses, and then leapt, toppling and tumbling, towards him. The seven hundred level, where the masses were quiet and still, and the only noises were those of humans and scurrying, friendly mice, had been heaven after that.

But now he was at the twelve, in the big stope that was always filled with vague hints of irresistible power, crushing weight and diabolical purpose, biding their time.

When Bill began to realize that his mate's inexplicable state was serious, he tried, with a clumsy good humour that was not free of patronage, to set his fears at rest. Standing with his heels dug into the rubble, he talked commonsense down to the pale face of a man whose mind had long since rejected logic as applied to his obsession.

'Crikey!' said Bill, in amiable, peaceful tones, unaware that all around him the earth was whispering promises to the devil. 'It ain't the ground that talks all the time you've got to get the wind up about. When it starts all of a sudden, stand from under if you like; but this noise that goes on for years an' years don't mean a thing. She might come down, same as she might anywhere; but you ought to know there ain't any more chance of it just 'cause of all the silly row. Surely t' Gawd you've worked in a level where the ground's been gruntin' a bit before now.'

Jim, a dozen feet below him, snarled. He had never admitted to Bill how he felt. He never would. He would wait for what was coming, and meet his end when it did, just for the joy of seeing Bill Lawton go under first, with his grimace of animal astonishment on his ugly, unintelligent face.

'Damn you!' said Jim. 'I know. I'm like you – I know everything – so you don't need to tell me. You don't need to tell me, do you hear? You're like the ground – you talk too much; but I don't give a damn for either of you.'

After that they had little to say to each other, though Bill, who felt that he had a just grievance, aired it occasionally in ways that pricked and rankled. He took to watching his mate with the amused interest with which one might examine a freakish and eccentric insect.

'I've got an idea, Jim,' he said one day. 'Why let th' ground do all the talking? Answer it back a bit, lad. Tell it to go to hell a few times, an' they'll soon put you where it won't worry you any more.'

'Listen to that one!' he would sing out when the fastness of the rock rumbled more heavily than usual. 'It's giving you the raspberry now. If I was you, I'd shove a few plugs of fracteur into the cheeky cow?'

Jim writhed, wavered at breaking point, and inwardly swore himself to what would be a joyous murder if he ever suspected that Bill had talked to any one else in that strain. But Bill never did that.

They were, of course, no longer friends off the mine. They kept as far away from each other as possible. And each eight-hour shift in the twelve hundred stope was an eternity of shameful misery for Jim. In the daylight, above ground, he knew it was ridiculous. In the mine he had no fear of a chattering rock-drill's hammering point striking an unexploded charge and splashing itself and the men around on the nearest wall. He had no fear of falls, or nervousness in the cage that dropped and leapt perilously in the narrow shaft. It was just the voices in the rocks, the secret evil conversations that went on in the bowels of the earth, that unnerved him. His face developed a permanent masklike stiffness of expression. He lost weight, and could not sleep for hating Bill Lawton.

Then one day when Jim, obviously a sick man, needed a lift on a job that was too heavy for him, Bill surprisingly made overtures towards friendship.

He was up on the rill, with his lamp illuminating the frowning rock behind and above him, and he sang out a little less confidently than usual.

'Wait a sec.,' he called, 'and I'll be down t' give you a hand.' Then he straightened. 'Crikey, Jim, we've been actin' like a couple o' nannies!'

Jim from the depths, looked up in silence.

'You're a bundle o' nerves,' Bill continued; 'and I know I've been kiddin' too hard. Git it straight, son. Forget the stupid noises for a week or two, an' we'll work a shift back to the seven hundred if I can manage it.'

Just then the murmur of the uneasy earth became perceptibly louder, but Bill was too earnest in his persuasive arguments to notice it. Jim was listening more to the creaking of the rocks than to him, though he gazed as if fascinated at his mate. Away in some corner out of sight a staccato noise that was more like straining timber than grating stone joined the weird medley of sound; but Bill continued.

'It's a bit uncanny sometimes, I know,' he said. 'P'rhaps I been noticin' it more lately, with you all of a dither. A man wants a mate down these damn' holes that he can talk to, an' forget what lousy places they are. It's no use makin' 'em more unpleasant than they've got to be.'

But Jim was not listening to his words at all now. The grunting of the mile-wide masses of stone was ringing in his ears like the sobbing breath of a giant struggling in bonds. A few tiny flakes dropped off behind Bill, and fell noiselessly into the rubble. Over his head a gigantic sharp-fanged lip of stone drooped slowly (like the lower jaw of a titanic, hungry beast) away from the main body. Jim's body seemed to slip away from him, and leave him standing, watching, without it. The tenseness was gone. He was not even afraid.

'If you'll call it quits – 'entreated Bill.

Then a scattered rain of small boulders was spewed from the crevice above his head. One of them caught him between the shoulders, and with surprising, elastic leaps and somersaults he came bouncing down the rill, with a little torrent of rubble in his wake. His lamp was out, but Jim's showed him, inert, at the bottom.

A few tons of rock peeled away, up above, with a rending noise, and settled with a sigh on the rubble. An ocean of dirt submerged the lower part of Bill, and pebbles pelting about his head brought him to consciousness. His face wore just that puzzled, uncomprehending expression Jim had often imagined upon it.

'Jim!' he called. 'For God's sake –'

But it was not that cry that affected Jim. A new river of dirt had started, near the top of the rill somewhere. The voice of the earth was angry, farther back, with the quaking upheaval that was upsetting it. The whispers had changed to a harsh challenge, and Jim snarled in reply, suddenly determined to beat the ground, to trick it of its prey. He leapt for his mate, and together they struggled against the mounting rubble.

It was only the loose stuff – the first light layer of the dirt that would soon be packed hard beneath hundreds of tons of rock – that held Bill. He came out of it like a cork out of a bottle, and together they ran. Careless of fingers and faces in the fearful darkness, stumbling and scrambling forward with desperate energy, they made the level. And as they sped along it they heard the voice of the earth behind them change to a roar as the avalanche engulfed the big stope.

At the plat, under electric lights and in the comforting company of solicitous inquirers, the unruffled Bill tenderly examined bruises on his legs, and explained their narrow escape with a wealth of vivid detail. He made a hero out of Jim, though that worthy sprawled beside him, colourless and limp, and fit for nothing as yet.

And Jim, shivering and dumb with shock, longing for the surface and the sunlight, felt a glow of appreciation of his mate. A great chap – tough, straight and decent. As good a cobber as a man could wish for – a man upon whom one could rely. Such mates were scarce enough to be valuable. It would be a long while before he would find another. But seek another he would have to, for Bill would never, in any circumstances, understand how he felt about talking ground.

His only satisfaction was that now, at any rate, he would be able to get away from it, to walk off the lease for good, and still be able to enjoy a friendly drink and a yarn with Bill when they ran across each other on paydays.

Peter Cowan

NIGHT

HE got on the end of the line and it shuffled forward. As they
came to the stack of trays he took one and started it sliding
along the rail. He looked at the first racks of food and saw
nothing that he liked. He stared out over the seated men and
the few girls moving among them, making alien splashes of
colour. The automatic phonograph was playing from one corner.
It's like that, he thought, it's like walking about where there is
no hope. It's like a lost lament. He lifted a plate with a roll and
butter and put it on the tray. It's like we shuffle along here, a step
at a time – I don't know where we're going any more. God, he
thought, I'm bored. The phonograph stopped and there was
the wall of voices.

The line moved so that he was a couple of paces from the
man in front. There were others behind him now. He moved
forward. He reached for a fruit salad and put it on the tray. He
saw the blue jumper and short white skirt of the girl behind
the counter. It registered that she was rather well built. She
moved so that her face was towards him, it was young, with
something that he felt in a way challenging in her expression.
Looking at her he thought suddenly, she is alive. She turned
towards the shelves behind her and he saw her faintly golden arms.
He thought she is quite nice. He looked again out over the tables
and the movement and the noise, the coming and going in the
path to the door between the tables. Then looking back at the
counter he saw the girl again. She reached towards something
on the shelves. Her bare arm was outstretched. He noticed
suddenly two dark marks on the back of her upper arm. He
thought, she got that from a man's fingers.

He moved slowly along, looking at the girl. The blue jumper
showed her full, young breasts. The white skirt was tight across

her hips that were immature. Her eyes were dark, her brows darker than her hair. Perhaps it is darker at the roots, he thought. Her features were clear cut. Her mouth was outlined rather smaller than its own shape.

He thought later she will be dancing. He pushed the tray along, and when he came to the end he paid, and going through the seated men got a table near the rail. He put his things down on it, and from where he sat he could see the girl behind the counter. The moving stream of drab garbed men obscured the colour of her, the blue and white and the freshness of her among the staled faces. But when there was a gap he looked at her, seeing her active movements that had something almost of the foreignness of eagerness in them, her step, the twist of her body, the movement of her hands. And when she turned he saw the marks on her arm. He thought yes, and it stirred in him so that he felt the deadness lift.

When he had finished, and he ate slowly, he saw there was still time before the dancing began. He got up and went to the rest room. The men stretched in attitudes on the lounges and chairs. He got the corner of a lounge and sat back. Outside someone was playing the piano. The sound was dragged heavily from it as a background to the noise of the singing of those around it. Yet it obstructed and mocked the voices. He heard without listening. The simple rhythms pulsed and beat, and he felt tired and let the tiredness come slowly over him like a welcome. Against the background of the voices and sound he went slowly to a vagueness and unawareness that was not sleep. When the sound stopped he came back as though waking, and he heard the band begin to play. He sat for a time trying to subdue the sense of unfulfilled sleep, and then he got up slowly and went out. Among the moving couples he could not distinguish her. He could not have picked her out from among those that lined the edge of the floor, packed in on each other. Then he saw her suddenly, coming past him. He looked after her. She did not dance particularly well, but she was light and active.

When the music stopped he saw she stood with two other girls by the railing that ran along one side of the floor, and he hesitated until the band had started and someone else had got her to dance. He looked at the moving dancers and he felt the deadness coming over him again. We are all dead, he thought. Who knows if we'll ever live again. I've heard combat men suddenly start to live as they got near their home towns on a leave train. They quite suddenly and a bit childishly came alive. But the rest of the time only the very young and the very stupid are not dead. There are enough of the very stupid. Yes. The girl came past and he looked at her active eager movements, her free stride, her young bare arms. He watched her. The next dance he went up to her. He looked quickly at her two companions. The three of them were half looking at him. He took her and they began to dance. He felt it would be hard to talk. He said:

'D'you come here often?'

She shook her head, looking up. 'No, not very often.'

After a time she said, 'Do you?'

'Now and again I do. When I get leave.'

'It's very crowded.'

'Yes.'

They moved among the moving couples. Her light coloured hair was close to his face, and if he leaned his head a little towards her its pleasant scent came to him. He leaned a little towards her and she looked up at him suddenly. She smiled. Something of the impersonality of her expression was gone. His leg against her thigh was intimate. When the music stopped he left his hand on her waist as they turned towards the band. As they began to dance again he said:

'D'you like dancing?'

She nodded. 'Yes.'

'You live here?'

'Yes.'

The suburb she named he did not know. He said: 'Can't say I know where that is.'

'It's a fair way out. Not very far though,' she added.

When the dance ended he walked back to her place with her. The other two girls had not danced. Men stood pressed in around the rail, watching. The two girls, one of them chewing gum quickly, watched him and the girl come across the floor. He put his hand on her arm as they went through the crowd, the flesh was soft under his fingers. He stood by her, talking, the other two girls joining in, and he danced with her again the next dance. The number on the floor had increased. The dancers wove their distorted pattern and the music beat at them, deadening them to subtleties. He did not try to think. He felt the physical sympathy from their closeness, and he closed his mind and let it all go on to what he did not think about. He bought supper. Talking, she told him where she worked, at one of the big city retailers, and something of what her day was. He listened, but she existed now for him without background, in a kind of suspension of time that yet was itself temporally limited. They danced again, and a little after ten he said:

'The place closes at half past, doesn't it?'

'Yes. I ought to get my things or I'll get caught in the rush.'

He said: 'D'you think – could I take you home?'

She smiled. 'Well – it might be too far – you've got to get back –'

'I can fix that.'

'I don't want you to be late.'

'It's all right tonight. I don't have to be back any particular time tonight.'

She said: 'If we're going I'd better get my things after this dance.'

He waited while she collected her coat and bag, and he helped her on with her coat. She shook her light coloured hair as she pulled the coat about her.

'It'll be pretty cold outside,' he said.

She laughed. 'You get used to it. Don't you grumble about our weather.'

They went out on to the street and walked along with the herded people. As they came near a crossing she began to hurry.

'There's a tram there,' she said.

They got across with the lights and on to the tram. They got a seat, and he asked her where they got out, to pay the fare. While they waited, before the tram started, they were silent. The tram filled up. It started and she began to talk, about something that had happened during the day. He could not hear all she said, but he nodded, and when she made the point laughed, though he did not understand. She talked without the eagerness he had noticed in her physical movements. She told him when they reached the stop and they got out. They went across the road where the shops closed in on each side, and along one of the side streets that gave on to the main road. He noticed that the clouds that had been evident early in the evening had gone and the sky was clear. It was cold. She brushed against him and he took her arm.

'I had a letter from my boy friend yesterday,' she said.

'Oh yes.'

'Yes. He's in the islands.'

'Is he?'

'He never says much in his letters.'

He did not say anything. He thought I do not know what that means. They walked along the empty footpath. She drew her arm close in to her side and his hand on her arm felt the movement of her body and then the looseness of her breast. She looked up suddenly at him and smiled.

He said: 'You look very nice, like that.'

'Thank you.'

He was not sure whether she was laughing at him. He thought I don't know. Once I could do this. Now I don't know. They turned down a short street and then along to the right so that they were going the direction they had been before.

He said: 'Funny if I get lost.'

'You won't do that.'

'I don't know.'

'With me?'

'That's possible.'

She laughed. 'You're funny.'

'What do you mean by that?'

'Oh – nothing. No, I don't mean you're funny. Just –'

'Too long in the service,' he said. 'Get's you that way. Doped. And I find you a bit – well, funny.'

'That makes us even.'

'Yes.'

'Down here,' she said. They went down a narrower street. 'That's the place just past the light.'

They came to the gate. The house was close to the pavement. There was little space on either side of the neighbouring houses. At the gate they stopped. He stood close to her. She was looking

down at the bag in her hands. He looked past her down the
narrow street. The houses made a black line against the sky. He
thought suddenly there's nothing there. It's no good. She said
unexpectedly:

'What are you thinking about?'

He said 'You.' He took her arms so that she faced him. She
raised her head. He bent towards her. Her lips were curiously
impersonal. She said:

'Goodnight.'

He said: 'Perhaps I'll see you again.'

'You might.'

'Well, will I?' This is useless, he thought.

'That depends.'

'On what?'

'Well, on you, I suppose.'

'Well, if we could arrange something –'

'Look,' she said. 'I'll be down there the same next week.'

He nodded. Then abruptly he pulled her towards him. His
hand closed on the softness of her covered breast and he felt
her body strain suddenly against him. She said:

'I'll have to go.'

'I don't want to go,' he said.

She stood for a moment and then she said: 'We can sit on
the verandah. Don't make too much noise though.'

They went across the short path. The end of the verandah was
partitioned off. There was a bed with a small stool beside it.
For a moment she stood just on the verandah, then she stepped
quietly towards the partitioned portion and put her bag down on
the bed. She sat down and he followed her, sitting on the end. He
looked at her pale coloured hair and he put one hand over hers,
resting on her knee. There was that in her expression he could
not relate to her. He thought of her as he had seen her standing
behind the counter, the pale hair and the blue jumper and white
skirt, the smooth arms and the bruise on her rich young flesh.
Then the memory was fused into the actuality of her and his hand
moved over her thigh and she leaned against him, the eagerness
deeper and more urgent, older in its demand, and in the time that
held the smoothness and softness of her and the pattern of the
blood and the harmony brief in discord he thought away from

himself who am I to destroy his memories and what perhaps keeps him for life in the unbelievable and the insanity, and he said I cannot destroy them for there is nothing now, and I destroy my own. And in the destruction there is living, and the denial of the slow death.

He pushed the gate open and walked along the narrow street. There was no traffic and the streets were silent. He looked up at the clear sky. His footsteps were loud. He walked quickly.

Alan Marshall

TELL US ABOUT THE TURKEY, JO

HE came walking though the rusty grasses and sea-weedish plants that fringe Lake Corangamite. Behind him strode his brother.

He was very fair. His hair was a pale gold and when he scratched his head the parted hairs revealed the pink skin of his scalp. His eyes were very blue. He was freckled. His nose was tipped upward. I liked him tremendously. I judged him to be about four and a half years old and his brother twice that age.

They wore blue overalls and carried them jauntily. The clean wind came across the water and fluttered the material against their legs. Their air was one of independence and release from authority.

They scared the two plovers I had been watching. The birds lifted with startled cries and banked against the wind. They cut across large clouds patched with blue and sped away, flapping low over the water.

The two boys and I exchanged greetings while we looked each other over. I think they liked me. The little one asked me several personal questions. He wanted to know what I was doing there, why I was wearing a green shirt, where was my mother? I gave him the information with the respect due to another seeker of knowledge. I then asked him a question and thus learned of the dangers and disasters that had beset his path.

'How did you get that cut on your head?' I asked. In the centre of his forehead a pink scar divided his freckles.

The little boy looked quickly at his brother. The brother answered for him. The little boy expected and conceded this. He looked at the brother expectantly and, as the brother spoke, the little boy's eyes shone, his lips parted, as one who listens to a thrilling story.

'He fell off a baby's chair when he was little,' said the brother.

143

'He hit his head on a shovel and bled over it.'

'Ye-e-s,' faltered the little boy, awed by the picture, and in his eyes was the excitement and the thrill of danger passed. He looked across the flat water, rapt in the thought of the chair and the shovel and the blood.

'A cow kicked him once,' said the brother.

'A cow!' I exclaimed.

'Yes,' he said.

'Go on, Jo,' said the little boy eagerly, standing before him and looking up into his face.

'He tried to leg-rope it,' Jo explained, 'and the cow let out and got him in the stomach.'

'In the stomach,' emphasized the little boy turning quickly to me and nodding his head.

'Gee!' I exclaimed.

'Gee!' echoed the little boy.

'It winded him,' said Jo.

'I was winded,' said the little boy slowly as if in doubt. 'What's winded, Jo?'

'He couldn't breathe properly,' Jo addressed me.

'I couldn't breathe a bit,' said the little boy.

'That was bad,' I said.

'Yes, it was bad, wasn't it, Jo?' said the little boy.

'Yes,' said Jo.

Jo looked intently at the little boy as if searching for scars of other conflicts.

'A ladder fell on him once,' he said.

The little boy looked quickly at my face to see if I was impressed. The statement had impressed him very much.

'No,' said I unbelievingly.

'Will I show him, Jo?' asked the little boy eagerly.

'Yes,' said Jo.

The little boy, after giving me a quick glance of satisfaction, bent and placed his hands on his knees. Jo lifted the back of his brother's shirt collar and peered into the warm shadow between his back and the cotton material.

'You can see it,' he said uncertainly, searching the white skin for its whereabouts.

The little boy twisted his arm behind his back and strove to touch a spot on one of his shoulders.

'It's there, Jo. Can you see it, Jo?'

'Yes. That's it,' said Jo. 'You come here and see.' He looked at me. 'Don't move, Jimmy.'

'Jo's found it,' announced Jimmy, his head twisted to face me.

I rose from my seat on a pitted rock nestling in grass and stepped over to them. I bent and looked beneath the lifted collar. On the white skin of his shoulder was the smooth ridge of a small scar.

'Yes, It's there all right,' I said. 'I'll bet you cried when you got that.'

The little boy turned to Jo. 'Did I cry, Jo?'

'A bit,' said Jo.

'I never do cry much, do I, Jo?'

"No,' said Jo.

'How did it happen?' I asked.

'The ladder had hooks in it . . .' commenced Jo.

'Had hooks in it,' emphasized the little boy nodding at me.

'And he pulled it down on top of him,' continued Jo.

'Oo!' said the little boy excitedly, clasping his hands and holding them between his knees while he stamped his feet. 'Oo-o-o.'

'It knocked him rotten,' said Jo.

'I was knocked rotten,' declared the little boy slowly as if revealing the fact to himself for the first time.

There was a pause while the little boy enjoyed his thoughts.

'It's a nice day, isn't it?' Jo sought new contacts with me.

'Yes,' said I.

The little boy stood in front of his brother, entreating him with his eyes.

'What else was I in, Jo?' he pleaded.

Jo pondered, looking at the ground and nibbling his thumb.

'You was in nothin' else,' he said, finally.

'Aw, Jo!' The little boy was distressed at the finality of the statement. He bent suddenly and pulled up the leg of his overalls. He searched his bare leg for marks of violence.

'What's that, Jo?' He pointed to a faint mark on his knee.

'That's nothin',' said Jo. Jo wanted to talk about ferrets. 'You know, ferrets . . .' he began.

145

'It looks like something,' I said, looking closely at the mark.
Jo leant forward and examined it. The little boy, clutching the crumpled leg of his trousers, looked from my face to his brother's and back again, anxiously waiting a decision.

Jo made a closer examination, rubbing the mark with his finger. The little boy followed Jo's investigation with an expectant attention.

'You mighta had a burn once. I don't know.'

'I wish I did have a burn, Jo,' said the little boy. It was a plea for a commitment from Jo, but Jo was a stickler for truth.

'I can't remember you being burnt,' he said. 'Mum'd know.'

'Perhaps you can think of another exciting thing,' I suggested.

'Yes,' said the little boy eagerly. He came over and took my hand so that we might await together the result of Jo's cogitation. He looked up at me and said, 'Isn't Jo good?'

'Very good,' I said.

'He knows about me and everything.'

'Yes,' I said.

There was a faint 'Hulloo' from behind us. We all turned. A little girl came running through the rocks in the barrier that guards the lake from the cultivated lands. She had thin legs and wore long, black stockings. One had come loose from its garter and, as she ran, she bent and pulled and strove to push its top beneath the elastic band. Her gait was thus a series of hops and unequal strides.

She called her brothers' names as she ran and in her voice was the note of the bearer-of-news.

'Dad must be home,' said Jo.

But the little boy was resentful of this intrusion. 'What does she want?' he said sourly.

The little girl had reached a flat stretch of grass and her speed had increased. Her short hair fluttered in the wind of her running.

She waved a hand. 'We have a new baby sister,' she yelled.

'Aw, pooh!' exclaimed the little boy.

He turned and tugged at Jo's arm. 'Have you thought of anything exciting yet, Jo?' His face lit to a sudden recollection. 'Tell him how I got chased by the turkey,' he cried.

146

'Brian James'

SHOTS IN THE ORCHARD

TEMPLETON was singularly free of crime – major crime, that is. Someone tried once to explain that it was the air, and the scenery, and the busy industry of the small farms that made it so. You just can't, he said, imagine anything happening in a place like Templeton – its neat rows of oranges and lemons and passion-fruit are a picture of a properly ordered life. Templeton was certainly beautiful in its orchards, miles of them breaking at irregular intervals into the drab bush of stringybarks and blood-woods and all the hard, tenacious growth of the sandstone country. It was on a plateau, too, where one looked over the edge of the world on to a blue mistiness, empty and endless, till the mountains rose against the western sky – and the world com-menced again. Not a place for crime – big crime. Even the very scent of citrus bloom, most of the year, did not fit it with the larger misdoings of man.

There were the smaller sins, of course. Full of interest they were too. But they happen anywhere; bound to happen any-where. That's only natural. Terry Heydon might get into trouble with the taxation people about his faked returns – well, you could hardly blame Terry, the way things were; but he was a damned fool not to have got 'an expert to help with the faking'. Old Prosser might be having trouble with that second girl of his – but he should have known better after what happened to the oldest girl. The insurance company might try to catch Peter Armstrong over his highly successful and profitable fire; but Peter *could* account for the kerosene on the chaff-bag – not that everyone else couldn't account for it, too, though their interpretation was different from the one Peter gave at the inquiry. There might be Elsie Youngtree with her illegitimate twins – *that* was a sensation. 'Put Templeton on the map,' said

Rolly Grey, the agent for the big fertilizer company. Rolly was fond of apt quotations. Twins! No one had ever heard of anything so ambitious as twins. There might be old Muir and his dispute with the Egg Board; the Board won handsomely because, as everyone said, old Muir was too truthful and honest. But Muir was like that; a bit simple really. There might be the hiding Jack Morgan gave Wally Prosser; good to hear of, that was – though it never got to court. There might be – well, dozens of things that just happen in a normal sort of way, as it were.

But the shooting over at Rath's place was different. That was a big event, something to last Templeton for all the years to be.

Enoch Rath lived on the ridge that led to Halfway. Quiet little man with eyes of no particular colour, and with a hopeless sort of mildness in them. He was so neutral in feature that he was really noticeable on that account. Gentle and religious, too, the very model of Mr Samuel Henderson's small flock. Samuel himself was a mild-seeming man, but when he preached he was inspired with such a divine anger that he almost seemed fierce. But Enoch was one of the Lord's lambs.

Enoch had married, years before, a woman who most decidedly wasn't one of the Lord's lambs. She was supposed to have come from 'down the coast somewhere', but, incredible as it may seem, no one ever found out a single item of her antecedents. She was a full, big woman, if you understand, with very red, thick lips; but not at all unpleasant to look on. She had bits of coral or something dangling from her ears, and a very rich growth of glossy black hair. Possessive looking, and not the sort of wife for Enoch – that is if anyone could imagine the right sort of wife for Enoch. He looked a shrimp beside her; or like a male spider perhaps. How he came to marry her no one ever heard, but the general view was that she had married him – why, the Lord only knew. Perhaps it was Enoch's property; he had a tidy bit of a place, well kept too, and as profitable as anyone's. People conceded that Enoch knew how to work an orchard, though they reckoned he wasn't much good for anything else. And those who didn't belong to Mr Henderson's flock were sure that the very name 'Enoch' had a lot to do with it. 'Them old Bible names don't sorter fit now,' was how 'Major' Brown summed it up. 'There's such – of a sort-er-ver-kind-er-ver twist about them that they never gets properly over it. Sort-uv insult to the rest-er-vus, they are, too.' The Major's first name was Kandahar; which in its way told quite a deal about *his* parents. And 'Major' was a purely honorary affair bestowed on account of the Kandahar, and the circumstances of a grandfather having been in the Indian Mutiny – or, at least, the Major believed that he had been in the Mutiny.

There was a contract carrier at the other end of Templeton called Tommy Ramsbottom, a husky big brute, full of life and strong language. But he was an efficient carrier, though it was always a sore point that Tommy made so much out of the carrying business – ninepence a bushel he charged, whatever fruit prices were: 'Makes more out of the damned fruit than we do what grows it,' Wiseman often said. And then Wiseman would hint darkly that he was thinking of getting a truck himself; and then you'd see. As a matter of fact, he did get a truck later – and charged a bob a bushel, and went into a maze of figures about running costs, as well as into a fine historical review of McCallum, the storekeeper, who wouldn't give him the job of 'back-loading'. However . . .

Tommy treated Enoch in a scandalous fashion. It really wasn't a fair thing at all. He would yell at Enoch whenever he saw him ' 'Ullo, old cock! 'Ow are you and Gawd getting on now?' Enoch 'tried to keep out of his way. Nor was that all. Tommy spent a lot more time at Enoch's than the carrying business seemed to warrant. Everyone knew that and 'all about it' – that is, everyone but Enoch. Not that it would make much difference, they said, if the poor sook did know. Then they agreed that Mrs Rath was a bitch, and that *they* knew what *they'd* do to Tommy Ramsbottom. Such matters weren't discussed or hinted at when Tommy was about, however. 'Like-ter-see *my* wife carrying on like that!' said Major. 'Just-like-ter!' Of course, Major didn't quite mean it that way – he merely wanted to show how distressing situations of the kind might be handled. In any case, Major's wife was a long, thin, very flat woman with a slight beard and a holy terror of a tongue. That she might ever, in her long life, have been detected in the process of 'carrying on like that' went far beyond the flights of the higher imagination. So Major could only use her as an abstract illustration – very abstract.

When Enoch went to McCallum's store he was generally in for a bad time, especially if the gangling youths of the district were there in force. They always did seem to be there. Enoch was a diversion to them. They addressed him as 'Mr Rath' with a mocking emphasis on the 'Mr', or as 'Nocky, old boy, how *are* you?' They made very earnest and serious inquiries about his oranges and then the 'hard case' would ask, 'How's the passions down your way, *Mr* Rath?' That was insuppressible humour, and one or two others always fell off packing-cases in their mirth. Or they tried out limericks, which were no better than that simple poetic form is often prone to be. They winked and nodded and nudged when the hard case inquired if Enoch had seen Tommy Ramsbottom of late, and someone was sure to fall off a packing-case at that. It was great sport, for Enoch didn't seem 'to know', and anyway he was so defenceless.

Perhaps Enoch knew a lot more than they thought. It may have been his chicken heart, or it may have been his religious creed, or both of these together, that made him take it all. But certainly something was going on in his mind all the time, and one day – a Thursday, when Tommy would be doing the return with empties along the ridge to Halfway – Enoch came to the store and 'acted peculiar'. Not easy to say just how, but even the hard case remembered it later. Looked straight at everyone for the first time in his life, queer sort of look too, and when he got into his cart he belted his horse over the rump till it galloped rickety-rockety down the road. After that no one knew exactly what happened, though everyone heard the two shots, and everyone knew when they heard them that something was wrong. 'Just sitting in the shade of an orange-tree,' it went, 'and those two shots went "bang!" and after a long time "bang!" again. I said to the wife, "Nellie, those shots are over at Rath's place. I don't like them." Just like that I said it. And the wife said, "Jim, you'd better not go over." Very careful the wife is. And I didn't go, but I couldn't get those shots out of my head at all.'

But the big news soon got round – Enoch had shot his wife and Tommy Ramsbottom: 'Got 'em both as neat as yer like.' So everyone went over – a lot of the women did, too, to see if they could help. The police were there already, and acting very importantly and officiously, nor would they tell anything. But those that got there first said that Enoch was sitting on the edge of the veranda holding the Winchester .32, and staring strange-like into nowhere. And he just said: 'I done it.' Nothing more, and went on staring again.

Tommy Ramsbottom's big red truck was still standing near the packing shed, loaded high with a square mountain of empties. They found Mrs. Rath near the grader, and Ramsbottom right at the end of the lemon-bed where the thick scrub begins – right at the end of the row, and one hundred and fifty yards away – all that, if it was an inch. Both dead – and he got Tommy at one hundred and fifty yards, and Tommy running hard and dodging! The tracks showed that. It was a wonderful shot. And that sook of an Enoch would tell nothing more than 'I done it!'

They took all three to town, of course, and then everyone went to look at Enoch's place – just casually – and tried to reconstruct everything, and measured the distance from where they reckoned Enoch fired to where Tommy was found. Some of them stepped it out as one hundred and sixty yards. There was a reluctant sort of admiration for Enoch when they said, 'A wonderful shot, that!' though some reckoned it must have been a fluke. Strangely enough – or perhaps it wasn't so strange – there was a lot of sympathy for Tommy Ramsbottom, even more than there was for his wife. He had a wife – a poor colourless little woman who was always complaining in sing-song tones which no one ever took any notice of. There were four young children, too. In all it was a ghastly business. Some of the women went along, and did what they could to help. It was really difficult to do much. Mr Samuel Henderson drove over too. Deep down in old Samuel – much deeper down, though he'd never recognize it, than all his lay-preaching – was a rich vein of gold. And when he found that Mrs Ramsbottom didn't think, as far as she was able to think, that it was God's will at all, he didn't pester her on those lines any more.

But most of Templeton and Halfway went into solemn judge-ment. In a strictly fair manner they weighed the evidence and did what otherwise fair judges often neglect – they reviewed the principal actors in the tragedy over many years. And so the findings ran:

'In all fairness you can't altogether blame Tommy Ramsbottom . . .' 'She encouraged Tommy . . .' 'I will say this for Tommy, that he was a decent enough fellow, though I will maintain that ninepence a bushel *was* a bit hot for fruit . . .' 'Something of the sort was bound to happen sooner or later – but who'd have thought Enoch could shoot like that? . . .' 'Well I blame Enoch for the whole thing – wouldn't have happened if he'd been half a man . . .' Then Wiseman went into gloomy prophecy (it was hard to say whether he enjoyed more the gloom or the prophecy). 'As I was saying to the wife, "They must find him guilty; and then the judge will have to sentence him to hanging. But with this crowd in power they'll remute to life, or something like that." ' Wiseman seemed to think it a pity, but you could only expect the worst from 'that crowd'. Also, Wiseman had a special insight into the workings of the criminal law by virtue of his cousin who had sat on the jury in many of the biggest (and worst) cases in the city. From him Wiseman had gleaned many features and highlights of crime that 'don't even get into the papers.'

In the meantime Templeton was duly put on the map. City papers featured Templeton for many days, and had long accounts of the district, and many photos of Enoch's house and orchard, and crosses to mark the spots, and even a photo of Wiseman, in his lemon-bed, in an attitude of strained listening ('Mr Wiseman Hears the Fatal Shots').

The inquest was held in due course, and was a most exasperating affair: Enoch had nothing to say, or would say nothing. Nothing at all beyond 'I done it!' No questions would shift him from that, or make him say more. He was committed for trial. Everyone said, 'He'll talk when it comes to the trial.' But he didn't. It was hard to get him to plead at all, but at length he became voluble to the extent of, 'Oh yes, I'm guilty, I suppose. I done it!' After that he relapsed into 'I done it!' Enoch was a shocking disappointment to those who thirsted for the details. Many of those who had admired his wonderful shooting were now inclined to concede that it must have been a fluke after all. In fact, Enoch fell even lower than ever in popular estimation, if that were at all possible.

They didn't hang poor Enoch: after much medical and psychological examination (in which the local hard case and his boon companions did *not* tender any evidence) it was decided that Enoch was insane, and he was sent to an institution. Mrs Ramsbottom, who in the generally held opinion was 'much to blame', left the district. Mr Samuel Henderson saw to it that she got a fair deal with her place, even if she didn't belong to his flock.

Wiseman remained dissatisfied. 'He knew . . . and – he always had said . . . and as I said to the wife only yesterday – but I will say this much . . .'

In his final findings, influenced not a little, no doubt, by his cousin the eminent juryman, he concluded that Enoch was mad all along, but that Enoch knew well enough what he was doing. His 'I done it!' was a piece of low cunning (the cousin had met cases like that before). And Enoch did the right thing, anyway, in shooting the 'pair of them', but the law should have had its course, and they should have hanged him. Wiseman was a great believer in hanging; he reckoned it was a complete cure – and a great example. 'But what can you expect from this crowd?'

Quiet, rural Templeton looked as beautiful as ever, and the citrus bloom smelt as sweet, but for all that Templeton had made history and had been placed on the map.

E. O. Schlunke

THE COWBOY FROM TOWN

ALL too frequently one reads in the newspapers of farm or station hands shooting their employers. On the other hand, one rarely sees a report about graziers shooting their employees. This, to one familiar with the position, indicates an admirable quality of forbearance on the part of the landowners, who are often sorely tried by their so-called workers. This state of affairs has come about quite simply. So many of the good old farm and station hands have gone to the city that a vacuum has been created in the country; and into this vacuum have been sucked some extraordinary creatures.

'I beg you, your Honour, not to send that boy to jail,' implored the zealous-looking young man, with something restrained about his clothes and uncontrolled about his emotions that branded him as an ardent social-worker. 'Let me take care of him.'

The judge looked doubtfully at Mr Birdey, whose type he was beginning to know very well. 'But this is a serious case.'

'All the more reason why we should want to save him, your Honour.'

The flashing blue eyes of Mr Birdey, his crown of shining gold hair, as well as his other-worldly tone and manner, made everyone in the court look on him with interest and, generally, with sympathy. He rushed on before the judge could adjust himself to this peculiar line of reasoning. 'I will have him sent to kind friends in the country. Away from the crime-breeding squalor and vice of the slums, to pure air and pure people.'

'A youth,' said the judge, in an earthy, factual manner, 'whom I allowed to be sent to the country, despite my better judgement, caused some very serious trouble.'

'Ah, but not one of *my* youths, sir,' Mr Birdey announced, as

154

if he had scored a notable point against someone. 'That would have been the responsibility of another organization, which shall be charitably nameless. They, I regret to relate, make mistakes; they don't exercise the discrimination I do. I realize that I have a responsibility to my friends on farms and stations, as well as to my boys. Moreover, I have university degrees in psychology, sociology –'

The judge made a resigned gesture and tapped for silence. 'Very well, Mr Birdey, if you are prepared to take the usual responsibilities, you may have him; and I hope that *he* won't be *your* mistake.' Then, turning to the overgrown, loutish youth in the dock he said in a very different tone of voice, 'Remember this! You thoroughly deserve to go to jail for two years. And if you misbehave in any way in the place you're sent to, *you shall*. Quite frankly, I'm sorry for the man who's going to knock you into shape. I hope he's a big, strong man who always carries a stockwhip.'

Three hundred miles inland a letter arrived, courteously addressed to H. Kraftmann Esq., Donnerwetter Station, Nogoluk P.O. Neither the 'Esq.' nor the 'Station' had any effect on Harry Kraftmann, though his boundingly successful father had taken great pride in meriting both, and his whiskered old German peasant grandfather, who had acquired in Australia the first little block of land the family had ever owned, would never have imagined either possible.

The contents of the letter made Kraftmann frown with a kind of resigned pessimism.

'. . . I am sending you Ronald Harby, a lad with great possibilities, who has not had the opportunities to fulfil himself in the city. He will respond well to kindness and understanding . . .'

Kraftmann skipped one and a half pages until he came to the date of arrival; then he called out to his wife, 'Another of Birdey's golden-hearted youths arriving tomorrow, Sophie. Don't leave anything valuable lying about.'

Mrs Kraftmann scarcely bothered to reply. Her husband's youths came and went as frequently as the novels from her circulating library, and made as little impression on her. She didn't even bother to learn the names of most of them, since they were almost certain to be sacked before she got them right. She was very unlike her husband, who, coming accidently across the names of past youths in his farm records, was apt to wince with pain or burn with indignation, no matter how many years ago the records referred to.

Kraftmann's trouble, so his friends told him, was that he couldn't take the bad with the good. But Kraftmann expressed his outlook thus:

'If it really was the "bad" with the "good", I could stand it; but what it really amounts to is the "worse" with the "terrible". Talk about the wool-growers' golden age,' he'd shout, 'have you ever thought about how much it would cost any of you to renew the fences and buildings on your properties? (and God knows there are plenty that need renewing). Have you? At the present cost of labour and materials? I have! I'll tell you! More than you could get if you sold your entire properties! So what do you really own, after working hard all your lives, and your fathers working twice as hard before you? Nothing! Nothing! Nothing!'

Most of his friends agreed that Kraftmann's outlook on life had been blighted by the worry of looking after his stud-sheep. Every year he had to give tremendous thought to the destinies of hundreds of highly expensive stud-rams. Those with good records had to be rewarded with seraglios of shapely young ewes of most select breeding. Those with poor progeny records were to be sold to people who wouldn't know any better; and those so bad that they'd spoil his reputation as a breeder must be desexed with what he called for brevity, his 'bloodless' – a form of retribution which seemed to give him a grim sort of pleasure. In fact, he was in the habit of carrying this instrument about with him and using it over-hastily on any ram that annoyed him by getting into the wrong paddock. There was even a legend, perpetuated by the oldest permanent employee, Old Tom, that he had once used it on an irreproachable and highly valuable ram which had had the misfortune, while he was examining it, merely to step accidentally on his sore toe. Other animals which had won his disapproval, chiefly dogs and cats, had had their futures blighted by this instrument, and countless times he had threatened to use it on his employees. It can thus be readily seen that running a stud does not have a refining effect on a man; but those who knew Kraftmann best forgave him most, because they knew how often and how sorely he was tried.

His nights were harried by doubts as to whether some idiot employee had really put top stud-ram BG-1041 into the Upper Kurrajong paddock (as he'd been told to three times and made to repeat back twice – as well as checked twice after he'd returned), or whether he mightn't have put the ram into the Middle Kurrajong, where he'd be having an incestuous orgy with his own offspring and, in one way and another, throwing the progress of the stud back ten or fifteen years.

A merino stud would not have been so bad, but Kraftmann had to have an English Longwool breed, every member of which regarded a fence as a challenge, and an arranged marriage as being as contemptibly humiliating and unacceptable as a wild career of paddock-to-paddock free love was grand and desirable.

Now, the old permanent hands like Old Tom, the only one left of a vanishing race, could be depended upon to notice, even in their time off, that TM-107 had got into the Ironbark paddock, and to do something to remedy matters. But the youths that were being sent to Kraftmann lately were quite capable, on seeing a ewe repelling the advances of her legitimate spouse and making advances to the lord of the next paddock through the fence, of pulling the wires apart so that all three could get together. Then they'd sit there watching the fun and games for a couple of hours, while Kraftmann was cursing them up hill and down dale for being so late.

And the kind of 'permanents' he'd been getting lately, men who had cottages provided for them and their families, as well as all sorts of perquisites like free meat and milk, were giving him nearly as much trouble as his youths. Often married to town or city girls, who had no intention of settling down in the country, they rarely stayed long enough to learn to be really useful.

'They only take it on,' he was in the habit of growling, 'because there's a house where they can get married and have their baby respectably. Then, as soon as they hear of something else, they're off.'

Apart from Old Tom, the only 'permanent' of any promise he now had was a man called Larkins, whose arrangement to be married had collapsed between accepting the job and moving in. For the time being he was being fed and housed at the homestead, an arrangement extremely unpopular with Kraftmann's wife, since it reduced the number of novels she could read. So Kraftmann had added to his burden an undertaking to find Larkins a suitable wife.

This, he realized, was no light undertaking, since none knew better than he how difficult it was to achieve a successful mating. Animals he'd paid shocking prices for, with a specific object in view, had either failed to produce any progeny at all, or sometimes progeny of an utterly unexpected type. And it was progeny he was concerned with now, too, because he had decided, after foolishly allowing all of Old Tom's big family to drift away to other occupations, that, if you wanted hands of any use at all, you'd have to raise them on the property.

The disadvantage, as compared with sheep, was that, if you made a mistake in the first year, you couldn't switch them round and try different combinations; another disadvantage was that sheep didn't introduce extraneous matters and want a hot-water system in the cottage that had been electrified for a previous couple, who hadn't stayed for more than six months after all.

However, he now had a pretty good candidate lined up. The daughter of a sharefarmer who had all the necessary physical qualities to compensate for Larkins's rather lean ranginess. He'd had her coming over to help his wife in the house several days a week, so that he could study her temperament and make sure of her outlook – that is, whether she liked country life; if she could be expected to settle down in a cottage; and whether she was likely to want to have children in reasonable numbers, and be capable of bringing them up sturdy and healthy.

He felt so pleased about this girl that he had actually sounded her out, cautiously, on her willingness to marry Larkins, and, though her reply was mostly giggles, the giggles had seemed to have an affirmative sound. Yet, a *marriage* was, relatively, so irrevocable, and as he so earnestly wanted to make sure (as the sheepmen put it) that they would 'nick', he was still hesitating.

In the kind of fine spring weather that a social worker couldn't help regarding as personal approval for the work he was doing,

a small English car drew up at Kraftmann's large and complicated set of sheep-yards. Social-worker Birdey got out, glowing
and beaming, to find out just what the pure air and pure people
were doing for the reclamation of Ronald Harby. The scene
looked charming and peaceful enough, to a man who knew as
little as Birdey about sheep studs. Dark-green cypress-pines shed
their dense shade over the yards where small mobs of sheep
drowsed with drooping heads. Here and there men and dogs
were attempting, without any jarring enthusiasm or hurry, to
move sheep from one pen to another, filling the warm air with
barkings and rustic sounds like 'Hoy!' 'Gettalong there!' and
'You bastards!' Only in the centre of the vortex of fences was
there any suggestion of intensity. Here, two men were holding
an enormous ram for Kraftmann to examine, while he was
studying its history in a large diary, meanwhile muttering to
himself, 'Even though I paid five hundred guineas for you, you
spunkless weed-chewer, nothing would give me greater pleasure
than to cut your blood-curdling throat.'

Then for the benefit of Larkins, for Old Tom had reached the
limit of his absorbing powers about fifteen years ago, he said in
a voice heavily loaded with exasperation, 'No matter what kind
of ewe I mate him with, all his bloody lambs have behinds like
castrated dogs.'

At that moment Birdey arrived, deliberately not hearing the
language nor the passion with which it was delivered, still
beaming, though he'd had a difficult passage through the maze
of yards. He greeted Kraftmann and his attendants as if he was
quite prepared to share his heavenly sunshine with them,
whatever their denomination.

'I'm spending my holidays on a tour of the farms and stations
where my boys are placed,' he told Kraftmann, 'to see them again.'

It took Kraftmann a few moments to get used to the idea of
anyone sacrificing so much, for anything so unworthy. 'You'll
be seeing a lot of the country too,' he said, as if he believed that
to be the true explanation. 'It's looking at its best now.'

'Oh, beautiful, beautiful,' Birdey went on, deciding he had
found the responsive chord in Kraftmann's heart, and deter-
mining to play on it to his best advantage. 'How wonderful it
must be to live always among such beauty and peace.'

Larkins and Old Tom looked as if they didn't know what in hell he was talking about, but Kraftmann, who hadn't quite forgotten all the poetry he'd learnt at his college, smiled at him sympathetically, because it was taking him so long to grow up. They might have found some mutually comprehensible topic sooner or later, if at that moment they hadn't all been compelled to turn about by a menacing thunder of approaching hooves.

A cowboy had arrived, straight from Texas, U.S.A. Black, velvety ten-gallon hat with silken tassels flying, a purely decorative waistcoat of plaited leather over a yellow shirt dotted with pink bathing-girls, something that looked like defensive half-trousers over the front of his pants, high-heeled knee-boots, and flashing spurs. Because there was an augmented audience, he jerked his sweating horse to a standstill in a few yards, just like the inhuman cowboys appear to do in the 'Western' movies. The ram-holders looked apprehensively at Kraftmann, expecting him to disgrace himself before Birdey, whom they took to be a parson; but before Kraftmann could say a word, Birdey was at it.

'Ronald Harby! *My* Ronald Harby! How wonderful! How magnificent! What a transformation!' Then he shouted, 'Ronald, Ronnie, come here; it's Mr Birdey come all the way from Sydney to see *you*!'

And while he waited for the youth to come, clambering stiff-legged over the fences, because of all his cowboy gear, he confided to Kraftmann in an excess of candour, 'To think that if I hadn't intervened, he would now be serving a sentence in jail.'

Kraftmann turned on Birdey, demanding sharply, 'Do you mean to tell me that?'

Birdey put on all his charm and plausibility to retrieve his error. 'Believe me, Mr Kraftmann, many fine lads get into trouble just because their natures need freedom and vigorous action, like riding horses. There's really nothing basically wrong with them–'

'I'm not worrying about him being a criminal,' Kraftmann interrupted him violently. 'They're all alike that come from *you*. But what gets my goat is the pity of it. If only you hadn't interfered *I* would have been spared having Ronald Harby, and *he* would have been getting what he needs so terribly.'

But Birdey, with radiant eyes on the dazzling cowboy, gave

a loud chuckle, because he'd been warned about the leg-pulling he was likely to get in the country. He vaulted several fences to greet Harby.

'Ronnie, my boy,' he said, seizing his hand in both of his, 'how marvellous you look.' And he swept the gaudy outfit up and down with the kind of admiration Harby had been yearning for ever since he'd bought it, but which he'd never yet received. Then suddenly Birdey stepped back in startled amazement. 'But surely you don't need to go that far, Ronald. Perhaps it's not real, is it?'

Harby flicked a small-bore revolver out of his holster and put an imaginary shot through a sheep to show his speed on the draw. 'Too right it's real; and too right I need it. The boss here threatens to shoot me on the average twice a week, and I've gotter have some way of defending myself, haven't I?'

'Oh, but Ronnie,' Birdey said, trying to get the right psychological angle on him, 'Mr Kraftmann is a kind man, he just has his little jokes.'

'Joke!' Harby sneered with his wide, ugly mouth. 'If you'd seen all the dogs he's shot, you wouldn't think it was a joke. Just let them disobey him once, and it's up with a rifle and, no matter how far away, he gets them through the head first shot.'

'Yes, well,' Birdey fumbled, thinking in city terms of dogs as beloved companions, cherished even unto decrepit old age, and not as Kraftmann saw them, working animals he'd bred with care, which either did their job well or had to be put our of the way for being intolerable, ungrateful nuisances, 'but still, there's a big difference between shooting a dog and shooting a man.'

'He shot a horse one day,' Harby assured him, with a big out-thrust of his lower lip to show that nothing was going to deprive him of the right to carry firearms, 'just because it fell with him. And he shot a neighbour's bull that cost three hundred and fifty pounds, only because it was breaking one of his fences.'

A lot more like this, delivered vehemently to overcome Birdey's repetitions of the judge's warning, and the reminders of the obligations, moral and financial, *he* had undertaken on *his* behalf. Not that Birdey was really worried, because what could happen out here under the warm September sun, where the pines were slowly exhaling the deep breaths they had taken overnight? It was really amusing, this dressing-up and leg-pulling, and quite wonderful for the boy from the slums, Birdey was thinking. Harby went on about the vast armoury of guns, rifles, and pistols Kraftmann owned, and his habit of always having some kind of firearm within reach. And about all the talk between Kraftmann and his men; how often they'd said, 'A man ought to be shot for that,' and really meant it; and how twice, in cold blood, they'd discussed the advisability of shooting *him* and throwing his body down one of the old mines. 'Nobody would ever miss a bastard like him,' they'd said.

'So I just had to get this.' Harby flourished the pistol, which had such a small hole in the pointing end that Birdey decided it was really little more than a toy. 'My life's going to depend on it. He always says "This is it!" before he shoots. That'll give me a chance to get in one shot first, and if I miss him, I'll be a goner, because *he never misses.*'

'If you don't want him to be shot, take him away with you,' Kraftmann said to Birdey, looking him so straight in the eye and speaking in so manifestly sincere a voice that Birdey was certain he'd somehow gained access to some of the textbooks used in training social-workers, and was making corrupt use of them.

The only thing Birdey could do was to laugh heartily and say, 'Ronald's a fine boy, and I think you know it as well as I do. But I ought to warn you that he's taking some of your talk about shooting him rather seriously.'

At which the ram-holders laughed with such apparent brutality that Birdey left, with reproachfully brief farewells. But after he'd failed to open two gates and climbed laboriously over three fences, an explanation struck him that was as dazzling and beautiful as the sunshine. Harby had become such a thorough countryman that he could beat them all at leg-pulling. He turned to wave an exultant arm, and was wafted over the remaining fences quite effortlessly by the uplift of his heart.

'Do you know what they do in the Orkney Islands?' Mrs Kraftmann asked her husband one night, looking up from her Linklater novel, which, after having the covers nearly worn off and many of the spiciest pages lifted in the city, was now circulating to the country subscribers. 'The young men creep into their girl-friends' bedrooms at night, and don't marry them until they're sure they're going to have a baby! Isn't it awful?'

Kraftmann thought it over slowly, with the deepest professional interest. 'Well, I don't know about it being awful,' he said. 'There's quite a lot to be said for it, really. If you wanted to make sure of having a family, that would be the best way to go about it.'

He resumed his study of the *Studmaster's Monthly*, to get himself thoroughly informed about a new and better process for artificial insemination, but he kept turning back to where he'd started, and fidgeting in his chair, as if urgent and pressing ideas were formulating in his mind. At length he said to his wife, 'There's more good in those novels of yours than I thought.'

He got up from his chair and went out to the room where Larkins slept. 'Look here, Larkins,' he said, trying to get an unusual heartiness and friendliness into his voice, so that Larkins would stop looking as if he was expected to get out of bed and drive several miles in the station utility to make sure a certain gate had been closed, 'when you take your holidays after dipping, would you like to stay at my seaside cottage?'

'Well,' Larkins said slowly, knowing very well there was more than honest generosity in the offer, 'thanks, Mr Kraftmann, but I don't know whether I'd like batching there alone.'

'Oh, you wouldn't be alone,' Kraftmann said, trying hard to kindle some spark of worldliness on Larkins's sleepy face. 'This girl who comes here to work some days. I've told you about her, haven't I? Well she's going down with a couple of other girls to have a holiday there, and to get the place ready for us later. You wouldn't need to be lonely, now, would you?'

And he gave Larkins a wink that was all the more scandalous for its fleeting brevity.

It was sheep-dipping time at Donnerwetter Station – always a time of crisis for Kraftmann, because it was the exacting end of a long period of trying work. Once it was over he could look for a brief interval of comparative peace. For one thing, he could sack those of his men who had become completely unendurable. Of these, the first was the fake cowboy Harby, the worst of Kraftmann's long line of terrible failures. Others would go on holidays, and there wouldn't be the daily grind of keeping a lot of half- or quarter-willing hands gainfully employed. Once the dipping was over the rams would behave better, too. The new type of highly scientific and fabulously effective dip he was using had an odd temporary after-effect on his rams, in that for the next three weeks or so they seemed to be without any of their normal masculine impulses. No jumping fences to compete fiercely with other rams for their legitimate mates – give them a shady tree, plenty to eat, a bit of rest, and they were quite happy.

Dipping sheep is exasperating work, even when the dip is the modern shower-type used by Kraftmann. A hundred sheep at a time are driven into a circular shower-room, and none of them go willingly. They know very well that the doors will be slammed and that dip will be sprayed at them from every angle by a powerful pump driven by a tractor. There needs to be only one fool among the workers, who makes the wrong move at the wrong moment, which checks the sheep when at length they have been induced to go forward – and Harby was always there to be that fool.

Let Kraftmann send him on jobs at a distance, he'd be back in a few minutes, panting to be one of the mob, having botched the job so terribly that he was no longer to be trusted out of sight. Let Larkins seize him by his cowboy neckerchief and lead him round like a badly behaved dog, and he'd still cause havoc by yelling or plunging about at the wrong time. That he was still on the place was only because these were the last days; because Kraftmann was determined that he should share the dust and discomfort of the hard work after being paid so long for riding uselessly about the place; that he should be the one to go into the dripping shower-room to push out the wet sheep; the one to be splashed every time a sheep shook itself; and the one to get his ear tweaked or a prod from a broom-handle every time he kicked the sheep that did it. Larkins was the only man who appeared to be enjoying himself, astonishingly lively for the man he usually was, working like a demon to get the dipping finished quickly, and only showing a sign of ill-humour in his harrying of Harby. Only Old Tom, veteran of forty years' dipping, was normal. So experienced was he in the ways of sheep that he could do more good by standing still in one place than any three others could by dashing about and yelling like mad.

Kraftmann, as usual, was postponing the morning-tea break as long as possible. No one knew whether it was because he had an unreasoning idea that he got more work out of his men that way, or because he wanted to put off for as long as possible this opportunity for trouble to arise. This interval, when all the men were together, was when all the morning's irritations were worked off onto someone else, when the underdogs bit back under the assumed protection of the boss. But it had to come at last.

'I know why Larkins is so larky!' Harby shouted into a brief silence. 'He thinks he's going away for a mating season with —'

Even on a stud farm there are some things which are not done, and Harby had done one of them; or rather, he had done it in the wrong way. Larkins cut the lady's name off with a back-handed blow, reinforced by the weight of a sandwich she had cut for him that morning. It not only knocked Harby onto his back, but it caused him to gouge his buttocks cruelly on his spurs.

Harby jumped up again, spitting out sandwich and so stung to rage by his spur-wounds that he exceeded all his previous follies. Out of his wide, ugly slit of a mouth he shouted in his guttery voice, 'She'll take me on before you, any day!'

Kraftmann jumped up with the look of a man too shocked for speech. He watched Larkins slogging Harby mercilessly, first with one hand, and then the other, then standing over him, waiting for some sign of life, so he could hit him again. Kraftmann came over to look at Harby, a cruelly worried man. Women had been known to do astonishingly queer things, even when the best possible arrangements had been made for them.

'Right-oh, boys, back to work again!' he shouted, knowing they'd be too excited to notice that they'd had only half of their usual spell. He continued to stand over Harby, thinking deeply. Harby opened his eyes slowly; he seemed about to relapse into unconsciousness again, when he saw that Kraftmann had his hand thrust deeply into that pocket where he usually carried that fateful instrument which he used with such relish on badly behaved rams. He jumped up with a fearful yell, and bolted into the corner of the big yard before facing Kraftmann again.

'Get to work,' Kraftmann snapped, grinning with pleasure at having frightened him so much.

And Harby rushed away, casting, every now and then, apprehensive looks behind him.

So the sheep were pushed forward again, saturated, and let out to dry, one mob after the other. Harby, not at his best after the beating he'd received, kept his eyes roving, warily for Kraftmann and revengefully after Larkins. Then, suddenly, he saw his opportunity. Larkins was delayed in the shower-room, when everything else was ready for the spraying to start; he was trying to make a sheep stand up, but it persisted in lying down, regardless, in its supine imbecility, of the risk it would run of being drowned. Harby slammed the door and started up the pump.

'That'll take the "larks" out of your holiday!' he yelled wildly, as whirling iron arms poured the dip over Larkins and jets streamed at him from floor and walls.

For a moment everyone was too shocked to do anything. Then Kraftmann started to run for the door of the dip, yelling orders to the others like a lunatic, seeing his best man and the vital part of his plan threatened with destruction, calling every kind of annihilation down upon Harby's head as he ran. Harby, half frightened now at the stir he'd caused, suddenly noticed that there was a rifle beside the door to which Kraftmann was running. He waited no longer; no doubt he thought that if he started now he'd have a good chance of getting in two shots before Kraftmann began.

The first went so wide that if Kraftmann hadn't happened to look across at Harby he wouldn't have noticed he was being shot at. But the second went so dangerously close that Kraftmann grabbed the rifle instead of the door. Harby fell to the ground almost, it seemed, before Kraftmann's shot, and for the moment Kraftmann took no more notice of him. One of the men ran to stop the pump, another to fling open the door, two to rush in and drag out Larkins, with a great bruise on the head where the flying arms had hit him, drenched like any of the sheep.

'Quick!' Kraftmann shouted. 'Two of you put him in a hot bath and scrub him like hell, with plenty of changes of water.' Then he looked round impatiently at a frightened youth who'd been trying to get his attention.

'What about Harby, Mr Kraftmann?'

'Oh, he's all right,' said Kraftmann irritably. 'I just broke his collarbone to stop him shooting.'

'He looks pretty bad to me,' said the lad.

Kraftmann strode across, rolled him on his back, and started to swear. 'Couldn't ever stop doing something foolish. Must have ducked the last moment. And look where it got him!'

Then Old Tom came and had a good look. He said thoughtfully, 'Every year we thought we'd have to shoot someone. But this is the first time we ever did it.'

Then he looked at Kraftmann, as if the full significance of it was slowly seeping into his old brain. He said, with enormous relief in his voice, 'Lucky for you, Boss, that you had to do it in self-defence.'

Birdey was the only one to cause any trouble. He turned up at the inquest, recalling Harby's fears, and Kraftmann's threats, and Kraftmann's reputedly unerring marksmanship, now convinced that neither Kraftmann nor Harby had been pulling his leg.

But country coroners do not attach much importance to what they call 'theoretical persons', when a man of good standing in their district is supported by witnesses on the spot. Moreover, since Birdey was obliged to admit his knowledge of poor Harby's city convictions, and of his habit of carrying an unlicensed revolver (which he, who was responsible for Harby's behaviour, hadn't reported to the police), he received a very unsympathetic hearing; in fact, one of the spectators was rude enough to call after him, 'You're the real cause of it all.'

Some little good did come of it, however. Kraftmann, either because he was shaken into temporary virtuousness by what had happened, or was worried about the possibility of the proverbial slips between cups and lips, had Larkins and the girl respectably married before they really knew what was happening. And then, although in his calloused view it was now quite unnecessary, he still allowed them the use of his seaside cottage for their honeymoon.

John Morrison

A MAN'S WORLD

JUST after half-past four came the last of the callers.

It had been going on all the afternoon, ever since twelve o'clock when the news first began to get around. Big sums of money don't come often to the residents of Tanner Street, Richmond, and Mrs McLean was beginning to weary of the urgent knocking on the front door, the more neighbourly call at the back – 'You there, Liz! Can I come in?' – the excitement on well-known faces, the constant repetition of the story of how she herself had taken the news and what she was going to do about it.

She wanted her husband home, quietness over the special dinner she was cooking, more than anything else confirmation of the fabulous telegram she'd received just after noon.

Still, Mrs Howe was a bit closer than the others, and when Mrs McLean heard the familiar voice at the back door, she resigned herself cheerfully enough to going over it all once again. Here, anyway, was another who wouldn't be butting in after Frank arrived.

Mrs Howe was a breezy young woman, obviously got up for an outing that called for the best she had. She came in with a crisp rustle of new clothes and more than a mere whiff of perfume.

'Liz, is this fair dinkum? I just got back . . .'

The happy smile that had sat on Mrs McLean's face for four hours quickened again. 'I hope it is, Ruth.'

Her plump face flushed with joy and the heat of the stove, she stood nervously fiddling with a tea-cloth. Two children, one only a baby, played quietly with some new wooden building-blocks at her feet.

'What d'you mean, you hope it is? Haven't you got word?'

'I got a telegram from Frank. I think it's all right.'

'You got a telegram from Frank – you beaut! Can't you believe it, love? My God, let's kiss you! It might bring me luck. I been taking tickets for years.'

They came together for a moment, then Mrs Howe sat down with the self-assurance of one who has no doubt about her welcome. 'This is the best I ever heard. How many's in it?'

'Six. Frank'll get about one-thousand-six-hundred pounds.'

'One-thousand-six-hundred!'

Mrs Howe gasped, and passed a hand across her forehead. 'Gee, say it again! No, Liz, don't go making tea; I got to go in two minutes.'

Mrs McLean had picked up the teapot. 'You might as well.'

'No, I told Bill . . .'

'Where is he?'

'Gone down for a couple of quickies. We been up seeing the old man. Sit down and talk, love.'

Mrs McLean sat down, and the two women beamed at each other across a corner of the table.

'I couldn't have been more pleased if it'd been Bill,' said Mrs Howe heartily. 'What does it feel like?'

'I couldn't believe it for a long time. It was like somebody was playing a dirty joke on us. Then I sat down and cried. Honest, I cried. I couldn't help it. To think it come now, after all this worry.'

Mrs Howe's smile was tender. 'God help you, you're still shaking. You don't want to let yourself get upset over it, love. You got nothing to worry about now.'

Mrs McLean nodded dreamily. 'I've been sitting here buying houses all the afternoon. It's funny, ever since we got the eviction order we've been saying that Tatts was the only thing that stood between us and Camp Pell.'

'When is it you're got to be out?'

'Friday week. Frank's sick with worry. He's been getting nightmares thinking about it.'

'It's a damn shame. It's all right for them magistrates . . .'

'They've got to do it sometimes. The bloke that bought this place has got four kids.'

'There should be houses for everybody. Anyhow, you're all

right now. The agents'll be falling over you now you've got money. There's houses everywhere for a deposit half of what you got. How's the kids? They wouldn't know what it's all about. Eh, Davey?'

Davey, the eldest, looked up as the visitor's hand ruffled his hair. But his blue eyes rested on her only for a moment, then turned, with a spontaneous little frown, to his mother, as if he'd suddenly remembered a half-forgotten grievance.

'You woke something up,' said Mrs McLean. 'I went out and got a duck to celebrate with. That's all he can think of.'

'Bless him!' Mrs Howe fondled the child again. 'Your belly thinks your throat's cut, does it love? Never mind, Dad won't be long now – then . . . whacko!' She glanced at the clock and got up. 'I got to go, Liz . . .'

'Frank'll be in any minute.'

'So will my Bill! But you don't want to bet on Frank. I know them wharfies. They're bound to have a few snorts on it when they knock off.'

'He said in the telegram he'd come straight home. "Happy Gang got first in Tatts. Home on the bat." Just like that. I've been reading it all the afternoon.'

'Well, I'm just telling you, don't get worked-up if he's a bit late. See you in the morning.'

As the door closed behind Mrs Howe the boy Davey dropped his bricks, stood up, and tugged at his mother's skirts.

'Isn't it ready yet, Mum?'

'As soon as Dad gets in, Davey. He's on the way now. Just another minute and we'll have it. Keep Joe quiet, there's a good boy.'

Satisfied that all was well with the dinner, she left the room. Davey wandered back to the baby and stood sulkily watching him heaping up the wooden bricks.

When, a few minutes later, she came back, the boy hadn't moved. His inquisitive little eyes took in everything; she'd changed into a bright frock, combed her hair, and touched up her face.

'You going out, Mum?'

'No, Davey.' Stepping cautiously among the bricks, she laid an investigating hand on the seat of Joe's rompers. 'I'm just making myself look nice for Dad. It's like a birthday tonight.'

'Whose birthday, Mum?'

'Nobody's son. I said: like a birthday.'

'Why, Mum?'

'Because we've got a lot of money. We're going to buy a nice big house.'

'Where, Mum?'

'I don't know yet. In some nice place. You'll be going to a new school.'

'You told me that before.'

'Yes, but it'll be a different one now.'

'Where, Mum?'

'Near where we go to live.'

'Where's that?'

She was very patient. The table was already set, and she seated herself near the stove with the boy at her knees. Joe still played on in the absorption of infancy with a new and novel toy. All kinds of noises came in from the street only a few feet away, backed by the ceaseless rumble of the peak-hour traffic along Punt Road. In the little room there was only the peaceful murmur of two voices, and an occasional clatter as Joe's bricks tumbled down.

He came in at a quarter to six.

It was one of those houses opening directly on to the street, with a picket side-gate attached, every closing thump of which could be heard from one end to the other. Her smile grew into one of childish excitement as she followed his footfalls along the narrow alleyway just at the other side of the wall, and caught the second familiar bump as he placed his bicycle against the back weatherboards. Joe had dropped his bricks and set off in a headlong stagger across the floor.

'Careful, Frank!' she called out. 'Joe's there . . .'

He opened the door slowly, just enough to get his head in and see where the baby was, and a moment later all four of them were in a hilarious mix-up on the threshold, both children in his arms, she nuzzling into his chest and reaching behind to take away the ugly bale-hook twisted under his belt.

She got it out and left him for a moment to place it in safety on the end of the mantelpiece. 'That hook – one of these days –

oh, Frank, it is true, isn't it! I still can't believe it . . .'

He was very tall, and had to stoop to kiss her even though she was on her toes. 'Spare me days, it's nothing to cry about!'

'I can't help it. It's been like a week since I got the telegram. Davey! Wait – we're going to have it now.'

'He's all right.' He was trying to disengage himself while her arms were still tight around him. She caught him looking over her head at the clock, and suddenly sensed something that didn't quite fit in with her own complete happiness.

'You don't look like a man that's just won Tatts,' she said, still laughing.

'It was a hard day, Liz. We had to work on just the same.'

He set Joe on his bottom on the floor, and playfully pushed Davey away.

'Let me get my boots off, son.'

Her smile became a little doubtful as she watched him take off his coat, hang it behind the door, and sit down to unlace his boots.

'I went out and got a duck,' she said. 'The electric-light money was still there . . .'

'Good on you, mate; I can smell it.' He lifted his head to sniff appreciatively, but dropped it again rather too quickly.

'You look worn-out, Frank. Would you like a cup of tea first?'

'Good idea.'

'Frank . . .'

'Make a cup of tea, Liz.'

He spoke with a firmness that startled her, his head still down as he pulled on a shoe with one hand and fended Joe off with the other. 'I've got something to tell you before we get stuck into that duck.'

'What's the matter with your slippers?' she asked. 'Are you going out again?'

'I might have to. Make the tea, there's a good girl.'

'Mum . . .'

'Davey, if you don't keep quiet for a minute . . .'

The atmosphere was quite changed now. No longer smiling, she brewed a pot of tea, picked Joe up, and sat down sideways at the table. 'Get the biscuit-tin, Davey . . .'

She remained silent while he rolled a cigarette. Then:

'Frank, you're frightening me. What's wrong? Didn't you win it?'

For the first time since coming in he looked straight at her. He had the pained, pitying smile of a man trying to temper bad news.

'I'm not sure, Liz.'

'I got a telegram.'

'Yes, I sent it. But something's happened since.'

'It was a mistake!'

'In a way, yes.'

He spoke softly and reluctantly each time, trying to ease the blows. He saw her jaw tighten to stop the sudden trembling of her lips.

'You'd better tell me, Frank.'

He had pulled Davey on to his knees, and the boy, sensing a crisis, sat there watching his mother, an untouched biscuit clutched in his fingers.

'You remember the shift I lost on the Norwegian ship last week?'

'When you went after that house, yes.'

'I got Arthur Glenn to work it, on my docket.'

'In your name, yes.'

'You remember me telling you afterwards there'd been a near-accident in the hold?'

'I remember you saying something at the time about an officer . . .'

'The second mate got trapped in some dunnage as they were dragging a big case out from the wing.'

'Yes, you told me.'

'He could have been badly hurt if the gang hadn't acted quickly. And Arthur Glenn was the first to yell out . . .'

'Yes . . .'

'Don't hurry me – that bit's important. Did I tell you what one of our blokes said to the officer afterwards?'

'I don't think so.'

'He said: "You ought to take a ticket in Tatts, mate!" '

'You didn't tell me that.'

'Well, he did. I got all this from Dally Spencer next day when I was back on the job. He said it, all right. And the bloke *did* take out a ticket.'

'Frank – it was *him* that won it!'

'No. It was the gang's ticket. He gave it to Dally for the gang.'

Frank, stirring his tea continuously for the past minute, had not taken his eyes off her.

'That's what you said in the telegram: Happy Gang...'

'Liz, girl, don't you see! I shouldn't be in on this. Arthur Glenn was in the gang that day.'

He smothered a curse and picked up his cup as he saw her face go white.

'Oh, Frank!'

'That lost shift could cost me hundreds of pounds.'

Silence fell between them. Both children were getting troublesome. Davey, sternly admonished, retreated to the other side of the table, a frightened little face just showing above the white cloth, darting puzzled glances first at his father, then at his mother. Joe had to be cuddled. Over his wispy hair Liz stared horror-stricken at her husband.

'*Could* cost you hundreds of pounds,' she repeated, her expression hardening. 'What do you mean – *did* you win it, or *didn't* you?'

'The Happy Gang won it.'

'Well, you're in the Happy Gang, aren't you? You've always paid in for the tickets; two a week ever since...'

'This one wasn't bought by the gang. It was bought *for* the gang, when I wasn't in it.'

'Who told you all this?'

'Dally Spencer. Dally always handles them. He told us at lunch-time the next day that we had an extra runner. The second mate had just pulled him up as he was coming down the gangway.'

'Dally wouldn't put anything over you, would he?'

'No, you can forget that.'

It was a strange dialogue. She, studying him with a fearful eagerness, full of suspicion, ready to pounce on anything that would save them. He, deliberately keeping his face averted, and giving the answers in the stubborn dejected way of one who has already covered every inch of hateful ground.

'Are you telling me,' she asked fiercely, 'that we've got to give all this money to Arthur Glenn?'

'If I know anything about Arthur Glenn he won't take it all. He'll cut me in. But I've got to tell him.'

'The ticket was given to the gang!' she wailed.

'It was given to the six men working below for that shift.'

'It was made out to the Happy Gang Syndicate, like all the others. You *said* so.'

She began to cry, noiselessly, thinking of the baby, holding him up over her shoulder so that he wouldn't see her face, and patting him ceaselessly on the back the way mothers do.

'Frank, you can't give it up, you can't!'

'What d'you want me to do?' he demanded.

'Nothing. You don't have to do anything. Arthur Glenn can't claim it. Your name's on the time-sheet. He wasn't supposed to be there.'

'I asked him to work the shift for me.'

'And you paid him for it. What more does he want? Does anybody else know about all this besides Dally?'

'Nobody. Nobody seemed to think of the extra ticket. They were all too excited. We've been taking tickets for so long ...'

'What did Dally say? Does he think ...' she broke off, biting her lip.

'Go on,' said Frank bitterly, 'finish it! Does he think we ought to tell Arthur? Now tell me we'd be doing the right thing! Hell, have I been through it this afternoon!'

He stood up, took a couple of turns across the floor, then sat down again as Davey crept back to the idle chair.

'Liz,' he said, stroking the boy's head, 'we've got to settle this all by ourselves. Dally won't have a bar of it. He didn't wake up to it himself till just after lunch, when he took another look at the ticket. And he threw the whole thing right into my lap. He's a funny bloke, Dally. He told me he was going to keep it under his hat at first, because he knows how we're placed. But he knows Arthur's battling too, and it worried him too much. He said he couldn't carry it. I'd have to make up my own mind. He knows Arthur lives just around in Coppin Street.'

'Is that why you put your shoes on?'

'Yes.'

'Then you had your mind made up when you came in?'

'Pretty well. I can bet on Arthur doing the right thing and

whacking it up with me. But when I opened that door and saw
your face . . .'

'You still want to do it, though, don't you?'

'Liz . . .'

'And I won't let you!'

She wasn't crying now. She was thoroughly angry, leaning
towards him with the baby still held to her shoulder, and
gesticulating with her free hand. Davey ran to her, whimpering,
and staring across at his father with frightened eyes.

'Hold on, Liz, you're scaring the kids. We've got to talk this
over . . .'

'Talk it over! You want to give it away. You *said* so.'

'We'll get half of it. I know Arthur Glenn . . .'

'You never know anybody once money creeps in.'

He seized on this eagerly. 'By cripes, you've said it! How
d'you think I've been all the afternoon? I never pinched a
cracker in my life. Now, when it's a question of really big
money . . .'

'You talk as if we'd be stealing it.'

'*You* might have another name for it. And I'm not blaming
you, in a way. It looked all right to me, too, when Dally first told
me. You can persuade yourself anything's right if you try hard
enough.' Only for a time, though – the little nigger keeps
creeping in . . .'

'You can't afford to be as fussy as that in this world. We've got to
live. We've got these kids to think of. Somebody's got to look
out for them. We're under notice to quit.'

'D'you think I'm forgetting that?'

'What if Arthur Glenn keeps the lot? He could, once you
told him, couldn't he?'

'The waterfront wouldn't be big enough to hold him. He'd
stink once it got around.'

'Would Dally Spencer ever tell?'

'No, but he'd hate the guts of me. And what d'you think my
feelings would be whenever I ran across Arthur Glenn?'

'You're thinking of everything except me and the children.
My God, it'd be worth your while . . .' She stopped, with a
sudden frightened glance.

'To what?' he demanded quietly.

She dropped her head, fumbling guiltily with the baby's fat legs.

'It'd be worth my while to leave the waterfront,' he said in the same gentle tone. 'That's what you were going to say, wasn't it? See where we get?'

A long silence fell, while he watched her lowered eyelids.

Reaching out a big hand and laying it on her knees to keep her steadied, he said: 'Liz, I don't blame you. I suppose in the long run it's a good thing that a woman will fight for the home, and to hell with everything else. But it's a man's world I've got to live in, not a woman's. I've got to go out in it. I've got to go down to the compound in the morning. Dally will be waiting for me. What am I to tell him? He's a nice bloke. He thinks I'm a nice bloke. What d'you want me to tell him?'

He waited, but she neither spoke nor looked at him.

'You do see, don't you, Liz? Say I do run away from it – I've got to live with myself, haven't I? And you?'

He shook her.

'Spare me days, girl, I'd see it sitting on the bed-rail for the rest of my life!'

With a weary little smile she lifted her head at last.

'Do what you think best, Frank.'

'You _do_ see, don't you?'

'Yes. Go and tell him. Go and tell him, quickly. And don't be long. I've got to give the kids theirs.'

Hal Porter

FIEND AND FRIEND

PERROT was young enough, at twenty-four, to be enthusiastic, energetic, sympathetic, to have all the softie bents of an inexperienced junior master in a Public School – doesn't matter where. He was hopeless; the boys offhandedly disliked him. That was the year – oh, long enough ago for *Cappuccino* to suggest a monk, Zen Buddhism to be a zealot's study rather than a fad; the Windsor Knot was just making Australia and Perrot and, while a cannery was a cannery, canned peaches were tinned peaches. Television was years off; people therefore sometimes looked at sunsets as though they were living in the nineteenth century. Perrot even, now and then, after cricket practice, blinked at Turner, Harrow-on-the-Hill sunsets from the disproportionately grandiose Italianate portico of The School which, on its last Victorian legs, nevertheless still took charge of a view that sloped down for miles, and was open to the common-cold- or hayfever-bringing gusts from . . . from an ocean needless to name. The School prospectus, sprinkled with Hollandse Medieval initials, used *panorama* and *ozone*, and extolled as *healthful zephyrs* largely southerly and often refrigeratingly antarctic winds.

The School's heyday had been also the bicycle's, Brittania's and Beardsley's; in Perrot's time all was flaking, cracked, sutured by Virginia Creeper, down-at-heel but not seedy. The place had *cachet* though doors would not lock, windows would not open, floorboards were so worn that knots stood up like carbuncles. Glass cases of stuffed hawks and unglittering geological samples stood in subfusc corridors. It was draughty as the Parthenon; the flywire screens of kitchens, sculleries and dining-hall were more ragged than the Bayeux tapestry.

The Head, the Common Room, Matron, Sister, the Housekeeper, the ex-Test-bowler cricket coach all intimated or brazenly kept on indicating that they had come from – how long ago? – somewhere better. *Somewhere better*, of course, meant *youth* and was the answer; jobs had been no better; they had been younger. While too intelligent, educated or experienced for hope, and aware they could be on their way nowhere else, they were not resigned to their own unhappiness though, the easy sagacity, they were to each other's. Fretfully they droned like senile bees; there was an atmosphere of Eventide Home. In the Common Room hung academic gowns like attire Villon might have worn. Perrot's gown alone seemed Byronic. It was new. Perrot, the one young master, alone represented the generation between boys and ageing staff. Perrot alone of the adults was on his way somewhere else. For others this was the last year because, after seventy years of lathing out judges, knights, diplomats, dipso-maniacs, professional bores and one undramatic murderer, The School was to close. Next year the desks incised with unthinkable dates, the FOO-haunted changing-rooms, The School barber like someone out of Jerome K. Jerome, the music master who affected a velvet-collared overcoat and Lisztian hair, all, everyone, would be gone, the boys doubly so.

Doubly? Gone as schoolboys of that School, gone irrevocably as boys for, turn one's back and temperamental tennis pro-fessionals took their places, quick-gnawing sub-deans, shy graziers, terse shire engineers, turners-and-fitters, tally-clerks, journalists, *divorcés*, no-hopers garnet-eyed and bender-skinny quavering, 'Two bob, dig', in a Russell Drysdale town. But, fleetingly, boys. Conventional as cannibals, secretive as stool pigeons, shrewish as little girls, sensitive, six inches above the footpaths of common sense, a rabble with its own two-up school protocol, they missed nostalgia, wistfulness, the end-of-an-era atmosphere. They acted *Boys will be Boys* with *éclat*. No one, indeed, can act a boy as well as a boy.

Except for Rymill. He overacted, at least for Perrot and largely for Perrot.

Rymill seemed the scandalous boy from nowhere. He was spare as if his spirit abhorred the luxury of flesh, Murillo-eyed changeling, the unsmiling gipsy at the manor gates. He travelled south from some unimaginable part of Queensland – hinterland, borderland, Goblin Market, God knew! – by shattered buses to board other shattered buses on teeth-splintering back roads, by trains with sandpaper seats through landscapes of glaring antagonism or where impermanent rivers, momentarily mad with seeming ginger beer, flushed like lavatories. End of term – abracadabra! – he disappeared. First day of term, while others were unpacking, there he was – whoosh! – as though riding it bareback to puncture yoo-hooing about on someone else's bicycle. He was Perrot's Old Man of the Sea, his nigger in the woodpile, his *bête noire*, his . . . 'I could give Dr Roget a hundred he hasn't thought of for *bane*,' Perrot would cry. 'A thousand! I'll disembowel the Rymill; I'll garotte him; I'll commit mayhem; I'll . . .' Perrot was thus desperately facetious as people are when they imitate Cockney at sticky moments. He hated Rymill. The Common Room smiled like a waiting-room of Mona Lisas, a club of Punches, a jury ardent to pronounce, 'Guilty!'

'I shall cane the next boy who . . .' Perrot cried, deliberately dramatically for the little monsters, sweeping about so that his gown was Hamlet's cloak on the swirl. Rymill was the next boy.

'Who said that?' called Perrot, spooning out rissoles at table. 'Who said "compost"? Ah, I might have known! See me after luncheon, Rymill.'

Perrot, looking up in prep., impelled to look up, met the intense and shocking gaze of a little man with an enormous *papier-mâché* Jewish nose and horn-rimmed spectacles who was sitting in Rymill's desk. 'Out here, Rymill!' he shouted.

'Hell!' yelled Perrot leaping like Buster Keaton from the thistle on his chair. He knew at whom to direct his outrage. Rubbing his behind, Rymill was already on his way, face bleak as a saint's.

Rymill's misdemeanours had the dreary innocence of japes and merry pranks conned from a 1913 *Boy's Own Paper;* they smelt of the lamp, of Baden-Powell and Goodnatured Boyish Fun: there were crackers, treacle in the inkwell, sewn-up pyjama legs, vile stenches, tin blots on pages, lizards in desks . . . It was persistence and repetition, impenitence and intensity that marked Rymill eccentric. Perrot was the target.

In choice of friend Rymill carried eccentricity further. He had screened The School to find an *alter ego* as like himself in appearance but as unlike in behaviour. Van der Velde, a Dutch consul's son, was the choice, a boy of his height, age, curls and colouring but bland, cautious and smilingly courteous. War and Peace, thought Perrot in distracted moments, Whisky and Water, Mad Hatter and Dormouse, Fiend and Friend. Van der Velde spent much of his time eating, an exercise Rymill seemed to like little, gorged as he was, Perrot thought, by plottings, plannings, and venom. The consul's son always ate Rymill's pudding; as left-handed as the King of Spades he was rarely seen without a bag of *éclairs* or grapes into which he south-paw dipped and dipped. He was affable and godly Rymill.

Tirelessly, sombre, with nicotine-stained fingers, skulls-and-crossbones inked on wrists, Rymill himself continued overacting Tom Sawyer, *Triumph* and *Stalky and Co.* until The School was bored to screeching, 'Ow, chuckit, Rymill!' 'Pipe down, Rymill!' 'Go to *buggery*, Rymill!' Only his friend, left-handedly pecking into caramel cartons, laxly indulged him. Only Perrot was beyond the shallows of boredom or forbearance; Rymill was to him the seventh wave, the deadly bumper, the slug in the salad, as ever-present as Satan as over-shadowing as a Doré one. Rymill was thirteen.

The older masters were invigorated, as with moral penicillin, by Perrot's distress; it graced their morose last year that he was rattled by a mere whippersnapper; young-manhood, with its imperfections of disciplinary technique, seemed less worthy of regret.

Even the Head, as classical of profile and as remote as a Carrera Olympian topping an insurance building, said with dispassion, 'My dear young man, Rymill is impermanent. Boys are, you know, quite.' He paused; reflection from some high-flying pigeon of thought flicked his rigid handsomeness. 'He's an only son, you know. And fatherless. Perhaps this campaign of terror is disguised affection, hero-worship. However, though I can't expel him *yet*, shall I cane him for you? Brutally?'

Cynical bastard, thought Perrot but, 'Heavens, no,' he said. 'Heavens, *no*, sir. I'll learn to cope.'

'Cope?' said the Head as though Perrot had used four-letter obscenity.

'Manage . . . that is, handle the situation, sir.'

'I'm certain you will. You – a vigorous, intelligent stripling

. . .' The Head looked at his knuckles as if they were new.

Perrot flushed. 'It's just, sir, that his behaviour's so incredible.'

'Nothing, Perrot; is incredible until one has said it is. And saying it . . . well, untruth, eh? I *myself* find it all credible.'

'Thank you, sir,' said Perrot as though imparting, after losing all toenails, the secret the Gestapo wanted.

The Head stared an unwinking four seconds at the air agitated by Perrot's exit, then returned with detachment to what he called a railway novel, a paper-back James Hadley Chase, whose bloodhouse world seemed calmer much than the one he had long inhabited – bickering Board, backbiting masters, pregnant maids, parents with delusions, neurotic housekeepers, imperious Matrons, hyperbolizing tradesmen, drunken ground-keepers, domineering archbishops, conveyor belts of boys transparent and meretricious as Christmas stockings, and, above all, an ex-actress wife who felt herself gifted and young enough to retreat into the costly fantasy of fashion from the cut-rate indelicacy of having fallen, almost immediately after marriage, out of love with him.

Then came the absurd affair of the Music Room ceiling.

Perrot was on evening duty which usually, for him, resembled the French Revolution. However, prep., showers, lights-out had passed in such peace, as though another master were on duty, that he should have warned himself. Instead, he went gulled to bed to find himself stark awake at some deep hour: horizon askew, raft sinking, the moon turned over. God, he thought, resident masters are like mothers. There was a wrong weight of silence; an area of breathing and dreaming and stirring had been subtracted from the sum of boarding-house night. He switched on. Two-o'-bloody-clock, *ante meridiem*. He padded seeking with electric torch. Dormitory One – dead to the world. Dormitory Two – eight-year-old Bernstein, frail as Tiny Tim, snoring like a warthog. Dormitory Three – 'I . . . might . . . have . . . known,' said Perrot to the twelve beds and their bulges that neither twisted, snorted nor dreamed. Midnight feast! he thought. Rymill!

As though seeking Jesus's lambs, but fuming like Etna, Perrot stamped here and there. No one in the gymnasium except the vaulting horse grazing tan bark under the trapeze; no one in the cricket pavilion except Callaghan's cricket boots, and a singlet abandoned like an after-birth in one corner; no one in the old science theatre except the memory of useless lectures; no one in any custom-sacred place. Within twenty minutes Perrot began to suggest to himself the notion of being in nightmare, himself ranging the famous slope for a dozen Jack-o'-Lantern sub-adolescents, his torch springing junior Erl Kings under olive-trees and stabbing the head-hunter rustles in canna plantations, barking, 'Rymill! Rymill!' in the provoking darkness.

On the boil, he returned to his study and waited, gnawing at the smoke of cigarettes, and deciding to become a jackeroo with an English accent and a *fiancée* called Christine. What else to do except turn on the sun like an electric light?

At last he heard sibilances and graveside shufflings that should have been theme-musicked by Grieg. These approached; it was reminiscent of *Alice in Wonderland*, something about Bill the Lizard, 'Hold up his head . . . Brandy now . . . Don't choke him . . .' Ahead of the tissue-paper hubbub Van der Velde appeared first at the doorway, his dressing-gown pockets bulged with Chocolate Royals. His eyes were too starry, were lunatic's. 'Oh, sir,' he cried, 'Oh, sir – Rymill's hurt!' Perrot disconcerted himself by stubbing the cigarette he had just lit.

And there, over-zealously supported by *all* the Lost Boys, everyone a finger in the pie, lying in a pansyish though awkwardly sustained pose, was Rymill. One leg, on deliberate foreground display, dripped blood and stained the pyjama-leg torn like a beachcomber's at a Fancy Dress Ball. Perrot transformed himself to a competent schoolmaster. There were cuts and more dramatic blood than seemed necessary. 'I'm perfectly all right, sir,' said Rymill. 'I'm perfectly, perfectly all right. I'm perfectly, perfectly, *perfectly* . . .'

'Take him,' said Perrot, suddenly raddled with a cutthroat's anger, 'take him to the nearest bathroom. We'll see if we need disturb Sister or Matron.' In a stimulating hush of doom Rymill's Caesar's body was borne to where his washed wounds were revealed as scarcely more than scrimshawing. Joy faded from the mob at this treacherous let-down. 'Get to bed, all of you,' said Perrot, angrier than they thought a dope could be. 'Get out of my sight. Except Van der Velde. You'll tell me everything, if I have to use torture. And for God's sake stop eating,' he said viciously. 'Your whole life is a litter of banana peel and a trail of paper bags. Stop it.' Ruthlessly, yet with a suffusion of paternal affection he had no cause to feel, did not care to harbour and certainly not to admit, Perrot iodined and sticking-plastered while Van der Velde, an undevilled version of the patient, told of the feast.

'It was my fault, sir,' said Rymill with death-bed weariness. 'I planned it. I am to blame. I . . .'

'Shut up,' cried Perrot. 'Do shut *up*. Don't come the noble, self-sacrificing schoolboy with me. I'm sick of you.'

Planning had taken weeks. Climbing to get tennis-balls from rain-gutters Rymill had prowled the elaborate valleys and steeps of the roof, and had so loosened a sheet of corrugated iron that the caveland of rafters was opened to him. Perrot perceived the value of this to Rymill; even those fed-up with his *Schoolboy's Annual* pranks could not resist a beano in such a setting. Old mattresses were filched from the infirmary store-room, a catwalk of planks was made across the rafters, an electric light circuit tapped. 'God, you little fools!' said Perrot and, bitterly, 'Then, *then*, all you waited for was a night *I* was on duty, eh?' Rymill stared with luminous fixity. Van der Velde gushed, 'Well, sir, not *really*. The day after tomorrow's end of term *and* . . .' Perrot disregarded him. 'You are to blame, aren't you, Rymill?' he said. 'Remember saying that? You waited until I was on duty, didn't you?' The stare, its quality untranslatable, continued. 'Didn't you, Rymill?' Perrot could just control his voice. 'Yes, sir,' said Rymill as though he were lying to save some face or other. He closed his eyes. Van der Velde continued.

Feast over, the boys were returning when Rymill had fallen from the catwalk; his leg had gone through the Music Room ceiling.

'How do you know it was the Music Room?'

'We flashed torches through the hole,' said Van der Velde. 'There's plaster all over the grand. It looks frightful, sir. Tons and tons of it.'

'Get to bed,' said Perrot. 'Get to your wretched beds. I shouldn't like to be in your shoes tomorrow when the Head sees all that mess.'

Rymill opened his eyes, said with passionate earnestness, 'Sir, couldn't we clean up the mess so that it won't look so bad, and then the Head wouldn't be so mad with us? *Please*, sir?'

Perrot could hardly speak; when he did he was astounded to hear, 'Rymill . . . Rymill, I hate you. Hate *you*. I have never in my life . . . Get out!'

When the two had gone, Perrot, distressed at anger but still angry, walked to the Music Room. Tons and tons was right; the hole in the ceiling seemed too small for the wreckage below. I wonder, he thought, if there's blood up there and, remembering the torn leg which seemed younger, as though it belonged to a child, as though it had a mother and could be loved, Perrot cleaned up. It took a long time, and became a labour of fantasy for he could not tell himself why he was repaying months of torment with furtive dirty work.

He did not see Rymill until next term. At breakup, the boy had disappeared across horrors of scarcely inhabited space, and had returned bearing a gift. The fact of the gift astounded Perrot, the nature of it electrified him: eleven feet of swamp-python's skin. Eyeing gift and what he felt was Greek with distaste, Perrot listened to Rymill attempting to consecrate the musty tribute. 'Belts, sir,' he chattered desperately on, 'and little pouches for money. Or combs. You *know*. Maybe a wallet or a portfolio. I know a bloke . . . a *man* who has shoes.' Perrot was able, just, to say, 'Thank you, Rymill.' This meant, 'O.K., I don't know what you're up to, but leave the repulsive thing and vamoose. I don't trust you. I don't like you.' Rymill got the meaning, faded-out his chattering, looked paler and shocked. Then, 'Is that all, sir?' he said, was it pleadingly? Is what all? thought Perrot. Should I burst into fireworks because he's sucking up to me? Run a hand over his curls and pretend that snake-skin shoes were what I wanted most in the world? 'That's *all*,' said Perrot. Rymill turned and left.

The final term was given over to ritual farewell: the last Old Boy's Cricket Match, the last Swimming Carnival, the last Knight-and-Bishop-studded Garden Party; bunting flapped continually; potted palms were always being borrowed from the City Hall. It was the *Titanic* sinking with lights ablaze, ragtime, and ornamental behaviour. The Head, distant behind railway novels, nevertheless conceived imperial notions, and sent the Second Master marathoning from him to Common Room like a Euripidean messenger – shields and silver cups were polished for the first time in memory; a six-fold School Magazine, gilt-embossed, and over-decorated with nineteenth-century fleurons, was distributed free and, *crescendo*, the messenger recited that *Peter Pan* was to be produced by the Head's wife who had been plucked, as it were, from the very sill of the Darling nursery for she had been being a notable Peter Pan almost till her wedding-day. Auditions happened as incontinently as nervous break-downs. Proud seniors, acne aflame like sprays of Cartier rubies, were returned from failing Hook or Smee to their degrading skill in the elementary properties of the parabola, whey-faced boys whose voices had not broken were pincered out of German classes to try for Wendy. Van der Velde – curls, slight build, Consular-English voice – was Peter Pan. Since no expense, ardour and hard work were spared, the Head's wife was able, on the second last night of the last of all terms to bring off a technical and dramatic success.

One moment seemed to Perrot to have oblique poignancy. Peter Pan cried, 'Look!' and rose on his invisible wires, cleaving the air with unforeseen grace. All fake, thought Perrot, and it's only Van der Velde and his smile on wires, someone who will be a molly-duked loud-mouth with false teeth and hairy ears. But, for a moment, a dream child flitted charmingly, Peter Pan, the dream no one should have. The show went on. The Indians stamped; the pirate cutlasses flashed; the show closed. The School closed. The School was pulled down and the appalling abode of a politician went up. The sloping view became sloping streets and crescents. The birds lost their Public School accents and, fidgeting in suburban birdbaths, acquired unsurer ones; the southerly 'zephyrs' scattered largesse of hayfever on house-wives in super-market head-scarves; the Head in retirement wrote a remaindered mystery novel containing five split infini-tives, and died, and Perrot became an anodized schoolmaster no boy could faze. Rymill had taught him much, and not to let ells be taken, never to give an inch.

Eleven, twelve, thirteen years passed.

Perrot, ambitious, unlovable, cultivating loneliness, moved from school to school. As such schoolmasters are, he was often disconcerted by unplaceable men who fired at him their 'Sir! Nice to see you!' These reunions with their hand-pumpings, post mortems and mediocre revelations had for him the garbled air of embraces at funerals. He did not know what to say to these strangers. But unwritten rules stated that schoolmasters were interested, and that the advancing unknown who might merely be wishing to ask where the next corner was, could not be repulsed when he cried, 'Sir!' – that invocation to boyhood lost in the quicksands.

So there was Perrot mincing wine matters with his favourite Basque waiter at the Trattoria Triaca, when 'Sir!' Two of them. Which school? Who? It was Rymill, they cried. It was Van der Velde, they cried. It was two men. It was two half-drunk men – one huge as Orson Welles, fleshed and flushed, the other slender and flashing smilelessly more teeth than a rajah. Perrot learnt with deep uninterest that Rymill and Van der Velde had bumped into each other, first time for years, below in Young and Jackson's Hotel. (Perrot: How did *they* recognize each other?) Now, to meet their schoolmaster (Perrot: Beloved? Revered? Respected? Disliked?) was coincidence worthy of over-drinking and un-relenting *brouhaha*. Perrot knew the grisly drill, resigned himself, drank quickly, arranged an expression and listened. It was necessary, as always, to submit to a depersonalizing and reper-sonalizing that made him feel that someone else had badly impersonated him years ago. Rymill and Van der Velde recalled what he knew nothing of, told an involved Perrot legend of a doing so contrary to his essential nature that he could not recognize himself. Did he remember this, and that, and the other? Oh, yes, he did, he did, he did, he lied, and shocked Leo the Basque by asking twice for double Scotch in the middle of claret. Did he remember one night, when Old Nodsy (who the hell was old Nodsy?), shortcutting through the basement, caught Halliburton (and who was *he*?) – did he remember Halliburton? 'Of course, of course. Old Halliburton, eh!') – well, Halliburton was in a pretty hot clinch with one of the sewing-maids in a niche, and nearly fainted, and all Old Nodsy said was, 'Goodnight, goodnight. You should be in bed!'

They roared. Perrot mimed roaring, idiot on the rack, and tossed off another drink.

Did he remember . . .? *And* did he remember . . .?

By the third bottle of claret Perrot had scraped together his own scant memories. Peter Pan flying in the spotlight, he thought. And the Music Room ceiling! No wonder at all that Rymill had crashed through for, within the boy who had nearly driven him bats, had hibernated this double-chinned, gutsy hearty who had just knocked over his claret. So this was what happened to naughty boys; this was justice! It warmed Perrot but he also felt old hatred like a re-awakened indigestion. He'd always hated Rymill, hadn't he? Wasn't there some odd back-blocks background? And something about a snake-skin?

Van der Velde had shed boyhood more effectively, his manners were gracious (consular background, Perrot recalled) – at least he hadn't knocked over two glasses of wine. Yes, Van der Velde hadn't turned out badly though he had been smug, always chewing at bits and pieces like a pregnant woman.

And then the fat man, the uncouth, the knocker-over, suddenly blundered to his feet. 'I think,' he said, 'I'm going to perk . . .' and walked out.

'Look after that man, please, Leo,' said Perrot. He had never spoken like a schoolmaster to the Basque before. I'm drunk, he thought. I hope Rymill is sick as a dog. I hope he crashes through the lavatory floor into Young and Jackson's. I hope . . .

'What are you thinking of, sir?'

'I don't think I was thinking. But I was before, you know, of the few things I do remember about the old School. Things you two wouldn't. The sunsets, the parklands sloping away. All gone – the big porch, the Virginia Creeper, the oak-trees. I'm drunk, you see . . . nostalgic flapdoodle. Hadn't thought of them for years. And you . . . Peter Panning away there. I'm not usually sentimental but I *am* drunk. And Rymill. I used to hate him. A fiend. I used to call you two fiend and friend, you know, war and peace. Absurd! You, of course, were peace and friend.' Perrot giggled. 'Rymill would plummet *right* through the ceiling now . . .' He seemed to hear a Marx Brothers' crash into a grand piano.

'Sir?'

'For Pete's sake, don't tell me you don't remember that? I've listened to so much tonight that *I* didn't remember . . .'

'Of course I remember, sir. I've still got scars. And I've never forgotten how kind you were.'

Scars? Kind?

'I *thought* you'd got us muddled, sir. That's Van der Velde who tottered out to the dyke. I'm Rymill.'

Perrot now observed that the man before him not only had a moustache like the Knave of Hearts' but that he held his wine-glass in his right hand as the Knave holds the nameless and baffling leaf. This was not the consul's left-handed son. This was the hellion who had vaccinated him against boys for ever. Here he was facing again in a restaurant smelling of *minestrone* and garlicked salad bowls, two untranslatable eyes set in luminous, unsmiling fixity. As once before, but drunkenly now, he was aware of something paternally unzipping: an *exeat* had to be given, an expiation made; words *had* to be said. Reluctantly Perrot said some, 'I didn't really hate you, Rymill.' But these were not right; they were, indeed, a lie.

Perrot frowned, closed his eyes, thinking: here – now – are two grog-soaked men who had nearly fought out something thirteen years ago, but merely nearly. Time's inevitable simplicity being revealed, it was easy to follow the paper-chase of greasy bags that led absolutely from Peter Pan to a fat man; it was difficult to chart what unfinished business, what trail of mis-givings led to this overdue confrontation in the Trattoria Triaca. He heard Rymill saying (insolently? gratefully?), 'Why, sir, did you clean up the mess in the Music Room?' The question left echoes in the soundbox of Perrot's conscience; fantastically he seemed to hear a dead man, the Head, intoning, 'Only son . . . fatherless . . . hero-worship . . .'

Perrot's frown melted; he opened his eyes with conviction; he realized what should have been said years ago instead of 'That's *all*.' Revolted, unwilling, but as enthusiastically as possible, he therefore said it now, 'Did you kill that enormous python yourself?' It was a confession of sin.

He saw Rymill smile *Yes, of course, silly sir* as he would have smiled thirteen years ago. Whether the smile was tinted sardon-ically or affectionately Perrot neither knew nor cared, but it was the appeased smile of one who has finished training his schoolmaster.

It was also, Perrot realized with horror, the first smile he had ever seen on Rymill's face.

Patrick White

DOWN AT THE DUMP

'Hi!'

He called from out of the house, and she went on chopping in the yard. Her right arm swung, firm still, muscular, though parts of her were beginning to sag. She swung with her right, and her left arm hung free. She chipped at the log, left right. She was expert with the axe.

Because you had to be. You couldn't expect all that much from a man.

'Hi!' It was Wal Whalley calling again from out of the home.

He came to the door then, in that dirty old baseball cap he had shook off the Yankee disposals. Still a fairly appetizing male, though his belly had begun to push against the belt.

'Puttin' on yer act?' he asked, easing the singlet under his armpits; easy was policy at Whalleys' place.

' 'Ere!' she protested. 'Waddaya make me out ter be? A lump of wood?'

Her eyes were of that blazing blue, her skin that of a brown peach. But whenever she smiled, something would happen, her mouth opening on watery sockets and the jags of brown, rotting stumps.

'A woman likes to be addressed,' she said.

No one had ever heard Wal address his wife by her first name. Nobody had ever heard her name, though it was printed in the electoral roll. It was, in fact, Isba.

'Don't know about a dress,' said Wal. 'I got a idea, though.'

His wife stood tossing her hair. It was natural at least; the sun had done it. All the kids had inherited their mother's colour, and when they stood together, golden-skinned, tossing back their unmanageable hair, you would have said a mob of taffy brumbies.

190

'What is the bloody idea?' she asked, because she couldn't go on standing there.

'Pick up a coupla cold bottles, and spend the mornun at the dump.'

'But that's the same old idea,' she grumbled.

'No, it ain't. Not our own dump. We ain't done Sarsaparilla since Christmas.'

She began to grumble her way across the yard and into the house. A smell of sink strayed out of grey, unpainted weatherboard, to oppose the stench of crushed boggabri and cotton pear. Perhaps because Whalleys were in the bits-and-pieces trade their home was threatening to give in to them.

Wal Whalley did the dumps. Of course there were the other lurks besides. But no one had an eye like Wal for the things a person needs: dead batteries and musical bedsteads, a carpet you wouldn't notice was stained, wire, and again wire, clocks only waiting to jump back into the race of time. Objects of commerce and mystery littered Whalleys' back yard. Best of all, a rusty boiler into which the twins would climb to play at cubby.

'Eh? Waddaboutut?' Wal shouted, and pushed against his wife with his side.

She almost put her foot through the hole that had come in the kitchen boards.

'Waddabout what?'

Half-suspecting, she half-sniggered. Because Wal knew how to play on her weakness.

'The fuckun *idea*!'

So that she began again to grumble. As she slopped through the house her clothes irritated her skin. The sunlight fell yellow on the grey masses of the unmade beds, turned the fluff in the corners of the rooms to gold. Something was nagging at her, something heavy continued to weigh her down.

Of course. It was the funeral.

'Why, Wal,' she said, the way she would suddenly come round, 'you could certainly of thought of a worse idea. It'll keep the kids out of mischief. Wonder if that bloody Lummy's gunna decide to honour us?'

'One day I'll knock 'is block off,' said Wal.

'He's only at the awkward age.'

191

She stood at the window, looking as though she might know the hell of a lot. It was the funeral made her feel solemn. Brought the goose-flesh out on her.

'Good job you thought about the dump,' she said, out-staring a red-brick propriety the other side of the road. 'If there's anythun gets me down, it's havin' ter watch a funeral pass.'

'Won't be from 'ere,' he consoled. 'They took 'er away same evenun. It's gunna start from Jackson's Personal Service.'

'Good job she popped off at the beginnun of the week. They're not so personal at the week-end.'

She began to prepare for the journey to the dump. Pulled her frock down a bit. Slipped on a pair of shoes.

'Bet *She*'ll be relieved. Wouldn't show it, though. Not about 'er sister. I bet Daise stuck in 'er fuckun guts.'

Then Mrs Whalley was compelled to return to the window. As if her instinct. And sure enough there She was. Looking inside the letter-box, as if she hadn't collected already. Bent above the brick pillar in which the letter-box had been cemented, Mrs Hogben's face wore all that people expect of the bereaved.

'Daise was all right,' said Wal.

'Daise was all right,' agreed his wife.

Suddenly she wondered: What if Wal, if Wal had ever . . . ?

Mrs Whalley settled her hair. It she hadn't been all that satis-fied at home – and she *was* satisfied, her recollective eyes would admit – she too might have done a line like Daise Morrow.

Over the road Mrs Hogben was calling.

'Meg?' she called. 'Marg-*ret*?'

Though from pure habit, without direction. Her voice sounded thinner today.

Then Mrs Hogben went away.

'Once I got took to a funeral,' Mrs Whalley said. 'They made me look in the coffun. It was the bloke's wife. He was that cut up.'

'Did yer have a squint?'

'Pretended to.'

Wal Whalley was breathing hard in the airless room.

'How soon do yer reckon they begin ter smell?'

'Smell? They wouldn't let 'em!' his wife said very definite. 'You're the one that smells, Wal. I wonder you don't think of takin' a bath.'

But she liked his smell, for all that. It followed her out of the shadow into the strong shaft of light. Looking at each other their two bodies asserted themselves. Their faces were lit by the certainty of life.

Wal tweaked her left nipple.

'We'll slip inter the Bull on the way, and pick up those cold bottles.'

He spoke soft for him.

Mrs Hogben called another once or twice. Inside the brick entrance the cool of the house struck at her. She liked it cool, but not cold, and this was if not exactly cold, anyway, too sudden. So now she whimpered, very faintly, for everything you have to suffer, and death on top of all. Although it was her sister Daise who had died, Mrs Hogben was crying for the death which was waiting to carry her off in turn. She called: 'Me-ehg?' But no one ever came to your rescue. She stopped to loosen the soil round the roots of the aluminium plant. She always had to be doing something. It made her feel better.

Meg did not hear, of course. She was standing amongst the fuchsia bushes, looking out from their greenish shade. She was thin and freckly. She looked awful, because Mum had made her wear her uniform, because it was sort of a formal occasion, to Auntie Daise's funeral. In the circumstances she not only looked, but was thin. That Mrs Ireland who was all for sport had told her she must turn her toes out, and watch out – she might grow up knock-kneed besides.

So Meg Hogben was, and felt, altogether awful. Her skin was green, except when the war between light and shade worried her face into scraps, and the fuchsia tassels, trembling against her unknowing cheek, infused something of their own blood, brindled her with shifting crimson. Only her eyes resisted. They were not exactly an ordinary grey. Lorrae Jensen, who was blue, said they were the eyes of a mopey cat.

A bunch of six or seven kids from Second-Grade, Lorrae, Edna, Val, Sherry, Sue Smith and Sue Goldstein, stuck together in the holidays, though Meg sometimes wondered why. The others had come around to Hogbens' Tuesday evening.

Lorrae said: 'We're going down to Barranugli pool Thursday.

There's some boys Sherry knows with a couple of Gs. They've promised to take us for a run after we come out.'

Meg did not know whether she was glad or ashamed.

'I can't,' she said. 'My auntie's died.'

'Arrr!' their voices trailed.

They couldn't get away too quick, as if it had been something contagious.

But murmuring.

Meg sensed she had become temporarily important.

So now she was alone with her dead importance, in the fuchsia bushes, on the day of Auntie Daise's funeral. She had turned fourteen. She remembered the ring in plaited gold Auntie Daise had promised her. When I am gone, her aunt had said. And now it had really happened. Without rancour Meg suspected there hadn't been time to think about the ring, and Mum would grab it, to add to all the other things she had.

Then that Lummy Whalley showed up, amongst the camphor laurels opposite, tossing his head of bleached hair. She hated boys with white hair. For that matter she hated boys, or any intrusion on her privacy. She hated Lum most of all. The day he threw the dog poo at her. It made the gristle come in her neck. Ugh! Although the old poo had only skittered over her skin, too dry to really matter, she had gone in and cried because, well, there were times when she cultivated dignity.

Now Meg Hogben and Lummy Whalley did not notice each other even when they looked.

> 'Who wants Meg Skinny-leg?
> I'd rather take the clothes-peg . . .'

Lum Whalley vibrated like a comb-and-paper over amongst the camphor laurels they lopped back every so many years for firewood. He slashed with his knife into bark. Once in a hot dusk he had carved I LOVE MEG, because that was something you did, like on lavatory walls, and in the trains, but it didn't mean anything of course. Afterwards he slashed the darkness as if it had been a train seat.

Lum Whalley pretended not to watch Meg Hogben skulking in the fuchsia bushes. Wearing her brown uniform. Stiffer, browner than for school, because it was her auntie's funeral.

'Me-ehg?' called Mrs Hogben. 'Meg!'

'Lummy! Where the devil are yer?' called his mum.

She was calling all around, in the woodshed, behind the dunny. Let her!

'Lum? Lummy, for Chris*sake*!' she called.

He hated that. Like some bloody kid. At school he had got them to call him Bill, halfway between, not so shameful as Lum, nor yet as awful as William.

Mrs Whalley came round the corner.

'Shoutin' me bloody lungs up!' she said. 'When your dad's got a nice idea. We're goin' down to Sarsaparilla dump.'

'Arr!' he said.

But didn't spit.

'What gets inter you?' she asked.

Even at their most inaccessible Mrs Whalley liked to finger her children. Touch often assisted thought. But she liked the feel of them as well. She was glad she hadn't had girls. Boys turned into men, and you couldn't do without men, even when they took you for a mug, or got shickered, or bashed you up.

So she put her hand on Lummy, tried to get through to him. He was dressed, but might not have been. Lummy's kind was never ever born for clothes. At fourteen he looked more.

'Well,' she said, sourer than she felt, 'I'm not gunna cry over any sulky boy. Suit yourself.'

She moved off.

As Dad had got out the old rattle-bones by now, Lum began to clamber up. The back of the ute was at least private, though it wasn't no Customline.

The fact that Whalleys ran a Customline as well puzzled more unreasonable minds. Drawn up amongst the paspalum in front of Whalleys' shack, it looked stolen, and almost was – the third payment overdue. But would slither with ease a little longer to Barranugli, and snooze outside the Northern Hotel. Lum could have stood all day to admire their own two-tone car. Or would stretch out inside, his fingers at work on plastic flesh.

Now it was the ute for business. The bones of his buttocks bit into the boards. His father's meaty arm stuck out at the window, disgusting him. And soon the twins were squeezing from the rusty boiler. The taffy Gary – or was it Barry? had fallen down and barked his knee.

'For Chrissake!' Mrs Whalley shrieked, and tossed her identical taffy hair.

Mrs Hogben watched those Whalleys leave.

'In a brick area, I wouldn't of thought,' she remarked to her husband once again.

'All in good time, Myrtle,' Councillor Hogben replied as before.

'Of course,' she said, 'if there are *reasons*.'

Because councillors, she knew, did have reasons.

'But that home! And a Customline!'

The saliva of bitterness came in her mouth.

It was Daise who had said: I'm going to enjoy the good things of life – and died in that pokey little hutch, with only a cotton frock to her back. While Myrtle had the liver-coloured brick home – not a single dampmark on the ceilings – she had the washing machine, the septic, the TV, and the cream Holden Special, not to forget her husband. Les Hogben, the councillor. A builder into the bargain.

Now Myrtle stood amongst her things, and would have continued to regret the Ford the Whalleys hadn't paid for, if she hadn't been regretting Daise. It was not so much her sister's death as her life Mrs Hogben deplored. Still, everybody knew, and there was nothing you could do about it.

'Do you think anybody will come?' Mrs Hogben asked.

'What do you take me for?' her husband replied. 'One of these cleervoyants?'

Mrs Hogben did not hear.

After giving the matter consideration she had advertised the death in the *Herald*:

> MORROW, *Daisy (Mrs), suddenly, at her residence,*
> *Showground Road, Sarsaparilla.*

There was nothing more you could put. It wasn't fair on Les, a public servant, to rake up relationships. And the *Mrs* – well, everyone had got into the habit when Daise started going with Cunningham. It seemed sort of natural as things dragged on and on. Don't work yourself up, Myrt, Daise used to say; Jack will

196

when his wife dies. But it was Jack Cunningham who died first.
Daise said: It's the way it happened, that's all.

'Do you think Ossie will come?' Councillor Hogben asked
his wife slower than she liked.

'I hadn't thought about it,' she said.

Which meant she had. She had, in fact, woken in the night,
and lain there cold and stiff, as her mind's eye focused on
Ossie's runny nose.

Mrs Hogben rushed at a drawer which somebody – never
herself – had left hanging out. She was a thin woman, but wiry.

'Meg?' she called. 'Did you polish your shoes?'

Les Hogben laughed behind his closed mouth. He always did
when he thought of Daise's parting folly: to take up with that
old scabby deadbeat Ossie from down at the showground. But
who cared?

No one, unless her family.

Mrs Hogben dreaded the possibility of Ossie, a Roman Catholic
for extra value, standing beside Daise's grave, even if nobody,
even if only Mr Brickle saw.

Whenever the thought of Ossie Coogan crossed Councillor
Hogben's mind he would twist the knife in his sister-in-law.
Perhaps, now, he was glad she had died. A small woman, smaller
than his wife, Daise Morrow was large by nature. Whenever
she dropped in she was all around the place. Yarn her head off
if she got the chance. It got so as Les Hogben could not stand
hearing her laugh. Pressed against her in the hall once. He had
forgotten that, or almost. How Daise laughed then. I'm not so
short of men I'd pick me own brother-in-law. Had he pressed?
Not all that much, not intentional, anyway. So the incident had
been allowed to fade, dim as the brown-linoleum hall, in
Councillor Hogben's mind.

'There's the phone, Leslie.'

It was his wife.

'I'm too upset,' she said, 'to answer.'

And began to cry.

Easing his crutch Councillor Hogben went into the hall.

It was good old Horrie Last.

'Yairs ... yairs ...' said Mr Hogben, speaking into the
telephone which his wife kept swabbed with Breath-o'-Pine.

'Yairs . . . Eleven, Horrie . . . from Barranugli . . . from Jackson's Personal . . . Yairs, that's decent of you, Horrie.'

'Horrie Last,' Councillor Hogben reported to his wife, 'is gunna put in an appearance.'

If no one else, a second councillor for Daise. Myrtle Hogben was consoled.

What could you do? Horrie Last put down the phone. He and Les had stuck together. Teamed up to catch the more progressive vote. Hogben and Last had developed the shire. Les had built Horrie's home, Lasts had sold Hogbens theirs. If certain people were spreading the rumour that Last and Hogben had caused a contraction of the Green Belt, then certain people failed to realize the term itself implied flexibility.

'What did you tell them?' asked Mrs Last.

'Said I'd go,' her husband said, doing things to the change in his pocket.

He was a short man, given to standing with his legs apart.

Georgina Last withheld her reply. Formally of interest, her shape suggested she had been made out of several scones joined together in the baking.

'Daise Morrow,' said Horrie Last, 'wasn't such a bad sort.'

Mrs Last did not answer.

So he stirred the money in his pocket harder, hoping perhaps it would emulsify. He wasn't irritated, mind you, by his wife – who had brought him a parcel of property, as well as a flair for real estate – but had often felt he might have done a dash with Daise Morrow on the side. Wouldn't have minded betting old Les Hogben had tinkered a bit with his wife's sister. Helped her buy her home, they said. Always lights on at Daise's place after dark. Postman left her mail on the veranda instead of in the box. In summer, when the men went round to read the meters, she'd ask them in for a glass of beer. Daise knew how to get service.

Georgina Last cleared her throat.

'Funerals are not for women,' she declared, and took up a cardigan she was knitting for a cousin.

'You didn't do your shoes!' Mrs Hogben protested.

'I did,' said Meg. 'It's the dust. Don't know why we bother to clean shoes at all. They always get dirty again.'

She stood there looking awful in the school uniform. Her cheeks were hollow from what she read could only be despair.

'A person must keep to her principles,' Mrs Hogben said, and added: 'Dadda is bringing round the car. Where's your hat, dear? We'll be ready to leave in two minutes.'

'Arr, Mum! The hat?'

That old school hat. It had shrunk already a year ago, but had to see her through.

'You wear it to church, don't you?'

'But this isn't church!'

'It's as good as. Besides, you owe it to your aunt,' Mrs Hogben said, to win.

Meg went and got her hat. They were going out through the fuchsia bushes, past the plaster pixies, which Mrs Hogben had trained her child to cover with plastic at the first drops of rain. Meg Hogben hated the sight of those corny old pixies, even after the plastic cones had snuffed them out.

It was sad in the car, dreamier. As she sat looking out through the window, the tight panama perched on her head lost its power to humiliate. Her always persistent, grey eyes, under the line of dark fringe, had taken up the search again: she had never yet looked enough. Along the road they passed the house in which her aunt, they told her, had died. The small, pink, tilted house, standing amongst the carnation plants, had certainly lost some of its life. Or the glare had drained the colour from it. How the mornings used to sparkle in which Aunt Daise went up and down between the rows, her gown dragging heavy with dew, binding with bast the fuzzy flowers by handfuls and handfuls. Auntie's voice clear as morning. No one, she called, could argue they look stiff when they're bunched tight eh Meg what would you say they remind you of? But you never knew the answers to the sort of things people asked. Frozen fireworks, Daise suggested. Meg loved the idea of it, she loved Daise. Not so frozen either, she dared. The sun getting at the wet flowers broke them up and made them spin.

And the clovey scent rose up in the stale-smelling car, and smote Meg Hogben, out of the reeling heads of flowers, their cold stalks dusted with blue. Then she knew she would write a poem about Aunt Daise and the carnations. She wondered she hadn't thought of it before.

At that point the passengers were used most brutally as the car entered on a chain of potholes. For once Mrs Hogben failed to invoke the Main Roads Board. She was asking herself whether Ossie could be hiding in there behind the blinds. Or whether, whether. She fished for her second handkerchief. Prudence had induced her to bring two – the good one with the lace insertion for use beside the grave.

'The weeds will grow like one thing,' her voice blared, 'now that they'll have their way.'

Then she began to unfold the less important of her handkerchiefs.

Myrtle Morrow had always been the sensitive one. Myrtle had understood the Bible. Her needlework, her crochet doilys had taken prizes at country shows. No one had fiddled such pathos out of the pianola. It was Daise who loved flowers, though. It's a moss-rose, Daise had said, sort of rolling it round on her tongue, while she was still a little thing.

When she had had her cry, Mrs Hogben remarked: 'Girls don't know they're happy until it's too late.'

Thus addressed, the other occupants of the car did not answer. They knew they were not expected to.

Councillor Hogben drove in the direction of Barranugli. He had arranged his hat before leaving. He removed a smile the mirror reminded him was there. Although he no longer took any risks in a re-election photograph by venturing out cf the past, he often succeeded in the fleshy present. But now, in difficult circumstances, he was exercising his sense of duty. He drove, he drove, past the retinosperas, heavy with their own gold, past the lagerstroemias, their pink sugar running into mildew.

Down at the dump Whalleys were having an argument about whether the beer was to be drunk on arrival or after they had developed a thirst.

'Keep it, then!' Mum Whalley turned her back. 'What was the point of buyin' it cold if you gotta wait till it hots up? Anyways,' she said, 'I thought the beer was an excuse for comin'.'

'Arr, stuff it!' says Wal. 'A dump's business, ain't it? With or without beer. Ain't it? Any day of the week.'

He saw she had begun to sulk. He saw her rather long breasts floating around inside her dress. Silly cow! He laughed. But cracked a bottle.

Barry said he wanted a drink.

You could hear the sound of angry suction as his mum's lips called off a swig.

'I'm not gunna stand by and watch any kid of mine,' said the wet lips, 'turn 'isself into a bloody dipso!'

Her eyes were at their blazing bluest. Perhaps it was because Wal Whalley admired his wife that he continued to desire her.

But Lummy pushed off on his own. When his mum went crook, and swore, he was too aware of the stumps of teeth, the rotting brown of nastiness. It was different, of course, if you swore yourself. Sometimes it was unavoidable.

Now he avoided by slipping away, between the old mattresses, and boots the sun had buckled up. Pitfalls abounded: the rusty traps of open tins lay in wait for guiltless ankles, the necks of broken bottles might have been prepared to gash a face. So he went thoughtfully, his feet scuffing the leaves of stained asbestos, crunching the torso of a celluloid doll. Here and there it appeared as though trash might win. The onslaught of metal was pushing the scrub into the gully. But in many secret, steamy pockets, a rout was in progress: seeds had been sown in the lumps of grey, disintegrating kapok and the laps of burst chairs, the coils of springs, locked in the spirals of wirier vines, had surrendered to superior resilience. Somewhere on the edge of the whole shambles a human ally, before retiring, had lit a fire, which by now the green had almost choked, leaving a stench of smoke to compete with the sicklier one of slow corruption.

Lum Whalley walked with a grace of which he himself had never been aware. He had had about enough of this rubbish jazz. He would have liked to know how to live neat. Like Darkie Black. Everything in its place in the cabin of Darkie's trailer. Suddenly his throat yearned for Darkie's company. Darkie's hands, twisting the wheel, appeared to control the whole world.

A couple of strands of barbed wire separated Sarsaparilla dump from Sarsaparilla cemetery. The denominations were

PATRICK WHITE

separated too, but there you had to tell by the names, or by the
angels and things the RIPs went in for. Over in what must have
been the Church of England Alf Herbert was finishing Mrs
Morrow's grave. He had reached the clay, and the going was
heavy. The clods fell resentfully.

If what they said about Mrs Morrow was true, then she had
lived it up all right. Lum Whalley wondered what, supposing
he had met her walking towards him down a bush track, smiling.
His skin tingled. Lummy had never done a girl, although he
pretended he had, so as to hold his own with the kids. He wondered if a girl, if that sourpuss Meg Hogben. Would of bitten
as likely as not. Lummy felt a bit afraid, and returned to thinking
of Darkie Black, who never talked about things like that.

Presently he moved away. Alf Herbert, leaning on his shovel,
could have been in need of a yarn. Lummy was not prepared to
yarn. He turned back into the speckled bush, into the pretences
of a shade. He lay down under a banksia, and opened his fly
to look at himself. But pretty soon got sick of it.

The procession from Barranugli back to Sarsaparilla was hardly
what you would have called a procession: the Reverend Brickle,
the Hogben's Holden, Horrie's Holden, following the smaller
of Jackson's hearses. In the circumstances they were doing things
cheap – there was no reason for splashing it around. At Sarsaparilla Mr Gill joined in, sitting high in that old Chev. It would
have been practical, Councillor Hogben sighed, to join the
hearse at Sarsaparilla. Old Gill was only there on account of
Daise being his customer for years. A grocer lacking in enterprise, Daise had stuck to him, she said, because she liked him.
Well, if that was what you put first, but where did it get you?

At the last dip before the cemetery a disembowelled mattress
from the dump had begun to writhe across the road. It looked
like a kind of monster from out of the depths of somebody's
mind, the part a decent person ignored.

'Ah, dear! At the cemetery too!' Mrs Hogben protested. 'I
wonder the Council,' she added, in spite of her husband.

'All right, Myrtle,' he said between his teeth. 'I made a mental
note.'

Councillor Hogben was good at that.

202

'And the Whalleys on your own doorstep,' Mrs Hogben moaned.

The things she had seen on hot days, in front of their kiddies too.

The hearse had entered the cemetery gate. They had reached the bumpy stage toppling over the paspalum clumps, before the thinner, bush grass. All around, the leaves of the trees presented so many grey blades. Not even a magpie to put heart into a Christian. But Alf Herbert came forward, his hands dusted with yellow clay, to guide the hearse between the Methoes and the Presbyterians, onto Church of England ground.

Jolting had shaken Mrs Hogben's grief up to the surface again. Mr Brickle was impressed. He spoke for a moment of the near and dear. His hands were kind and professional in helping her out.

But Meg jumped. And landed. It was a shock to hear a stick crack so loud. Perhaps it was what Mum would have called irreverent. At the same time her banana-coloured panama fell off her head into the tussocks.

It was really a bit confusing at the grave. Some of the men helped with the coffin, and Councillor Last was far too short.

Then Mrs Hogben saw, she saw, from out of the lace handkerchief, it was that Ossie Coogan she saw, standing the other side of the grave. Had old Gill given him a lift? Ossie, only indifferently buttoned, stood snivelling behind the mound of yellow clay.

Nothing would have stopped his nose. Daise used to say: You don't want to be frightened, Ossie, not when I'm here, see? But she wasn't any longer. So now he was afraid. Excepting Daise, Protestants had always frightened him. Well, I'm nothing, she used to say, nothing that you could pigeonhole, but love what we are given to love.

Myrtle Hogben was ropeable, if only because of what Councillor Last must think. She would have liked to express her feelings in words, if she could have done so without giving offence to God. Then the ants ran up her legs, for she was standing on a nest, and her body cringed before the teeming injustices.

Daise, she had protested the day it all began, whatever has come over you? The sight of her sister had made her run out leaving the white sauce to burn. Wherever will you take him? He's sick, said Daise. *But you can't*, Myrtle Hogben cried. For there was her sister Daise pushing some old deadbeat in a barrow. All along Showground Road people had come out of homes to look. Daise appeared smaller pushing the wheelbarrow down the hollow and up the hill. Her hair was half uncoiled. *You can't! You can't!* Myrtle called. But Daise could, and did.

When all the few people were assembled at the graveside in their good clothes, Mr Brickle opened the book, though his voice soon suggested he needn't have.

'*I am the resurrection and the life,*' he said.

And Ossie cried. Because he didn't believe it, not when it came to the real thing.

He looked down at the coffin, which was what remained of what he knew. He remembered eating a baked apple, very slowly, the toffee on it. And again the dark of the horse-stall swallowed him up, where he lay hopeless amongst the shit, and her coming at him with the barrow. What do you want? he asked straight out. I came down to the showground, she said, for a bit of honest-to-God manure, I've had those fertilizers, she said, and what are you, are you sick? I live 'ere, he said. And began to cry, and rub the snot from his snivelly nose. After a bit Daise said: We're going back to my place, What's-yer-Name – Ossie. The way she spoke he knew it was true. All the way up the hill in the barrow the wind was giving his eyes gyp, and blowing his thin hair apart. Over the years he had come across one or two lice in his hair, but thought, or hoped he had got rid of them by the time Daise took him up. As she pushed and struggled with the barrow, sometimes she would lean forward, and he felt her warmth, her firm diddies pressed against his back.

'*Lord, let me know mine end, and the number of my days: that I may be certified how long I have to live,*' Mr Brickle read.

Certified was the word, decided Councillor Hogben looking at that old Ossie.

Who stood there mumbling a few Aspirations, very quiet, on the strength of what they had taught him as a boy.

When all this was under way, all these words of which, she knew, her Auntie Daise would not have approved, Meg Hogben went and got beneath the strands of wire separating the cemetery from the dump. She had never been to the dump before, and her heart was lively in her side. She walked shyly through the bush. She came across an old suspender-belt. She stumbled over a blackened primus.

She saw Lummy Whalley then. He was standing under a banksia, twisting at one of its dead heads.

Suddenly they knew there was something neither of them could continue to avoid.

'I came here to the funeral,' she said.

She sounded, well, almost relieved.

'Do you come here often?' she asked.

'Nah,' he answered, hoarse. 'Not here. To dumps, yes.'

But her intrusion had destroyed the predetermined ceremony of his life, and caused a trembling in his hand.

'Is there anything to see?' she asked.

'Junk,' he said. 'Same old junk.'

'Have you ever looked at a dead person?'

Because she noticed the trembling of his hand.

'No,' he said. 'Have you?'

She hadn't. Nor did it seem probable that she would have to now. Not as they began breathing evenly again.

'What do you do with yourself?' he asked.

Then, even though she would have liked to stop herself, she could not. She said: 'I write poems. I'm going to write one about my Aunt Daise, like she was, gathering carnations early in the dew.'

'What'll you get out of that?'

'Nothing,' she said, 'I suppose.'

But it did not matter.

'What other sorts of pomes do you write?' he asked, twisting at last the dead head of the banksia off.

'I wrote one,' she said, 'about the things in a cupboard. I wrote about a dream I had. And the smell of rain. That was a bit too short.'

He began to look at her then. He had never looked into the eyes of a girl. They were grey and cool, unlike the hot, or burnt-out eyes of a women.

'What are you going to be?' she asked.

'I dunno.'

'You're not a white-collar type.'

'Eh?'

'I mean you're not for figures, and books, and banks and offices,' she said.

He was too disgusted to agree.

'I'm gunna have me own truck. Like Mr Black. Darkie's got a trailer.'

'What?'

'Well,' he said, 'a semi-trailer.'

'Oh,' she said, more diffident.

'Darkie took me on a trip to Maryborough. It was pretty tough goin'. Sometimes we drove right through the night. Sometimes we slept on the road. Or in places where you get rooms. Gee, it was good though, shootin' through the country towns at night.'

She saw it. She saw the people standing at their doors, frozen in the blocks of yellow light. The rushing of the night made the figures for ever still. All around she could feel the furry darkness, as the semi-trailer roared and bucked, its skeleton of coloured lights. While in the cabin, in which they sat, all was stability and order. If she glanced sideways she could see how his taffy hair shone when raked by the bursts of electric light. They had brought cases with tooth-brushes, combs, one or two things – the pad on which she would write the poem somewhere when they stopped in the smell of sunlight dust ants. But his hands had acquired such mastery over the wheel, it appeared this might never happen. Nor did she care.

'This Mr Black,' she said, her mouth getting thinner, 'does he take you with him often?'

'Only once interstate,' said Lummy, pitching the banksia head away. 'Once in a while short trips.'

As they drove they rocked together. He had never been closer to anyone than when bumping against Darkie's ribs. He waited to experience again the little spasm of gratitude and pleasure. He would have liked to wear, and would in time, a striped sweatshirt like Darkie wore.

'I'd like to go in with Darkie,' he said, 'when I get a trailer of me own. Darkie's the best friend I got.'

With a drawn-out shiver of distrust she saw the darker hands, the little black hairs on the backs of the fingers.

'Oh, well,' she said, withdrawn, 'praps you will in the end,' she said.

On the surrounding graves the brown flowers stood in their jars of browner water. The more top-heavy, plastic bunches had been slapped down by a westerly, but had not come to worse grief than to lie strewn in pale disorder on the uncharitable granite chips.

The heat made Councillor Last yawn. He began to read the carved names, those within sight at least, some of which he had just about forgot. He almost laughed once. If the dead could have sat up in their graves there would have been an argument or two.

'*In the midst of life we are in death,*' said the parson bloke.

JACK CUNNINGHAM
BELOVED HUSBAND OF FLORENCE MARY,

read Horrie Last.

Who would have thought Cunningham, straight as a silkyoak, would fall going up the path to Daise Morrow's place. Horrie used to watch them together, sitting a while on the veranda before going in to their tea. They made no bones about it, because everybody knew. Good teeth Cunningham had. Always a white, well-ironed shirt. Wonder which of the ladies did the laundry. Florence Mary was an invalid, they said. Daise Morrow liked to laugh with men, but for Jack Cunningham she had a silence, promising intimacies at which Horrie Last could only guess, whose own private life had been lived in almost total darkness.

Good Christ, and then there was Ossie. The woman could only have been at heart a perv of a kind you hadn't heard about.

'*Forasmuch as it hath pleased Almighty God of his great mercy to take unto himself the soul . . .*' read Mr Brickle.

As it was doubtful who should cast the earth, Mr Gill the grocer did. They heard the handful rattle on the coffin.

Then the tears truly ran out of Ossie's scaly eyes. Out of darkness. Out of darkness Daise had called: What's up, Ossie, you don't wanta cry. I got the cramps, he answered. They were twisting him. The cramps? she said drowsily. Or do you imagine? If it isn't the cramps it's something else. Could have been. He'd take Daise's word for it. He was never all that bright since he had the meningitis. Tell you what, Daise said, you come in here, into my bed, I'll warm you, Os, in a jiffy. He listened in the dark to his own snivelling. Arr, Daise, I couldn't, he said, I couldn't get a stand, not if you was to give me the jackpot, he said. She sounded very still then. He lay and counted the throbbing of the darkness. Not like that, she said – she didn't laugh at him as he had half expected – besides, she said, it only ever really comes to you once. That way. And at once he was parting the darkness, bumping and shambling, to get to her. He had never known it so gentle. Because Daise wasn't afraid. She ran her hands through his hair, on and on like water flowing. She soothed the cramps out of his legs. Until in the end they were breathing in time. Dozing. Then the lad Ossie Coogan rode again down from the mountain, the sound of the snaffle in the blue air, the smell of sweat from under the saddle-cloth, towards the great, flowing river. He rocked and flowed with the motion of the strong, never-ending river, burying his mouth in brown cool water, to drown would have been worth it.

Once during the night Ossie had woken, afraid the distance might have come between them. But Daise was still holding him againt her breast. If he had been different, say. Ossie's throat had begun to wobble. Only then, Daise, Daise might have turned different. So he nuzzled against the warm darkness, and was again received.

'If you want to enough, you can do what you want,' Meg Hogben insisted.

She had read it in a book, and wasn't altogether convinced, but theories sometimes come to the rescue.

'If you want,' she said, kicking a hole in the stony ground.

'Not everything you can't.'

'You can!' she said. 'But you can!'

She who had never looked at a boy, not right into one, was looking at him as never before.

'That's a lot of crap,' he said.

'Well,' she admitted, 'there are limits.'

It made him frown. He was again suspicious. She was acting clever. All those pomes.

But to reach understanding she would have surrendered her cleverness. She was no longer proud of it.

'And what'll happen if you get married? Riding around the country in a truck. How'll your wife like it? Stuck at home with a lot of kids.'

'Some of 'em take the wife along. Darkie takes his missus and kids. Not always, like. But now and again. On short runs.'

'You didn't tell me Mr Black was married.'

'Can't tell you everything, can I? Not at once.'

The women who sat in the drivers' cabins of the semi-trailers he saw as predominantly thin and dark. They seldom returned glances, but wiped their hands on Kleenex, and peered into little mirrors, waiting for their men to show up again. Which in time they had to. So he walked across from the service station, to take possession of his property. Sauntering, frowning slightly, touching the yellow stubble on his chin, he did not bother to look. Glanced sideways perhaps. She was the thinnest, the darkest he knew, the coolest of all the women who sat looking out from the cabin windows of the semi-trailers.

In the meantime they strolled a bit, amongst the rusty tins at Sarsaparilla dump. He broke a few sticks and threw away the pieces. She tore off a narrow leaf and smelled it. She would have liked to smell Lummy's hair.

'Gee, you're fair,' she had to say.

'Some are born fair,' he admitted.

He began pelting a rock with stones. He was strong, she saw. So many discoveries in a short while were making her tremble at the knees.

And as they rushed through the brilliant light, roaring and lurching, the cabin filled with fair-skinned, taffy children, the youngest of whom she was protecting by holding the palm of her hand behind his neck, as she had noticed women do. Occupied in this way, she almost forgot Lum at times, who would pull up, and she would climb down, to rinse the nappies in tepid water, and hang them on a bush to dry.

'All these pomes and things, he said,' 'I never knew a clever person before.'

'But clever isn't any different,' she begged, afraid he might not accept her peculiarity and power.

She would go with a desperate wariness from now. She sensed that, if not in years, she was older than Lum, but this was the secret he must never guess: that for all his strength, all his beauty, she was, and must remain the stronger.

'What's that?' he asked, and touched.

But drew back his hand in self-protection.

'A scar,' she said. 'I cut my wrist opening a tin of condensed milk.'

For once she was glad of the paler seam in her freckled skin, hoping that it might heal a breach.

And he looked at her out of his hard blue Whalley eyes. He liked her. Although she was ugly, and clever, and a girl.

'Condensed milk on bread,' he said, 'that's something I could eat till I bust.'

'Oh, yes!' she agreed.

She did honestly believe, although she had never thought of it before.

Flies clustered in irregular jet embroideries on the backs of best suits. Nobody bothered any longer to shrug them off. As Alf Herbert grunted against the shovelfuls, dust clogged increasingly, promises settled thicker. Although they had been told they might expect Christ to redeem, it would have been no less incongruous if He had appeared out of the scrub to perform on altars of burning sandstone a sacrifice for which nobody had prepared them. In any case, the mourners waited – they had been taught to accept whatever might be imposed – while the heat stupefied the remnants of their minds, and inflated their Australian fingers into foreign-looking sausages.

Myrtle Hogben was the first to protest. She broke down – into the wrong handkerchief. *Who shall change our vile body?* The words were more than her decency could bear.

'Easy on it,' her husband whispered, putting a finger under her elbow.

210

She submitted to his sympathy, just as in their life together she had submitted to his darker wishes. Never wanting more than peace, and one or two perquisites.

A thin woman, Mrs Hogben continued to cry for all the wrongs that had been done her. For Daise had only made things viler. While understanding, yes, at moments. It was girls who really understood, not even women – sisters, sisters. Before events whirled them apart. So Myrtle Morrow was again walking through the orchard, and Daise Morrow twined her arm around her sister, confession filled the air, together with a scent of crushed, fermenting apples. Myrtle said: Daise, there's something I'd like to do, I'd like to chuck a lemon into a Salvation Army tuba. Daise giggled. You're a nut, Myrt, she said. But never *vile*. So Myrtle Hogben cried. Once, only once she had thought how she'd like to push someone off a cliff, and watch their expression as it happened. But Myrtle had not confessed that.

So Mrs Hogben cried, for those things she was unable to confess, for anything she might not be able to control.

As the blander words had begun falling, *Our Father*, that she knew by heart, *our daily bread*, she should have felt comforted. She should of. Should of.

Where was Meg, though?

Mrs Hogben separated herself from the others. Walking stiffly. If any of the men noticed, they took it for granted she had been overcome, or wanted to relieve herself.

She would have liked to relieve herself by calling: 'Margret, Meg wherever don't you hear me Me-ehg?' drawing it out thin in anger. But could not cut across a clergyman's words. So she stalked. She was not unlike a guinea-hen, its spotted silk catching on a strand of barbed-wire.

When they had walked a little farther, round and about, anywhere, they overheard voices.

'What's that?' asked Meg.

'Me mum and dad,' Lummy said. 'Rousin' about somethun or other.'

Mum Whalley had just found two bottles of unopened beer. Down at the dump. Waddayaknow. Must be something screwy somewhere.

'Could of put poison in it,' her husband warned.

'Poison? My arse!' she shouted. 'That's because *I* found it!'

'Whoever found it,' he said, 'who's gunna drink a coupla bottlesa hot beer?'

'I am!' she said.

'When what we brought was good an' cold?'

He too was shouting a bit. She behaved unreasonable at times.

'Who wanted ter keep what we brought? Till it got good an' hot!' she shrieked.

Sweat was running down both the Whalleys.

Suddenly Lum felt he wanted to lead this girl out of earshot. He had just about had the drunken sods. He would have liked to find himself walking with his girl over mown lawn, like at the Botanical Gardens, a green turf giving beneath their leisured feet. Statues pointed a way through the glare, to where they finally sat, under enormous shiny leaves, looking out at boats on water. They unpacked their cut lunch from its layers of fresh tissue-paper.

'They're rough as bags,' Lummy explained.

'I don't care,' Meg Hogben assured.

Nothing on earth could make her care – was it more, or was it less?

She walked giddily behind him, past a rusted fuel-stove, over a field of deathly feltex. Or ran, or slid, to keep up. Flowers would have wilted in her hands, if she hadn't crushed them brutally, to keep her balance. Somewhere in their private labyrinth Meg Hogben had lost her hat.

When they were farther from the scene of anger, and a silence of heat had descended again, he took her little finger, because it seemed natural to do so, after all they had experienced. They swung hands for a while, according to some special law of motion.

Till Lum Whalley frowned, and threw the girl's hand away.

If she accepted his behaviour it was because she no longer believed in what he did, only in what she knew he felt. That might have been the trouble. She was so horribly sure, he would have to resist to the last moment of all. As a bird, singing in the prickly tree under which they found themselves standing, seemed to cling to the air. Then his fingers took control. She was amazed at the hardness of his boy's body. The tremors of her flinty skin, the membrane of the white sky appalled him. Before fright and expectation melted their mouths. And they took little grateful sips of each other. Holding up their throats in between. Like birds drinking.

Ossie could no longer see Alf Herbert's shovel working at the earth.

'Never knew a man cry at a funeral,' Councillor Hogben complained, very low, although he was ripe enough to burst.

If you could count Ossie as a man, Councillor Last suggested in a couple of noises.

But Ossie could not see or hear, only Daise, still lying on that upheaval of a bed. Seemed she must have burst a button, for her breasts stood out from her. He would never forget how they laboured against the heavy yellow morning light. In the early light, the flesh turned yellow, sluggish. What's gunna happen to me, Daisy? It'll be decided, Os, she said, like it is for any of us. I ought to know, she said, to tell you, but give me time to rest a bit, to get me breath. Then he got down on his painful knees. He put his mouth to Daise's neck. Her skin tasted terrible bitter. The great glistening river, to which the lad Ossie Coogan had ridden jingling down from the mountain, was slowing into thick, yellow mud. Himself an old, scabby man attempting to refresh his forehead in the last pothole.

Mr Brickle said: '*We give thee hearty thanks for that it hath pleased thee to deliver this our sister out of the miseries of this sinful world.*'

'No! No!' Ossie protested, so choked nobody heard, though it was vehement enough in its intention.

As far as he could understand, nobody wanted to be delivered. Not him, not Daise, anyways. When you could sit together by the fire on winter nights baking potatoes under the ashes.

It took Mrs Hogben some little while to free her *crêpe de Chine* from the wire. It was her nerves, not to mention Meg on her mind. In the circumstances she tore herself worse, and looked up to see her child, just over there, without shame, in a rubbish tip, kissing with the Whalley boy. What if Meg was another of Daise? It was in the blood, you couldn't deny.

Mrs Hogben did not exactly call, but released some kind of noise from her extended throat. Her mouth was too full of tongue to find room for words as well.

Then Meg looked. She was smiling.

She said: 'Yes, Mother.'

She came and got through the wire, tearing herself also a little.

Mrs Hogben said, and her teeth clicked: 'You chose the likeliest time. Your aunt hardly in her grave. Though, of course, it is only your aunt, if anyone, to blame.'

The accusations were falling fast. Meg could not answer. Since joy had laid her open, she had forgotten how to defend herself.

'If you were a little bit younger' – Mrs Hogben lowered her voice because they had begun to approach the parson – 'I'd break a stick on you, my girl.'

Meg tried to close her face, so that nobody would see inside.

'What will they say?' Mrs Hogben moaned. 'What ever will happen to us?'

'What, Mother?' Meg asked.

'You're the only one can answer that. And someone else.'

Then Meg looked over her shoulder and recognized the hate which, for a while she had forgotten existed. And at once her face closed up tight, like a first. She was ready to protect whatever justly needed her protection.

Even if their rage, grief, contempt, boredom, apathy, and sense of injustice had not occupied the mourners, it is doubtful whether they would have realized the dead woman was standing amongst them. The risen dead – that was something which happened, or didn't happen, in the Bible. Fanfares of light did not blare for a loose woman in floral cotton. Those who had known her remembered her by now only fitfully in some of the wooden attitudes of life. How could they have heard, let alone believed in, her affirmation? Yet Daise Morrow continued to proclaim.

Listen, all of you, I'm not leaving, except those who want to be left, and even those aren't so sure – they might be parting with a bit of themselves. Listen to me, all you successful no-hopers, all you who wake in the night, jittery because something may be escaping you, or terrified to think there may never have been anything to find. Come to me, you sour women, public servants, anxious children, and old scabby, desperate men . . .

Physically small, words had seemed too big for her. She would push back her hair in exasperation. And take refuge in acts. Because her feet had been planted in the earth, she would have been the last to resent its pressure now, while her always rather hoarse voice continued to exhort in borrowed syllables of dust.

Truly, we needn't experience tortures, unless we build chambers in our minds to house instruments of hatred in. Don't you know, my darling creatures, that death isn't death, unless it's the death of love? Love should be the greatest explosion it is reasonable to expect. Which sends us whirling, spinning, creating millions of other worlds. Never destroying.

From the fresh mound which they had formed unimaginatively in the shape of her earthly body, she persisted in appealing to them.

I will comfort you. If you will let me. Do you understand?

But nobody did, as they were only human.

For ever and ever. And ever.

Leaves quivered lifted in the first suggestion of a breeze.

So the aspirations of Daise Morrow were laid alongside her small-boned wrists, smooth thighs and pretty ankles. She surrendered at last to the formal crumbling which, it was hoped, would make an honest woman of her.

But had not altogether died.

Meg Hogben had never exactly succeeded in interpreting her aunt's messages, nor could she have witnessed the last moments of the burial, because the sun was dazzling her. She did experience, however, along with a shiver of recollected joy, the down laid against her cheek, a little breeze trickling through the moist roots of her hair, as she got inside the car, and waited for whatever next.

Well, they had dumped Daise.

Somewhere the other side of the wire there was the sound of smashed glass and discussion.

Councillor Hogben went across to the parson and said the

right kind of things. Half-turning his back he took a note or two from his wallet, and immediately felt disengaged. If Horrie Last had been there Les Hogben would have gone back at this point and put an arm around his mate's shoulder, to feel whether he was forgiven for unorthodox behaviour in a certain individual – no relation, mind you, but. In any case Horrie had driven away.

Horrie drove, or flew, across the dip in which the dump joined the cemetery. For a second Ossie Coogan's back flickered inside a spiral of dust.

Ought to give the coot a lift, Councillor Last suspected, and wondered, as he drove on, whether a man's better intentions were worth, say, half a mark in the event of their remaining unfulfilled. For by now it was far too late to stop, and there was that Ossie, in the mirror, turning off the road towards the dump, where, after all, the bugger belonged.

All along the road, stones, dust, and leaves, were settling back into normally unemotional focus. Seated in his high Chev, Gill the grocer, a slow man, who carried his change in a little, soiled canvas bag, looked ahead through thick lenses. He was relieved to realize he would reach home almost on the dot of three-thirty, and his wife pour him his cup of tea. Whatever he understood was punctual, decent, docketed.

As he drove, prudently, he avoided the mattress the dump had spewed, from under the wire, half across the road. Strange things had happened at the dump on and off, the grocer recollected. Screaming girls, their long tight pants ripped to tatters. An arm in a sugar-bag, and not a sign of the body that went with it. Yet some found peace amongst the refuse; elderly derelict men, whose pale, dead, fish eyes never divulged anything of what they had lived, and women with blue, metho skins, hanging around the doors of shacks put together from sheets of bark and rusty iron. Once an old downandout had crawled amongst the rubbish apparently to rot, and did, before they sent for the constable, to examine what seemed at first a bundle of stinking rags.

Mr Gill, accelerated judiciously.

They were driving. They were driving.

Alone in the back of the ute, Lum Whalley sat forward on the empty crate, locking his hands between his knees, as he forgot having seen Darkie do. He was completely independent now. His face had been reshaped by the wind. He liked that. It felt good. He no longer resented the junk they were dragging home, the rust flaking off at his feet, the roll of mouldy feltex trying to fur his nostrils up. Nor his family – discussing, or quarrelling, you could never tell – behind him in the cabin.

The Whalleys were in fact singing. One of their own versions. They always sang their own versions, the two little boys joining in.

> '*Show me the way to go home,*
> *I'm not too tired for bed.*
> *I had a little drink about an hour ago,*
> *And it put ideas in me head . . .*'

Suddenly Mum Whalley began belting into young Gary – or was it Barry?

'Wadda *you* know, eh? Wadda *you?*'

'What's bitten yer?' her husband shouted. 'Can't touch a drop without yer turn nasty!'

She didn't answer. He could tell a grouse was coming, though. The little boy had started to cry, but only as a formality.

'It's that bloody Lummy,' Mrs Whalley complained.

'Why pick on Lum?'

'Give a kid all the love and affection, and waddayaget?'

Wal grunted. Abstractions always embarrassed him.

Mum Whalley spat out of the window, and the spit came back at her.

'Arrrr!' she protested.

And fell silenter. It was not strictly Lum, not if you was honest. It was nothing. Or everything. The grog. You was never ever gunna touch it no more. Until you did. And that bloody Lummy, what with the caesar and all, you was never ever going again with a man.

'That's somethink a man don't understand.'

'What?' asked Wal.

'A caesar.'

'Eh?'

You just couldn't discuss with a man. So you had to get into

217

bed with him. Grogged up half the time. That was how she copped the twins, after she had said never ever.

'Stop cryun, for Chrissake!' Mum Whalley coaxed, touching the little boy's blowing hair.

Everything was sad.

'Wonder how often they bury someone alive,' she said.

Taking a corner in his cream Holden Councillor Hogben felt quite rakish, but would restrain himself at the critical moment from skidding the wrong side of the law.

They were driving and driving, in long, lovely bursts, and at the corners, in semi-circular swirls.

On those occasions in her life when she tried to pray, begging for an experience, Meg Hogben would fail, but return to the attempt with clenched teeth. Now she did so want to think of her dead aunt with love, and the image blurred repeatedly. She was superficial, that was it. Yet, each time she failed, the land-scape leaped lovingly. They were driving under the telephone wires. She could have translated any message into the language of peace. The wind burning, whenever it did not cut cold, left the stable things alone: the wooden houses stuck beside the road, the trunks of willows standing round the brown saucer of a dam. Her too candid, grey eyes seemed to have deepened, as though to accommodate all she still had to see, feel.

It was lovely curled on the back seat, even with Mum and Dad in front.

'I haven't forgotten, Margret,' Mum called over her shoulder.

Fortunately Dadda wasn't interested enough to inquire.

'Did Daise owe anything on the home?' Mrs Hogben asked. 'She was never at all practical.'

Councillor Hogben cleared his throat.

'Give us time to find out,' he said.

Mrs Hogben respected her husband for the things which she, secretly, did not understand: Time the mysterious, for instance, Business, and worst of all, the Valuer General.

'I wonder Jack Cunningham,' she said, 'took up with Daise. He was a fine man. Though Daise had a way with her.'

They were driving. They were driving.

When Mrs Hogben remembered the little ring in plaited gold.

'Do you think those undertakers are honest?'

'Honest?' her husband repeated.

A dubious word.

'Yes,' she said. 'That ring that Daise.'

You couldn't very well accuse. When she had plucked up the courage she would go down to the closed house. The thought of it made her chest tighten. She would go inside, and feel her way into the back corners of drawers, where perhaps a twist of tissue-paper. But the closed houses of the dead frightened Mrs Hogben, she had to admit. The stuffiness, the light strained through brown holland. It was as if you were stealing, though you weren't.

And then those Whalley's creeping up.

They were driving and driving, the ute and the sedan almost rubbing on each other.

'No one who hasn't had a migraine,' cried Mrs Hogben, averting her face, 'can guess what it feels like.'

Her husband had heard that before.

'It's a wonder it don't leave you,' he said. 'They say it does when you've passed a certain age.'

Though they weren't passing the Whalleys he would make every effort to throw the situation off. Wal Whalley leaning forward, though not so far you couldn't see the hair bursting out of the front of his shirt. His wife thumping his shoulder. They were singing one of their own versions. Her gums all watery.

So they drove and drove.

'I could sick up, Leslie,' Mrs Hogben gulped, and fished for her lesser handkerchief.

The Whalley twins were laughing through their taffy forelocks.

At the back of the ute that sulky Lum turned towards the opposite direction. Meg Hogben was looking her farthest off. Any sign of acknowledgement had been so faint the wind had immediately blown it off their faces. As Meg and Lummy sat, they held their sharp, but comforting knees. They sank their chins as low as they would go. They lowered their eyes, as if they had seen enough for the present, and wished to cherish what they knew.

The warm core of certainty settled stiller as driving faster the wind payed out the telephone wires the fences the flattened heads of grey grass always raising themselves again again again again.

Elizabeth Harrower

ENGLISH LESSON

So after a little indecision, and baring her teeth at the letter-box, Laura posted the letter. It dropped from her fingers, slid out of her control. She felt an instant's blank surprise as if the letter fell in her. Then she thought: oh well, that's done. And went away from the red letter-box, across the road and into the park, harkening all the while to Leslie's difficult conversation. It was about himself. Surrounded by invisible lime trees, skirting the invisible pond and boys playing cricket, he addressed her right ear. She forgot the letter.

It was not important. She did not think it was important. But sensible people thought it was sensible to write it and send it. They sank back with folded hands on hearing that their will had been done, bereft not of the *right* to bully (for what thing is that?) but of the stuff, the wherewithal. Their will was done.

And alack! They were deprived. Their satisfaction was frustration before their very eyes.

As for Laura – touch me not; lay no further words on me. I have gone your way. I am not assailable.

The letter was written, the ground cut from beneath the feet of sensible persons. They champed gloomily and searched as if waiting for specific things though they were not. Unless the return of their reason for living.

It was only a sort of business letter to a man who was purported to look after Laura's interests. She told him some news and asked for some advice. She had no idea what he was like, but he was purported to be looking after her interests. Anyway, the letter was polite. Laura wondered if it might not be ingenuous. Advisers set their jaws uncertainly when she allowed them to infer this. *No*, they said tremulously. He has some obligations towards you.

(*Had he?*)

What else is he for? they insisted.

No one answered.

Laura put discussions and well-phrased paragraphs behind her. After all, this was not the only thing in her life. The doing, the acquiescence, had pacified the country for miles around. Concord – everyone to be, if not happy, at least not looking bitter thoughts at people – is more to some natures than others. She would seem ingenuous or even quite peculiar if necessary, to any number of business men, for concord's sake. It was a question of what mattered most to whom. And how she appeared and what she did mattered little to her. And that obligations were nicely fulfilled in all directions mattered much to others. A bun for a bun.

All that happened was that the man had been given a chance to say: Dear Laura, Yes. (Or, alternatively, No. Or practically anything.) An amiable exchange. Concord. Folded hands. For her – no words. For them – incipient, approaching satisfaction *here*.

And non-existent.

Propelled by Leslie, the letters skated on the glossy starched tablecloth. Last down for breakfast, acting postman, he had delivered mail at five other tables. Laura had watched him: American in a strange land and het up about it. Conspicuous and glad to be. Trying not to seem contemptuous of inferior Anglo-Saxon ways and not succeeding. Bearing his prodigious education heavily. And uneasy. Uneasy.

Airmail striped red-white-and-blue. A catalogue with pictures of Italian shoes in it.

Oh. And that one.

Leslie recognized it, too, and languidly expressed his fore-knowledge that it contained the most sanguine of replies. He stirred his coffee and shook salt and pepper over his plate.

Laura read the letter, and her surroundings vanished.

Pausing over his egg, inviting news, Leslie as it were paused a second time. Yet again he paused and looked at Laura. Then he took the letter up, read it and replaced it on the table.

Laura's hand lay on her bare collarbone. The bone was scorching. Indeed, her whole body burned, recoiled, retreated from her skeleton. She had been insulted. Someone almost a stranger had hit her across the face. *Why?*

Unable to raise their eyes from the flip little note, the two spoke simultaneously and, it might as well have been, in a language foreign to both and understood by neither. The dining room was submerged fathoms deep. Everything echoed.

What the motive? Where the wit? Why the knife in the ribs? What had she done? Almost total strangers . . . Surfacing briefly, Laura began to say words in English to Leslie, and he spoke back to her in American, and they were able to hear each other with difficulty, very faintly.

For years unconvincing examples had been reported in books of human beings reeling under blows. Laura reeled, literally dizzy. Yet she had never been a sheltered person! Still, though she had known real malevolence and survived it, she was awed by the malice of the note. Its very littleness, its unexpectedness, its having less than no reason to it, made it strange.

Her heart hammered. She was insufficiently acquainted with physiology to know what else was happening inside her because of a dozen casual words, but she was learning. For instance, an insult recorded by the eye could cause an entire organism to react as though it had been violently smitten with an axe.

Consider calmly. Had she not been insulted in the old days many times, and borne it with an even mind? Why the fuss now? Today? Yes, but rarely, never by anyone she cared about; never by anyone who cared about her. (She temporarily shelved this remarkable and complicated fact, merely giving it a startled look in passing.) But she and this man did not know each other! No question of emotion one way or the other! . . . Anyway. Anyway, she was grateful to have been reminded what it felt like to be angry. She had forgotten. It was interesting, too, to find that a man could be so . . .

Oh, *was* it? Was it? Let the world, the walls of this room and these rickety bits of furniture understand: she felt herself to have been insulted! What use all this retaliatory chatter with Leslie's American accent over poached eggs? She was anguished, struck back, hacked to the ground. The man's very unknownness made it seem that the universe had gratuitously spoken against her.

Nothing but today's lecture would have drawn Leslie from the fascinating case she represented to him. Laura rallied him, urging him to go, groaning soft asides to her spirit till she would be free to attend to its wounds. Reluctantly, he analyzed his way to the front door and disappeared. He would like to have *studied* . . .

Upstairs, distraught, holding herself with her arms, stopping now and then to read the note again, Laura trailed about her room.

And yet wasn't her behaviour extreme? *Think*. A moment's spite, ennui, thought of private troubles, on the part of a man she hardly knew, and this reaction. Come . . .

Unexpected, unexpected, uncalled for, unprovoked, unkind, unusual, unbearable . . . She had a second shower and dressed again. Unusual, unexpected, uncalled for . . . She looked in no mirrors.

Most peculiar (she addressed herself chattily) but I understand that this is how people start ulcers. Her body was considering whether or not to begin one. A true story she had once heard of a man who had a heart-attack and died when his special restaurant table was given to a stranger made sense. If you were old and so indignant, you could die of it.

In the communal kitchen she tried to drown herself with cup after cup of coffee. She ate a large piece of stale cake. In her room, on the bed, she read *The Fall*, splitting her mind neatly in two so that she at one and the same time debated that novel, and gently humoured her fevered spirit, whispering softly and soothing it.

She finished that book and started another. Oh, my heart, my heart, she thought, through its pounding. The insult was hours old, yet the heavy thuds would not abate for cake or Camus.

People (the unshaken Laura addressed her languishing body with an increasing hardness and lack of sympathy) are insulted every day. Salesmen. Politicians. All kinds of people. Did they collapse if someone said a brutal word? Did they fall down in the streets? Did they lie about as if their loved one had been seen dropping poison in their porridge? Was this the worst thing that had ever happened to her? Ludicrously far from it! It was trivial. Trivial. Well then. Enough is enough. The scornful and the wounded both agreed. A moment's grim standing-fast.

But unusual, unexpected, unkind, uncalled for, unprovoked, unnecessary . . .

That man . . . There had to be some suitable names for him in the language, but her efforts to recall any were strikingly ineffectual. To be natural at all, she saw, she ought to dig up some invective and fling it, at least mentally, at him. She had to *want* to. Leslie had done it for her at breakfast. One of them was wrong – either she or the man. He had a will to be unpleasant; she had no will to name-call. Pig. Lousy thing. *Rude*, she had thought him. He was bloody awful and not nice into the bargain.

Obligations. She had an obligation to pay Mrs Chaloner for the milk. Sandals flapping, unconscious of legs, of mouth without lipstick, she dropped downstairs. A hollow cave. A beating drum.

Money for milk, Mrs Chaloner. I owe you money for milk. She handed it over. Mrs Chaloner stared, but Laura had left her face to its own devices. She was off somewhere under anaesthetic. If her face was grey, if the cheeks cleaved to the bones, if the eyes were glazed and blank, she knew nothing about it.

Upstairs she read the letter again and drank coffee and drifted and was racked with futile wonder. Still her heart pounded. Lying down, she saw it lift the pink blouse she wore, felt its deep unnatural reverberations through her body. Its capacity for feeling insulted, astonished and exhausted her.

If she were ever to meet him . . . *Are you always so bad-mannered?* Oh, killing. He would curl up and die. She had a genius for sarcasm. Terrible to unleash a talent like that on a perhaps quite sensitive man!

She moved her head on the pillow restlessly. Death, death . . . Death, she thought, while her heart struck deafening chimes through her body.

If she were to meet him . . .

Oh, sickening. Out of all proportion. Too frail for this world. When things *mattered*, she fortunately refrained from this sort of performance. It was ridiculous beyond words in the person who had lived her life. Face it. To mind *this* much you have to be a megalomaniac. No. Just – just . . . It was not *right*. Think what he said! Oh, what he said, what he said. The burning smoking strokes of her heart continued. The very bed shook under them.

Laura! Laura!

Disembodied, she jerked herself up and meandered to the landing. Yes?

A drink for you, gasped Mrs Chaloner, looking at her amazed. I thought you might be able to do with it. It's so hot. Here.

She offered up a clinking tumbler, icy, lemony, ginny. She was kind.

Oh, thank you! How kind of you! If ever I needed anything! Laura said with alarming vivacity.

It's so hot up here, Mrs Chaloner told her.

Laura gazed about in a vague stupor. Yes, it is, she agreed insincerely, beginning at once to sweat now that the fact was pointed out.

Indeed it was hot. It was roasting, boiling, and had been for hours. Laura simmered slowly, drinking the icy drink, burning, hammering and insulted.

Sagging, far from convalescent, she sat on the edge of her bed. Out through the window she could see children playing on the lawn of a distant school. Little did they know ... Shock. That was all that was wrong. Brandy, blankets, a St Bernard dog ... No, sweet tea, blankets ... But could shock have the effect of bringing about a permanent physical change? Could she doubt it? Everything about her, physical and metaphysical, had sunk, shrunk. She was shorter, pruned, slightly murdered.

The world, human beings. Her mind reviewed every fact she had ever learned. She recollected all the significant scenes of her life, and the meaningful words. She contemplated the perfect love that casts out fear, rested in it, knowing that to be reality and herself to be, in truth, beyond harm. Smiled.

But just the same ...

Dinner-time and Leslie returned to his room along the corridor and to the table. All day, in his mind, he had written letters to that guy. He stated doubtfully his opinion that Laura would survive. Then he repeated it. Appointing himself chief distractor and analyst, he distracted and analyzed while the undiverted heart thumped.

Late that night when she was alone, the banging stopped quite suddenly. Hurt pride and vanity, her whole vast sense of the dreadful wrongness of what had happened, up in smoke. The heart that knew how to act temperately in crucial situations gave up being a burning mountain on this inappropriate occasion, and was all at once lightless.

I know something, Laura thought before falling dead asleep. It did not speak against me; it spoke *to* me. And I know what insulted means. I was never insulted before. I'll never be insulted again. I'll always know what insulted means. As I know what some other words mean.

Desmond O'Grady

BARBECUE

VICTOR Naughton had scrubbed his teeth, swigged down a cup of tea and stood under the shower, running it alternately hot and cold for ten minutes, before his head cleared and he recognized that liquor was not the only cause of his feeling so foul on awakening.

As he dressed in his fawn slacks and open shirt, he focused on the cause of his sourness. He connected the electric razor and, while pretending to examine his beard, had a good look at himself. His blue eyes stared back at him photographically from the mirror until he decided he could not tell what expression they had; he then noted impersonally his black hair, slicked back after the shower, and free from any trace of grey, his lined, tanned skin, the straight nose and mouth. It was a narrow face, and his friends called him Indian, meaning Red Indian. Indian was Jacky's name for him; sometimes he felt like laughing at that, but not this morning – Indian, the hunter. Well, looking at his face would not get him anywhere, after all it was no different now from any other morning. As the razor did its work, he reflected that his friends saw the same impassive features as the mirror: his face might just as well be a mask.

Clean shaven, he felt the need to eat something, because he could not do the work ahead on an empty stomach. He did not want to wake Jacky, so he sliced a banana into a dessert plate, covered it with cereal, and, taking the milk from the refrigerator, swamped the cereal with it. As he shovelled the pap into his mouth he walked to the lounge room.

From the wall opposite the door, the buffalo's head stared eyeless at him. Naughton crossed the room and opened the windows which gave on to the front garden. He felt the sun on the small of his back as he turned to survey the remains of the party. It was warm for eleven thirty. The job should have been done before the heat of the day. He would tidy up this mess later, he told himself, thinking that if it hadn't been such a mess of a party there would be no need for the sacrifice this morning.

As he finished the cereal, he saw again the scene of the previous night. He had been talking with guests in the kitchen for twenty minutes before his return to the lounge room, so he did not know for how long Jacky had been performing. He had stood transfixed at the sight of her, a glass of beer immobile in his hand as he heard Morrison's incredulous comment: 'He's got everything there but the green eye of the little yellow god!'

The sight of Jacky balancing on one of the new chairs had chilled Victor. For in her left hand she held the maplewood box in which he kept the eyes. She was holding one of the fox's eyes in the buffalo head's empty eye-socket, to the amusement and amazement of all the guests, but for Morrison's benefit in particular. He had a mad desire to knock her down, and started into the room to shout: 'Jacky, what the hell are you doing?' but even as he began he knew it was far too late.

The guests had turned at the strange, rent sound of his voice, and some had started to offer comments, but fell abruptly silent at the sight of Victor's face. For that moment, so out of keeping with the robust bonhomie of the evening, Jacky, poised beside the one-eyed bullock, looked down at him with malice and surprise, and Morrison's eyes flickered from one to the other as if he were assessing clients' strengths and weaknesses.

'Where did you get them?' he had asked, and his voice had been hoarse as if he had been shouting for hours. Mercifully the chatter had resumed. She had taken them from his cabinet, of course. That's not what he had meant to ask her, rather, 'Why did you take them?'

They were a collection of animals' eyes, stones, marbles, anything which could be fitted into the bullock's eye-sockets in place of the original eyes which Victor had removed some years ago. He had inserted then the fox's eyes, but after some time he could not stand them either and had substituted sheep's eyes, then marbles. So it had gone on until, as there was a limit to his supply, he had returned to the beginning of the series by using the fox's eyes again, without ever restoring those of the bullock. It was a subject he never discussed with Jacky; at first curious and ready to joke about it, later she had pretended to ignore it. She was well aware that it was taboo to touch his box of eyes, just as he knew he must not suggest that the bullock's head be taken down altogether.

He had not missed the fierce enjoyment in Jacky's face as she exposed his secret to Morrison. And Morrison had obviously been relishing the entertainment. Jacky had been badgering Victor to invite Morrison home, for she argued that Morrison would make her husband go ahead by leaps and bounds once he had met her. As the new assistant accountant for his advertising agencies, Victor was not in close contact with Morrison, not at his ease in his company.

Left to his own devices, he would not have invited him, but he considered that Jacky's idea might work after all. Jacky had been extremely interested in Morrison's reputation as a hunter, his war-time exploits, his business flair. He appeared to be a more successful Victor, and it annoyed Victor that he could not tell his wife the less flattering stories about his boss, such as his doubtful business deals and his womanizing.

He had decided against telling her these stories for a number of reasons, some of which he could not enumerate even to himself, but it left intact the picture of Morrison as a dazzling adventurer, and he was quite capable of playing that part, especially to a female audience. Early in the night Morrison had invited them, through Jacky, to a barbecue at his place the following day, but that was before Jacky had made such an exhibition of herself.

Morrison had left almost immediately after that scene, but he had repeated his invitation to Jacky, saying that he looked forward to seeing her – and Victor, he had added as an after-thought. Well, Morrison would not be seeing her, Victor told himself, and that's for sure, she would not be at that barbecue.

He took down the rifle and tiptoed out to the bathroom where the bullets were stored, loaded it and, still on tiptoe, stole along to the bedroom. Jacky lay at an angle across the tangled bed, one arm flung out along the pillow. She had not removed her make-up, and the artificial colour on her sleeping face made her seem much older than her thirty-nine years. Suddenly she stirred, and Naughton stepped silently backwards from the doorway in case she awoke. But she slept on soundly, lying on her back with her mouth slightly open.

He slipped along the passageway and into the back garden. In the far corner, stretched out asleep in the surprisingly warm sun, was the victim, the black-and-white tabby, which had been with them for three months now.

Victor lay on his stomach, and adjusted the rifle to his shoulder, moving with deliberation to prevent himself thinking and feeling. He trained the rifle on the cat but then lowered it. He could not shoot it while it slept: he called it for some minutes without effect, before scraping together some pebbles which he lobbed on to the cat.

It rose groggily and took a few steps towards Victor. When the yellow eyes were staring him full in the face, he fired.

The report crashed through the calm of the Balwyn morning, and a scream was heard as the blast faded. Victor turned to see Jacky on the backdoor step with her hand clapped to her mouth. He had been a fool to use such a gun on a cat; he had blown it to smithereens.

He heard Jacky again: it was as if she had drawn in a great lungful of air and the last of it hurt. This was the closest she had been in years to crying, it might have been a sob. Something had broken in her; Naughton felt a sudden elation as he rose.

He had not recognized why he had awoken with the unpleasant knowledge that today he had to kill the cat which he had avoided disposing of in the last three weeks, despite Jacky's insistent requests. Now he half realized that it had become imperative because of last night's incident, and that he had gone about it in a clumsy compulsive way, using a gun of ridiculously high calibre. It wasn't a buffalo that had to be killed.

But, as he poured a Pimm's for Jacky, who was sitting on the sun-porch, he was not reproving himself: he saw that the shooting had shaken Jacky and now, surprisingly, she might listen to him. Seeing Jacky so hard hit, he realized, had stopped him from getting the shakes.

When he gave her the drink, she was staring out at the field of slaughter, and as he spoke she remained with her forehead pressed against the sun-porch windows, but he was confident that his words were getting home.

He found that he could talk about the eyes. Jacky had always wanted to believe that he was a great hunter. At first he had encouraged the lie, and later he had been afraid to deny it because she banked so heavily on the image of him as hunter; everything was built around it, her interests in outdoor life, her desire to go on hunting trips, her search for friends among those who had money and did make trips.

He described the last hunt he made in the Territory during the war. With his mates from the Katherine camp, he had gone bullock shooting – and far from it being a dangerous sport, the bullocks were so tame that one could walk within twenty yards of them before they would walk away. His victim had studied him with trusting eyes until he had stopped at twenty-five yards and fired. They were the eyes which he saw, as if still alive, when the bullock's head was installed in the lounge – or, rather, when the lounge was built around the bullock's head.

After his confession he was sure he had finally killed the bullock, even though Jacky merely looked at him as if stunned as well as shocked. But, as Victor began his usual Sunday morning car washing, he was sure she had understood, that she would see things his way.

They lunched from the left-overs of the party, and then he asked, as casually as he could manage, whether she wanted to go for a drive. She answered yes just as casually, and he knew that he had won. Their usual Sunday drive would bring them home too late to attend Morrison's barbecue, and that was the acid test.

If Jacky saw things his way, she would realize that that party was out. He could easily enough invent some excuse for Morrison tomorrow and during the week start looking for a new position once again.

Their car joined the long line of vehicles edging outwards from Melbourne on the Sunday afternoon pilgrimage to nowhere in particular. Victor was blissful, poised between the old life which he had rejected and the new whose difficulties he had not yet experienced. He felt an unfamiliar tenderness towards Jacky and regretted he had not trusted her sufficiently to have told her before. He surveyed the new life they would lead: they could keep the car, it had always been a bit of disgrace in their street, but it would go unnoticed in Camberwell or Brighton. They would have to retain all the things they had bought on hire purchase, but they would not have to mortgage themselves any more just because their friends could afford the latest fashions and they could not.

They had passed Ferntree Gully and were starting to climb into the Dandenongs when Jacky protested 'not this again', so he turned and headed for the beach. He was thinking how much a quiet life would suit him; he'd be happy enough to look after a garden and leave the rat-race to the others.

Jacky started to report the Musgroves' comments on their European trip. They had raved on about marvellous this and marvellous that and Jacky's envy was obvious as she imitated them. The Naughtons were the only couple in their circle who had not made at least one trip to Europe, and how could they on his salary? It was better that Jacky admit this, and find friends who would not make her envious by tripping around the world every two or three years.

'It's a lot of money to spend, just to go rubbernecking for six months,' said Victor.

'We could do it on the cheap without anyone knowing,' Jacky replied; 'It would give us something to talk about.'

What was she up to? Did she expect him to pay for a world trip also by instalments?

'Doesn't sound as if Ted Musgrove had much interesting to say,' he countered sulkily.

'At least he doesn't sit there like a statue.'

'I suppose you enjoy hearing him babble about Bombay or Bangkok.'

'Soon he's off to ski in Japan.'

Victor lost control altogether. 'Morrison's seen the lot five times over, and he says he knows which place will do him,' he rapped out, immediately regretting that he had mentioned Morrison and his prowess.

'Everyone knows this is number one, it's just to have made the damn trip,' replied Jacky in a tone which made Victor apprehensive.

He shied away from the subject and drove in silence. Would

she always be bitter in their new home because they hadn't made a trip to Europe? Knowing Jacky, he feared she would, she was used to getting what she wanted. But they would have to start living within their means or he would have only grey hairs.

Finding a space among the cars facing the seafront, he parked, rested his forearms on the steering wheel and relaxed: Morrison's barbecue would be under way already. Rather than leave the car, they just sat, and on either side saw older couples likewise seated in silence in their cars.

From the small promontory of Point Ormond, the seafront stretched away below them to Port Melbourne, tightly packed as far as the eye could see with cars as ordered as a congregation.

Victor glanced at Jacky's reflection in the rear vision mirror. Her alert face, handsome despite its engraved lines, had the bored and testy expression he had feared to find there. Would she want to drag along the bullock's head then, when they shifted? No, he would have to be firm, it must be a clear break, he would sell that with the house.

From their slightly elevated position, they looked down on the waves that broke tamely as they reached the beach. It was the only movement in the wide expanse of the bay.

Jacky stirred restlessly, and Victor noticed the blackness of her slacks. She filled them too tightly, he considered. And her nail polish was too striking; she should recognize that she was nearly forty.

Like the others in those cars congregated along the seafront, they watched mutely as the sun sank into the chalice of the Port Melbourne gasworks. When it disappeared, a solemn sadness invaded the air, as if they had witnessed the death of a hero. Some traces of cloud which caught the rays of the sun lay like bloody smears against the fading sky. The car-dwellers' faces flushed red in the last blaze of the sunset and Victor felt unnaturally hot. He wound down the car window to get a breath of air, thinking that if he had a clearer head the spectacle might mean something to him.

'What do you want to do with the head?' he asked, looking down at the waves.

'Nothing,' Jacky answered.

'Nothing?' he echoed, so as not to betray his relief.

'What did you expect me to do – take it down and put up a wall bracket and artificial flowers? What would I say at the next party, Indian?'

His thoughts and feelings were churning with such confusion that he didn't tell her they had had the last of those parties.

'But this morning . . .'

'She was only a damn tabby,' said Jacky forcefully, letting all her scorn weigh on the last word.

'And afterwards when I told you how I killed the bullock and about the eyes . . .' He was consciously relaxed in order to keep his voice level. But she was laughing, and as always it made you think of someone running giddily up a spiral staircase.

'So what?' she said. 'That was sixteen years ago.'

She reached out impulsively to grasp his forearm. He had been conscious of her as hard, distant and hostile since she had broken his bliss by her talk of an overseas trip, but now he felt the suasion of her feminity.

'Oh, Vic,' she said coaxingly, 'you're larger than life. You exaggerate everything. You've got to go on living just the same.'

She was close now and his tension ebbed.

'What are we sitting here for, Indian? Whose funeral is it?'

Mine, he felt like answering. Some bruise easier than others, he thought, or some have longer memories. The light was fast draining from the sky and the bay faded in the darkness. The dusk was isolating them in their car with only the beach still visible.

He could slam the car into gear, accelerate forward and they would plunge over the edge into the bay. It would be a quick spectacular end, and she would plead for mercy when she realized what was happening.

He would have to take the initiative. 'We might still be able to get to Morrison's barbecue,' he ventured, knowing that he had said the right thing at last.

'Yes, the fun will just be starting.'

He had anticipated the answer, but still wished that she had been less avid in her agreement. He slipped into reverse and edged the car out, pausing a moment to fix in his mind the whiteness of the tame waves before shifting to forward gear and pumping the accelerator. That whiteness gave him an idea; it was a pity he was not on the creative side of advertising. He would go ahead by leaps and bounds there. Just a word to convey that whiteness, to evoke it, and you had a brand name that would sell a soap. He had it, it was short enough to fit on a packet, too – surf, that was it, SURF.

'You won't throw an act like last night's, will you, Vic?'

There was no need to answer. Of course he wouldn't, least of all at Morrison's place.

Thelma Forshaw

THE DEMO

THE morning of the demonstration nobody could be bothered with the Odd Bod who came into the milk bar the moment it opened at seven o'clock and asked did they sell French letters. He was always asking – could they sell him a comb, postage stamps, rosary beads, porridge – everything, in fact, which a milk bar did not stock.

Mr Hele Ganor, half wild with nervousness, could not face the regular encounter with the Odd Bod, when he would utter his usual protesting howl: 'You're in the way! You've been sittink there for hours!' or 'If you don't want to buy anythink – buzz off! Buzz off!'

These peremptory outbursts unleashed Mr Ganor's accent at full blast, and the overlay of Australian idiom built up over twenty years cracked and was swallowed up in a veritable eruption of foreignness. He turned now, gnashing, on the Odd Bod.

'I have no time! I have worries! Why must you come today? You must wait till the chemist opens for your bloody French letters. What you think I am, eh? A bloody pedlar, maybe. Buzz off! Buzz off!'

The Odd Bod, his youthful face emaciated and unshaven, slunk into a chair at one of the tables and ordered tea and toast.

'Too early! Too early!' Mr Ganor cried hoarsely. 'The girls have not come yet. No tea and toasts. I have my hands full and today a demo. Maybe my shop will be smashed. How do I know? I have worries and you come here and make me mad, mad!' He struck his own brow with a clenched first, since he could not strike the Odd Bod.

'A milk shake, then,' said the Odd Bod immovably. He had a penchant for Mr Ganor's milk bar and came there almost daily with his irrelevant requests – perhaps conversation-starters, for when refused these absurd things he made no attempt to find them elsewhere. Mostly he sat for hours, watching people coming and going, making an occasional abortive attempt to chat with the staff, lapsing into silence, but in some way comforted by the atmosphere of burring milk shake mixers, the clash of the till, the laughter and chiacking of the girls behind the counter.

He had been a divinity student who had suffered a nervous breakdown, and only five weeks ago two passing strangers had prevented him from leaping off the Harbour Bridge. Mr Ganor viewed him with distaste and uncomprehension, but could find no way to banish him from his shop, short of calling his darlings the police and charging the Odd Bod with vagrancy or loitering. That, however, he stopped short of.

As the girls arrived, Mr Ganor flew at them gabbling: 'The demo, the demo! My Christ, what a terrible thing! Twenty years in Australia and now this. We're not safe any more. Give them what they want. Don't argue. We want no donnybrook. Jesus, my shop! What if they smash my shop!'

May yawned. 'Oh boy, talk about a heavy night at the South Sydney Leagues – we hit a jackpot and then it was on! Let me take you one night Mr Gay. Hell, don't tell me the Odd Bod's turned up already.'

Cheryl tied her pink overall sullenly. 'I should be studying this morning, instead of coming here to help you out.' She was a veterinary science student.

Mr Ganor could not make his girls understand. They were completely unperturbed by the demonstration which was to take place just down the street from his shop when Air Vice-Marshal Ky of Vietnam arrived at Admiralty House. They grumbled only at the prospect of the heavy work. They did not understand Mr Ganor's conflicting terror and exhilaration. Nor did they believe in violence as Mr Ganor believed in it. He remembered election days in his native European city, the killings, the armed police; above all he remembered the Second World War when Hitler's gangs roamed the streets, enforcing, terrorizing. Today he was filled with both elation and fear. Elation because of the prospect of big takings for his milk bar – and fear of riots in which maybe his car would be overturned, bottles broken and biscuits stolen from the display stand near the door.

For twenty years he had lived in Australia and found them a quiet if sceptical and sardonic people. They were not the demo type. Hadn't he seen them laughing and ridiculing the rebels and rabble-rousers who shouted their views in the Sydney Domain on Sundays? He could not believe in an Australia seething with protest and violence. Twenty years and now a demo on the very doorstep of his milk bar. His heart beat hard with apprehension and dread, then skipped with hope, his sallow face strained, tensely lined as if he were enduring great inner pressures.

Mr Ganor's business both masked and compensated what would have been loneliness, a lack of social ease as a foreigner and every kind of personal failure, for he was either suspicious or envious of his own countrymen and avoided them. The shop flowed into all his voids and filled them. He was full of love for the money it brought him, he had the girls and the customers as company without need of the graces and social techniques he lacked. The shop *was* Mr Ganor. Like an artist he made it, and like the artist's work it made him.

Therefore any threat to it endangered not merely glass and chromium and money, but a solid edifice which had become himself. Strip the shop from Mr Ganor and there would have been left a naked, empty, lonely and loveless exile. The shop protected Mr Ganor from the modern malady of alienation. In his shop he was marvellously in touch with life. He knew nothing of alienation. At the first chill breath, instinct had swiftly created a protective carapace, and it was for this carapace he feared.

And so today was not a day like any other when he cuffed the heads of rowdy schoolboys, or cursed the Odd Bod for 'smelling up' his shop with fish and chips. Today he could not sing with passionate fervour:

Pale hands I loved beside the Shalimar-ar,
Where are you now, who lies beneath your spell?
I would have ra-ather felt them round my thro-oat
Crrrrrushing out life than waving me farewe-ell,
Crrrrrushing out li-i-i-i-fe than waving me-ee farewe-e-ell.

It was unnerving to hear Mr Ganor bellowing out 'Pale Hands I Loved' while he shook all over. May said it was the hands pushing money across the counter that *he* loved – never mind about beside the Shalimar. Bloody money-grubber.

The song could never have referred to Mr Ganor's ex-wife whose hands had been blotched by hard work and who, on no account, however romantic, would he have suffered to strangle him rather than depart. He had in fact accepted her farewell with relief rather than regret. She had found a less obsessed man with time for her kind of love. Mr Ganor sang with frightening intensity, and confounded those who speculated on his sexual proclivities by preferring the song to a mistress's obstructing reality. We all have some unlived life in us, and so we sing, or recite or savagely dream. Mr Ganor sang his unrealizable romance. But not today.

His pallor, the lines of suffering in his face were a source of amusement to the girls, who had never experienced, never ever thought about, nor some so much as read of the outbreaks of violence in other countries. They viewed the demo with amusement and the demonstrators were dismissed as 'a pack of nuts'. Even the patrolling police, though disgruntled at being deprived of their week-end leave, wore deprecating grins and were lavish with winks.

As the time of the demonstration approached, Mr Ganor ran down the street to see if he could assess the situation and found the way lined with an unprecedented number of police – 'Just like a foreign country,' he said with agitation. He seriously thought of shutting the shop – an unheard-of procedure, for Mr Ganor's shop was open all the year round, every day of the week, including Good Friday and Christmas Day. He was torn in two. He suffered all the torments of the schizoid – his heart bounding with exultation at the prospect of a good day, yet unable to shake off a sense of terror and foreboding. He wrestled with himself . . . and wrestled. In the end . . . He would stay open.

Courage is as relative as anything else. For Mr Ganor to keep the shop open in the face of possible rioting by the demonstrators was an act of courage. That his motive was greed for extra profits and that this motive proved stronger than his terror did not make his stand less courageous. He would risk life and limb by keeping his shop open in the face of what he saw as the onslaught of ravening hordes who would either make or break him.

As he saw the crowds passing on their way to watch the demonstration or join it, Mr Ganor's bowels moved frequently and ever and anon as he fled, his anguished cry: 'May, watch the shop – I must *go!*' became the object of indelicate jokes between the girls.

'He's got the runs because of the demo,' May jeered, then, wheeling swiftly, in a lilting voice: 'Yes, sir, what can I get you?' as a customer breasted the counter.

In his extremity – perhaps inspired by his own discomfort – Mr Ganor had an hysterical vision in which he saw the demonstrators effectively de-activated. He tested this vision on his girls. 'I tell you what I do – I go to the chemist and buy cascara and put it in their drinks when they come here – ha, ha, you laugh, eh? – Good idea? Then they think of nothing but shitting.'

The girls doubled up with laughter, catching underlips between their teeth as a sketchy gesture of modesty, for Mr Ganor always used the crudest words in English with the abandon of one who does not fully feel their impact in the adopted language.

Outside, shouts and chanting had begun and grew stronger and more impassioned, indicating that the Vietnamese Premier had arrived. Peering from the doorway, Mr Ganor saw at the bottom of the street hundreds of people surging forward against the linked hands of the police. The fire brigade stood by with hoses at the ready. He withdrew, trembling. Just like a foreign country. What was happening to his haven, quiet Australia? When would it be guns instead of fire hoses?

Standing like a sentinel behind his counter, brave as could be, he served the numerous people who strayed in off the streets, many of whom he knew, who grinned and winked and referred to the demonstrators as a 'bunch of fanatics' or a 'pack of crackpots', and he felt comforted by these Australians who had not changed.

He dreaded the mood of the demonstrators if the police thwarted their will to protest. He understood perfectly well the expression 'pecking order'. He had been a victim of it often enough. Frustrates, foiled of their original target, who came into the milk bar and made trouble, abusing and threatening him, calling him a 'wog', 'a dago', 'a bloody foreigner'. Yes, he knew all about pecking order. And he had a Caesar's enthusiasm for festivals, carnivals and fêtes of all kinds – a Caesar's shrewd dread of the people's mood and a desire to see it deflected into pleasurable activities. He would have approved of the arenas of ancient Rome. He wanted to get on with what he was doing and not be troubled by the fury of a populace desperate for emotional outlets. Mr Ganor was neither a Freudian nor a politician but, as a dedicated shopkeeper – a man, therefore, with a purpose – he dreaded everything that conflicted with his purpose: to be left to make money in peace.

The Odd Bod, who had been meditating ever since his thwarted attempt to leap from the Harbour Bridge, chose this moment, while the roaring and chanting of the demonstrators rose like a wild surf outside, to communicate the result of his meditations. He stood up and said quietly and firmly: 'The Hound of Heaven is on my trail. He wants me.'

'Yeah, and He's about all that *does* want you.' May grinned, as she wiped his table. 'Look, love, clear out, will yuh – you're gonna be in the way.'

Several customers stared and smiled and turned back to their drinks. The poor crazy nut.

The Odd Bod approached Mr Ganor confidently. 'You have read, of course, "The Hound of Heaven" by Francis Thompson,' he asked, surely not unreasonably.

Mr Ganor did not look at him blankly, because you only look at people blankly when you wish you knew what on earth they meant. Mr Ganor did not give a rap for anything he did not know. Frightened people can barely contend with what they already know. Any more may shake – even destroy – the crude or elaborate fortifications they erect to defend themselves. Mr Ganor's identity was well sandbagged against mysticism.

'I have been waiting for grace,' explained the ex-divinity student. What was so irrational about that?

'She is not here, so wait for her somewhere else,' Mr Ganor retorted, supremely unaware that he had been witty, even when a customer, standing near by, laughed aloud. Mr Ganor had felt many things, but never embarrassment.

'You see, I have been fleeing the Hound of Heaven,' the Odd

Bod pointed out. Mr Ganor, who understood pecking order so well did not, however, disdain its practice himself.

'For Christ's sake,' he cried with unwitting aptness, 'go, go with your Hound of Heaven. You have bought nothing for two hours.'

'He wants me,' said the Odd Bod out of his obsessed dream, at the same time slapping down twenty cents for the chocolate bar which would buy him another two hours in Mr Ganor's milk bar. He looked triumphant.

Mr Ganor interpreted the triumph as directed towards himself and pushed away the twenty cents. 'I sell you nothing. Buzz off. I will need all the tables when *they* come.'

The Odd Bod knew a thing or two. 'You can't refuse to sell me a bar of chocolate.'

In the end he got it and went back to his table.

And now they came – the demonstrators and their amused or sympathetic observers, streaming up the street, the sound of their voices, their footsteps, causing Mr Ganor to flex and tremble. The demos, oh God, the demos. What would be their mood? If the police had suppressed them would they take it out on *him*? The window of the shop darkened as a mass of figures surged towards the milk bar doorway. Young men came carrying placards with the flaring legend KILLER KY looking, Mr Ganor thought, themselves like killers. Numerous Save Our Sons ladies bustled in, taking over tables and chairs as if they owned the place, ordering tea and sandwiches. Mr Ganor was offended by what he saw as high-handedness and aggression. They were only women. His voice hoarse and wavering he shouted, 'No tea and sandwiches. Not enough staff.' It was *his* shop and he would declare his rules if they killed him for it – these – these *untypical* Australians. He confronted the annoyed women, trembling, but with his sense of possession stiffening him to anger. They were only women.

Just then half a dozen huge policemen entered, towering over the heads of the crowd in the shop. An expression of deep content erased the lines of strain from Mr Ganor's face. Here were his protectors against all unruliness and disorder. Lovingly, he cried, 'Officers, what do you wish?'

'Can you do tea and sandwiches for six?'

'Certainly, officers, certainly.'

Several demonstrators protested: 'Thought you said the tea and sandwiches were off.'

'Yes – off. Off!' Mr Ganor said with open hostility. Hadn't they scared the living daylights out of him?

'How come they're on for the coppers?'

Loudly Mr Ganor said, 'A very special favour for the officers.'

'That's not fair!'

At that moment the demonstrators saw no difference at all between the police and themselves – only outside in the street earlier, chanting, and straining against the linked beefy hands. Inside Mr Ganor's shop all men were equal. Not so. In Mr Ganor's shop the police were more equal than others. The police who would protect his beloved property. No one could be *more* equal than the police. In a low caressing voice Mr Ganor added: 'It's on the house, officers.'

When he refused tea and sandwiches to the demonstrators he was punishing them for the terror they had aroused in him and at the same time literally curtseying to the police – as ostentatiously flattering as a mayor's wife greeting royalty. Had the police been more popular they could have afforded to despise Mr Ganor's petty bribery – his effort to keep them in his shop as long as the demonstrators were still at large. But beggars can't be choosers and their smiles were gratified as trays of tea and sandwiches were borne under the very noses of the hungry demonstrators to the tables of the favoured. What Mr Ganor knew of men was what he knew of himself, which was, so to speak, brief and to the point. Quite a number of people had agreed to 'play ball' with Mr Ganor after a carton of cigarettes or a box of chocolates had been pressed into their hands. It was said he had a local M.P. on lay-by. Mr Ganor, a foreigner and a charmless man, believed that people would do nothing for him out of sweet Christian charity. It was all very much a bargain-basement affair, a sort of mini-politics. The grand scale was not Mr Ganor's. Free tea and sandwiches for the police would gain him what he wanted.

For a moment there was restiveness among the demonstrators; some stormed out, but the rest remained, discontentedly accepting the drinks and chocolate which was all Mr Ganor vouchsafed them – so long as six policemen sat at his tables. Everyone clamoured to be served and now they were served with a will.

Mixing drinks, selling bottles of cordial, slapping down cigarettes and sweets, running, bustling his girls, breathing fast as a lover, now Mr Ganor flew on the wings of delectable exertions, while the cash register chimed like a carillon. The shop seethed and swarmed as people came and went, or clustered together talking, groups surged in and struggled out pushing their way past the packed shoulders of others. The cash register chimed continually, Mr Ganor whirled like a prima ballerina from customer to customer, while his girls flagged and began to complain of feet, varicose veins, headaches.

Eventually the tempo slowed, the shop began to empty. The police rose, winking here and there at those they knew, and departed with a now-we're-square nod to Mr Ganor. The musical clamour of the cash register became no more than occasional hiccupping. The girls drew off their clammy overalls, eager to leave and soak their feet in a Radox or salt bath.

'Oh, Christ!' glowed Mr Ganor with heartfelt religiosity. 'What a bloody lovely day!' *His* feet might never have touched the cement floor.

Serious but exhilarated, lives bursting with meaning, the demonstrators trailed off home, and Mr Ganor began to count the day's takings. The Odd Bod loped away, happily pursued by the Hound of Heaven, telling it to himself:

> *'Now of that long pursuit*
> *Comes on at hand the bruit,*
> *That voice is round me like a bursting sea . . .*
> something something something
> *Lo, all things fly thee, for thou fliest Me!*

. . . Oh, yes, God, oh, Yes!'

In the milk bar, Mr Ganor indulged himself in a little well-earned passion as he wrapped his multitudinous coins for banking. His voice soared tremulous:

> *'Pale hands I loved, beside the Shalimar-ar,*
> *Where are you now,*
> *Where are-are you no-o-owwwwwww?'*

Dal Stivens

WARRIGAL

'YOU'LL have to get rid of that dingo before long,' my neighbour Swinburne said to me across the fence. 'Why, he's an Asiatic wolf –'

'No one of any authority says that the dingo is an Asiatic wolf,' I said. 'The Curator of Mammals at the Australian Museum classifies the dingo as *Canis familiaris* variety *dingo* – that is, a variety of the common dog. Another eminent authority says it's most unlikely that the dingo is descended from the northern wolf –'

'I know a wolf when I see it,' this classic pyknic said. 'I don't care what some long-haired professors say. I was brought up in the bush.'

As my wife Martha says, I can be insufferable at times – particularly when I'm provoked. I said: 'So much for your fears of this animal attacking you – it's most unlikely as long as he continues to look on you as the *gamma* animal. Of course, you need to act like a *gamma* animal at all times.'

I thought for a moment he was going to climb over the paling fence that divided our properties and throw a punch at me.

'You be careful who you call an animal!' he said. His big red face and neck were swelling like a frog's. It was pure Lorenz and Heidigger I was throwing at him. This was during my animal behaviour period.

'I'm not calling you an animal,' I said. 'I'm just explaining how the dingo sees you. He sees me as the *alpha* animal – *alpha* is Greek for A. I'm the pack leader in his eyes. He sees my wife, Martha, as the *beta* animal. *Beta* is B and *gamma* is C. He probably sees you and your wife and kids as *gamma* or *delta* animals. *Delta* is D. While you behave like *gamma* or *delta* animals, you'll be O.K. He'll defer to you.'

He seemed a little assured – or confused, anyway.

'This *gamma* stuff,' he began uncertainly. 'You're sure of it, now?'

'I'll lend you a book,' I said.

'All the same, he's got pretty powerful jaws,' he said, pointing to Red, who was crouching at my feet, his eyes not leaving me. The jaws were, as he said, powerful, and the white shining canine teeth rather large. The head was a little too large, the prick ears a bit too thick at the roots for Red to be a really handsome dog, but there was a compact power in his strong tawny chest and limbs.

'No more than a German shepherd's,' I said. There were two of them in Mansion Road – that wasn't the name but it will do.

'I suppose so,' he said doubtfully.

'If I hadn't told you Red was a dingo you wouldn't be worrying,' I said. 'I could have told you Red was a mongrel.'

'Are you trying to tell me I wouldn't know a dingo?' he started in belligerently.

Before I could answer, his own dog, a Dobermann Pinscher and a real North Shore status job, came out and began challenging Red. Both dogs raced up and down on their sides of the fence, the Pinscher growling and barking and Red just growling. (Dingoes don't bark in the wilds. When domesticated some learn to do so but Red hadn't.)

Red ran on his toes, his reddish-brown coat gleaming and white-tipped bushy tail waving erect. His gait was exciting to watch: it was smooth, effortless and one he could maintain for hours.

'This is what I mean,' he said. 'Your Asiatic wolf could savage my dog to death.'

'Yours is making the most noise,' I said. The Pinscher was as aggressive as his master.

'Noise isn't everything,' he said. 'Look at that wolf-like crouching.'

'Innate behaviour,' I said. 'Dingoes have acquired that over thousands of years of attacking emus and kangaroos. They crouch to avoid the kicks.'

'So your wolf is getting ready to attack, is he?'

'Not necessarily,' I said. 'No more than yours is. Of course, if one dog were to invade the other's territory, then there would be a fight. But they won't invade.'

'Yours could jump the fence,' he said. 'I've seen him. He could kill my dog and clean up my fowls.'

'Not into your place,' I said. I was beginning to lose my temper. 'He wouldn't. He knows it isn't his.'

'So he's moral, is he?' he shouted. 'This wild dog –'

'They're all moral although the term is anthropomorphic. Wild dogs or domestic dogs usually won't invade another's territory.'

'So you say,' he said. His face was purpling. 'I warn you now yours had better not. If he does I'll shoot him. The law's on my side.'

I was so angry I went inside and got a hammer. I started knocking palings out of the fence.

'Hey!' he shouted. 'That's my fence. And I meant what I said about shooting that Asiatic mongrel.'

'Pure-bred dingo,' I grunted. I was out of condition and the nails were tough. 'Our fence.'

I got four palings out and, as I knew would happen, the dogs kept racing past the gap and ignoring the chance to enter and attack. I was dishing out pure Lorenz.

'It's just bluff,' I said. 'You can see it for yourself. They talk big. After they've said their bit, they'll knock off.'

'Perhaps,' he said, doubtfully.

'Call your dog out into the street,' I said. 'I'll call mine. They'll meet in the middle and sniff each other's anal quarters but they won't fight. There's nothing to fight about – none lays claim to the centre of the road. Of course, the footpath is different.'

'I won't risk it,' he said and he called the Pinscher and started off. 'You may be right and your dingo ought to be at home in your garden.'

It might have sounded conciliatory to you. But there was a crack in it. This was during my Australian native flora period. When I bought this block I had the house built well down the hillside and left all the trees and shrubs. I wanted a native bushland garden and I had left what the other people in Mansion Road called 'that rubbish' in its near-natural state. I had planted some more natives – waratahs like great red Roman torches, delicately starred wax flowers and native roses, piquantly scented boronias, flannel flowers, and subtly curving spider flowers. This was in keeping with my newly acquired feeling for *furyu*, which is often used to describe things Japanese. It can be translated as 'tasteful', but the Japanese characters convey a fuller meaning of 'flowing with the wind' – the acceptance of nature, of the material itself, and of the patterns it imposes. Transferring the concept to Australia, I was accepting nature and learning to appreciate the muted beauty of Australian shrubs and flowers.

The neighbours didn't approve. They all had lots of lawns and terraces and beds of perennials and annuals. They'd chopped down most of the native trees and planted exotics. They thought my garden lowered the tone of the street. And they thought the same about our unobtrusive low-line house, blending with the slim eucalypts and the sandstone outcrops. They preferred double-fronted mod. bungs.

We'd have got on a lot better if we had lived in Mansion Street during my azalea and camellia period. At our last house Martha and I had gone in for landscaping – vistas, focus points, and the rest. And we'd used azaleas and camellias for much of the mass planting. I'd got myself wised up on azaleas, particularly, and I knew as much as most about Wilson's fifty Kurumes; I once engaged in some learned discussion in a specialist journal as to whether or not some experts were correct in thinking Pink Pearl (*Azuma Kagami*) was, indeed, the progenitor of all the pink-flowered forms.

That was some time ago, and although I still like azaleas, the love affair was then over. Not everyone appreciates Australian natives. We went away for a week once and when we came back someone had dumped two tons of rubbish into our place. We had no fence at the street level and someone had thought it was a virgin block. The house is well down the slope and hard to see from the street. Of course, he should have noticed the rather heavy concentration of native flora. He had tipped the rusting tins, galvanized iron, mattresses, and so on, onto a stand of native roses, too.

We didn't really fit into Mansion Road for a number of reasons. First, there was my profession as a journalist and writer.

And moreover, Martha and I were in our Chagall period; our earlier Rembrandt love affair might have been accepted.

And there was the car business. They all had one or two cars but we didn't see the need when there was a good taxi and hire car service. When they finally got the idea that we could afford a car but wouldn't have one, it struck them as un-Australian or something.

The dingo business was merely another straw, though Swinburne seemed to be trying to push it a bit further.

'Why get yourself angry?' Martha reproached me when I went inside.

'A conformist ass!?' I said.

'You can't educate him,' she said.

'I know,' I said. 'I was having a bit of fun.'

'Whatever you call it, we'll probably have to get rid of Red,' she said.

'Where?' I said.

That was the question. I wasn't giving him to the Zoo, as some in Mansion Road had hinted I should. Dingoes are far-ranging, lively, intelligent creatures and it would be cruelty to confine him. And I couldn't release him in the bush now that he was a year old and had had no training in hunting for himself. Normally, he would have acquired this from his mother, but I'd got Red as a pup. A zoologist friend had brought him to Sydney and then found his wife wouldn't let him keep a dingo.

I didn't see Swinburne again until the next week-end. He called me over the fence.

'What you say about that dingo might be true at present but he'll revert to type,' he said. 'The hunting instinct is too strong. It will be someone's chicken run eventually even if it's not mine.'

'He hasn't been taught to hunt fowls – or anything else,' I said. 'So why should he? He's well fed.'

'Primitive instincts are strong,' said Swinburne.

'We don't know what his primeval instincts are,' I said.

'He's a wild dog.'

I said, insufferably: 'Professor Konrad Lorenz, who is one of the world's greatest authorities on dogs, says that the dingo is a descendant of a domesticated dog brought here by the Aborigines. He points out that a pure-blooded dingo often has white stockings or stars and nearly always a white tip to its tail. He adds that these points are quite irregularly distributed. This, as everyone knows, is a feature never seen in wild animals but it occurs frequently in all domestic animals.'

'Has this foreign professor ever seen a dingo in the wilds?' he asked.

I couldn't see what his question had to do with the paraphrase I had given him, but I told him that while Lorenz had not been to Australia so far as I knew, he had bred and studied dingoes.

He changed the subject abruptly.

'You seem to know all about animals and birds,' he said. 'Perhaps you have a cure for a crowing rooster? Mine is up-setting some of the neighbours by crowing during the night. He answers other roosters across the valley.' (There were farms there.) 'In a street like Mansion Road, you have to fit in.'

He was getting at me but I ignored it.

'I think so,' I said.

'I'd like to hear it,' he said, too sweetly.

'You have to get on with people, as you say,' I said, also too sweetly. 'But roosters can be stopped from crowing in a very simple fashion. A rooster, as you know, has to stretch its neck to crow. I'd suggest tacking a piece of hessian over the perch, a couple of inches above his head. When he goes to stretch his neck, he'll bump the hessian and won't be able to crow.'

He took it in after a few questions and said he'd try it. It took him and his fifteen-year-old son most of the afternoon. I must say they were thorough. It took them ten minutes to catch that White Leghorn and then they held him with his feet on the ground and measured the distance to a couple of inches over his head. They measured the hessian meticulously and then they had a conference during which they kept looking towards me. I was sowing some flannel flower seeds. I'd gone to the near-by bush-land reserve several times to observe the soil and aspect of flannel flowers so that I could plant the seeds in the right place in my garden.

Swinburne came over to the fence finally. 'I'm sorry to trouble you,' he said. This was a change. 'But there are several perches in the hen house.'

'The top one,' I said. 'He's the *alpha* animal.'

They fixed it there and Swinburne asked me to come and have a beer at his place. But he hadn't changed his mind much about the dingo because he and his wife started telling me about the merits of budgerigars as pets.

'Now, budgerigars make marvellous pets,' he said. 'Our Joey is a wonderful talker.'

The bird, a male pied blue, was perched on his hand, and while Mrs Swinburne smiled dotingly, it displayed and then, with wings down-dragging, it tried to copulate with Swinburne's big red hand.

'Isn't he quaint?' asked Mrs Swinburne. 'He does that by the hour.'

Poor bloody bird, I thought.

'No wonder,' I said aloud.

'What do you mean?'

'Nothing,' I said. 'I mean it's wonderful.'

'And they tell me budgerigars don't talk in the wilds,' said Mrs Swinburne.

'No,' I said. 'Only when they're caged.' I refrained from saying anything about mimicry being due to starved sexuality, to banked-up energy.

I couldn't see Mansion Road letting up on Red – Swinburne was just the official spokesman as it were, one of the *alpha* members in the street, the managing director of a shoe factory. I knew the others were saying the same things among themselves.

They said them to me a few nights later. Mrs Fitter called. If Swinburne was an *alpha* male, she was *the alpha* female. Her father had been a drapery knight and had built the big house in which the Fitters lived with a feature window and two cars.

'I've come on behalf of the mothers of Mansion Road,' she started in. She was a large dark woman with a hint of a moustache. 'They're very frightened that ravening wild dingo will attack their children. They have to pass it on their way to school and it crouches in the gutter.'

She was laying it on. Most of the children were driven to school.

'It won't attack them,' I said. 'He lies in the gutter because that's his territorial boundary. Like ourselves animals are land owners.'

'And what's more he barks at them,' she said, going too far.

'Dingoes don't bark,' I said, gently, but I was getting angry. Martha was making signs.

'And at cars, too,' she said. 'I had to swerve to miss him. And he slavers at the lips.'

'He has well-developed salivary glands,' I said. 'I assure you he won't attack anyone, but in any case the solution is simple. Your Schnauzer owns your footpath, Mrs Fitter – or thinks he does. I respect his property right and don't walk on his footpath and we get on very well.'

It wasn't tactful but I didn't want to be.

After Mrs Fitter had left, Martha said, 'Red has been going out after cars the last couple of days.'

'But not barking?' I asked.

'No,' she said.

Three nights later a young policeman called. Mrs Fitter had complained that Red had killed one of her fowls.

'Did she see him?' I asked.

'No, but she is convinced it could only have been the dingo,' he said.

'Well, constable, you know the legal position as well as I do,' I said. I didn't like it but I had to tack a bit. 'Every dog is allowed one bite – but not two. I don't admit that Red did kill the fowl. It could have been any one of the dogs in the street. And, further, Red is not necessarily a dingo. He could be a mongrel. I don't know his parentage. He was found in the outback by a friend and brought to Sydney.'

He went away but was back the next night.

'Mrs Fitter says that you have admitted that the animal is a dingo,' he said.

'I admit nothing,' I said tacking again. 'I have called the dog a dingo without any accurate knowledge and purely out of a spirit of fantasty. I wanted to indulge in a little fancy. It has been fun to think of Red as a dingo.'

He was a bit shaken and I went on, 'I'm no expert on dingoes, nor is anyone else in this street. Have you ever seen a pure-bred dingo?'

'I think so – at the Zoo –' he said, uncertainly.

'Exactly,' I said. 'And how do you know it was a pure one

and even if it was, would you be able to point to any dog with certainty and say that is a dingo or that another was a Dobermann Pinscher –'

'A Dobermann what, sir?'

'Mr Swinburne's dog is a Dobermann Pinscher. Mrs Fitter, on the other hand, has a Schnauzer. Of course, the two have points in common, according to the experts. I am told that a Manchester Terrier is even closer in appearance to a Dobermann Pinscher and that only the well informed can pick one from the other. Now when you come to mongrels, the question of identification is much more complicated –'

There was a bit more of it. He fled in some confusion and Martha and I rolled around the floor, helpless with laughter, and went to bed earlier. But it was getting serious. If I didn't cure Red of going out on the road, Mrs Fitter, or someone else, wasn't going to swerve next time.

What I did was undiluted Lorenz.

If you want to stop a dog chasing cars you have to fire a small stone at him from behind from a catapult when he is in the middle of chasing. When you do it this way the dog is taken by surprise. He doesn't see you do it and·it seems to him like the hand of God. That is anthropomorphic, but you know what I'm getting at; it's a memorable experience for the dog and usually cures him completely.

I stayed home the next day. It took me an hour to make a catapult that worked properly and I had to practise for twenty minutes. Then I was ready. I cured Red that morning with two hits, which were, I hope, not too painful. The gutter and the street were abandoned by him. Encouraged, I decided to cure him of establishing himself on the footpath. I achieved that, too.

I knew it only won a respite for the dingo. I had to return him to the wilds. The alternatives of giving him to the Zoo, or having him put away, I'd already rejected. Swinburne came home early that day.

'I see you're still insisting on keeping that Asiatic wolf,' he said.

'*Canis familiaris* variety *dingo*,' I corrected. 'But you're wrong about keeping him. I'm returning him to the wilds.'

'But they're sheep killers.'

'Not where there are no sheep.'

'There are sheep everywhere,' he said stubbornly.

'Australia's a big place,' I said. 'There ought to be a place somewhere where he can live his own life. But he'll have to be taught to hunt before I can release him.'

'You mean on wild animals?'

'What else?' I said.

'You'll soon have the fauna protection people after you,' he said.

'Rabbits aren't protected,' I said.

'They're vermin – and so are dingoes!' he said.

They didn't give me time to put my plan into operation. I had thought it just possible that they might give Red a bait. But I couldn't believe they hated him so much. Besides it's an offence to lay baits and they were most law-abiding in Mansion Road. They didn't poison Red. What happened was that Red went wandering off one day through the bushland reserve and a poultry farmer on the other side of the valley shot the dingo, as he was legally entitled to do.

'Sorry to hear about that dog of yours,' said Swinburne later.

'But why should he go off?' I asked.

'I know a bit about dingoes,' he said and his eyes were gleaming. 'Most likely he followed a bitch on heat. It's a question of studying animal behaviour.'

I knew then that he'd done it with a farmer in on the job. They were legal in Mansion Road. But I wouldn't be able to prove anything.

'It's better to keep budgerigars as pets,' I said, blazing inside. 'You keep them sex-starved and they'll try to mate with your hand.' Only I used a blunter word. 'It's all nice and jolly and they'll talk, too.'

I was sorry afterwards for losing my temper. Swinburne wrung the budgerigar's neck the next time it displayed on his wife's hand.

We sold out soon afterwards. I was coming to end of my Australian native flora period, anyway.

Frank Moorhouse

FIVE INCIDENTS CONCERNING THE FLESH AND THE BLOOD

The incident of the lifeless skin

'I'm disintegrating,' she said.

'Oh Louise, really . . .' Cockburn grinned patiently.

'I'm serious. I'm disintegrating.'

The styling of her hair was both appropriate and fashionable. Her slacks suit, soft, grey, quiet. Her feet well shod. She stood, one knee on a chair, turned away from him, staring out at the dark lane.

'Living gives me nothing,' she said, matter-of-factly. 'That's why I'm disintegrating.' She emptied her glass and, without turning around, held it back from herself towards him, 'Please.' He rose and poured her a scotch, using tongs for the ice. By the next drink he wouldn't be bothering with the tongs. He took her hand and kissed it.

'We are all disintegrating,' he supposed.

'But I feel it – and it's faster than it should be . . . it's because I'm sick to death of living.'

They'd been back from dinner for an hour and during that hour she had been saying the same thing in various ways. Though not at dinner. She had gaiety at dinner. It had come out after – with the drinking. He'd kept telling her that her physical appearance and her animation belied it – that although she was in her late thirties she retained the complexion and figure of her twenties which were supported by her personality which was *comme il faut*.

He'd not been flattering her. It was her sexuality and her luxuriant charm which had led him to take her to dinner and had led him now to her flat. He did not want his image of her fractured by self-attack and depression.

'I'm becoming bored by your attacks on yourself,' he smiled.

She turned from the window, 'I'm sorry – I am becoming a bore.' The remark had obviously pinched her. 'A lady can be a cheat, a liar, a bitch must never be a bore.'

She kissed him. He took her hands.

He felt the situation, decided it was right, and said, 'Let's go to bed.'

'Yes, why not?'

He caught the heavy, 'Why not,' with both mental hands.

'Do I detect a lack of enthusiasm?'

'No – don't take it personally – you're a darling and superbly handsome and terribly attractive.' She smiled apologetically. 'I'm just moody.'

She put her head against him. 'I keep telling you,' she said, 'I'm defeated.'

He kissed her on the lips. She did not have full lips and the kiss was a thin kiss. Her mouth did not open freely but not as though from resistance – more from indifference. It was not a forced kiss and she held to him and held the kiss.

They undressed separately and quietly. She gave him a coat hanger. In his more passionate days, he thought, his clothes would have been left on the floor where they had fallen. The days of headlong rushes to bed must have passed. But his experience in recent years was meagre – his marriage had been enough. It was two years or nearly three since he'd been with another woman. Now Louise, and certainly no headlong rush to bed.

Undressed, her body was firm. He stood naked, she pulled on a housecoat.

'Get into bed,' she said, 'I'll take off my make-up.'

'OK.' He got into the clean, tightly made bed. She left the room and he heard her in the kitchen pouring drinks. She brought him a drink.

'Drink this while you wait.'

'This waiting is tantalizing.'

'I'm glad – for me it's a bore.'

She turned on a beside light and turned out the main light. She sat at the dressing table. 'You'll see the real disintegrating me,' she said. At least she was joking about it now. He watched her using Kleenex and cleansing cream and then the astringent – like his wife. Sipping her drink as she did it.

'That word again,' he said. 'You run a bad press for yourself.'

She brushed her hair.

Then she rose from the dressing table and smiled wanly. The make-up was gone and had taken away the highlights of her face and left it placid. Its natural colourings and structure were soft.

She took off her housecoat and came to bed beside him, entering his embrace.

She was tense.

Even after alcohol. Even at their age – her age – she was tense. Her kiss pushed with a forced enthusiasm.

As their bodies became aware of each other for their full length he realised that her body was clammy. His fingers moved down the body but met a clammy resistance. He stopped and left his hand at her waist, feeling himself grow tense.

Her skin was lifeless.

He lay still, frozen in the half-light of the bedroom. The refrigerator beat came from the kitchen. Her skin was like that of a frog, he thought, a frog. Lifeless skin. It gave off stale perfume which attempted to give the body some artificial attractiveness. He had not felt that sort of skin before. She now gave away the forced enthusiasm and collapsed to a sort of sexual apathy and was lying still in his arms. She moved under him and whispered, 'Be quick,' and added, 'I'm tired.'

He was relieved she wanted it that way. It gave him little pleasure. After they finished, he tried to stay away from her. He resented the situation. They lay unspeaking, his hand obligatorily in hers. His legs could feel the lifeless flesh of her thigh. His nose tried to close itself to the perfume. She could be dead, he thought.

In five years time he would be as old as she.

Throughout the drive home the thought stayed with him – shooting up like flak. He wanted to talk to his wife about the lifeless flesh and whether it came with age. He wanted to be reassured. But he knew he couldn't talk to her about that.

He showered and then went to bed. His wife's skin was warm and alive and he soothed himself with it. With the living warmth of it.

He lay there thinking of the lifeless skin and of disintegrating Louise. He believed Louise now about that.

The incident of the young girl in the rose garden

He had wandered into the back garden after feeling bombarded by the party. Too many conversations in too short a time. Too many switches of subject matter and too many people, all requiring an artillery of response.

The garden covered an acre or more and was professionally tended, although he knew that Julien and Frederick liked to think they did most of it. They did at least *plan* it.

He'd reached the roses when he saw the girl sprawled on a garden seat, a drink on the seat beside her. Her arms spread along the back of the seat. Her head was back. The moonlight lit an unhappy face.

She was a girl who had had an expensive upbringing. Professionally tended. Good diet, good dentistry, strict hygiene, deportment training – all showed in her skin, hair, teeth, and sprawl. And her clothes showed taste more than fashion. Her prettiness depended heavily on her careful tending.

'You don't appear to be in the party mood,' he said, standing before her.

She looked up at him and shook her head.

'I'm not sure whether I am myself,' he said, wondering about it.

'Join the club,' she said.

He moved her glass and sat down.

'Why so dejected?'

She shrugged, went to say something, and gave up. Then she said, 'I'm just being neurotic.'

She was young to be recognizing herself as neurotic, probably meant depressed.

'How old are you?' she asked abruptly.

He was instantly defensive, realizing distantly that he was conscious of his age. He decided to be frank. 'Thirty-three.'

'How do you bear it?' she said, without a smile.

He laughed, 'For Godsake.'

He guessed she was about twenty-one or two. With a private flexing of his leg muscles he affirmed his fitness.

'I look into the mirror every day and say I'm dying,' she said, 'and I'm only just twenty.'

'A little morbid,' he said, irritated.

258

'What do you see when you look into the mirror?'

He knew the answer. Not that it worried him much.

'Well?'

'Well, yes, I sometimes think –"I'm dying"– but I think it . . . academically,' he drank, 'of course.'

She looked at him sceptically. 'I see death in my face,' she said, 'and in my hands and in my breasts.'

She made a desperate gesture with her mouth and drank from her glass.

He smiled at the histrionics.

He felt obliged, though, to say something . . . in defence of life. He laboured to find something.

'I suppose ideally one should lead a life that doesn't give time for morbidity,' he said, 'a strong argument for burning the candle at both ends.'

'But I've only to see someone like you and I become aware of death.'

'Thank you,' he said, almost offended.

'I didn't mean to be rude,' she said looking at his face and touching his hand.

In reflex he took her hand. But he wanted to cancel it as soon as it happened.

Her hand was warm and alive. He touched her arm, feeling the light, healthy hairs and the solid girl tenderness of her flesh.

'There are a lot of kicks in life,' he said.

He thought what Hemingway had said about life only having taste or meaning when death was in the wings. No that was wrong, when danger was in the wings. Or which was it?

'Of course, he was referring to danger and not to dying,' he said·

She looked at him, puzzled.

'It's all right, I was thinking aloud,' he said, embarrassed, 'I was thinking about what Hemingway said about danger giving life a meaning,' he added, scrabbling for sense.

'But I'm not talking about – danger – sudden death – I'm talking about the excruciating process of dying.' she said.

She seemed more detached about the subject now.

'Actually, danger – death through dangerous living – is a way of escaping it all. Instead of being a victim of inevitability.'

'Could be.' He was surprised, even a little diminished by her insight.

'I don't want to live past twenty-five,' she said, 'I'll kill myself. That's why I like fast cars.'

He smiled. He'd said it at twenty-five, then thirty, and sometimes he said forty.

He told her that.

'Yes, I guess we have a pretty frantic grip on life,' she said, 'no matter how ugly.'

'I wouldn't equate ageing with ugliness,' he said. 'Change, perhaps, but not ugliness.'

'That's not true,' she said strongly. 'People do just become ugly and their personalities change, become ugly, you know – dogmatic – oh – inflexible – and all that. Little funny things grow into ugly big warts.'

'Sitting out here bitching isn't going to stop it,' he said.

That was avoiding the issue. Perhaps that was all that one could do – about ageing.

'Going in there,' she said, taking her hand away and gesturing to the party, 'is not going to help me forget it.' The withdrawn hand released him from the implication of it.

'Life is not a continually pleasant thing,' he said, 'but it has things to offer – love, the mastering of something. Making beautiful things. And, if you like, fast cars.'

'But take the idea of mastering something – you only get really good at it when you're old and ready to die.'

'They say the mastering is the best part,' he said. But this drummed hollow. 'I mean that there are stages which give the pleasure.' This drummed less hollow but still sounded empty. He thought how fleeting these pleasures were compared with some of the groaning hours.

He was nervously agitated in the stomach. It was caused by the girl being stronger in her arguments than he was. She was bringing home to him things he had not thought for some time. In her mouth they seemed freshly and cruelly correct. And too many of the things he was saying seemed downright untrue. He needed to prove his wisdom. For his vanity as well as for the girl.

But why was he finding it so bloody difficult?

'Love's a good thing,' he said, 'and the making of beautiful things.'

'I've never been in love,' she said, 'Perhaps love is dead.'

'Come, now, you're only twenty.'

He was thinking though of the doubts you suffered both in love and in the making of beautiful things. You doubted whether the things you made or did were beautiful and you doubted whether you were loved and whether you really loved.

He told her that, 'But there are short periods when you do. It's pretty good then.' He was thinking, strangely, about his cooking, which was about the only time he made anything that could be called beautiful.

'But what if we're incapable of either,' she persisted.

'You don't know yet.'

She took his hand and kissed it, then sighed, 'No ... love is dead. Art is dead. Everything an artist spent a lifetime striving for any old hippie can do with two hundred milligrammes of LSD.'

'Then there is LSD,' he said, smiling. Glad of even the simple response of a kiss on the hand. He wanted now to pull out of the conversation and its disturbance. 'The pleasures of drugs and grog,' he laughed, drinking a toast. Although he had never tried drugs.

'Alcohol is a bore and pot and LSD are affectations,' she said, she could have been serious.

'The new sophistication. The unhappy princess of the mid-twentieth century,' he said tightly.

She looked at him, a little surprised by his tone.

'I guess that was a little sarcastic,' he said.

In a sudden change of mood unrelated to anything he'd said, she said, 'I'm ready to go to the party now.'

She pulled him into a run across the lawn.

As they entered the party she said, 'You're a very attractive man for your age,' and laughed.

'Wait until I'm fifty – and I'll really have a distinguished sexuality,' he said, grinning artificially, conscious of the sham humour groaning under sham optimism.

He went over to his wife.

'I've just saved a young woman from despair and futility.' And he made this and another genial remark and as he did he felt sick to the stomach.

'Must try your line on me some time,' she said.

Standing there, for an instant he felt a fear of the darkness of death and felt himself also cringing back from the incandescence which burnt out from the party around him. His wife bent forward to avoid dripping the juice from the rollmop she was eating. The young girl, laughing, was talking to a young man and her gloom seemed to have passed.

'Let's go home soon,' he said to his wife, 'I'm tired.'

She gave him a slightly exasperated glance, 'Soon,' she said, leaving him suspended in it all.

The incident of the suspended exercises

The alarm had buzzed only twice before his hand slapped it off. It buzzed the time to rise and study the American Civil War, do some work on the sand-trays, and do his exercises. He rose, went to the bathroom, ran the tap until the water became warm, and then sloshed it on his face. His wife slept on, her arm fallen from him on to his vacant place.

He was sour. His body struggled to get away and back to bed.

In his study, with a sand-tray regiment of Confederate soldiers watching, he commenced exercise one – *feet astride, arms upward, touch the floor outside left foot between feet, press once* . . .

He began the propaganda. About him being an attractive man in his thirties, because of exercise. And not having a beer gut. He didn't lose his breath on stairs. His body said, 'So what?'

His body was straining as he sat down for exercise two – *back lying, legs straight, feet together, arms straight overhead* . . . hardly any of his acquaintances did exercises . . . *sit up and touch toes* . . . he was, though, more disciplined than his friends . . . *keep the arms straight* . . . always had been . . . hadn't done him much good . . . keep arms in contact with the sides of the head . . . perhaps a little healthier . . . *front lying, hands and arms stretched sideways* . . . was he? . . . and what good did it do him? . . . *lift the shoulders and arms* . . . so he'd be the fittest man in the North Shore crematorium . . . his wife didn't exercise . . . *keep legs straight, raise chest and both thighs completely off the floor* . . . why didn't he just accept it . . . he was growing old . . . why fight it . . . you couldn't fight it . . . you probably wore the body out faster fighting it . . . *approximately one from the ears directly to the side of the head* . . . the fact that exercises distressed the body . . . that couldn't be good . . . that must mean something was wrong with exercising . . . *straighten arms to lift the body* . . . it was all too unpleasant . . . *chest must touch the floor for each completed movement* . . . it was the boredom too . . . most boring eleven minutes . . . no matter how short one told oneself it was . . . it was crazy . . . *straighten up* . . . lunatic . . . *lift knees waist high* . . .

He stopped in the middle of the last exercise.

Bugger it. No more. Bugger it.

He stood panting in his study. In surrender before a regiment of impassive Confederate soldiers. The sun was just beginning and the birds were moving.

Bugger it. He wiped his forehead with a towel, and returned to the bedroom. He undressed and got back into bed.

Bugger the exercises. He'd go on with the Civil War. Not the exercises.

His wife stirred, 'You finished?' she murmured.

'No, I've taken the day off from exercises.'

Seeming not to comprehend, she kissed him, put her arm across him and went back to sleep.

He didn't sleep. He wondered why he hadn't told her. Because he felt guilty, that was why. He felt he'd broken a contract. With himself more than her. He put his hands under his head. He felt he owed it to her to keep fit. As well as for vanity.

He would have to find another way. Isometric exercises – what the hell were they? He couldn't face a sport. He had enough obligations at work, without having to worry about a team and competitions.

He realized he felt the same way about stopping exercises as he had about contact lenses. He'd suffered smarting eyes and the whole dreadful business because he didn't want to admit publicly that his eyesight was failing.

He thought about Louise. That was almost enough to get him

up. But there must be more to lifeless flesh than age. Attitude to life perhaps.

He drowsed on a nervous stomach, woken sharply now and then by anxiety.

On the fourth day his wife said, 'Have you stopped exercising?'

'I'm having a holiday,' he said.

He continued to argue the problem for the next two weeks and once even tried to resume but found his body even more refractory.

'You haven't done your exercises now for weeks,' she commented with slight curiosity.

'They're a bore,' he said, 'I don't think I can be bothered.' He watched her.

'Don't blame you,' she said, fixing coffee, 'I never could understand how you did them day after day.' She passed him the stewed fruit. 'Actually it impressed me when we were first married.'

He felt a bind. But she'd said it casually. There didn't seem to be a reference in it to 'the contract'.

'They're an agony,' he said, 'I didn't mind them that much for the first few years. But recently they've become an agony.'

'I hadn't realized,' she said, unrolling the newspaper. 'Why did you bother?'

'I've finished with them now.'

She yawned, 'I intend to slide into decadence without a fight'.

'Perhaps I'll slide with you,' he said, taking the newspaper and running away into it.

She didn't seem to remember. He'd told her when they were first married that he did it for her. He kept fit for her. Not that the giving up now meant anything about his feelings for her. He valued their marriage. He had very deep affection for her. Giving up the exercises only meant something about him. Not the marriage. He wanted to be released from the obligation. She didn't seem to remember. But he couldn't raise it with her. Not yet anyhow. He wasn't ready to acknowledge. It was all too troublesome now.

The incident of the second meeting with Louise

His meeting with Louise was accidental although he accepted the responsibility for what followed. His wife had flown to New Zealand to see her parents and this was a contributing circumstance.

'Have a drink with me,' she had said when they met in the street.

'Sure,' he replied. He had intended to dine alone and expensively – in the pleasure of his own company. The newly discovered pleasure of being alone.

Once the compulsion had been to dine with *someone*, or to have drinks with *someone*, and, before marriage, to spend the night with some woman.

However he abandoned the idea of eating alone and they went to a quiet bar. But he was determined to have no sex.

She was as charming as before – with a touch of vivacity which he had not noticed before – perhaps she was making an effort to please as some sort of compensation for what she must have accepted as rather a dismal sexual encounter on the earlier occasion and which had not been followed up by him or by her. Not that he really felt she was to blame for the dismal nature of it.

'I'm still selling the British,' she told him, 'still publicly relating. Now it's Swinging Britain, of course.'

She sipped her drink, 'Actually I think the BIS could find a more suitable person – I'm not really the sort to sell Swinging Britain – I am, after all, of another generation.'

'Nonsense, Louise, you're a with-it woman.'

'And you're a darling for saying it,' she said touching his hand.

'But,' she said, 'I was happier selling Conservative Grey Britain. What I'm terrified of is . . .'

'Not disintegration again – please,' he laughed.

She laughed with him lightly.

'No, I'm not in that mood,' she said. 'What scares me today is those ridiculous old ladies in boots and mini skirts and coloured stockings.'

'. . . and Twiggy haircuts,' he laughed.

'Yes, it's a delicate problem for a Lady. The young fashions are so terribly tempting.'

'You're safe for a while yet, Louise.'

'As long as I know when the Swinging Divorcee has become the Ridiculous Old Lady.'

Soon the alcohol and the fact they obviously both had no commitment for the evening brought about a casual, light, intimacy.

'It's not as though I don't love her,' he said, 'but her absence made me realize that one loses the pleasure of being alone.'

'I'll go immediately,' she laughed.

'You know, that when she returns I think I'll even scheme to have time to myself – alone.'

She nodded.

'After marriage one never considers dining alone.'

'I know, darling, I know.'

Their eyes caught and satellited desire. His thinking stopped but he looked away and broke the glance. He wanted to get back to the safety of words.

'It's not as though I'm becoming a recluse,' he said.

She took up the conversation again, acknowledging his unwillingness to go with desire.

They talked. They lightly held hands. Her hands did not feel dead. Her hands gave off a warmth. The holding of hands was, though, simply a gesture of the moment. It was not an early stage on the progression to physical intimacy. He was determined. He wanted only to talk for a while.

'Come home and I'll make you something to eat – a snack,' she said.

He hesitated but realized, anyhow, he would have to drive her home. He was hungry as well.

'That would be perfect.'

They drove.

'New car?' she asked.

'Yes.'

'I love the smell of new cars.'

'I do too!' he said with some surprise. 'I like my newly painted rooms. I like the smell of all new things.'

'What is it? I can't tell cars.'

'A Rover.'

They drove in silence. He said after a while, 'I don't like women to have blemishes in their dress either – holed stockings, peeling finger-nail paint. I like things to be in good shape and repair.'

He wondered if he'd embarrassed her. No, she was one of those women who had everything in good shape. Except their psyche.

They reached the flat. He poured the drinks while she hurriedly picked up a few things from the floor of the bedroom and living room. Then she made open sandwiches on black bread.

'Why do you go with other women?' she asked as they ate.

'Well, in fact, I seldom do.'

She grinned with gentle disbelief.

'Seriously,' he said, 'you were the first for years.'

'I suppose I should be flattered.'

He shrugged. He wouldn't have called it an affair.

'Why the rare occasions?'

He thought and then said, 'On two occasions I did it for pure sexual satisfaction. Another city. And once it was a gesture to an old affair.'

They were silent for a while. He thought she was probably wondering what her category was – sexual satisfaction or something else.

He worried that she might be heading for depression.

But she came back to the conversation brightly.

'I have something to tell you,' she said.

'Oh?' he was alert, cautious.

'It's one of those things which is difficult to tell friends – I mean everyday friends. It involves loss of face – even though it is a good thing to have happened. Do you know the sort of thing I mean?'

He said, 'I don't think I do.'

'Well, I feel I can tell you because we don't really expect that much of each other – we don't see each other frequently and so on.'

He agreed, wondering.

'But even then what I have to tell you is embarrassing.'

She was enjoying creating the suspense.

He couldn't imagine. Was she pregnant?

'You're intriguing me.'

'I just don't know how to say it.'

She filled her glass.

'Surely, Louise, at our age . . .' he gave her his legal smile, to encourage confidence.

She buttered herself a biscuit.

'I had my first orgasm recently,' she said.

She blushed. He smiled, unsteadily. He felt very wary of unwanted intimacy.

'Great,' he said.

'And I'm not actually at the beginning of my sexual experience,' she said.

'That's really great.'

She continued, more freely, 'It's not as though I have not had – well, had a sex life – but orgasm, no.'

'It must have been some experience,' he said, uncomfortably, finding it difficult to say anything appropriate. A feeling he had on rare occasions with an over-frank client. 'Are you in love?' he asked, feeling somehow that the question was naive.

'No, not really – not really at all,' she thought aloud. 'The man was . . . only instrumental.' She giggled, 'If that's the word.'

He smiled.

'I didn't mean to sound cold about it,' she rushed to say. 'It wasn't cold at all.'

'No, you didn't,' he assured her.

He was having great difficulty in expressing himself. At university when he had drunk with the Push it had been a bit easier.

But that was talk about sex in a tough undergraduate vocabulary. He didn't seem to talk about sex much now.

'Telling you how it happened is more difficult,' she said, 'But I feel pretty amazed about it. And there's nothing worse than being terribly *amazed* and not being able to share it.'

'I know,' he said; he guessed he knew.

'What happened was – that he went up my . . . anus,' she said, with a tone of mature coyness. 'Of course, he went in my . . . as well.'

Her sentence broke down with the same shyness. She blushed again.

'Was it the first time . . . that way?' he asked.

'Yes, why? Is it . . . usual?'

'I guess it isn't,' he said, and then laughed. 'You don't always think to do it.'

'It was the pain of it and the thrill of it and his way of talking and the sort of man he was. All those things.'

'That sounds rather beautiful,' he managed to say.

'I hadn't thought of myself as frigid,' she said, 'I've always liked sex. But it was probably more a way someone showed *interest* or *affection* rather than for itself.'

'Probably means you've resolved something in your mind.'

'Perhaps. I find a few hard truths aren't hard anymore.'

He took her in his arms. Mainly as a gesture of affection, somehow appropriate to the experience just shared with him. He hadn't meant to kiss, but they did. Her kiss was still restrained in the way it had been the first time, but not tense.

They stood in each other's arms, rocking, not saying anything.

Then she said softly, 'Do you want to go to bed with me?'

He looked at her, kissed her lightly, with the memory of the lifeless skin fading in his mind screened off by alcohol and creeping desire. 'Yes, I do,' he said, not knowing, as he answered whether he did or not.

They moved to the bed, undressing themselves and each other in interplay.

She quickly wiped off her make-up while he held her from behind. They rolled then together on to the bed, lying outside the bed clothes. The temperature seemed right for that.

Her skin was not dead. She was not clammy from tension. She was responsive in a tentative way.

'I don't subscribe to the mumbo jumbo of the orgasm,' he whispered to her, 'but you seem happier in bed.'

'Perhaps we just know each other better,' she said.

'Perhaps.'

It was freer, still a little restrained, but freer and more responsive. He did what she had found she liked.

Afterwards he lay close to her, tired and released.

He wondered about it. Whether it was the last flare of her body before it died away. The last bright burning before the disintegration she had felt so strongly.

'Are you still disintegrating?' he asked, quietly.

'It's slowed down,' she said, smiling. 'Perhaps it's stopped for a while.'

'Do you see much of the man?'

She didn't answer, as though thinking of who he meant. 'You mean *the* man,' she said. 'Yes, fairly often.'

'Is it still good?'

'Yes, still good.'

'That's good.'

They lay in silence. He smoked.

Then as if she felt she should, she said, 'You're a good lover.'

'Thanks.'

'You are, I mean it,' she emphasized.

He had no reason to go home but he felt he owed it to his absent wife – as a ritual – a gesture.

'I'm going now,' he said, kissing her.

'Phone me,' she said, sleepily.

He dressed and left. Driving home, he wanted to also tell his wife about this, the revitalization of Louise. But he could not because (a) that was not the way they worked their marriage and (b) she was in New Zealand.

The incident of the birthday dinner

The dinner had reached cheese. Roger and Cindy were smoking His wife had asked about coffee but everyone seemed content t stay on wine.

The conversation had fragmented into three smaller groupings He and Julien were talking across the table.

'Tell me, Julien – what do you think about death?'

'My God,' she said, 'why so morbid?'

'Well, birthdays are like that – at my age – no, seriously I'm curious.'

'What can one say?' she said, cutting some cheese, 'it' unthinkable in – the logical sense.'

'You can speculate – and some things might seem mor probable than others.'

'Which do you consider the most probable?' she asked.

'I used to favour the Disintegration Theory – you know, that's it – dead – the end. But now I'm more inclined to Transmutation.'

'What!?' Cindy broke across the table into the conversation, cutting across Sally and Roger.

'What do you think of death?' he said, turning to her.

'Are you becoming all mystical?' There was a touch of derision in her voice.

'Just interested,' he said, smiling. 'You're probably too young, Cindy.'

'What's transmutation?' Julien asked.

He turned back to her. 'Reincarnation was probably the primitive form of the theory,' he said, 'the idea that we change into complete whole new forms. Transmutation would have it that we change into another living form – ashes become part of the living soil and through the soil we become part of living plants, and in turn part of a living creature. We go on changing form.'

'Oh *really*,' Cindy said, sarcastically.

'Well, what do you think happens, Cindy?'

'Nothing. We just die – turn to dust. Nothing,' she said impatiently.

'Well, I suppose no one at this table would support the Christian view.'

'That's the next thing – you're obviously on the way,' Cindy said aggressively.

'Take it easy, baby,' Roger said to her.

'I will not,' she said back to him, in a private-public tone.

'I'm intrigued with how people view death as it approaches them,' he said, mainly to Julien. 'It's the big inevitable event about which we know nothing.' He caught his wife looking at him with interest. He had never discussed it with her.

'We know it's just the end,' Cindy said loudly, 'and it's not worth discussing.'

'I'm terrified,' Sally said, 'simply terrified.'

They laughed, except Cindy.

'What makes you so sure there is no *felt* experience after death, Cindy?' he asked, perhaps a little irritably.

'I think you're becoming a neurotic old man,' Cindy said toughly. 'Now you're a success you'll start worrying about immortality – youth drugs – and next you'll be screaming for a priest.'

'It is a rather normal interest, I would have thought,' Frederick said.

The conversation was reclustering.

'It's morbid,' Cindy said, 'and sick.'

'It's nothing to get angry about,' Roger said to her quietly.

'You shut up,' Cindy said, without looking at him.

'It's the finality,' he said, 'the separation from everything we know and understand. Plunged into an unknown situation.'

'It's the inevitability which I find hard,' Frederick said. 'As Cindy said – I'll be looking for youth drugs.'

'We can't accept the loss of our essence or spirit, or whatever it's called.'

'Spirit!' Cindy cried, 'you *are* becoming religious.'

'There's more to feeling than just nerves, isn't there? Don't we believe we're more than flesh and brain?'

'How incredible, how bloody incredible,' Cindy said with disgust. The others were listening and watching with some interest.

'Just electricity, dad, just electricity,' Roger said. 'When we go, the electricity is discharged – we're just flat batteries.'

'I'm leaving,' Cindy said, standing up. He grinned at her. He thought she was joking.

'I'm leaving,' she repeated at Roger. She moved away from the table.

Roger realized that she was serious and said, 'Now don't be silly, Cindy.'

'You're scared, Cindy,' Sally said humorously.

'I'm furious,' Cindy said.

'I'm terrified,' Sally said, 'simply terrified.'

'Oh shut up, Sally, you're as big a bore as he is,' she said, gesturing at him.

'My, my,' Sally said.

Cindy went to the bedroom to get her coat.

Roger followed her and he followed Roger.

He heard Sally say in a loud voice intended for Cindy, 'Cindy's the youngest and obviously the most upset. We should discuss it with her,' and then called out to Cindy, sarcastically, 'Cindy, darling, come back – we're going to have Group.'

In the bedroom Roger said, 'Come on now, we'll go soon, but don't run off like this.'

'It's my fault really,' he said, coming closer to her.

Cindy stood pouting.

He went over and kissed her on the cheek. 'I apologize for upsetting you.' He took her hand. 'I shouldn't have pursued it when you found it distasteful. It was dreadfully insensitive. I'm sorry.'

She half smiled. 'I hate talking about ageing,' she said sadly.

Roger and he led her back.

They didn't raise the subject again.

They talked in a strained way about Dos Passos and then the party broke up.

After everyone had gone and they were clearing the table his wife said, 'D-e-a-t-h was a lead balloon.'

'Yes. I thought Cindy over-reacted.'

'I hadn't realized you were worried about death.'

'I'm not as worried as Cindy seems to be,' he said, kissing his wife on the back of her head. 'Mine's purely academic – or nearly.'

'I suspect you're going through the trauma of the mid-thirties,' she said, carrying wine bottles to the kitchen.

He paused. 'I guess there is something of that in it,' he called to her, emptying the ashtrays into a sheet of newspaper.

She came back and put her arm around him. 'We've got a few years more sex in us yet.'

'But one day we'll have to say – "that's it".'

'It doesn't happen like that,' she said, 'and it's never been the centre of our life anyway.'

'I guess not.'

'If it ever gets bad we'll take poison together,' she said and kissed him.

They kissed in the dinner party air, rich with the breath of conversation, warmed by bodies, a smell of candle wax, aroma of food and spilled wine, the air slightly fogged with the comfortable smell of cigarettes.

The only sound was a cistern dribbling.

Michael Wilding

AS BOYS TO WANTON FLIES

LIONEL's world was a narrow honey-smeared jar into which
insects were lured and from which they could not escape. But
buzzed and drilled around him, striking themselves against the
invisible walls and cloying their wings with a sweet tackiness that
dragged them down.

He hated cockroaches which crushed like chestnuts, a white
coagulate powder, a paste, extruded from their crisp glossy cases.
After he had first seen that, he would never eat chestnuts, the
soft white insides protected by that brown scaly skin. And
vomited at tea one day when his mother served ice cream
garnished with chestnut purée.

It was a clean neat suburb, dried white by the sun, with no
ramshackle weatherboard extensions to houses, no rows of
outside lavatories; the garbage collector came twice a week
and the houses were new, each set in its own garden and shaded
by its own trees. Besides, they had a maid. And yet, in the
evenings, lines of cockroaches would file across the cooling
pavement, from the gardens to the nature strip, from the nature
strip to the gutters and drains. Yet the gutters were kept swept.
And what could they have found in the gardens?

As he lay in bed, he could hear the soft, scratching progress,
as they filed along the pavement, the mindless invasion. And he
would wake up screaming, that they had trooped across the
floor and up the wall and across the sheet and into his mouth;
and were cramming into his mouth, one after another, choking
him. And he would wake screaming, his mouth and throat dry,
the mucus scraped off on their scaly shells, their wiry legs.

And if his parents were home, his mother would rush into his
room, and draw his head against her, pressing him against her
heavy breasts, consoling him by fondling his hair. Till he would

almost choke with suffocation again, but dared not break away for fear she would be offended, and leave him to the resonant emptiness of the room. Because so often she was not there; but at concerts in the town hall, or at art galleries. There was little enough culture in their new land, so they determined to see as much of it as they could; and went out more often than ever they had done in Europe. Or so it seemed to him. Though he had been younger then, of course; and now they kept saying he was old enough to be left on his own. Which was not even on his own for there was Erica, the maid.

Each morning before she went to work, his mother would repeat to Erica: 'You must watch him carefully; I have told him not to run across the road without looking, not to talk to strange men, not to pick up stones in the garden.' He would hear her repeated instructions; and he picked up no strange stones in the garden, poked into no holes. For under stones and tin cans were cavities where poisonous spiders lurked; and in cavities hid thin centipedes and lizards, whose bites infected. And he heard his mother rebuke Erica for cockroaches that intruded to the kitchen, heard her issue warnings of bubonic plague, glands swelling till they burst with pus, heard her inveigh if meat were left out of the refrigerator the briefest time, lest it should become fly-blown. And the flies buzzed around them as they talked.

He believed the horrors that dropped from his mother's lips. When a flea leapt on his bedroom carpet, he would examine himself minutely for the sign of a bite, watch himself in the mirror for the signs of swelling heralding the plague. There had been no noxious insects where they had lived in Europe. Ladybirds were happy things, and to kill a spider had been heinous slaughter, precipitating bad luck. His grandmother had had a pet fly, and each night put out grains of sugar for it to feed on.

But here each insect was potential death; here were spiders as large as a dinner plate; ants here more than nipped, they destroyed whole houses, ate whole joints of meat, and living flesh. Beneath each strip of flaking bark on the garden trees, lay a myriad beetles, grubs, and worms; breeding, multiplying, hatching. And in the branches hung ticks, ready to drop and suck out the blood of their host, and, settled on the head or spine, paralyze and kill. They could not keep a dog, because of the ticks. He recoiled from every cat he saw, knowing it inevitably carried its portion of parasites, was being sucked to death. The noise of the cicadas drilled through him with fear; he recoiled from the scuttle of lizards as from the lash of a whip. At night, lying in bed, the touch of moths' soft wings was a brush of death. When his parents' music stopped, his room was filled with the insect sounds of the garden.

In the afternoons the sun shone golden over the city. And home from school he would sit on the lawn beside Erica, whose honey blonde hair shone, and whose body glowed a rich, sweet orange brown. She wore only the briefest bikini, whose top she would untie to prevent strap marks from forming across her back. He squatted on a rug and watched her. 'You should take your clothes off and lie in the sun,' she said to him; but his skin burnt in the sun. 'Why do you never come with me to the beach?' she asked: 'The sands are all warm and golden to dance on and the waves wrap you in their arms. They are the arms of mermen,' she said, 'coming up to love you. Oh, not you, Lionel; they'll be little mermaidens for you, and when the waves break over you that's their hair spreading all around you.'

'I don't want waves breaking over me,' he said, 'and besides, there are sandflies and crabs and all those things, everywhere.'

'They don't hurt,' she said, 'they're all too happy in the sun.'

He watched wide-eyed as an ant crawled up her side and along her back; it went slowly down to her belly, beneath her, towards her navel.

'There's an ant,' he said.

'I know,' she said, 'I can feel it; it's like fingers tickling over you. When you're a big boy, Lionel,' she said, 'you'll know all about that.'

'About what?' he asked.

'About having hands stroke all over you,' she said, and she suddenly, convulsively, stretched out her legs and arms at that and, smiling, shut her eyes in the gentle afternoon sun. He wondered if she had crushed the ant in her movements.

He did not want to know about that. At night he thought of it, of the ant moving towards her belly-button; and he shuddered and shuddered in horror at the thought. And slept with his hand covering his belly-button over, so nothing could creep within it in the night.

He feared flowers brought into the dark dining room, lest poisonous spiders hid amongst their unfolding petals, crouched beside their honey.

'Look, Lionel, this lovely flower I have just picked from the garden,' Erica would call, and bring in some bold bloom, hold it towards him for him to sniff its fresh scents. But he would shake his head, draw back, refuse to touch it, refuse to reach his nose near its yearning petals.

'Oh, you silly boy,' she would say, annoyed at his silliness; till, happy in the sunny day, she would laugh, and put the single flower in her bosom, its stalk lodged between her breasts, its head nodding at her neck. And she would sing at that. So that her singing aroused such vibrations of fear as the sound of the cicadas that were always present in the evening, that reasserted their presence between all his parents' music.

He hated Aboriginals who fed on plump white witchetty grubs. His school reader that had told him of that, he hid beneath his other books at the bottom of his desk. And when for one lesson he had to get it out again, his fingers groped in terror in the dark recesses, lest some creature lurked there. Kookaburras which he had always loved as funny laughable birds, he hated after he had seen them pictured with worms and lizards wriggling from their jaws. His stomach tensed, he nearly vomited, at the thought of insects in the intestine, perhaps not fully devoured, unchewed, groping, scratching, scraping, scuttling, and wriggling to get out. The story of Jonah and the whale did not trouble him; the dimensions were large, Jonah was not constricted but in palatial accommodation. And escaped. But the minute insect life trapped and burrowing in soft intestine, hard scaliness scratching the tender entrails, nauseated him. What if it bred there?

Salads he prodded with trepidation, lest poisonous slugs like asps clung to the underside of lettuce leaves; and to do that prodding, to entertain the possibilities he prodded against, was almost as nauseating for him as to have encountered a beetle immersed in mayonnaise, to have closed his teeth on a spider's case.

Nights were times of terror. When he undressed, the shadows

of moths projected on to walls as they battered against the burning electric globe, were vampires' wings flailing around him, scratching his eardrums, eyeballs, grazing his lips, till they bled red cries of terror. Despite fly screens, mosquitoes entered the bedrooms at night, just as cockroaches penetrated Erica's kitchen. Bitten, his flesh would swell in huge flat spreading weals. Woken by the pain he would put on his light and run wild, hurling his pillow at mosquitoes settled on the wall or ceiling, sometimes squashing them to leave a damp stain of blood shared between wall and linen pillowslip, often only disturbing them, so that he had to wait for them to settle before he could throw again. The thumps would waken his parents, his father tired, irritable in the hot weather; his mother so, too, but maternal and solicitous, billowing in her nightdress and dressing gown, surging in to embrace him, comfort him, lull him to sleep, beside him on the soft bed, assure him the insects were all killed. And through the door she left open at her entry, others would sidle in.

And if his parents were out at some concert or entertained by friends, he would lie in the hot night exhausted with his futile onslaught on the mosquitoes; and terrified to go to the kitchen for a drink of orange from the refrigerator. At certain seasons slugs left trails across the kitchen floor, and he was terrified lest his unwary foot should tread on their soft pulpiness, terrified indeed lest his eyes should encounter their obscenity – the white trails they left for the morning nauseous enough to him.

'Oh you silly thing,' Erica would say when he called her. She did not like being woken from her dreams, but the warm night gentle against her body, the scents of garden trees and the warm exudations of the hot land rising and stirring across her bosom, rising up to her thighs and belly, as she stood in the soft moonlight outside the open door, calmed her. She would stand there in the rustling night and, appeased, take him his orange juice and put her hand against his hot brow, reassure him. And when he was restful again, she would stand outside for her own restfulness, longing to walk naked beneath the scented gums, but aware that the family might return at any moment, or that a sleepless neighbour might look from his window. And there were no neighbours she wanted to see her naked in that street.

One afternoon Lionel had come home from school and was

sitting in the dark living room, with his homework. He heard, close by, a cicada croak, feebly, weakly, in its final throes. He looked round carefully, fearfully, but could see it nowhere, the cat following his every movement, watching. Till he realized that the croaking came from the cat, that the cicada was encapsulated in the cat who stood with dulled surprise. He screamed at the realization before him of his horror, at the cicada forever buried in the cat's intestine, forever giving voice to its entombed presence, laying eggs perhaps that would hatch into a whole choir of buried, croaking horror. Erica held him against her as he told her of what had happened, reassured him that it would be all right. But he screamed again as the cat stroked itself against his leg. Erica picked it up at that, forced open its mouth and removed the soggy cicada, drenched in saliva; she was about to throw it into the waste bin, but took pity on Lionel and went outside and lodged it on the branch of a tree. But though she went back to Lionel and stroked him and held him to her breasts, she told him he was silly, babyish, childish.

'Grown up people don't run away from insects and grubs,' she said. 'What ever harm could a little thing like that do?'

He sucked his thumb, miserable, sucking, isolated.

'You big baby,' she said, 'you suck your thumb but what's the difference in sucking a big worm or a thick swollen maggot or anything else?'

'Stop it,' he cried, 'stop it, stop it,' and he ran, his hands clasped over his ears, his stomach churning at her words.

She followed him through to his room: 'You must grow up,' she said. 'Something must be done, I shall have to cure you.'

'No,' he cried, 'no, no, no, I don't want to be cured, I hate them, I hate insects, I don't want to like them, I don't want to touch them, I'd rather die than be cured.'

'You're just a silly spoilt boy,' she said. 'What if you lived in France and had to eat frogs and snails, or in Mexico and ate lizards?'

But he held his hands over his ears and would not listen to her.

She was a monster to him. Her golden prettiness was only the prettiness of a butterfly that had been chrysalis and caterpillar and egg; those were her real nature, not this transitory prettiness. She was a butterfly that at night turned back to its grovelling caterpillar; a moth that at night became a vampire; the cockroaches in her kitchen were laid by her, squatting there at night, letting them pour out of her and spread along the floor. Her voice was the drilling of cicadas, the whine of mosquitoes; her embrace the clasp of the black widow; in her navel lived ants and woodlice and termites. When she peeled off the casing of her bikini, her exposed flesh was the soft, crumbling white paste of a cockroach; the tap of her high heels on the floor was the croak of the swallowed cicada, which she had gone outside to ingest herself, which she had stolen from the cat. And the mermen who fondled her in the glistening sea were hosts for the eggs she lodged in them, that hatched and lived parasitically in cocoons along their back, eating them slowly as they lived. He would not let her touch him again for fear of what she implanted in him; he would not eat foods she had prepared for fear of the eggs he would swallow and that would hatch. He would close his ears against her voice that burrowed and settled in his ears like earwigs. He told his mother who said he was not to be silly, and he heard his mother and Erica talking about him, saying he must be cured. But he would not be cured, he would never be cured. He waited in fear of her cure, knowing she would plan some evil against him.

One evening she took him to his bedroom at the usual time – his parents were at a concert – and helped him to undress. He feared her touch, that one of her scarlet nails might draw his blood.

'Where are my pyjamas?' he asked, fearful in the musicless house.

'In the bed,' she said. And when he walked over to the bed in his nakedness to find them, she pulled back the upper sheet in one swift movement, and pushed him naked into bed, with a squashing, crushing, splintering, pulping sound, down amongst a collection, so laboriously assembled, of cicadas, christmas beetles, woodbugs, ants, caterpillars, worms, snails, slugs, silverfish, centipedes, chrysalises, loopers, spiders, tarantulas, blowflies, moths, grubs.

He screamed, his scream an uncontrolled single ceaseless howl of horror, a scream of helpless terror as, his eyes pressed against her excited cleavage, his back, his legs, his buttocks, crawled and itched and slimed with all the maimed and trapped, and self-devouring, resisting, awoken insects. And she pushed him into the slippery scaly pulp till, with a dreadful force, he thrust her away, thrust her off balance and onto the floor, and ran, screaming, howling, naked through the house, the garden, the street, screaming one single high note as he ran, smeared over with slime and crushed paste and pulsing dying living insects, being eaten and stung and torn as he ran, his eyes blinded and his mouth and nostrils filled to suffocation, his flesh being eaten from his bones and pumped and drilled full of eggs and parasites and borers, burrowing through into his entrails, his heart, his throat, his mind.

'Come back,' she called him, 'Lionel, come back. Now you will be cured. Come back Lionel, now there will be no need to scream.'

But he ran, impelled on his single ceaseless note of terror, and he would never come back.

Peter Carey

REPORT ON THE SHADOW INDUSTRY

1

My friend S. went to live in America ten years ago and I still have the letter he wrote me when he first arrived, wherein he describes the shadow factories that were springing up on the west coast and the effects they were having on that society. 'You see people in dark glasses wandering around the supermarkets at 2 a.m. There are great boxes all along the aisles, some as expensive as fifty dollars but most of them only five. There's always Muzak. It gives me the shits more than the shadows. The people don't look at one another. They come to browse through the boxes of shadows although the packets give no indication of what's inside. It really depresses me to think of people going out at two in the morning because they need to try their luck with a shadow. Last week I was in a supermarket near Topanga and I saw an old negro tear the end off a shadow box. He was arrested almost immediately.'

A strange letter ten years ago but it accurately describes scenes that have since become common in this country. Yesterday I drove in from the airport past shadow factory after shadow factory, large faceless buildings gleaming in the sun, their secrets guarded by ex-policemen with alsatian dogs.

The shadow factories have huge chimneys that reach far into the sky, chimneys which billow forth smoke of different, brilliant colours. It is said by some of my more cynical friends that the smoke has nothing to do with any manufacturing process and is merely a trick, fake evidence that technological miracles are being performed within the factories. The popular belief is that the smoke sometimes contains the most powerful shadows of all, those that are too large and powerful to be packaged. It is a common sight to see old women standing for hours outside the factories, staring into the smoke.

There are a few who say the smoke is dangerous because of carcinogenic chemicals used in the manufacture of shadows.

Others argue that the shadow is a natural product and by its very nature chemically pure. They point to the advantages of the smoke: the beautifully coloured patterns in the clouds which serve as a reminder of the happiness to be obtained from a fully realized shadow. There may be some merit in this last argument, for on cloudy days the skies above our city are a wondrous sight, full of blues and vermilions and brilliant greens which pick out strange patterns and shapes in the clouds.

Others say that the clouds now contain the dreadful beauty of the apocalypse.

2

The shadows are packaged in large, lavish boxes which are printed with abstract designs in many colours. The Bureau of Statistics reveals that the average householder spends 25 per cent of his income on these expensive goods and that this percentage increases as the income decreases.

There are those who say that the shadows are bad for people, promising an impossible happiness that can never be realized and thus detracting from the very real beauties of nature and life. But there are others who argue that the shadows have always been with us in one form or another and that the packaged shadow is necessary for mental health in an advanced technological society. There is, however, research to indicate that the high suicide rate in advanced countries is connected with the popularity of shadows and that there is a direct statistical correlation between shadow sales and suicide rates. This has been explained by those who hold that the shadows are merely mirrors to the soul and that the man who stares into a shadow box sees only himself, and what beauty be finds there is his own beauty and what despair he experiences is born of the poverty of his spirit.

3

I visited my mother at Christmas. She lives alone with her dogs in a poor part of town. Knowing her weakness for shadows I brought her several of the more expensive varieties which she retired to examine in the privacy of the shadow room.

She stayed in the room for such a long time that I became worried and knocked on the door. She came out almost immediately. When I saw her face I knew the shadows had not been good ones.

'I'm sorry,' I said, but she kissed me quickly and began to tell me about a neighbour who had won the lottery.

I myself know, only too well, the disappointments of shadow boxes for I also have a weakness in that direction. For me it is something of a guilty secret, something that would not be approved of by my clever friends.

I saw J. in the street. She teaches at the university.

'Ah-hah,' she said knowingly, tapping the bulky parcel I had hidden under my coat. I know she will make capital of this discovery, a little piece pf gossip to use at the dinner parties she is so fond of. Yet I suspect that she too has a weakness for shadows. She confessed as much to me some years ago during that strange misunderstanding she still likes to call 'Our Affair'.

It was she who hinted at the feeling of emptiness, that awful despair that comes when one has failed to grasp the shadow.

4

My own father left home because of something he had seen in a box of shadows. It wasn't an expensive box, either, quite the opposite – a little surprise my mother had bought with the money left over from her housekeeping. He opened it after dinner one Friday night and he was gone before I came down to breakfast on the Saturday. He left a note which my mother only showed me very recently. My father was not good with words and had trouble communicating what he had seen: 'Words Cannot Express It What I feel Because of The Things I Saw In The Box Of Shadows You Bought Me.'

My own feelings about the shadows are ambivalent, to say the least. For here I have manufactured one more: elusive, unsatisfactory, hinting at greater beauties and more profound mysteries that exist somewhere before the beginning and somewhere after the end.

NOTES ON THE AUTHORS

BARNARD, MARJORIE (b. 1897)

Marjorie Barnard collaborated with Flora Eldershaw (1897–1956) on novels like *A House is Built* (1929) and *The Glasshouse* 1936). Independently, she has written works of Australian history as well as short stories.

BAYNTON, BARBARA (1862–1929)

In the course of a life which began at Scone, New South Wales, which brought her three husbands, which admitted her to English aristocratic society, and which ended in Melbourne, Barbara Baynton wrote three books. *Bush Studies* (1902) has achieved classic status in the literature of the outback.

'BRIAN JAMES' (JOHN TIERNEY) (1892-1972)

For much of his life 'Brian James' was a school teacher, a profession to which his two novels, *The Advancement of Spencer Button* (1950) and *Hopeton High* (1963) are devoted. His short stories have a predominantly rural setting.

CAREY, PETER (b. 1943)

Peter Carey was born in Bacchus Marsh, Victoria, and now lives in Sydney. He is the author of *The Fat Man in History* (1974).

CASEY, GAVIN (1907–1964)

Casey was born in Kalgoorlie, Western Australia, and many of his stories are concerned with the miners of its famous Golden Mile. Nearly all his fiction has a strong strain of social criticism running through it.

COWAN, PETER (b. 1914)

Born in Western Australia, Peter Cowan is now on the staff of the English Department of the University of Western Australia. His first book appeared in 1944, and he has been steadily producing stories and novels ever since.

DAVISON, FRANK DALBY   (1893–1969)

Most of Davison's fiction is set in the bush, of which he had personal experience in Victoria and Queensland. His best known works are the animal tales, *Man-Shy* (1931) and *Dusty* (1946). His last work, *The White Thorntree* (1968), is a study of sexuality in a predominantly urban setting.

DYSON, EDWARD   (1865–1931)

A freelance writer for most of his career, Dyson dealt in his stories not only with the bush but with mining life and urban, industrial experience.

FORSHAW, THELMA   (b. 1923)

Thelma Forshaw was born in Sydney, where she now lives. She is married with two children, and has published one volume of short stories, *An Affair of Clowns* (1967).

HARROWER, ELIZABETH   (b. 1928)

Elizabeth Harrower lives in Sydney, and is best known for her novels, such as *The Long Prospect* (1958) and *The Catherine Wheel* (1960).

LAWSON, HENRY   (1867–1922)

Lawson was born at Grenfell, in the central west of New South Wales. The verse and prose that he wrote, mainly in the 1890s, make him one of the canonical figures of Australian literature.

MARSHALL, ALAN   (b. 1902)

I Can Jump Puddles (1955), Marshall's account of his own childhood, is the story of a boy, crippled by poliomyelitis, growing up in a Victorian country district. He has written several sequels to *I Can Jump Puddles*, as well as an impressive body of short stories.

MOORHOUSE, FRANK   (b. 1938)

Frank Moorhouse was brought up on the south coast of New South Wales. Books like *Futility and Other Animals* (1969), *The Americans Baby* (1972), *Conferenceville* (1976) and *The Everlasting Secret Family and Other Secrets* (1980) have placed him in the front rank of the younger short story writers. He edited the 1973 *Coast to Coast*.

MORRISON, JOHN (b. 1904)

Morrison came to Australia from his native England in 1923. Thoroughly assimilated into Australian life, he has produced some of the best modern stories in the democratic tradition which stems from Lawson. His latest collection *North Wind* was published in 1982.

O'GRADY, DESMOND (b. 1929)

Born and educated in Melbourne, O'Grady has lived for a number of years in Rome. His stories are collected under the titles *A Long Way From Home* (1966) and *Valid for all Countries* (1979).

PALMER, VANCE (1885–1959)

For a large part of a long life, Palmer was the doyen of the Australian literary community. In addition to short stories, his own writing included novels, verse, drama, criticism and belles lettres.

PORTER, HAL (b. 1911)

Born in Melbourne, Porter began writing in the 1930s. Since then he has produced a large body of highly individual work including novels, drama, verse and autobiography, as well as short stories.

'PRICE WARUNG' (WILLIAM ASTLEY) (1855–1911)

Born in England, Astley came to Australia with his parents when he was four years old. He followed many occupations before settling into journalism. During the 1890s, while he was writing his convict tales, he was closely associated with the political movement towards Federation.

PRICHARD, KATHARINE SUSANNAH (1883–1969)

One of Australia's leading novelists and short story writers in the first half of the twentieth century, Katharine Susannah Prichard dealt with many aspects of the national life, often from a politically radical point of view.

ROBINSON, LES (1886–1968)

Born in Sydney, Robinson drifted in and out of a variety of jobs. Most of his work was originally contributed to newspapers and journals.

SCHLUNKE, E. O. (1906–1960)

A Riverina farmer of German origin, Schlunke wrote almost exclusively of the people and community he knew at first hand.

'STEELE RUDD' (ARTHUR HOEY DAVIS) (1868–1935)

'Steele Rudd' started writing his selection stories for the *Bulletin* in the 1890s, while he was a civil servant in Queensland, where he was born. *On Our Selection* (1899) was one of the first Australian bestsellers.

STIVENS, DAL (b. 1911)

Stivens has been one of Australia's best known short story writers since the 1930s. He has also written several novels, one of which, *A Horse of Air*, was awarded the Miles Franklin Prize in 1970. He was actively involved in organizing the Australian Society of Authors.

WILDING, MICHAEL (b. 1942)

Born and educated in England, Wilding is now a Reader in English at the University of Sydney. His first book of Australian stories was *Aspects of the Dying Process* (1972).

WHITE, PATRICK (b. 1912)

White's international reputation dates from the publication of the novel *The Tree of Man* in 1955. Since then he has established himself as Australia's greatest contemporary writer of fiction. In 1973 he was awarded the Nobel Prize for Literature, the first Australian to gain that distinction.

Some other books published by Penguin
are described on the following pages

THE PENGUIN BOOK
OF AUSTRALIAN VERSE

*Edited with an Introduction
by Harry Heseltine*

In this widely acclaimed anthology, Professor
Harry Heseltine has collected Australian poetry
from every major period, covering the work of
more than one hundred of Australia's leading
poets – from Charles Harpur, Henry Kendall
and Adam Lindsay Gordon to Les Murray,
Geoffrey Lehmann and Michael Dransfield.

In addition to providing brief biographies of
each poet, the Editor has contributed an introduction to the book, in which he discusses his
choice of material and provides a scholarly
review of Australian poetry.

THE LITERATURE OF AUSTRALIA

Edited by Geoffrey Dutton

Since it was first published in the mid-1960s, *The Literature of Australia* has become a popular and widely-used classic in its field.

This revised edition has important new chapters on contemporary novelists, poets and playwrights, as well as original material which has been updated. The book also provides a comprehensive bibliographical guide, which will continue to make the book an indispensable reference work for many years to come.

THE PENGUIN BOOK
OF AUSTRALIAN BALLADS

Edited by Russel Ward

Australia's songs and ballads grew as swiftly as
her history. They did not record all of that
history, but certain aspects of the young and
vast country's traditions, legends, true and tall
stories are expressed in the ballads with a
simplicity and zest not to be found elsewhere.
Dr Russel Ward is an expert in the subject who
has collected many old bush songs and ballads
himself. From the vast amount of material
available he has made a selection which shows
all its liveliness and variety: from anonymous
convict and bushranging songs and ballads to
the literary ballads of *The Bulletin* and modern
verse in the ballad tradition.